Praise for
New York Times **bestselling author**
Sharon Page

"Merging the flavor of *Downton Abbey* with her own special touches, Page crafts a vibrant novel and a dramatic love story [that] completely captures the angst and glamour of the era."
—*RT Book Reviews* on *An American Duchess*

"With danger and erotic intrigue at every turn, *The Club* is a fast-paced, blistering page turner that evokes the emotional and erotic with every scene."
—*USA TODAY* bestselling author Kathryn Smith

"A winner."
—*Publishers Weekly*, starred review, on *The Club*

"[A]n intensely emotional love story. It isn't only the sizzle that rivets readers, it's the true passion and love that [Page] infuses into the story that makes it a deep-sigh read."
—*RT Book Reviews* on *Engaged in Sin* (Top Pick)

"Anticipation...smolders on every page."
—*RT Book Reviews* on *Deeply in You* (Top Pick)

AN AMERICAN DUCHESS

SHARON PAGE

HQN™

HQN™

ISBN-13: 978-0-373-78938-2

Recycling programs for this product may not exist in your area.

An American Duchess

This book wouldn't exist without the influence of my mother, who, years ago, introduced me to the 1920s through *The Great Gatsby* and Agatha Christie's mysteries. She fostered my lifelong passion for the era and also encouraged my love for reading and writing. These are gifts that last forever.

1
OFF THE ROAD

May 1922
The Estate of Brideswell Abbey, Hertfordshire

NORMALLY, ZOE ANASTASIA GIFFORD was a spectacular driver. Now she found herself with her rear wheel stuck in a muddy rut on a positively medieval road somewhere in rural England.

A flock of bleating sheep surrounded her, attempting to eat her skirt. Zoe shooed the stubborn animals. Her car was unharmed, but the wheel was up to its axle in mud.

"What are we going to do?" wailed her mother from the passenger seat.

Zoe stood, tugged the end of her tasseled scarf away from a black-nosed sheep and tossed it over her shoulder. "Unless you plan to push out the car while I steer, Mother, we are going to walk."

Her mother's face crumpled and she began to cry.

Perhaps she was being a bit harsh, but it was Mother's fault she had to marry in haste, and she felt a distinct lack of sympathy. If they had not needed almost immediate access to her trust fund to sort out Mother's disastrous debts, she would have had time to actually mourn her lost fiancé before she'd had to find a new one and marry to get at her trust fund to save Mother from disaster.

It was sheer luck she'd met Lord Sebastian. She was an heiress who needed a quick marriage to access her fortune; he was an impoverished aristocrat. The perfect ingredients for a marriage of convenience that would end in a divorce almost before the ink dried on the license. A marriage that would cost her a relatively small settlement to Sebastian for his trouble.

Now she had an abbey to find. That was the name of Sebastian's home—Brideswell Abbey.

Zoe plucked her raccoon coat from the rear seat and slipped it on. Ever since the *Olympic* had docked in Southampton, she had been frozen stiff. And this was May.

"You can stay here if you wish," she informed her mother. "I'm going to walk. There was a farmhouse behind us and I'll bring someone to pull us out."

"That stone house, do you mean?" Mother looked distraught, staring behind the car in utter panic. "It was *miles* back there. I didn't see an automobile there at all. No one in this country has a vehicle. It's simply *uncivilized*."

"Wait here, then. It's not going to take hours."

"I should hope not. We'll be late for dinner. Really, Zoe, if we're going to have to suffer this journey, I wish you were at least marrying the *duke*."

Mother, I am doing all of this for you. But she didn't say that. In truth, it wasn't all for her mother. Once she had decided to make this marriage to free her trust fund, she had got rather excited for her upcoming independence. She wanted to manage her money her own way, spend it how she wished, invest it as she saw best. She wanted to be autonomous—a prize now available to a modern woman.

The truth was, she simply wasn't going to fall in love again. After her trust fund was released and her divorce settled—when she knew Mother was safe and she could finally breathe again—then she would take up her airplane, and she would drink a toast to Richmond in the sky with a bottle of champagne. She would finally, properly, say goodbye to him. And when she landed she would cry until she could do it no more.

"Mother," she said, "I have never met the duke."

"Well, you are going to meet him now, honey. Why in heaven's name did you agree to marry his brother before you met *him?* You would have been a duchess."

"According to Sebastian, his brother is scarred, reclusive, emotionless and thoroughly dislikes American women."

Mother gave a sly look. "I bet you could change his mind about that, Zoe."

"Sebastian has said his brother has vowed to never marry."

"Never marry?" Mother echoed. "Then his brother..." A cunning smile lifted her mother's lips. "You *will* be the duchess."

"In a country you just called uncivilized."

Her mother's large violet-blue eyes gleamed. "There are a lot of sacrifices that could be endured for a coronet—"

"Mother, Consuelo Vanderbilt just ran away from hers. Apparently it's not as great a treasure as so many heiresses have been led to believe. And I'd better go if I'm to get us out of this muck before dark."

Mother flicked open her compact and painted on a

new scarlet mouth. "Just think, Zoe, we will even be presented at *court.* All those snobs in New York can stick that in their pipes and smoke it."

"I'm sure they will. For now, I'm going to get *help.*" She would never be a duchess. Her union with Sebastian would be dissolved long before that, but there was no point in poking her mother with that particular sharp stick right now.

Her determined steps tried to swallow up the road, but her heels sank in the mud. Down the way, hidden by a muddy hill, plumes of light gray smoke rose against the darker gray sky. If she could see the smoke of the chimney, she couldn't be far away.

She pulled her heels out of the mud, found a firmer place to walk and trudged on with no idea how close to nightfall it actually was. As far as she could tell, the English countryside was perennially dark. A bitter wind rushed across the fields, whipped across the wall and raced up her skirt—one of the shortest in New York that year, cut above the knee.

She pulled her raccoon coat tighter around her. But the English cold seemed to penetrate everything.

Drizzle began then, of course. Rain spattered on her cloche hat, struck her nose and lips. She could not wait to plunge into the warmth of Sebastian's home. A long soak in a great big bathtub filled with steaming water would be heavenly.

Zoe turned a corner. Two things stood ahead of her: the simple stone farmhouse and a solid mass of sheep. She'd never be able to wade through them.

A grunt at her side and the scent of smoke startled her. She whirled around, confronting a deeply lined, ruddy face and a pipe held close to what appeared to be a toothless opening with no lips at all. It was an old man; a stout one with muddy boots, dirty trousers, a brown coat and a tweed cap. He was curled up in a crumpled way, seated on the low wall.

The elderly farmer studied her with small, dark eyes from beneath the low brim of his cap. He pulled on his pipe and didn't say a word.

"Good afternoon." She walked up to the man and stuck out her hand.

He remained utterly still, except for his lips, which released his pipe and sent a ring of smoke into the air. He might have been made from granite himself. He certainly made no move to shake her hand.

She knew, in general, the British did not shake hands, except in some business matters. In New York, she'd hired Lady Fannering, an elderly, broke viscountess, to teach her how to curtsy to Sebastian's family and how to address them. No one had told her what to do with ordinary people.

"My name is Zoe Gifford. I'm here from America— New York City—with my mother. We were driving to Brideswell Abbey when our automobile got stuck in the mud."

She paused, expecting some sort of sympathetic response. The farmer merely smoked his pipe and didn't say a word.

"My wheel is stuck. Do you have an automobile?" she asked. "You could tow me out. Just have to loop a chain around the bumper, hit the gas pedal and out I come."

Again silence.

Her shoe sank again, as if realizing she was getting nowhere. She gave a hard tug and her shoe came free, but it fell off her foot. She was *not* going to put her stocking sole down in this freezing English mud, liberally peppered with sheep poo. Hopping on the other foot, she lifted her leg, knee bent, to slip her shoe back on.

Her coat fell open as her skirt hiked up. Cold, damp air whisked between her legs.

The farmer made a sputtering sound, like a conked-out engine. His pipe dropped from his lips and landed in the muck between his worn boots. His eyes bulged, and he stared at her exposed thigh.

At least she had his attention. She was freezing and desperate enough to use the sight of her legs to get what she needed. People in New York called her wild and sophisticated. But she wasn't truly. At heart, she was still a girl who had grown up dirt poor and who felt a knife-twist of pain every time anyone looked down on her. But she had learned, in the frenetic, moneyed world of Manhattan, that demure didn't get a woman very far. More people respected her for her daring than ever would if she followed rules.

Zoe plucked up his pipe and handed it to the farmer. Up close, the gnarled old man smelled of smoke, damp wool and an earthy scent that she was sure came from his barn. But she was used to being at the aerodrome, where everything smelled of motor oil and gasoline. She batted her lashes. "Could you help me?"

"Bur urn gar burn," the farmer said, or at least that was how the series of grunts and mutterings sounded to her.

It must be his accent. She couldn't grasp it yet. After all, she'd had trouble understanding exactly what people had been saying when she and Mother had disembarked at the pier, and their luggage and her automobile had been unloaded.

"Excuse me, I didn't quite understand. *Do* you have a motorcar? It's what we need to have our car pulled out of the mud. Perhaps even horses could do it—"

He broke in unintelligibly, gesturing toward his house with his pipe. Then he gave a satisfied nod of his head.

This was not going to work. "How far is it to Brideswell Abbey?"

His answer was yet another guttural rush of incomprehensible sounds.

She tried again. But there was not one word in his speech she could recognize. Unfortunately, she had been misled. The inhabitants of England did not actually speak English.

Finally the farmer spat on the ground, then uttered a word she did understand. "Daft."

"I'm not daft," she declared with the full force of Gifford pride. "I can't understand your accent. Probably you don't understand mine either."

Tipping her chin in the air, she turned. She was going to have to walk in the other direction and blindly hope she found Brideswell.

But as she turned to begin marching back toward Mother—who would go off in hysterics when she returned with no automobile or horse to pull them out— Zoe saw a huge black gelding galloping across the fields, ridden by a tall man in a black top hat, immaculate breeches and long gray coat.

The horse's long legs moved so smoothly the animal looked to be soaring over the meadow. The strong neck stretched forward, the mane and black tail streamed back, and the gelding accelerated as if he were truly trying to take off and fly.

She hadn't ridden a horse in forever. Once she'd learned to drive and fly an airplane, she'd forgotten how glorious riding could be.

The rider moved fluidly with the horse's strides, raised out of the saddle. He leaned along the smooth black neck like a brilliant jockey.

He exuded power—in his broad shoulders, his tall frame, his endless, muscular legs. Much of his body was hidden by the long gray coat with its many tiers at his shoulders, but it was obvious how well built he must be. The hat was worn low on his head, shielding his eyes. He was like something out of a nineteenth-century novel.

"Hello!" she called, waving at him. "Over here!"

His head jerked toward her, and she knew he'd heard her, but he continued to thunder off in the same direction, and her heart sank.

Then his course changed. He wheeled the horse toward her.

A low stone fence separated the fields—a wall just like the one that ran along the road. He raced toward it. The rider urged his mount to soar over the fence, and they jumped in perfect unison.

Hooves struck the ground, and the gentleman—he most definitely fit the definition of that thoroughly British word—gently reined the horse in and cantered toward where she stood.

Thankfully, she could actually understand the English spoken by British gentlemen. A man of his class would obviously know where to find the home of the Hazelton family.

As he approached, she couldn't help herself. She clapped with abandon. "Bravo," she called out. "You're an excellent rider."

The rider made a curt acknowledgment of her compliment—an abrupt nod of his head. An American man would have smiled, but this man's face appeared carved of stone. As he approached, the gloom and the brim of his tall hat kept his face in shadow, but she could see his lips were drawn in a hard line. Those lips parted, and words slid out. Cool and austere, they were more chilling than inviting. "Good afternoon, madam."

He turned to the farmer, who had snatched off his cap. "Evnern, Yer Grr," the farmer called out in a reverential tone.

The gentleman on the horse reined his mount to a stop. "The lady is in distress, you say?"

Had he? How this gentleman had mined those words from the sounds, she didn't know, but relief made her almost giddy.

"I'm Zoe Gifford," she shouted, leaning on the stone wall. "I was on my way to Brideswell Abbey when my car went off the road. We're stuck, and we have no idea how to get to the house. Do you know where it is?"

The gentleman drew his horse to a halt more than six feet from the wall that separated them. Perhaps this was what was meant by British reserve—a good few yards were required between people or an interaction became too familiar.

Still, she was not going to shout as if across a chasm. Zoe planted her bottom on the wall, swung her legs over. Her coat once again fell open and her skirt flew up, revealing her stockings and a glimpse of her garters.

The horse reared as she jumped to the ground.

The huge legs pawed at the air, and Zoe's heart banged against her rib cage as if it were dancing the Charleston. She scrambled back, expecting to be crushed—

"Easy, easy," the man commanded, as he pulled on the reins and controlled the horse with his thighs. The enormous hooves thudded against the ground, two feet to the side of her body. She fought not to sway on her feet as she gulped cold breaths of relief.

"Brideswell is my home. I am the Duke of Langford." His voice was cool, calm, utterly without emotion. She would never have known he'd almost been tossed off a horse if she hadn't witnessed it. "So you are Miss Gifford. My brother has told me a great deal about you—it helped to reinforce the impression I had already made, given what I have read about you in American newspapers."

So this was her fiancé's brother and, as Sebastian had warned, ice coated his every word. It was true there had been several stories about her in the papers. But she had chosen not to care what was said about her. "Don't believe everything you read."

The duke sat on his horse, glaring at her—at least she believed he did since she could not see for the shadow cast by his hat—so she approached, putting out her hand. At this moment, she had no desire to curtsy. Not to a man who was peering down his nose at her.

The duke did not take her hand.

"Can you do anything about my car?" she asked, letting her hand drop to her side. "My mother is waiting there for me to return. She's afraid she'll be stuck in the car overnight."

"You should take better care on these roads."

"Aye," the farmer added, with startling clarity. The man drew on his pipe, before stating, "Aye, said that to the lass meself, Yer Grace."

That was news to her. But the duke nodded, as did the farmer, and the two men seemed to share some sort of quiet communication about her inadequacy behind the wheel.

She pursed her lips. "America has some bad roads, I'll admit, but your roads are horrible. There are sheep everywhere. I had to pull off to avoid a flock as I came around a corner, and then we ended up stuck."

"Then perhaps next time you will know to slow down."

"I'll keep that in mind, Your Grace. And while we're discussing how things are done over here, doesn't a gentleman tip his hat?"

The farmer let out a muttered sound of shock, but she didn't care. It didn't matter to her where the duke believed he was positioned socially— she put no stock in that kind of thing. If he chose to be cold and austere, then she would choose to point out where his behavior was at fault.

"My apologies, madam. I am no longer in the habit of doing so—the War left me with scars and my face is not pleasant to look at."

The farmer let out a sharp whistle and both she and the duke jerked to stare at him. The man tipped his cap, then lumbered away across his field. Again he whistled and a small black dog raced to his side, scampering around him as he walked.

Suddenly she and the duke were alone, surrounded by a patchwork of small, sloping fields and a wind that threw misty rain on them. "I think I will survive," she said gently. "I don't faint."

With an elegant sweep of his long leg, the duke dismounted. Holding the reins in one large hand, he lifted his hat and gave her a bow that spoke of a lifetime of dipping his torso in this old-world greeting. She had to admit: experience and schooling could make a man's bow positively dreamy.

It was her invitation to respond with a curtsy, but Zoe found she just couldn't do it, despite the training she'd received before leaving New York. The duke's bow was not really intended to show any respect. It was a perfunctory thing, offered only after she'd insisted on some basic courtesy.

She watched as he straightened, curious now. She'd seen the ravages of war on young American men. Boys who'd come back with missing limbs, or some who were what they called shell-shocked; who shook all the time and jumped at loud noises.

The duke was not all that bad. Scars marred the left side of his face. But it wasn't enough to horrify her.

He had Sebastian's features, but on Langford, every plane and line was harsher, more angular, as if his face had been sculpted with hard slashes—abrupt cheekbones, a blade of a nose, straight, dark brows and a strong chin with a deep cleft in its center. His eyes were a brilliant blue and his lashes were thick and black.

He obviously expected her to look away or gasp with shock.

Sympathy rose. Perhaps it wasn't disgust with his brother's inappropriate American fiancée that had led the duke to keep his distance. He put his hat on quickly, and for one second, he'd looked awkward and unhappy instead of condescending and annoyed, and she knew revealing his injuries had made him vulnerable.

"I lost a brother to the War," she said simply. "It was a horrible thing."

He said nothing for a moment. It was amazing he could look at her so directly without feeling any need to respond, as one would in conversation. Though, she had to admit—what could he say? She changed the subject. "What do we do now, Your Grace? Is it far to walk to Brideswell?"

"I will escort you back to your automobile," he said stiffly. "You may wait there with your mother, and I will send the Daimler for your persons and your belongings."

His expression was that of a man who had bit into a lemon.

Her heart sank. She was going to be trapped in a house with this man for a month. Perhaps the house was enormous and she wouldn't encounter him very often. Hopefully, he had a dining table the size of one of the *Olympic*'s decks and he sat at the opposite end of it.

They walked in silence along the uneven, muddy road, stepping around piles of manure left by the sheep. Then Langford stopped, and she halted, too. The duke cleared his throat and glared down at her. He intended to say something but, just as with the farmer, it seemed to take forever for an Englishman to speak.

"Is there something you wished to discuss, Your Grace?"

"Sebastian tells me you are marrying so you can have access to your trust fund." His words came in a rush, as if they'd burst out on a geyser of emotion he could no longer contain. "That you plan to divorce immediately after you have achieved that goal."

"That's right."

"Good God, Miss Gifford, have you no breeding? Only the most appalling women get divorced. As for planning to end a marriage before you have even wed… this I will not allow."

Zoe squared her shoulders, ready to do battle just as her father would have done when dealing with a cut-throat business opponent. What had Sebastian been thinking? They'd agreed not to explain their plan to either family, knowing it would just cause trouble.

"I have better breeding than you are displaying, Your Grace," she answered coolly. "Sebastian is a chivalrous gentleman. He's saving me from a disaster, and he's happy with the terms of our agreement. I have the contract drawn up, ready for his signature, and I don't believe your consent is required at all. I assure you I'll become Sebastian's wife, just as we've planned. The settlement I am giving him is money he said your family desperately needs. We're making a modern version of a transatlantic marriage—I need a marriage, he needs money, and we don't need to make matrimony last."

"You have no idea what you are doing, Miss Gifford," he snapped.

If the Duke of Langford thought his scowls could make her retreat, he was wrong. "Sebastian intends to use the money to help your family. My trustees, who are solid financial men, are going to work with him to invest it. I think your brother is being very noble."

"I refuse to allow you to drag my family into scandal—"

"A little scandal is a small price for financial rescue, is it not?"

His eyes narrowed. His eyes were vividly blue—

like the sky over the beaches of California. The Duke of Langford had the same smoldering gaze as Valentino, who had once crept into her girlish fantasies about passionate lovemaking. From the right side, with his dark hair, slashes of black brows and glittering eyes, the duke looked so much like the seductive movie star, she almost forgot to breathe. "A decent young woman avoids ignominy. She does not embrace it," he growled.

That shattered the mesmerizing spell of his sapphire eyes. "You're a relic from medieval times. Sebastian and I both need a marriage of convenience. You're stuck with me, whether you like it or not."

"No bold, calculating American heiress is going to disrupt my family."

"Your Grace, my arrangement will *help* your family. But it'll be a pleasure to disrupt *you*."

He glowered. "You are exactly what I expected of an American woman. Americans set my teeth on edge with their explosive, vulgar emotion. You gush, you flaunt and you have no idea of proper restraint. Your behavior in this is both vulgar and repugnant, madam."

She yearned to slap him. But with his scars, she could not bring herself to smack her palm against his face. Apparently, she'd been misled on another aspect of the British. They were more blunt and straightforward than she'd expected.

Taking a step closer to him—her eyes were on level with his lips—Zoe lifted her chin with pride. "You set *my* teeth on edge. You are the most irritating and prejudiced man I've ever had the misfortune to meet. I'm visiting my fiancé's home. It's unfortunate you happen to be in it. And I suppose you don't intend to send a car for my mother and me now."

He bent toward her. A warm, exotic aroma clung to the duke—sandalwood, she believed it was, and he smelled of leather. For a moment, they traded breaths, his scented with tooth powder and smoke.

"I will, Miss Gifford. What sort of host leaves guests stranded in the countryside?"

She almost laughed. "Good." She flung back her arms and stretched, as if thoroughly bored with the whole conversation. "I am looking forward to a long, luscious, hot soak."

"A what?" the duke asked sharply. His boot twisted in a rut on the road and he fell forward an inch, his mouth almost bumping against hers. Up close his lips were full and sensual, and she was suddenly, breathlessly waiting for their mouths to collide. But before it happened, he jerked back and she did, too, and in a heartbeat they were two awkward steps apart, each standing at the edge of the cart track that was called a road.

Her stomach felt as it did when her airplane hit wind shear and suddenly dropped.

She had to be out of her mind. She hadn't let a man kiss her since Richmond had, just before he took off on his flight over the Atlantic. She hadn't even done it with Sebastian. She was hardly going to let it happen with an obnoxious, insulting duke.

Zoe jutted out her hip. "What I meant was a bath. You know: turn on the tap and fill a nice big tub with a lot of hot water and then soak in it. You do have baths over here, don't you?"

Abruptly she was looking at the duke's back. Without a word, he had swung away from her. Then he stopped and motioned for her to follow. "We do, indeed, have baths, madam. What we do not have are taps."

2
DRESSING FOR DINNER

THE FIRST DINNER gong sounded.

Nigel Hazelton, the seventh Duke of Langford, stood in front of the mirror of his dressing room as his valet adjusted his collar and white bow tie, then gave one final tug to the shoulders of his coat.

"Very good, Your Grace," Higgins said.

Even dressing for dinner had become a battle—a clash between the old ways and modernity. He wore full dress for dinner, which meant a tailcoat, white waistcoat and white tie. Sebastian usually appeared for dinner in the style of the Prince of Wales: a tuxedo jacket, once considered too vulgar for female sensibilities, and a black tie…and he slouched around with his hands stuck in his pockets.

Sebastian would look effortlessly elegant and laugh at his brother for being overdressed.

"A relic of an antique age," Nigel muttered.

"Not at all, Your Grace," Higgins assured him. "Such classic attire is always correct."

Since Higgins had been his father's valet, and now approached eighty, Nigel merely said, "That will be all, Higgins."

With a bow and another respectfully murmured "Very good," Higgins disappeared through a connecting door like a shadow into darkness. Nigel ran his hand over his now-smooth jaw, having been shaved within an inch of his life in preparation for dinner.

He believed in formality. He believed in the old ways, the old standards, in showing respect to one's class and position.

But facing the mirror, he had no doubt Miss Gifford thought like Sebastian, considering the fashionable hat crammed on her short, sleek blond hair, the bright red mouth that smirked at him, the astoundingly short skirt she wore. When she'd swung her leg over the wall, the skimpy skirt had flown up, showing the entire length of her shapely legs, right up to the garters securing her stockings at her suntanned thighs.

He'd done the gentlemanly thing and looked away— at everything but those stunning legs. As a result, he'd jerked on Beelzebub's reins and almost unseated himself.

He had almost embarrassed himself again when she'd stretched like a seductive houri and he'd stumbled and almost fallen against her vibrant, scarlet-painted mouth.

It had been a misstep, not an attempt at a kiss. With his scars, he wouldn't think to kiss any woman.

"I should have known I would find you skulking in here," chided a soft female voice, "when you should be in the drawing room."

No American accent flattened the words and drew out the vowels, and he smelled the subdued scent of ladylike lavender. Not Miss Gifford. Nigel knew it was Julia, even before he saw his sister's reflection in the mirror.

"I am not skulking, I am dressing." He turned, and his eyes almost popped out of his head.

Julia had his silver cigarette case open in her hand. She took out a Turkish cigarette and put it between her lips.

"What are you doing?" He stalked toward her.

His sister picked up his lighter. "Attempting to smoke. Miss Gifford does it. She claims that smoking calms nerves. She also claims it keeps a woman thi—"

He relieved Julia of her unlit cigarette, plucking it from her lips. "Smoking is a man's habit. A lit gasper has no place near a delicate lady's mouth."

"Really, Nigel?" Julia crossed her arms in front of her chest. "So? What do you think of her?"

Julia was never so direct or blunt. Nor had she ever considered raiding his cigarette case before. Good God, were American ways contagious?

At least their manner of dress was not. His sister wore a demure gown of dark blue silk and it reached the middle of her calves. Her hair was long and rolled into a chignon. She was very like their mother, though her hair was jet-black, not gold, but she was just as beautiful with her oval face, her curling dark lashes and her wide pale pink mouth that she never touched with paint.

"Since you have seen her, I don't think I need to say more."

"Nigel, you can be hopelessly stuffy." Julia sighed and walked to the windows of his dressing room, pulling back the faded velvet curtains.

He followed. The rain had blown in hard. It ran down the windowpanes, turning the world beyond into a blurry palette of subdued color. Sheets of it sliced through the dark skies and slammed into the stone terrace and the green lawns.

"I showed her and her mother to their rooms," Julia

said, arching a brow, "since you appeared to have abandoned them."

"I instructed Mrs. Hall to take her and her mother to their apartments. It is customary for the housekeeper to do so." He frowned. "Sebastian is nowhere to be found, of course. I have no idea what to say to either of them. The mother was chattering on about the paintings and fixtures as they went upstairs—it sounded as if she were cataloging the contents of the house to auction them off. Miss Gifford finds me both prejudiced and irritating. However, she is determined to say things that both irritate me and prove my prejudice well-founded. The woman is Sebastian's fiancée. He should be here to keep her entertained."

He felt Julia's stare and he turned to her.

His sister regarded him with an amused expression. "I thought you'd only spent a short time in her company, Nigel. It sounds as if you had a lot to discuss."

"American women are not backward in coming forward." He raked his hand through his hair. He couldn't tell Julia the whole truth about this damnable, scandalous business. "She told me *she* proposed to him."

"Nigel, women in America—"

"Are not ladylike."

Julia laughed. And that was a rare treat these days. She was usually quiet, somber, troubled. He wished she would fall in love again. Yet he could not do his duty as head of the family and ensure she was presented to eligible men. Her dowry was quickly evaporating, along with the rest of the money.

"I thought she looked very ladylike," Julia argued. "Even you can't deny that she is very lovely."

"Her skirts are too short. She paints her face. Her hair is cut like a boy's."

"It is the fashion now, brother dear. It is called the Eton crop."

"That's because schoolboys have their hair cut that way. It's hardly feminine."

"I do love you, Nigel," Julia said. "Miss Gifford has what the Americans call 'it.' You know—sex appeal."

He did know what was meant by "it." But the word *sex* on the lips of his sister brought a strangled cough from his chest. Nigel sputtered, unable to catch his breath. He had to stalk to the chest of drawers, where he'd set a glass of brandy, and down a mouthful before he could stop choking. Suddenly, he saw what Miss Gifford was already bringing into his household.

The bloody modern world.

He didn't want it here.

He'd come back from war to find that, while he spent four years in mucky trenches, the world had changed— it was as if he'd stood still while the planet had revolved around him at top speed. There had been too much change, enough to upheave the world. At his home, at Brideswell, he'd planned to ensure change never breached the ancient walls.

Instead it had slithered in wearing an abbreviated skirt and scarlet lips and carried with it an absolute fortune.

"Julia, you cannot speak like that. You are an—" Another sharp cough. He had been about to say "unmarried woman." What in God's name was he thinking, to remind her of how much she'd lost?

"So you still disapprove of the marriage?" Before he could answer, she added quickly, "The thing is, Nigel,

I think *I* disapprove. I think this is wrong. You know what…what Mother was like. How terribly unhappy she was with Father."

Here, Julia wasn't being blunt. She was being careful with her words, but he knew how miserable their mother had been because of their father's infidelities.

"I like Miss Gifford," Julia rushed on, almost defiantly. "I think I will like her even more as I grow to know her better. I don't want to see her unhappy."

He had wanted to dislike Miss Gifford, and the woman had given him every reason to do so. She intended to disgrace his family because it was convenient to her.

But he also could not forget how she had looked him in the face without a gasp or flinch after he'd doffed his hat. Or the composed way she had told him she had lost a brother to combat.

There had been no gushing, no display of emotion at all. Just a cool acknowledgment she had experienced the destruction and loss that came with war, and in her direct American gaze, he'd felt she understood something of what he'd been through.

It was a moment in which he'd respected Miss Zoe Gifford. A very brief moment.

"I think Miss Gifford will get her heart broken." Julia's soft voice broke in on his thoughts. "Sebastian has never fallen in love with any woman. I think he's incapable of it."

Nigel almost dropped his glass. Only quick juggling saved him from throwing brandy on his chest. His heart thundered like it had when shells had been exploding around him.

Could Julia know about Sebastian? Four decades

ago, Oscar Wilde had gone to prison for the same appetites he knew Sebastian possessed, under a charge of gross indecency. That scandal still reached delicate female ears. Had Julia guessed what Nigel knew for a fact—that their brother was in love with a Captain John Ransome? Good God, how did he ask her?

"I mean Sebastian is rather selfish, and he's exactly like Father was," Julia said pensively.

Nigel relaxed. She did not know. Their father had been a womanizing rogue.

"I love him dearly," she went on, "but I would never let one of my friends marry him."

"Miss Gifford went into this proposition so she could get hold of her inheritance, as it is held in trust until she marries. I do not believe our steely-eyed American heiress is going to have her heart broken," he said coldly.

"And most heiresses want titles. If she wants Sebastian, she must be in love with him." Julia lifted her head and stared at him with huge, stricken blue eyes. "Oh, I'm so sorry. I didn't mean—"

"I know I am shirking my duty by avoiding marriage. I was doing it as a favor to both myself and any prospective bride. I will not do so any longer."

"You are going to marry?"

"I am going to have to," he said grimly. "Sebastian agreed to this marriage to obtain funds. It is my responsibility as duke to find a way to support Brideswell. I have to do my duty."

Julia touched his shoulder. "I know losing Mary broke your heart, Nigel. I know what that feels like."

He clasped his hands gently over Julia's. He had frightened Mary away when he'd come back from war, scarred, haunted, wounded. Frightened her so badly, she'd married someone else.

Julia frowned. "No, you can't make a duty marriage. I hate to think of you doing that. I don't want you to be as unhappy as Mama and Father were."

"You need not fear I will make a wife unhappy. I will keep my distance from her. After all, as you say, she would be in it for the title." He had to keep his distance. He certainly couldn't share a bed with a wife, to sleep the night with her, the way some couples now did. Not when he screamed with nightmares or had to fight to control the shaking of his body when a loud noise erupted.

"You cannot keep your distance from a wife and have children, Nigel. That simply won't work. If Sebastian and Miss Gifford are in love, why not let Sebastian go through with marriage?"

"I cannot." At her frown, he added, "I have a very good reason."

Julia rolled her eyes. Then she smiled—an impish smile that made his heart ache—and she waved her hand airily. "Then perhaps Miss Gifford has well-to-do American friends for you. I shall ask her—"

"I would not go near any woman who claims friendship with Miss Gifford."

"That won't stop me from asking her, unless you give your reasons."

"I assure you that Miss Gifford would not attempt to marry me to any woman she calls a friend."

The gong rang again—the final summons after the warning shot. He offered his arm. "Let us go for dinner."

Julia sobered. "I am not looking forward to this,

Nigel. Grandmama is appalled by Sebastian's choice, and she has not been hiding her displeasure. Mama has been attempting to put it all in the best light, but you know how stubborn Grandmama can be. I think dinner is going to be a disaster."

"It will not be," he said darkly. But he could easily imagine the battle over dinner between the dowager and Miss Gifford. And he could readily guess how Miss Gifford would behave. Much like he had when he'd had to race through bullets to save one of his soldiers—too stubborn to duck.

Strangely, Nigel found he was actually looking forward to seeing how she handled herself.

What was he thinking? When he'd come home, he hadn't wanted any more battles or confrontation. Brideswell had been the promise of normalcy after four years of living hell, albeit a far poorer normalcy than before the War.

Yes, he was a relic of an older age—of the way the world was before war had ravaged it. And he wanted his dinner in peace. There would be no wars tonight at his dining table.

"ZOE, YOU REALLY must wear jewels tonight." Mother sailed through the door. Encased in a formal gown that displayed her thin figure, her mother surveyed her with narrowed eyes. "That dress is all wrong. It's too modern for the occasion."

Zoe had dismissed the maid sent to help her dress—her maid and Mother's were arriving later by train. The girl's jaw had almost struck the carpet when she'd adjusted the skirt and discovered it went no lower.

"I like it," Zoe said. "There's no point in trying to

make it look as though our family goes back to Henry VIII, Mother. We don't." She touched her neck. "I was thinking a string of white beads—"

"Diamonds, Zoe." Lifting her gloved hand, rings sitting on top of the satin, Annabelle Gifford counted off the pieces that had been shipped by trunk and were now in the duke's safe.

"Mother, it's dinner, not a ball at Buckingham Palace. If I wear all of that I will look like a walking sandwich board for Tiffany & Co. Anyway, I want to look modern. I *am* modern," Zoe added, suddenly aware of how coldly she said it.

Mother looked pained. "The duke himself is quite handsome, you know. Once you ignore his scars. He looked at you, my dear, with a great deal of interest."

"If by interest, you mean dislike, then yes, he showed a lot of it. When the duke looks at me, it's down his nose. He's obnoxious and rude."

"I am sure if you were to get to know him—"

"I would be even more likely to want to run him over with my car. Every word exchanged with that man feels like shots fired in a war."

She would not think of that moment when their lips had almost touched. When she'd *wanted* their lips to touch. It had been a moment of insanity.

A modern girl kissed men—she had kissed a few. She'd known sizzling kisses. Her lips hadn't even touched the duke's, and the air had crackled like the aftermath of a lightning strike.

Yet the man was insufferable.

"Zoe, you must not antagonize the duke." Mother's large violet-blue eyes widened in panic. "Think of your father—it was his fondest dream that you be accepted in

New York society. No one will turn up their noses if you have a title. No ballrooms will be barred to us; there will be no invitation list that does not feature our names."

The things that drove Mother seemed so trivial. They had been through a war. The world was a place of manufacturing, of making things—airplanes, telephones, motion pictures.

That world had made Father a rich man—Zoe had grown up in Manhattan, after Father had made his money in steel. Columns and beams and rivets from his mills were used in most of the brand-new buildings that reached into the sky, and she knew a little of the ruthlessness that coup had taken.

What did it matter that Zoe, as a debutante, had been purposely excluded from most balls or that when her family hosted them, people took malicious pleasure in not showing up?

All that had mattered to her was following her heart. She'd fallen in love with Richmond DeVille, the famous and daring aviator. Richmond had taught her how to fly a plane. With him, she had touched heaven with silver wing tips. Every moment with Richmond had been filled with excitement and challenge. But they'd kept their relationship a secret, because Richmond had just got a divorce.

On the day of his departure, flashbulbs had popped everywhere, but she and Richmond had found treasured private moments. He'd slipped a diamond ring on her finger. With tears of joy and excitement in her heart, she had wished him a safe voyage. She had waved at his airplane until it had disappeared over the ocean into the early-morning sky like a silver star winking out. Then she had sat by the wireless for hours and hours, waiting for the word he'd arrived.

He hadn't made it. Days later the wreckage of his plane was found. His body never was.

Zoe snatched up a brush and smoothed her hair. "I don't care if they do snub us. Daddy might have come from a shack with a dirt floor, but he made something of himself. The duke hasn't even earned his advantages. He has them because of the luck of his birth. I don't need to wear diamonds, Mother. Everyone in the dining room knows I have a fortune. Money gives us the only things worth caring about in the world now—"

She was about to say the words *freedom* and *independence,* but in the large cheval mirror, she suddenly noticed how pale her mother was. She whirled.

Mother put her hand over her heart and took shallow breaths. "I know why you are doing this, Zoe. I know you are marrying to help me."

Zoe rushed to her mother, suddenly feeling helpless. "It will be all right—"

Mother trembled. "Oh, Zoe, I am so afraid. Those letters I received…they got downright threatening. If your uncle were ever to find out about that check, I'd be ruined. He would never forgive me. Brother-in-law or not, he would prosecute to the full extent of the law. I might end up in jail. I meant no harm by it. I was so certain I would be able to put the money back right away—"

"He's not going to find out. I'll have access to my funds long before Uncle Hiram comes back. You made a mistake, Mother—" She said it softly and reassuringly, though she could not understand her mother. How could Mama have forged a check? How could she not have seen that would obviously lead to disaster? But recriminations would get her nothing but maternal hysteria, and that she couldn't bear. "You will not go to jail," Zoe said firmly.

"But I want you to be happy married to Lord Sebastian," Mother said.

"Of course I'll be happy," Zoe lied smoothly.

"You aren't in love with him."

That startled her but she tried not to show it. "I will make the best of this, Mother."

"If you don't love him, there's nothing to stop you marrying his brother. You could have him, Zoe, if you just try. The deal's not done yet. You could still change your mind. And if you sew up the duke first—"

"Mother, no."

Her mother took quick, fluttery breaths and her hand trembled over her heart. "Dear Zoe, I've been having such pains. I'm so worried about you. It would ease my heart to know you had married the right man."

"Mother, you've been as healthy as a horse your entire life. This may have worked for Mrs. Vanderbilt, but I've heard Consuelo's story, and it's not going to work on me. You're not dying, and I'm not going to be pressured to chase a duke because of a fictitious bad heart. I will never be a duchess."

"What are you talking about? If the duke does not marry, you will."

Zoe shook her head. Mother might use quivering breaths, batting eyelashes and tears to get her way, but she was as strong and formidable as the steel her father had been famous for producing. The duke knew the truth and he had probably told his family. Mother might as well know it, too. "I won't be married to Sebastian long enough."

NIGEL ESCORTED JULIA to the south drawing room, where it was customary to gather for cocktails before the meal. They reached the open doors just as their grandmother, the dowager, exclaimed, "Good heavens, are those her knees? Is she in her shift? Where is her skirt?" Then, her voice higher pitched, "Sebastian, what are you doing on *your* knee? Are you rehearsing for a play?"

Julia looked around the doorway and gasped, "Oh, how romantic."

Nigel saw the scene in the room and his gut twisted with anger. He agreed with his grandmother: What in hell did his brother think he was doing?

In front of his fiancée, his hair soaked from the rain, his tuxedo jacket obviously thrown on in haste, Sebastian had dropped to one knee. He held a small velvet box in the palm of his outstretched hand.

Smoothing her skirt with nervous hands, Miss Gifford sparkled like a handful of stars in the glow of the candles and lamps. A white-and-silver dress with delicate straps fell from her slim shoulders, coasted over her slender figure, ended in gauzy, floating bits of fabric that swirled just above her knees. She stared down at Sebastian with huge, surprised violet eyes.

Whatever Sebastian was doing, she was not in on it.

Sebastian took her hand and bestowed a kiss on her fingertips, his gaze focused on nothing but her. But pure shock registered in her eyes...and in the dropped jaws and gaping mouths of his mother, Grandmama, his sister Isobel and Mother's two male guests—Quigley, a writer, and Sir Raynard, an older local squire.

"We did it over the telephone before, and I knew you deserved more, Zoe," Sebastian said, his expression deceptively earnest. "I'm sorry I'm late. I hopped off to town this morning and picked this up. I had it made especially for you. Took me a deuced long time to come up with the right inscription, then get it engraved. But you deserve a proper proposal of marriage."

It was satisfying to watch Miss Gifford squirm with embarrassment as Sebastian flicked open the box with a twist of one hand. In white velvet sat a heart-shaped ruby the size of a quail's egg, surrounded by diamonds.

"Marry me, my beloved Zoe," his brother said huskily. "Make me the happiest romantic fool in England. Now kiss me, love."

Nigel wanted to haul his brother to his feet. There was no need for a proposal. Sebastian should have been proposing the date for the blasted divorce.

But in one swift movement, Sebastian jumped to his feet and pulled Miss Gifford into his arms. In front of horrified guests, Sebastian sealed his mouth to his fiancée's lips.

A hot red flush of embarrassment rushed up the back of Nigel's neck. As duke, he had to put a stop to the scandalous display—

A cane sharply struck the floor. The dowager duchess's voice soared to fill the drawing room. "Good heavens, Sebastian, desist. How will I face my dinner with this image burned on my eyes?"

3

DINNER AT BRIDESWELL

WHAT DID HE mean by *proposing* to her?

They had a business agreement already. What more did they need beyond an intent to sign a contract and a handshake to seal it?

A footman bowed at Zoe's side, presenting a silver tray filled with oysters, redolent with garlic and lemon. Her appetite had evaporated but she plopped an oyster on her plate to be polite, alongside two wafer-thin slices of cucumber topped with cream cheese and caviar, also taken to make it appear she was not at all troubled, that she was thrilled Sebastian had made her a gushily romantic offer of marriage.

He had kissed her. Not just a sweet peck, suitable for viewing by his mother and grandmother. He'd swept her into a flamboyant, passionate kiss, long and intense. But she hadn't felt anything except surprise.

Sebastian sat across from her, down the table from his brother. Zoe couldn't read Sebastian's heavy-lidded, cool and jaded gaze. They were a small, intimate party housed in a gigantic dining room. There was the duke; the dowager, who had found Sebastian's romantic proposal shocking; the duchess; Sebastian; his sister Julia; his fourteen-year-old sister, Isobel; two older gentlemen friends of the duchess; herself; and Mother.

Zoe glanced down at the ostentatious ruby ring. The proposal and the kiss must have been gestures to distract his family. To make them believe this marriage was the real thing. But it wasn't, and the Duke of Langford knew it.

He hadn't told the rest of the family. Why not? Why not try to turn them all against her, if he was so against this marriage?

She applied a fork to the oyster, drawing out the plump treat and swallowing. Tart lemon, rich cream, the bite of garlic exploded on her tongue. Exquisite, but she was too startled to really think about the food going down her throat. Champagne was poured into her glass.

Conversation droned around her. The dowager—a tall, thin woman in a dress of the prewar style—was making an emphatic point. She knew how to make her voice cut through all others. Sebastian was talking to Mother, and Mother, who now knew the truth of the arrangement, was determined to change their minds about ending the marriage. She appeared transfixed by Sebastian's every charming word.

Zoe had been just like that on the first night she'd met Sebastian.

She'd thought jazz music, dancing and cocktails would help her think up a solution to her problem— her need for a marriage when her heart ached for Richmond. Lord Sebastian Hazelton had spent the entire night trying to coax the sorrow out of her eyes. In the end, she had poured the whole story out to him. He'd given her his story: an estate in ruins, a way of life crumbling, and his need to marry for money—something it offended him to do.

It wasn't supposed to be about love. She'd made that

very clear. Yet that proposal had seemed so sincere. So had his kiss. What was he doing?

She bit into a cucumber-and-caviar canapé and chased it down with a sip of champagne.

Langford was staring at her over his champagne flute, with an intensity that burned brighter than the candles struggling to illuminate the room. He had not said a word to anyone yet, but in white tie and an elegant black tailcoat, with his severe black hair and arresting blue eyes, he dominated even this massive dimly lit room.

Lifting her chin with pride, Zoe raised her glass slightly in a subtle, defiant toast to him. The duke put his glass to his lips, and his mouth softened as they touched his glass. An inappropriate shiver rushed down her spine, and her tummy dipped again.

A gilt-rimmed bowl was set in front of her, and soup of a soft, spring green was ladled into it. She smelled a light watercress soup.

Lady Julia was also presented with soup, but didn't dip in her spoon. Despite all the sumptuous food, she had not touched a bite.

Julia Hazelton was what must be meant by an English rose—ivory skin, rose-pink cheeks and huge blue eyes. A graceful, demure beauty. Julia had the sort of haunting gorgeousness that was made for austere, lovely Brideswell and the incessant rain, the ordered gardens, the rich green lawns. Sebastian's sister had been welcoming—the only one in the house who had—but in unguarded moments she looked sad.

Zoe knew all about being sad. She beamed a bright smile at Julia. She ignored the sharp glance from the dowager, who had the air of the *Olympic* bearing down on a harbor, if that liner had been dressed in throat-high purple silk with an anchor of amethysts around the neck.

"Lady Julia, I would like very much to go riding," Zoe said. "Would you be interested in a morning ride? If the weather lets us. I'm beginning to fear England is located beneath a permanent rain cloud."

Julia looked startled. "Oh—oh, I should love to."

"I am afraid that will be impossible," declared the dowager. "You have a meeting with the Women's Institute."

Zoe had known loneliness in New York society and in Julia's slightly hesitant, then ebullient tone, she sensed a girl happy with the idea of making a new friend.

She wanted a friendship with Julia. It probably wouldn't survive the divorce. But she wanted to try, and no ocean liner of a British matriarch was going to stop her.

"I should be happy to go with you to the Women's Institute meeting," Zoe said to Julia. "And see how these things are done."

She felt Langford's glare, but ignored it.

The dowager harrumphed. "Sebastian told us some nonsense that you plan to be married in America."

"That is correct. In New York."

She pursed her lined lips. "You should be married here, in England. Sebastian, why did you not insist?"

Sebastian did not answer. He finished his champagne and touched his glass. At once, the young footman refilled it to the brim.

"I think it's perfect that my darling will marry where she's grown up," Mother gushed, "where all her friends can be witness to the happy event. We'll have a huge reception and the wedding will be at—"

Thump. Even at the table, the dowager slammed her cane on the floor. "Mrs. Gifford—"

"Every June bride hopes for sunshine," Zoe broke in cheekily. "I don't think I could guarantee that here."

The two footmen hurried in with another set of silver trays bearing two fish dishes. Their presence did not even slow the dowager as she snapped, "Marrying Sebastian will make you British, Miss Gifford. This will now be your home. It is preposterous to think of holding your wedding elsewhere."

"Then I shall embrace being preposterous."

"No granddaughter-in-law of mine shall be so poorly behaved. You will listen to me."

"I will do as I wish."

The dowager's cane clattered to the floor. Utter quiet fell. Even the servants ceased to move, though the dowager needed her cane back. For a crazy moment, Zoe thought the bubbly pouring into Mother's glass had stopped in midstream.

The youngest girl, Isobel, stared in openmouthed shock at Zoe. Mother was apparently attempting to keep pace with Sebastian's champagne consumption. Sebastian's mother, Maria, the duchess, was putting all her attention on her dinner and did not even look up. The duchess looked exactly like him, slender, exquisitely beautiful, with golden hair. She was frail and pale, and had said nothing more to Zoe than a stuttered greeting in the drawing room, where they'd had cocktails before Sebastian's unexpected and dramatic proposal.

The dowager's lips moved, but no sound came out, as if she had been robbed of her voice.

"That is a careless and selfish attitude to take, Miss Gifford." The slow, deep drawl was the Duke of Langford. "If soldiers had taken such an attitude, our respective countries would be in smoldering ruins."

"We are speaking of my wedding," Zoe said brightly. "Not of war."

He stared at her with open dislike, and the dowager said sharply, as a footman jerked into motion and retrieved her cane, "You seem determined to launch a war, yet I thought Americans liked to keep out of skirmishes until all the dangerous work was done."

Zoe's chin went up. "If you are speaking of the War, we arrived just in time to help win it." She thought of her brother, Billy, and a cold anger settled around her heart. She knew about pain, loss and sacrifice, but it was as if the British thought they were the only ones who had experienced suffering, and everyone else should be condemned for having it easy.

She was not a criminal here. She had promised Sebastian a substantial amount of money as a settlement, and his family could use it. Brideswell obviously needed repair—and electricity, not to mention indoor plumbing.

As for scandal—really, divorce was not so horrifying anymore.

But the duke had pegged her as a scarlet woman, the dowager was determined to find fault with her, and Sebastian's mother appeared to want to ignore her.

Defiantly, she went on, "The War was in the last decade. Time has marched on. You should install electric lights, Your Grace. Perhaps, twenty-two years in, it is time to embrace the twentieth century."

The dowager sniffed. "The rooms are best suited to display by candlelight."

"The rooms are best suited to being gloomy?" Zoe asked. Langford glared at her with brooding intensity, so she sweetly asked, "What about plumbing or central heating, Your Grace? Surely you would wish some modern convenience."

Sebastian laughed. "Langford has no desire to be modern, my dear."

"Then I will make him more comfortable and speak of the past." She resented him calling her selfish. She was not doing this for herself, but for her mother. And the duke was going to benefit a great deal. "In what regiment did you serve in the War, Your Grace?"

Lady Julia's fork clattered to the table. The dowager gasped and pursed her lips, looking distinctly like a fish. Isobel stared at her brother, a bite of food balanced on her lip.

Everyone stared at the duke, waiting for something to happen.

"We don't— We can't—" Lady Julia began, but she stopped abruptly. Her face was pale, her eyes wide.

The duke cleared his throat. Cold anger radiated from his gaze. "We will not discuss war at my dining table. It is not done. My family have all suffered a great deal because of the War."

"It's something we all have in common, isn't it?" she argued. "I'm quite happy to field all the awkward questions you can throw at me. I'm not marrying Sebastian for his title, and I don't give a fig for social strictures. We've all suffered loss, life is short and I'm in it for the fun and the happiness now. I don't see there's any sense at all in pretending there's no world beyond those rain-streaked windows of yours. You cannot pretend the world is not changing around you. My goodness, even Britain now has the vote."

"Two years before America," Langford shot at her.

"But with so many strings attached, even an intelligent woman like your sister cannot exercise what should be her right."

"Zoe!" Mother gasped. She looked as if she might faint into her fried filleted sole in anchovy sauce.

"I can see you paid a horrible price for war, Your Grace. I lost a brother. I can't just not talk about it. I can't act as if he never existed. We Americans did fight in the Great War, after all."

"Zoe, no," Mother breathed.

"Are you quite finished, Miss Gifford?" inquired Langford stonily. "If I visit your home, I shall expect to be required to pour the contents of my soul onto your dining table. Here, at Brideswell, I will ask you to follow *my* social strictures."

She had opened up her heart. How could he continue to snap at her after what she'd said about her brother? "All right then, Your Grace. What do you speak of at dinner, then? So far I've heard you utter barely a word, while I've been condemned for wanting to wed in my native country, for daring to ask the name of your regiment and for suggesting intelligent women should vote."

The doors opened, the footmen strode in wordlessly and everything stopped while plates of fish were traded for larded fillets of rabbit. More wine was poured. This time, red.

"A lady should be taught how to engage others in conversation. In the *proper* sort of conversation." The dowager snapped the words to the room in general.

"I prefer meaningful conversation." Tears welled beneath her words, and Zoe fought to hold them back. All she could think was how she wished she were dining at the Waldorf with Richmond, instead of here. "If I'm going to endure a whole lot of anxiety at the dinner table, I would rather it be over something worth caring about."

"If we are going to dissect our lives at the dining table," Langford returned, "I would begin with yours, Miss Gifford. Tell me where you were born, what life is like in America. How did you meet Sebastian? I believe it was at a speakeasy. And I believe it was after you had broken up another gentleman's marriage."

The dowager gasped and the duchess threw a mortified glance at Sebastian.

"That last part isn't true, Your Grace," Zoe said. "I've broken up no one's marriage. But I did meet Sebastian at an underground club in Harlem. Sebastian and I indulged in rather too many cocktails, and we ended up dancing in a fountain. Of course, it was April, and much too cold. But bathtub gin will do that to you. And lo and behold, we decided to marry."

They expected her to shock them. The Hazeltons all seemed so grim or restrained—it was as if they were all preserved beneath glass.

"But we did fall in love," Sebastian added quickly. "Her charming American ways swept me off my feet."

"Perhaps they would not have done so had you been sober," the dowager said tartly. The lady turned to the duke in a flash of purple. "Langford, this is your fault. What were you thinking to allow Sebastian to travel alone? You should have accompanied him."

"Accompany him?" Zoe echoed. "Sebastian is a grown man."

"He rarely behaves like one," the dowager snapped. "His brother knows it is his duty to keep Sebastian out of trouble."

"Well, Langy refuses to leave Brideswell," Sebastian threw in with a careless smile. "And I refuse to be trapped here. When Zoe and I are married, we'll set up house in London. I know she will take good care of me and keep me out of trouble. Perhaps you can visit us. Certainly, you'll want to come after we begin to fill our nursery."

Sebastian's easy lie speared her with guilt. Suddenly she hated all this. She had been wrong to throw their expectations at them in bold defiance. She should treat them with respect at least, even if they did not return it. That meant she had to be up front about their arrangement. "There is something all of you must know about this wedding—"

"That can wait until later, Miss Gifford," the duke interrupted. "I, for one, would much rather talk about dancing in fountains. Tell me more."

His lips mouthed more words to her. *Do not tell them.* For a moment, his icy demeanor dropped, and he faced her with an almost pleading expression.

That stunned her.

But she recovered as swiftly as she could. "I don't think I should, Your Grace. I suspect discussing such a topic would be improper."

"Then we have come to an agreement," he said sharply. "Neither of us will plumb the depths of anyone's soul. I, for one, would like to finish my meal in an atmosphere of peace."

His tones could have frozen the dinner right to the table. Langford did not say one more word, and neither did anyone else. But at the end of four more courses, as the other men left for port and Zoe and her mother were directed to follow the ladies, the duke appeared at her side and he touched her wrist.

The brief contact made her stop in her tracks. The others filed out, and for a moment, she and Langford were alone, their faces close, just as they had been on the road, when their lips had almost touched.

His fingers curled around her wrist, holding her in place. Strangely, the air felt thick and heavy around them, as if lightning might fork through the shadows of the dining room.

"Please do not tell the ladies about your deal with Sebastian, Miss Gifford," he said.

"I would rather be honest, Your Grace. I don't regret my arrangement with Sebastian, but I do think now it is wrong to fool your family and pretend this marriage is real."

"There is something you have to know." When he spoke softly and low, his voice changed. No longer did it sound sharp with frost. It was smooth and rather caressing. "Our mother will never accept a divorce."

"It's not going to make much of a scandal, Your Grace," she stated. "In America, it is said that over fifteen percent of marriages now end in divorce, as people choose to find happiness rather than endure in misery."

"Our mother is a Catholic," he said. "This goes against her faith. She is already gravely weakened by our father's death, the War and losing William after that. The scandal would destroy her."

This was why he'd said nothing to his family. Zoe's stomach dropped away. "Who is William?" Her older brother's name had been William. They always called him Billy.

"He was my youngest brother. The Spanish flu epidemic claimed him, after the War."

"I—I'm sorry."

The duke's expression remained hard, as if carved of granite. But was it not because he felt no emotion, but because he was fighting to keep his feelings contained?

She was really sorry. Sorry for him, for his lost brother, his grieving mother.

His blue gaze bored into her. "You see, what you propose to do is not so harmless after all. Perhaps it is time you thought of more than yourself, Miss Gifford."

"It might surprise you, but I am. I am sorry you lost your brother. I know what that's like. But I know we also have to go on living. That's what I intend to do. Grasp life and live it as much as I can, so I can do his living for him as well as mine. I think we have an obligation to do so."

The duke glared at her. "Live how you please, but do not tell them of the arrangement tonight," he said. Then his fingers released her wrist. He walked away from her, just as he had on the road, but this time he did not look back, and he left her all by herself in the cavernous dining room.

4

THE JAZZ CLUB

From the arched stone doorway of the wine cellar, Nigel watched as Sebastian jauntily drew out a bottle of Château Cheval Blanc and tossed it from hand to hand.

"What in hell do you think you are doing?" he demanded.

Sebastian spun on his heel. A smug grin spread over his face. "Courting."

"No. You are not."

A guffaw met that. Sebastian scooped up two crystal goblets he had left on the floor and whistled his way to the cellar steps, where Nigel barred his way with an outstretched leg.

Sebastian rolled his eyes. "Hell, you should be helping me, Nigel. If I can woo Miss Gifford, we won't divorce, thus the family will be spared the scandal and notoriety. I've arranged to meet her in the gallery at midnight. What woman can resist an '04 Bordeaux and a suitor who praises her beauty to the stars?"

"Miss Gifford, I expect. I saw her face when you proposed. This game ends now, Sebastian. I have devised a solution."

"I'm supposed to drop to my knees and supplicate before you, oh great duke?"

Nigel glared. "I am adopting an American business strategy: making you a counteroffer."

"You want to marry me? It's illegal and you don't come with a trust fund."

Nigel gripped the doorway so hard he was amazed he didn't break off stone. "I will find a bride who comes with a substantial dowry. Once Brideswell is taken care of and Julia's dowry restored, you will receive an allowance. You can continue your dissolute London lifestyle, drinking and gaming. For Mother's sake, I'll keep you happy."

God, he hated this. He had vowed not to marry. Now he had no damned choice.

Sebastian prodded him in the chest with the bottle. "But on a short leash. Even if you could snag an heiress, I would have to refuse your proposal."

Nigel grabbed the bottle out of his brother's hand. He felt the dull throb in the back of his skull. Sometimes the pain started this way: building slowly until it exploded. Other times it hit him like a bursting shell. "You have a duty and an obligation to this family—"

"For once, I *am* putting this family before my personal desires, Langy. I need a way out of trouble, and marriage is it."

"What kind of trouble?" he asked slowly.

"The sort of trouble that gets a man dunked in fountains at Oxford by mobs of brawny, drunken louts. But I suppose you don't want to talk about it. No one in this family speaks openly of anything. No one does in any family of the bloody British aristocracy. That's what we do—adopt a stiff upper lip, pretend there is no rot in the foundations and carry on. But I can no longer do that. There are rumors, and I don't want to be rumored into a prison sentence. If I produce a lovely, rich bride and eventually an heir, I can sweep the gossip away. You're bloody worried about a scandal? The family will have a hell of a bigger one if I don't wed."

He had never understood Sebastian—not because his brother was drawn to men, but because Sebastian had been filled with a burning rage all his life. Underneath the charm, he was a powder keg that often exploded. He looked for trouble, just like their father had.

"Sebastian," he began, but his brother jumped neatly over his leg, snatched the Château Cheval Blanc out of his hand and vaulted up the stairs.

Nigel stalked after Sebastian, down the corridor and through the green baize door that separated the servants' part of the house from the family's living areas.

He caught Sebastian in the gallery. Lit lamps bathed the length in a golden glow that shone on three hundred years of Hazelton ancestral portraits in heavy gilt frames. Rain slammed against the windows.

He grabbed his brother's shoulder and hauled him around. "The answer to your problem is not a marriage where the woman has no idea what she's getting into, Sebastian. I won't let you woo this woman under false pretenses." He knew his brother was bitter and in pain, but that was no excuse to hurt Miss Gifford.

Sticking a screw into the cork, Sebastian shrugged. "I need to marry her. You aren't going to stop me, brother. Short of marrying her yourself."

"I could marry her myself," he said, without emotion.

His brother's blond brows shot up. The cork came free with a pop. "She doesn't want your blasted title, Langy, which is all you have to offer."

Even before his brother's insult, he'd dismissed the

idea. But he hated that nickname. "This woman is too clever to be fooled. Once she knows she's been duped, she won't meekly remain your wife. And you can't imagine she'll be discreet. Every sordid detail of your life will be paraded by the muckraking press."

"That's where you're wrong." Sebastian poured two glasses of wine and set them on the floor. "I can fool her. My blessing and my curse is that women tend to fall in love with me. It's the irony of my life—a smile, some sweet words, my full and devoted attention, and women swoon. Zoe will be as easily convinced as the rest of them. Though it may take some time with her, as she just lost her fiancé in an aeroplane crash—"

"What? What in the bloody hell did you just say?" Icy coldness shot through Nigel's body.

"That's what precipitated the whole scheme. She needed to marry, but could not face the idea of finding a husband while her heart was broken by the loss of her fiancé. I proposed a marriage of convenience. She took me up on the offer. Obviously, this wooing business will be a slow one." Sebastian drained half his wine and refilled the glass.

"Her heart was broken," Nigel repeated.

"I guess it was. But she'll get over it—"

"Julia is mourning a lost fiancé." Everything seemed strangely, eerily still. He remembered moments like this on the front. As if everything had stopped, and the only sound to be heard was the breathing of other men before they went over the top, and at the moment they did, guns would fire, shells would explode and most of those chests would stop sucking in air forever. "Have you not seen how much that loss has devastated your sister?" Nigel asked slowly.

"Yes."

Nigel struggled to breathe. "Miss Gifford must be feeling just as much pain. You are taking advantage of a woman in mourning. No gentleman has the right to behave this way."

"Who says I aspire to be a gentleman?"

"You are a Hazelton. You will aspire to be a gentleman if I have to beat you until you do."

"I won't hurt her, damn it. I'll be circumspect in my…affairs."

"If you marry her, you will be faithful to her."

"Bugger off."

The next thing Nigel knew, his gloves were split at the knuckles, his hand hurt like the blazes and Sebastian was sprawled on his arse on the floor. Had he really punched his brother?

But like a bobbing puppet perched on a spring, Sebastian jumped to his feet. Blood dribbled down from his nose.

Nigel didn't move as Sebastian's left fist hit his cheek, broke scarred skin and sent his head reeling back with the force of the impact. Absorbing that blow, he took another to his gut without complaint. Sweat poured off his brow, leaking like a stream of salt into his eyes. Ragged breaths tore at his chest.

He didn't lift his fists.

He couldn't. He had fought hand to hand, when rifles had jammed, when pistols had been spent. Once, with a twist of his arm, he had broken a man's neck. He knew how easy it was to kill—

He didn't dare hit his brother again.

Sebastian's fist slammed into the right side of his

face, twisting him around. Nigel spat blood. It landed just in front of a dainty, silvery-white satin shoe.

"Is this what brothers do in this civilized country? Beat each other senseless beneath portraits of their ancestors?"

"Zoe!" Panic in his green eyes, Sebastian lowered his fists. He jerked out a handkerchief and wiped away the blood, then chased after his fiancée, who had spun on her heel and was swiftly retreating across the floor.

His brother's foot hit the precious '04 and sent it rolling across the parquet, spilling wine.

Gushing and dark red, it made for a sickening sight. Nigel's hand shook. As if he were controlled by strings, his arm started to tremble, then his shoulders and his back.

His brother had to marry—it was the only way to avoid scandal. But right now all he could see was red.

"Who in blazes did this?"

"Weren't me. I don't 'ave a sweetheart. My money's on Lord Sebastian."

Zoe got out of bed and pushed open the drapes to see what was happening under her bedroom window. She stared down, unable to breathe. A stocky, gray-haired gardener and a young, fair-haired one stared at the lawn. On it, hundreds of petals spelled out the message: *I adore you.*

"Bleeding 'eck," the older gardener grumbled. "'Alf the flowers in the greenhouses must have been be'eaded. The dowager will want someone's 'ead. And it'll be one o' ours. Not 'is."

Zoe let the drapes fall back and paced in her room. This was carrying the ruse too far. She would go and tell

Sebastian, except he'd warned her he rarely woke before noon. She'd intended to tell him last night, until she had seen the duke and him knocking each other about.

A knock sounded at the door, and then her maid, Callie, who had arrived in the evening, hurried in carrying a silver tray on which sat a pot of tea and a plate of what appeared to be plain toast. "They gave me this tray to bring up to you. Your mama said to keep your breakfasts small."

Zoe rolled her eyes. Mother had instructed her to maintain a dainty appetite. If Mother had her way, she would be measured every morning to ensure she was maintaining a sufficiently svelte figure. It wasn't necessary. Eating was not an occupation that kept you busy. When you chewed, you had too much time to think.

"Do you want me to open your window, miss?" Callie went to the window, opened the drapes and stopped dead. "Ooh, miss, how romantic! He's so very much in love with you—" Callie broke off. "I'm sorry, miss. It's not my place to say such things."

"It's all right, Callie." Zoe sat on her bed. Sebastian didn't have to make gestures like these to fool his family...

But what if it wasn't just to con his family?

Father had told her to look for an angle when a man was too smooth. Father had wanted to protect her of course, but his words had *hurt*. Was there any man who would overlook her trust fund and see *her*?

Even with Richmond, she hadn't been sure. She'd never told him where she'd come from. Men might claim they would love you even if you had grown up barefoot in a dirt-floor shack, but she'd never wanted to put one to the test.

Could Sebastian be falling in love with her?

She didn't want love anymore. She'd told Langford she wanted to live—that she had an obligation to do it, and she believed she did. She just didn't want to risk her heart ever again.

"I must get dressed, Callie."

In the drawing room Julia had approached her and whispered, "I can go riding in the morning, before my meeting. Please say you will. I should like to give you a tour of Brideswell."

NIGEL SAT AT the head of the dining table, a cup of coffee in his hand. A newssheet was propped in front of him so he could hide his bruises behind it.

Last night it had taken a long time to gain control over his body and the strange ways it betrayed him: the trembling and sweating. The raw, nonsensical panic. The nightmares.

Maybe he was weak and mad, because why else was he such a physical wreck? But he would be damned if anyone else would know about it. Nigel knew what happened to men who were diagnosed with shell shock. The hell that was inflicted on them to "cure" them.

Heels clicked on the stone tiles of the hall outside the door, a hint of exotic perfume assailed him and he had just pushed to his feet when Zoe Gifford strode into the dining room, lit by sunlight pouring in the two-story windows.

She was wearing *trousers*. Beige trousers, tall leather boots and a trim-fitting leather jacket that nipped into her waist and swelled out around her bosom.

Miss Gifford was not fashionably flat-chested.

But he should not be looking at her curves. "Good

morning, Miss Gifford," he grunted. He intended to skirt around her and escape. He assumed she had as little desire to speak to him as he did with her.

She stood in his path, hand on her hip, barring his way while his coffee cup burned against his palm.

"You will soon learn that your brother denuded half the flowers in your greenhouses, Your Grace," she said, in her firm, husky American voice. "The gardeners had nothing to do with it. They'd better not be punished. I won't stand for men being wrongfully abused, simply because one group of people considers them to be of a lower class."

Could they not spend a moment together without an argument ensuing? He had not even finished his coffee. "I assure you, I do not punish either blindly or unjustly—" Then her words filtered in. "For what purpose did my brother do this?"

"Something pretty foolish," she began. Then she peered at his face, a gesture that made him step back and twist away from her. "You have a stunning set of bruises, Your Grace."

"And you are dressed like…like a gardener."

"I often wear trousers when I'm tinkering with an airplane engine. Or riding."

He had started to walk away, but he found his steps slowing. Last night, she'd been glossy and beautiful, with scarlet lips and a glimmering silver dress. "You tinker with aeroplane engines? In the grease and oil?"

"That's what an engine requires to run smoothly."

He frowned. "Isn't that what mechanics are for?"

She walked with smooth, confident strides to the buffet and picked up a plate. Taking the silver lid off the eggs, she glanced at him. "I like to know how my plane is going to perform when I'm betting my life on her. Have you never fiddled with an engine?"

He wouldn't know where to begin. That was why they had chauffeurs. In houses where they had electrical generators, a man was employed full-time to wrangle with the contraptions. Yet now Nigel hated admitting he did not tinker. "No," he said abruptly. He had cursed any number of seized machine guns and bogged-down tanks, but he had not the skill to deal with the blasted things.

Miss Gifford bent to spear a sausage, and her trousers pulled snugly against her derriere.

Nigel was equally speared with an image of how she would look, bent over an engine, her heart-shaped bottom the only thing visible beneath the hood.

"I could teach you," she said.

He had the distinct impression she was making an attempt to scare him away. Dukes did not scare easily. "Thank you, Miss Gifford. I would love the opportunity to have you teach me how to tinker. Let me know when you would find it convenient to begin."

With that, he tossed back a slug of coffee. Too hot, damn it, but he refused to flinch as he swallowed. Then he left the breakfast room, dignity intact.

ZOE APPROACHED THE stables prepared to shock first, then defend herself. It was how she negotiated New York society, and her first night at Brideswell had shown her that stuffy English society behaved in the exact same way.

She could refrain from being shocking. But since she would never fit in and it would hurt too much to try and fail, she was determined to stand out.

Lady Julia was already atop a black Arabian mare. Her eyes widened, but before Zoe could speak, Lady Julia smoothed her pretty features into an expression of elegant calm. Perched in a side saddle, Julia wore a long skirt of blue velvet, a snug jacket, white silk at her throat, a black hat and veil on her sleek jet-black hair. Smiling politely, she said, "Good morning, Miss Gifford. Your trousers look so much more comfortable and easy for riding."

Zoe hadn't expected this. Unflappable manners. "Thank you. I do find them that way."

"O'Malley," Lady Julia called, "you will have to change Miss Gifford's saddle."

"Wot's wrong with the one that's on Daisy, m'lady?" A broad-shouldered, redheaded man emerged from the stable, leading a pure white mare by the bridle.

He stared at Zoe as if Lady Godiva herself had strolled down nude to select a horse. "Trousers? Ladies use the side saddle, miss."

"I would prefer not to since I am not wearing skirts."

The groom gave a desperate look to Lady Julia. "Don't know if this is right, m'lady."

"It's a saddle," Zoe pointed out firmly. "Hardly the end of civilization as we know it. I am sorry if it is additional work, but in the future, you will know how to saddle my horse."

"Yes, O'Malley. Let's change the saddle and be done with it."

Lady Julia's polished, smooth tones gave the final word. The groom unbuckled the saddle on the mare and carried it back to the tack room, muttering under his breath all the while. He continued to mutter while fastening an English saddle intended for trouser-wearing gentlemen.

The servants were every bit as supercilious and snobby as the duke and the dowager. Maybe more so.

"Let's go, shall we?" Lady Julia flicked her reins.

Zoe followed. They set off along the gravel path together, and she had her first view of Brideswell that was not obscured by rain.

The lawns stretched endlessly, a carpet of lush green and bluebells, dotted here and there with stone benches and statues. In the distance, water rippled on a small lake. Deer grazed at the edge of a forest, and in the distance, the spires of a church struggled to be noticed over the trees.

Her father, Thaddeus Gifford, had built his own country house outside New York. He'd filled it with everything she could see around Brideswell, as if he'd asked a duke to give an inventory for his grounds. But these statues were evidently much, much older than her father's.

"I am being derelict in my duty," Lady Julia said. "I promised you a tour. You look as though you're an accomplished rider, Miss Gifford. Can you take jumps?"

Zoe liked Lady Julia. There was an air of reserve about Sebastian's sister, but also of genuine welcome. She could count on one hand her female friends, and that made her say impulsively, "Call me Zoe, please, my lady. I rode like a fiend when I was younger, but it's been years since I last did it. Once I learned to drive I spent most of my time in my car. Then when I learned to fly... Well, I find it dull to keep my feet on the ground now."

"You can fly?" Lady Julia pulled up her horse. "An aeroplane, do you mean?"

"Yes."

"I've seen them. Goodness, they look as if they are made of paper and string, but they are marvelous. I should be absolutely terrified to go up there—" Lady Julia broke off. Her face became as still as a pond, as colorless, too. "No, I would never be able to do anything so brave."

"Lady Julia, I am certain you would. You've lived with your two brothers and I should think that has given you a lot of courage." Lady Julia looked at her in surprise. Zoe's heart sank—she'd intended the words as a joke. "If you would like to fly," she offered, "I'd be happy to take you."

"Oh, no, I couldn't do that," Lady Julia declared, but she bit her lip and looked up at the sky with such longing in her eyes that Zoe's heart twisted.

Zoe suspected Lady Julia was refusing because of some kind of social stricture. Perhaps one that said a lady couldn't aspire to be more than a drawing-room ornament. "Wouldn't you like to touch the clouds?"

"You are teasing me, Miss Gifford. Clouds are just water droplets in the sky. If I tried to touch one, my hand would go right through." She gave a graceful smile. Mother would approve of it, Zoe thought—it was the sort of smile that would never add a wrinkle to a lady's brow.

"Now, I promised you a tour," Lady Julia said quickly. She pointed toward the edifice that was Brideswell, a square building of beige stone, paned windows and ironwork; with towers and spires that made it look like a castle. Zoe knew the house contained forty major rooms on the ground and first floors, along with eighty so-called lesser rooms. Gold gates were set in the outer wall, and inside them were oak doors with handles as big as her arm.

"The house itself was built between 1560 and 1603, during the reign of Elizabeth I," Julia said, "though it's been added to many, many times over the years. The east wing was added in the late seventeenth century and the west wing is Georgian. Unfortunately, that made it into a bit of a dog's breakfast. It's why the corridors inside are an absolute maze. I shall show you the chapel later—Father built it for Mama shortly after their wedding, and it is my favorite place of the whole estate. Down there—" Lady Julia nodded toward ornate buildings made of glass "—are the greenhouses. Though the flowers within are not quite as spectacular as they were yesterday."

"You know about Sebastian's message."

They cantered along a gravel path that wound toward large evergreen hedges, sculpted into spheres and rectangles and columns.

"The whole house does now," Julia said.

"Is your grandmother furious?"

Julia's brow rose as if she hadn't expected the question. "Grandmama will surprise you, Zoe."

"Do you mean take me by surprise? Jump out and get me with her cane?"

Lady Julia—Julia—giggled. "I mean Grandmama is very, very practical. Now, Miss Gifford, do you want to gallop? We'll go down past the lake, cross the bridge at the stream then take the higher trail into the woods."

Julia amazed Zoe—the talented horsewoman could take jumps in a side saddle that she didn't dare attempt.

Julia was charming, but there were moments as they cantered along when Julia's mouth turned grim and her eyes looked haunted.

She looked like a woman in grief. Was it over her younger brother? Mother had learned more details from the dowager. William Hazelton had died of the Spanish flu at fifteen. It would have been after the duke returned, scarred and wounded, when war was done and everyone thought the worst was over.

She remembered the day the telegram had come about Billy. Up until then, the War had been a distant thing, about loss and sacrifice, but not for her. For her it was about dances with young officers in uniform, about passionate kisses with passionate men who were pressed for time and eager to go all the way before they shipped out. A sensible girl always said no—though the girls hadn't really understood they might never see their men again.

She'd never dreamed she wouldn't see Billy again.

"Zoe, are you all right?"

Julia's voice, filled with worry, snapped Zoe back to where she was. "I was just thinking about my brother," Zoe said. But no amount of thinking would bring him back. "Let's gallop again," she called to Julia, and she spurred her horse to run. She leaned along her horse's neck like a jockey, tearing along the gravel path that encircled the house. She laughed with the exhilaration, even if she didn't really feel joy.

When she reined in on the long front drive that led to the house, Julia caught up.

"Your hat hasn't moved, Julia," Zoe said. "If I'd worn one, it would have sailed into the lake by now."

Julia fixed the veil. "Oh, it's practically nailed to my head with pins."

From there, they had a clear view of Brideswell; of the enormous house that had stood there for over three hundred years. Her father would have been so proud of her marriage—but if he had been living, she wouldn't have to marry to save Mother from scandal or prison. "You have a beautiful home."

Julia shook her head. "It's not my home—not anymore. Now it is a house in which I stay because I have not yet married and taken over management of my husband's house."

It was the first time Julia had sounded bitter, had sounded like anything other than a perfect lady. "Of course it's your home," Zoe said. "You grew up here."

"Eventually another woman will rule the house, and she may not wish to have me under her roof. She will want to give preference to her own family. Sometimes spinsters live on the estate—if there's a spare cottage that doesn't cost much to run. Whoever Nigel marries will have more rights to a home on the estate than I would."

"A woman who is only here by marriage would have more rights than you? That's shockingly unfair. But you'll have an inheritance—"

"Very little. I do have a dowry, which is only if I marry."

Zoe could always buy her own house. Never had she really understood what power that gave her until now. "Then you must marry."

The shadow darkened Julia's eyes. "I do not think that's possible. My fiancé, Anthony, was killed at the Somme. It is years ago now, but the loss…has not gone away. I do not think I could ever fall in love again. My mother and grandmother think me foolish, but I cannot marry without love."

"My fiancé was killed in a plane crash. He was lost over the Atlantic Ocean. I do understand what you mean. I can't—" But of course, she couldn't tell Julia she understood it was impossible to fall in love again— Julia thought she loved Sebastian.

Women did survive—they did get over loss. Zoe knew it was possible. Just not for her. But it had to be so for Julia.

"I think you can open your heart again," she said, making it sound like the gospel truth. "I did, after all. I met your brother Sebastian."

"I do not think it will be that way for me."

"Julia, do you do things for fun?"

"I have not felt very much like having fun."

Zoe would not have survived losing Richmond at all if she hadn't at least grabbed hold of life, rather than lock herself away to mourn.

Julia deserved to be happy. And after Zoe and Sebastian divorced, Julia would not listen to her scandalous former sister-in-law. If she wished to help Julia, she must do it now. "After your Women's Institute meeting, Julia, we are going to drive down to London. It's time you begin to have fun again."

"I don't think I could."

"You can. Do you think the man who loved you would want to see you wither away in sorrow? The best way to make his sacrifice mean something is to live the life he was fighting for."

"Where do you think she took her?"

Horns blared as Sebastian, dressed in a duster and

driving goggles, took a corner wide and crossed into oncoming London traffic. Nigel's heart jumped into his throat. Despite the thunder of his heartbeat in his ears, he said, with forced sangfroid, "Bloody hell, Sebastian. You have to stay on the left side of the road."

"This *is* the left side of the road."

"Not in England, it's not. Move over."

"Spoilsport. It's a lot easier to get through traffic when people are fighting to get out of your way. I'll head for the 400 Club."

Nigel did not doubt Miss Gifford had been able to ferret out the most popular dancing club in London. "No. Try Murray's," he growled. "On Beak Street."

"Murray's?" As usual, Sebastian took his gaze off the road to embark on a conversation. "How do you know about the jazz clubs in town, brother? You never leave Brideswell."

"I know about Murray's. Turn here." He'd heard about it in letters from friends. From war comrades who didn't understand why he was hiding away at Brideswell.

Sebastian swung the wheel, cut across traffic and made a hazardous left turn that aged Nigel by a decade. Having been shot at for four years, Nigel had no intention of dying in an automobile crash. "Pull over and let me drive."

"You don't drive," Sebastian protested. "You'd be worse than me."

"That would be impossible. Watch where you are going."

Nigel had never been in a London dance club. The only club he frequented in town was White's, which had been favored by the Dukes of Langford for almost one hundred and fifty years. Murray's had the staid, imposing facade of a bank. Sebastian located the curb by hitting it with the tires. Nigel jumped out, and within moments, he stood at the bottom of the stairs in the massive ballroom, straining to spot Julia.

"There is my beloved." At his side, Sebastian smoothed his slicked-back hair.

Nigel stared. "What in blazes is she doing? It looks like she is having a seizure."

"Dancing, brother."

Nigel watched Sebastian claim Miss Gifford. Her legs jerked behind her, kicking like a mule, and her hands waved wildly around her head like a drowning woman begging for rescue. Tall feathers showed every contorted motion of her head. Hundreds of beads jumped off from her indigo dress as her hips moved in a vulgar swing.

The dress shifted as she moved, giving him a glimpse of the garment beneath it. White fabric and lace banded her back, but below the one small strip there was nothing but bare skin. No corset. No shift.

He blinked. Miss Gifford sported a lot of bare skin. Her upper arms were bare, as were her thighs—in the gap between her short skirt and her rolled-down stockings. Underneath the dress, much of her must be naked.

Heat washed over him and he moved behind a potted palm to hide what must be a blindingly obvious erection in his trousers. Anger and embarrassment hit him. She was his brother's fiancée—albeit his convenient one—and he had no business feeling anything about her skin.

On the dance floor, Sebastian rushed Miss Gifford through the crowd in a waltz that looked like his brother was racing to find a bathroom.

Where was Julia? Nigel's gaze scoured the small round tables at the far side of the large room. Egyptian-style pillars separated that section from the dance floor, and couples lounged in the shadows. Nigel did not see any woman who looked like Julia—black hair in a neat bun, elegant and understated.

"Nigel!" At the edge of the dance floor, a woman with bobbed dark hair waved wildly at him. He could see the tops of her stockings below her short skirt, rolled down just below her knees like Miss Gifford's.

He had no idea who she was, though she'd addressed him intimately. Her partner's legs appeared to be made of India rubber, wobbling back and forth as the man passed his hands over his knees. Making wild gyrations, the girl moved toward the floor's edge.

"Nigel, come and dance," she called.

Her lips were a vivid scarlet, her eyes darkened with kohl. Some cosmetic, thick and black, was clumped on her eyelashes. There was something familiar about her, something that got under his skin...

"Julia!" Her name came out in a roar of shock.

The creature in front of Nigel was nothing like the demure English lady who had climbed into Zoe Gifford's motorcar that morning. Several feet of her dark hair had been cut. Her face was made up like an actress on Drury Lane. As for her dress—

It revealed so much of his sister's legs that his hands clenched into fists. Julia's entire body moved with the jazz beat, her hips flowing back and forth in shocking invitation.

Nigel grasped her wrist and hauled her off the floor. "Did *she* do this to you?"

Tugging against his iron grip, Julia's expression became one he readily recognized. She glared. "If by 'she,' you mean Miss Gifford, then yes. And if by 'this,' you mean that she is trying to coax me to have fun, then yes. This *is* fun, Nigel."

"Fun." He spat the word. "You are barely dressed."

"This dress is fashionable. And not quite shocking if every other woman in the room is wearing the same thing."

Someone tapped on his shoulder. It was Julia's partner—a pasty-looking young man who was obviously at university. "Look here," the lad began. "She's my partner."

"Bugger off," Nigel snarled.

Quaking, the boy retreated. Nigel rounded on Julia. "You were giving him ideas."

She burst out laughing.

"What is so funny?" he barked.

"Nigel, he is a sweet young man. We were simply dancing. You think my behavior is shocking? That young man is the son of Viscount Hardley and, to quote, you just told him to—"

"Never mind what I told him." This was Zoe Gifford's fault. He refused to lose control due to her—even control over his language. "That is not what I would call dancing. Married people have less contact during their private relations."

This made Julia double over, helpless with laughter. It was good to see her enjoying herself. Irritating to have it at his expense.

"What has she done to you?" Two days. That was all the time Miss Gifford had spent under his roof, yet Julia's hair was now gone, her demure face was painted, and she was making rude gyrations in a public place.

He hauled off his coat and threw it around Julia's shoulders. It reached her knees and engulfed her in an envelope of decency. "We are returning home."

"I am not leaving, Nigel. I want to dance."

A slender hand landed on his arm, and the scent of exotic roses surrounded him. As he jerked around, Miss Gifford, the culprit, smiled up at him.

"You are making a scene, Your Grace," she said. "Why don't we discuss this at our table?"

"I am making a scene?" The words came out with all the calm that pervaded the atmosphere before men rushed out of a trench with rifles. "My sister is cavorting half-naked on a public dance floor."

"Which is perfectly natural in a dance club," Miss Gifford pointed out. "Dragging her off the floor and throwing your coat over her is more fitting to the last century. If you are so concerned about appearances, look around you, Duke. You are creating the scandal here."

Dimly, he became aware of the stares. Hundreds of them. Grunting with anger—how dare she be in the right?—Nigel watched Miss Gifford lead Julia to a table. Sebastian was there, along with a group of rainbow-colored drinks. Two glasses in front of his brother were already empty.

Miss Gifford handed him a full one in a revolting shade of yellow-green. Nigel put it down. He didn't drink things the color of urine. "What in hell were you thinking?" he growled at her. "Julia is in mourning."

Julia threw off his coat so it landed on the back of the chair and sipped a pink drink.

"Don't be ridiculous," Miss Gifford said. "Lady Julia can't be mourning for the rest of her life."

Julia set down her drink and Sebastian whisked her onto the dance floor. Damn his brother.

Miss Gifford jumped to her feet and stood in front of him. From this view, he could see a considerable amount of her smooth, bare thighs. He grabbed his drink, downed it and sputtered. "Sweet," he choked.

"You certainly are not. Dance with me."

"I do not dance."

"I can teach you."

"Leave me alone, Miss Gifford."

"I won't. Not until you have one dance with me."

The loud, raucous music pounded in his head. It grew louder, slamming through his skull like relentless explosions. The thunderous beat became the burst of shells. It was engulfing him. Nigel shut his eyes—a fatal mistake. With every screech of the music, he could see the endless showers of flying mud and men. Roaring filled his ears and sweat trickled down his back.

"Dance with me, Your Grace. Surely you can't be afraid of attempting to dance."

His hands were shaking hard now. He had to get out—

He jolted to his feet. Turning his back on Miss Gifford, he ran to the stairs and took them three at a time. The dining room was a roar of noise. Cigarette smoke hung in the air like fog, like the ash-filled air of no-man's-land.

He shoved past the doorman, slammed open the door and stalked out into the night.

A car horn sounded and Nigel plastered his body against a brick wall beside him. His entire body shook. His mind was like Pandora's box—demons poured out and he couldn't jam them back in.

"Nigel, what is wrong?"

He whirled. Miss Gifford came up to him and put her hands on his arm. "Nigel—"

"Langford. The appropriate form of address is to refer to me by my title," he snapped, turning his back to her. What in hell would she see in his face? Why had she come after him? "Go dance with my brother," he barked.

"No." Her hand skimmed up his arm and rested on his shoulder. "You are shaking and are pale as a ghost. You ran out of the club as if someone was chasing you."

"Stop touching me."

But she did not listen. Her body moved closer until he could feel her softness pressing against his side. He felt the warmth of her bare skin through his clothes. Her breath brushed over the back of his neck.

He needed distance. Grasping her hands, he propelled her back. He had to face her to do it.

"What happened to you?" Her large violet eyes searched his face.

He fumbled for a cigarette. A mistake, for it revealed how much his hand still shook. It would take a long time for the physical reaction to subside. But he got the damned smoke out and stuck it between his lips. "I was upset at the sight of my sister."

Miss Gifford shook her head. "No, this is not anger. This is panic. I understand now. You're suffering from shell shock."

"I am not. There is nothing wrong with me."

"There are many things wrong with you, Langford, and this explains them all. No wonder you didn't want to talk about war. I apologize for everything I said. You're obviously suffering."

"I am not suffering."

"It's nothing to be ashamed of—"

"I am not ashamed. And I am not weak."

Her plucked brow arched. "You're afraid to admit there is anything wrong with you. Good heavens, how could there not be? My brother died in France. He wrote letters home. He tried to be strong and stoic for a long time. Then he began to fall apart. He wrote about how he couldn't stand the shooting and the shelling, the mud, the wet trenches, the sickness any longer—"

"There is absolutely nothing wrong with me, Miss Gifford. The only things I brought back with me from the War are the scars on my face and on my soul. My mind is completely intact."

She shook her head. He despised sympathy, but her soft, sad expression ladled it over him by the bucketful. "You can't deny what you feel. You may actually have to face your emotions—"

"I do not have emotions. Now, return inside. Dance in whatever shocking way you want with Sebastian. But send Julia out to me. I am taking her home."

Her look of concern hardened to iron-strong determination. "Why? So she can be alone, with nothing to do but think of the man she lost? That is not going to help her get over grief. That will force her to wallow in it. She needs dancing and excitement and fun, Langford."

"You cut her hair, for God's sake."

"Even you can't be afraid of a woman's haircut."

"I am *not* afraid. There is no reason for Julia to change. She is a lady, not a dance-hall floozy."

"You can't lock her away as if this were Victorian England."

"Julia is under my protection. I shall take care of her as I see best."

For the first time, he realized his voice had risen. Everyone in line outside the club was staring at them. Blast Miss Gifford.

"She is not your chattel, Your Grace. Julia is a grown woman, and every change she made today is one she chose to do. If she wants to cut her hair, she can. If she wants to go to university, she could do that, too. The world is changing, Your Grace."

"My world bloody well is not—"

A flashbulb exploded in his face. All he could see were spots before his eyes. The instant his vision cleared, a horn blared so loud, it sounded as if it were inside him. Jolting back, he took in the scene in an instant. A weaving car, going too fast.

Miss Gifford froze. Nigel caught her up in his arms. She weighed almost nothing—far less than a wounded soldier. He jumped back as the car lurched into the curb, its tires crunching over the spot Miss Gifford had been standing on.

The door opened, and the drunken driver fell out as he tried to get out.

"Oh, God, I could have been crushed like ice," she muttered.

He set her on her feet and turned her roughly. "It's not a joke," he said heatedly, his chest heaving, his heart pounding. Something was burning through him, something he didn't understand. It wasn't the usual cold that hit him before the battle memories attacked him.

He looked down; she looked up. Her eyes were huge violet circles beneath the bright club lights, but her usual expression was back on her face. Jaded amusement.

She had no idea what danger was about. She made him want to—

"I should thank you," she said, "for saving my life—"

His mouth slammed into hers.

Heat. The sweetness of a cocktail. Lightning shot through him, riveting him to this moment in time. Her mouth answered his fierce kiss with hunger. Her kiss was scorching. She was so utterly unlike any woman he'd known before. Vibrant, infuriating but so damn alluring.

Her tongue found his, making him sweat beneath his evening dress. His body had been cold for as long as he could remember. Now he was heating up.

Brilliant light exploded around him. The glare of it froze him. His brain registered two words—*scandalmongering newspapers*—just as Zoe Gifford pulled out of his embrace.

Sebastian shouted something at him in an inebriated slur, and his brother hit him for the second time in two days.

5

AT THE SAVOY HOTEL

SEVERAL HOURS LATER, Nigel pressed a towel filled with ice against his eye, the ice chipped from a block in the kitchens of the Savoy Hotel around the corner from Murray's. If he were to open the door of his suite, he would hear the strains of the orchestra in the ballroom downstairs, playing jazz for the partying crowd. Drunken laughter. And witness more couples stumbling through the hallways, sinking to the floor to kiss passionately and indecently before they even reached a bedroom. Indecent.

He had ripped off his tie. Now he paced his hotel room like a caged cat.

He had told reporters he was Oswald Warts, Oxford student, and the girl he'd kissed was an actress's understudy. Luckily, none of the press recognized him, as he was practically a hermit at Brideswell—except for the few times he came up to London to see his man of business and to visit his friend Rupert, who had been badly wounded at the Somme and was in a charity hospital. Given the late hour, he'd insisted they spend the night at the Savoy, and he had taken two suites: one for Julia and Miss Gifford, one for Sebastian and him.

A snore sounded from the adjoining bedroom. Sebastian was sprawled across the bed, fully dressed and unconscious.

"I don't know what in hell to do." He wouldn't sleep tonight. After what had happened, he was certain he would have nightmares. He didn't want to wake his brother with his screams and have Sebastian witness them.

What could he do? He couldn't let the wedding go ahead, but what could he do with Sebastian? The problem was not just the rumors; it was Sebastian himself. He was drinking more. He'd grown even angrier, edgier.

Nigel didn't know how to give his brother any peace. He couldn't just say: do your duty and prefer females. Father had tried that and it had sent Sebastian on a self-destructive path that had seen him spend much of his time dead drunk.

If the blasted marriage ended in divorce, wouldn't that lead to more rumors about Sebastian? *Of course his wife kicked him out—he was batting for the other team.*

Sebastian wasn't going to be able to fool Zoe Gifford. Her kiss had been hot enough to melt the soles of Nigel's shoes to the sidewalk. He had never been kissed like that.

It made him hot, when he was so accustomed to feeling empty and cold. It made him hunger for more. But—

"It cannot happen again," he muttered to his brandy glass. "Not with my brother's fiancée."

A soft knock sounded at the door. It was 3:00 a.m. The party in the ballroom was still roaring at full speed—he could feel the rhythm of the music through the floor.

Groaning, he got up. What if he hauled the door open and faced bobbed blond hair, huge violet eyes and painted lips? He remembered discovering traces of her red lipstick on his mouth.

Heat seared him just thinking about it. Perhaps he had better not answer that door. He'd never had his control snap like that. Was it another symptom of shell shock—hauling unsuspecting women into scorching kisses? He didn't think so, but losing control like that left him stunned.

Another knock. "Langford, open the door. It is Zoe and Julia. We want to make sure you haven't beaten each other senseless."

Both of them. At least it meant he wouldn't be tempted to—

No. Hell, he would never be tempted to do that again.

He took his bag of ice from his eye and opened the door. Miss Gifford walked in, beautiful in a dark blue silk robe tied at her waist and frothing around her ankles. Feathers adorned the neckline and the cuffs. Julia wore a new robe of scarlet silk.

"You have quite a shiner, brother," Julia observed. "I'll go check on Sebastian." She quietly went into their brother's room.

Miss Gifford walked up to him with her arms folded over her chest. Her face was scrubbed free of makeup. Soft pink lips. Unusual purple eyes with long, gold lashes. Soft, ivory skin.

She was beautiful. Luminous.

Then her finger jabbed his chest. "Julia is afraid she has made you angry. She's worried she hurt you. Don't you think she's grieved enough?" she asked in a quietly furious voice.

She always put him on the defensive. "Of course

Julia has not made me angry," he said. "And of course I want her to stop grieving."

"Then tell her that. She can't live in the past. She believes she won't have a home to live in once you are married. She fears she will be displaced by your wife, and that if she is very lucky, she might be allowed to live in a cottage." Miss Gifford's voice vibrated with indignation, though it stayed low in tone. "If this is true," she went on, "Julia's only hope for a future is marriage. And she doesn't want to marry because she is still in love with the man she lost. I can understand what that is like. But she needs to fall in love again, and she can't if you insist she must act as though it is still 1914. You are like that madwoman in Dickens—Miss Havisham or whatever her name was. Let your sister brush off the cobwebs and take off her unused wedding dress and find love!"

He gazed into her snapping violet eyes. "Thank you."

"What does that mean? Will you do something? Or are you going to tell her to drop her hems back below her knees this instant?"

"I will talk to her," he said stiffly. Without the ice on his eye, it stung again.

"Then do it now." Miss Gifford turned and walked out.

Damn it. All he wanted to do was kiss her. He slapped the bag against his black eye. The pain of doing that helped cool his ardor. Just barely.

Then Julia came out of Sebastian's room. Cautiously, and that in itself broke his heart.

"Are you very angry? I shouldn't have done it." Julia sank down to the wing chair and she looked up at him with tear-filled eyes. "Is it very wrong to go dancing when Anthony never will?"

He didn't want her to spend her life mourning. He felt like a wretch. She had been grieving, and he was making her worry about his reaction. "It's not wrong to go on living. Miss Gifford is right about that."

His little sister looked so different. She had always been elegant, even as a little girl. Now even the way she tilted her head looked lively. Her bouncing hair drew his gaze. She looked freer, lighter, and she glowed in relief from her worry.

"You are extraordinarily beautiful, Julia. You look even lovelier with bobbed hair." And he meant it. "Do you want me to take you home tomorrow?"

Julia wiped away her barely fallen tears. She gave him a wobbly smile as she stood to return to her room. "No, Zoe will drive me. But we are going to leave you to bring Sebastian home."

He closed the door after Julia, then lay down on the sofa. He must have slept, but he woke up shouting, bathed in sweat. Jerking upright, he listened, heart pounding. Soft snores came from his brother's bedroom. His brother was in a deep, drink-induced sleep.

Nigel sank back in relief. He stayed awake until morning, staring at the ceiling. Then he went downstairs, had breakfast and walked into the Savoy's smoking room.

A high-backed wing chair and a newspaper hid his view of the occupant, but long legs stuck out—shapely legs revealed by a short skirt. Nigel identified the legs at once with a deep sigh.

It was Zoe Gifford—a cigarette held between her fingers, a newspaper in her hands.

All around, elderly gentlemen were muttering. Who had let her in? What were the standards of the Savoy coming to? What was the world coming to?

For a moment, Nigel sympathized with Miss Gifford. A devastating war had killed millions, had recarved Europe, had torn wounds that might scar over but would never heal. And what shocked Englishmen was a woman in the smoking room in a short skirt with her legs crossed.

He took a seat across the room, facing the window, and opened his newspaper.

A shadow fell over him. He lowered the paper. Those legs were in front of him. Zoe blew a smoke ring. "I heard what you said to your sister."

"You listened in on a private conversation?"

"I was closing the door. It wasn't my fault you started speaking before you were sure I'd gone. Thank you for what you said to her. She was worried about your disapproval." Her now-painted lips curved in a smile. "She recognizes she does not have to obey you, but she does not want to fight with you."

"I told her the truth. Thank you for urging me to." He cleared his throat. "About what happened outside Murray's—"

"Don't worry, Your Grace. You know what American girls are like. We meet a boy at a dance at eight, and we're necking in a rumble seat with him by midnight."

He dropped his newspaper. Smiling, Miss Gifford walked away, and he had to loosen his tie.

But she cared about Julia. In the light of morning, he saw she had done a wonderful thing for his sister.

Zoe took the elevator up to Sebastian's room. She rapped on the door—repeatedly—until Sebastian threw it open.

His eyes were bloodshot, his golden hair a disheveled mess, his clothes rumpled. "Oh, it's you, Zoe." He leaned against the door frame. "I'm in here alone. You shouldn't come in, angel. It'd be a scandal without a chaperone."

"In the state you're in, I doubt anything could happen. Your head must be pounding."

He groaned. And let her in.

He sprawled in a silk-cushioned chair, long legs spread out in front of him. This time he held the monogrammed towel filled with ice against his head.

Blunt and honest. That was what a Gifford was. "Sebastian, our engagement is a ruse, and it can't be anything more. I—I was in love with someone else, and I lost him, and I don't plan on falling in love again. No matter what."

Sebastian had changed. When she'd met him in New York, he'd oozed charm. Now he seemed to be smoldering with anger all the time. She felt it in his tension, his drinking, his wildness.

On a groan of pain, he got down on one knee before her to take her hand. "I know, Zoe. But I'm falling in love with you. And I can't help it."

He gazed up at her, looking hungover, but vulnerable and gorgeous. With his blond hair, long-lashed green eyes, full, pouty lips, Sebastian was breathtaking.

But she didn't want to kiss Sebastian and she couldn't stop thinking about that kiss with Langford.

She'd thought him icy? He had been filled with fiery desire. His kiss set all her nerves aflame. She'd almost turned into a puddle on the sidewalk, she'd been so hot.

"I'm not going to fall in love with you, Sebastian. I can't."

Because of Richmond. "That's the only reason why," she said under her breath as she left Sebastian's room.

A LOUD, SPUTTERING sound came from the gray, cloudy sky over his head.

Nigel froze, reining in Beelzebub so they were motionless on the long stretch of Brideswell's gravel drive. He knew the sound. It was the tempestuous choking of an aeroplane's engine. His heart pounded. He expected to hear the explosion of machine-gun fire. That was what you heard—the engine roar over your head, then the cracking sound as the ground around you was blasted by gunfire.

The war was over. Had been for four years. Four years that didn't seem real at this moment....

Was he just imagining the sound? It was so damn clear against the other sounds he knew of Brideswell— the whip of the wind through trees, the caws of crows.

A bright yellow biplane flew out of a bank of thick cloud. It banked and made a wide turn over the trees that flanked the road at the end of the drive. The plane started to drop, and Nigel realized it was going to land on the lawn.

Then the engine stalled and his heart almost stopped in his chest.

The plane dropped fast. Then the engine roared and it swooped upward, clearing his head generously. As if it had struck Beelzebub, the spooked animal reared.

Nigel had let the reins go slack to watch the aeroplane. Too late, he gripped them, but he lost his balance—

He tumbled from his horse to wet ground. As he hit the earth, he saw the plane touch down.

He pushed up, his back sore and his arse aching. The yellow plane rumbled over the ground, coming to a stop just before the stone wall that bordered the lawn.

Zoe Gifford jumped out, pushed up her goggles and ran to him. "Are you all right? The damn engine is fickle. It ran fine yesterday when I purchased her, but on the way here, she decided to get temperamental."

For two days after their run-in in the Savoy smoking room, he had avoided Miss Gifford. Dinner had been the only meal that had forced them into the same room at the same time. She would say things about women's rights to goad him, but he refused to be drawn into the conversation.

He felt that if he started arguing with her, everyone in the room would know he'd kissed her. The incident hadn't appeared in newspapers, so apparently his Oswald Warts story had worked.

But Sebastian knew. His brother had come to his study the next afternoon, demanding to know what had happened.

"It won't happen again" was all Nigel had said.

He didn't know why it had happened. Miss Gifford should be the last woman he wanted to kiss. She drove him mad.

Now she had flown her aeroplane too close to him and sent him falling off his horse onto his arse. So why was his blood thrumming as she reached for him?

Nigel jumped to his feet. He did not want her helping him up. He kept hearing a sound in his head—the droning sound an aeroplane made when it was shot down, just before it crashed.

"The engine had stalled. You could have killed yourself."

She shrugged. "I got it going again. The trick is to not panic."

"I saw more men than I can count crash in aeroplanes." He'd seen the burned, mangled bodies of the pilots hauled by medics to ambulances. Most of them didn't survive the crash.

She folded her arms over her chest. "And if a man can't handle an airplane, obviously a woman can't?"

"Why risk your life by flying, damn it?" His chest was heaving and his hands shook. He was losing control. "You don't need to die. Millions of men had no choice but to go to war and be blown away. Why in God's name would you want to die? Most of the beggars I saw at the end would have traded anything to hang on to life."

She'd gone very white.

Bloody hell. He'd forgotten she had lost her brother. "I apologize, Miss Gifford." He said it stiffly. If he unbent for a moment—or got too close to her—he feared he would kiss her again.

"I'm sorry I spooked your horse," she said softly.

They both looked to Beelzebub at the same time. The horse had trotted close to the offending aeroplane and was nibbling grass.

Miss Gifford fell into step with him as he walked toward his horse. "Where are you riding?"

The mere sound of her voice made him hot, uncomfortable. He had no idea why. "I'm doing a tour of the estate. Visiting the tenants."

"Let them get a glimpse at the grand duke?"

"No, I find out how they are faring, assess repairs

that need to be made to their homes. In short, I learn about the problems the tenants are facing, then put in measures to fix them. Though right now, there is very little work that can be done, given our financial state."

"Don't you have a secretary or steward who does that for you?"

"Brideswell does have men in both those positions. However, I like to see for myself."

"Do you? That surprises me."

"Brideswell is my responsibility, first and foremost. In addition, Beelzebub needs to be ridden."

"I'd like to go. I rode a mare named Daisy yesterday. Give me a minute, and I'll get her saddled up and join you. I'd like to see what it's like to be the tenant of a great house."

"Probably no different than a manual worker or farmer in America," he responded drily. "I thought my mother and Grandmama were taking you around for social visits."

"For the past two days, that's all I've done. I've met every peer within shooting distance. I've had battles with your grandmother over everything from tea to motorcars to music to the peerage. As to the last, I think it's useless. Your grandmother thinks the world would collapse without it." She smiled, and then a concerned look touched her face.

"Your mother is very kind," she said, "but I can tell she is very sad and in pain over your brother. It's... awkward."

"Awkward because the engagement is a farce."

"I'd rather be honest about it. I think that would be for the best. Even for your mother."

"No," he said softly. Dangerously. "It would not."

"Can I come with you?"

He should say no. But it was not his head thinking when he said, "Yes."

He watched her walk away to dress for riding with her jaunty, strong stride. She behaved as if the kiss had been of no account. It hadn't seemed to unsettle her at all.

But as she'd said, kissing meant practically nothing to American girls.

The trouble was that kissing Miss Gifford had meant something to him. And it shouldn't.

THE CLOUDS SHE'D flown through earlier were thicker now and a darker gray. Zoe shivered as she trotted Daisy beside the duke and Beelzebub.

Two days ago, the Duke of Langford had saved her life and kissed her senseless. It had all burst into a kind of explosion. Reporters had been swarming; flash-bulbs went off. Sebastian had pulled Langford back and punched him. All hell had broken loose after that. People streamed out of Murray's, hoping to see a brawl.

There hadn't been one. The duke had not retaliated. She had taken care of a drunken Sebastian, pulling him away. The duke had taken hold of Julia, who was tending to his bleeding nose. Not caring about his injury, the duke had insisted they all spend the night at the Savoy.

Julia had apologized. "Nothing like this has ever happened. Sebastian frustrates Nigel—that's what he's always done, but they've never hit each other."

"They did on the first night I arrived."

Julia had been startled. "Nigel said he got those bruises when he walked into a door in the dark. But they were actually fighting?"

"They were," Zoe had said. And she'd felt guilt. For ten seconds, and then she'd been angry. She didn't want them punching each other over her. She was supposed to have a simple arrangement with Sebastian. Why did the men have to have such hot emotions over it?

Why had she kissed Langford back?

She'd never kissed a man who irritated her, who drove her mad, who disapproved of her. She'd never had any need to. There were enough men who had liked her.

"We stop here, Miss Gifford," Langford said, and he reined in in front of a small cottage. Roses rambled up the walls, covered with tight buds tipped with red and pink.

As Zoe dismounted, the duke came close to her. "Mrs. Billings lives here," he said. "She lost all four of her sons to the War."

Zoe put her hand to her mouth. "All her sons, gone?"

Langford nodded. "They were the only family she had. Her husband died during the War, too. His heart gave out."

She stared at the house. Curtains of grayish-white lace hung in the windows, old but tidy. "How could anyone live through that much pain?"

"I don't know," he said simply.

He straightened his coat and smoothed his shirtfront. It surprised her how much Langford tidied himself up before rapping on the door to the humble cottage. Zoe expected to meet a grieving woman, seated despondently in a chair, surrounded by cobwebs. Instead a plump woman with gray hair and a round, flushed face saw them and dropped into a curtsy. "Yer Grace, how honored I am to have ye visit. I'll put the kettle on."

Langford dipped his head to step through the low door. "I don't want to trouble you, Mrs. Billings."

"'Tis no trouble at all, Yer Grace. Won't you have a seat in the parlor? I've barn cakes, fresh today. I remembered this was the day of the month ye usually stop by," she said with a fond smile.

"Then I am a fortunate man."

Langford looked truly anticipatory, delighted to get what must be a treat. When he could have anything he wanted made by the cook at Brideswell. The cottage was filled with heat and steam. Zoe stepped in, too, and Langford introduced her. As Sebastian's fiancée, which startled her. She didn't know why—that was what she was. The woman beamed but kept staring at Zoe's trousers until she bustled out of the room to her tiny kitchen.

As Mrs. Billings made tea, Zoe walked around the parlor. It was a quaint room with a stone hearth, a low-timbered ceiling, simple furniture. What looked out of place were four photographs in silver frames. They were images of four young, handsome men. Zoe picked one up.

"Photographs were taken of all men before they left for the Front. A woman like Mrs. Billings would have had no record of her lads otherwise. I ensured they were framed for her."

"That was…very good of you." It was clear that the poor woman couldn't have afforded a photograph and frame.

A yellowed paper sat on the mantel beneath the first photograph. Zoe unfolded it and the words leaped up at her. It was an army form, with the information filled in by pen. The soldier's name, number, rank. Then the cold words: *The report is to the effect that he was killed in action.* There were words of regret and a message of sympathy from Their Gracious Majesties the King and Queen.

She couldn't swallow. Her throat was too tight. They had received a letter for Billy. Mother kept it tucked in with Billy's picture in a locket that she never wore, but had instead wrapped in a lace handkerchief. Zoe knew Mother took it out, sometimes at night, clasped it to her heart and cried.

War gave you the knowledge that every good thing in life—beauty, fun, security, pleasures, love—could be gone. So you had to dance harder, drive faster, pack everything in.

Beneath her leather jacket, Zoe felt hot and was perspiring. "It's steamy in here."

Langford turned—he was standing at the window, far from her. His blue eyes looked somber. "With her boys gone, she takes in laundry to earn money."

She stared at him. "She is forced to take in laundry?" Zoe left the room and went to the kitchen doorway where the most heat billowed out. Mrs. Billings had her back to her, arranging cakes on a plate. Steel tubs sat everywhere, filled with sudsy water.

Zoe hurried back to the living room to confront Langford. "How can you let her do manual labor after she has sacrificed her sons for this country? Surely you could help Mrs. Billings. A monthly amount or something invested—"

"Give me money? Why would His Grace do that?" Carrying in a simple tea tray, Mrs. Billings looked mortified. "My laundry provides for me. I won't take charity."

"But you should not have to work your fingers to the bone," Zoe protested.

But Mrs. Billings was adamant.

"It's not charity to take money to help you because you sacrificed the men who would help you run your household." Zoe hesitated, realizing that some landowners would have evicted Mrs. Billings. Langford hadn't.

"Well, I won't accept it. Though—" The woman's small blue eyes twinkled. "I do find piles of logs on me doorstep some mornings. No idea where they come from. And baskets of food."

"Wood is needed for the fires for your laundry," Nigel said gently.

"Aye, and a little fairy sees fit to leave some for me. And me rent was lowered."

Zoe understood. Langford wanted to do something for Mrs. Billings—he'd kept her rent low, provided her firewood and food. She sensed he wanted to do more. But Mrs. Billings had pride and was too stubborn to bend and accept anything more.

The Duke of Langford might be old-fashioned, autocratic and irritating, but looking at him with Mrs. Billings, Zoe could see that he was a good man.

6
THE ENGAGEMENT PARTY

THE NEXT DAY, Zoe returned with Julia to the village. Julia had visits to make of her own with villagers. They took a track through the estate's fields, crossing several farms, then walked up a back road into the village. Zoe wore a trim blue suit. The bite of the sea was in the air, something that surprised her because she couldn't see it, but the sea was only five miles away. Sheep lumbered on the track; lambs gamboled. The sight of them made Zoe smile. Despite the clouds—which she was growing used to—she felt a tug of happiness at her heart.

Brideswell was a beautiful place.

Julia visited elderly ladies, new mothers and the reverend's wife, where they had tea. Everyone stared at Zoe. She couldn't resist telling the reverend's wife, Mrs. Wesley, that all women in America were expected to drink gin and dance in fountains. The woman's look of shock was priceless. "Goodness," she twittered. "I should not want to go to America."

"I don't know," Zoe said teasingly. "You might have fun."

Julia knew everything about these people. Zoe saw Julia truly did care for them, just as Langford did.

She'd thought he would be autocratic with his tenants, but with ordinary people he was actually more natural. And now she barely noticed his scars. When she did, they gave him a dangerously...attractive appearance.

"Penny for your thoughts," Julia said lightly.

They were walking down the village's High Street. Zoe blushed. She didn't want to reveal her thoughts had been on Langford. "I was just thinking that Brideswell is a lovely place, and the village is so quaint and attractive."

Julia turned to her. "When you marry Sebastian, will you live here? I should love it if you lived close."

Zoe felt terrible. She was going to give Sebastian his money and never return. Julia was imagining a future that was all a lie. "I don't know. We haven't thought that far."

"Well, if you do look for a house, I would recommend Waverly Park. It is three miles from here, closer to the coast. My favorite house growing up was Wrenford, but that was bought by an industrialist last year. He married Lady Mary Denby—she was once Nigel's fiancée. But when Nigel returned from the War, Lady Mary couldn't bear how he had changed. He was so dark and cold and brooding then. So much worse than he is now."

"Worse? Were his nightmares worse, too? His shell shock?"

"Shell shock?" By the stone wall of the village church, Julia stopped and stared at her. A cart and pony rattled by, the driver tipping his hat. "Nigel doesn't have shell shock," Julia said. "Those poor men—their minds are gone. Nigel isn't like that."

He is, Zoe thought. She could see all the evidence now she knew to look for it. Obviously he had hidden it from his family. Casually, she asked, "Did Lady Mary or Langford break off the engagement?"

"She did. I'll never forgive her for it. She married Sir Harold Denby and they bought Wrenford. It broke my brother's heart."

Zoe had lost Richmond, but she wondered: What was it like to lose someone and know they were having a happy life without you?

It must hurt deeply.

Then Julia gave a bright, ecstatic smile. She was gazing at something over Zoe's shoulder. Zoe turned. A young man was walking through a gate in a low stone wall. A sign hung by the gate. *Brideswell Charitable Hospital.*

Julia brought her bubbly smile under control. Now she looked composed and ladylike as she made the introductions. But her voice lifted with soft excitement on his name: Dougal Campbell. "Mr. Campbell has just joined the hospital," she explained to Zoe. "He studied surgery at the famous Royal College of Surgeons of Edinburgh. He is working with Dr. Drury at Brideswell's hospital."

Zoe held out her hand. Auburn-haired Campbell shook her hand, his grip firm but not crushing. He had an admirable handshake. A surgeon's touch, she guessed. She would feel assured if he were her doctor, with his earnest eyes and handsome face.

Dr. Campbell fell into step with them, walking at Julia's side. He spoke of cases he was working on while keeping the name of his patients a secret.

Julia said breathlessly, "Dr. Campbell saved the leg of a ten-year-old boy last winter. He was run over by a car's wheel. It was believed the leg would have to be removed, that the break was too bad for it to be saved. But Dr. Campbell performed a miracle."

The doctor blushed. When he looked at Julia, his brown eyes softened and he caught his breath. "You are too generous, my lady. I cannot work miracles. I do the best that I can. And I'm fortunate to be here. Your family is very generous in your patronage of the hospital."

A shadow touched Julia's face. Then she masked it and said brightly, "We are honored to be able to benefit such a worthwhile cause and such noble men as you and Dr. Drury."

Were the Hazelton's financial troubles the reason for Julia's look of sadness? Zoe thought of her settlement— she had thought of her money as just keeping the family from having to sell the house. But Langford obviously was the major patron of the hospital. The entire village relied on the great house. It was a large responsibility. It had to say something that Langford didn't want Sebastian to marry her, even for money.

After, as she and Julia walked back to Brideswell, Zoe said, "I think you like him."

Julia glanced down demurely. "I admire him very much."

"I think you might be falling in love."

Julia looked up. "I don't know. Not yet." But she smiled.

Julia looked happy. Zoe was so pleased Julia was opening her heart to life and to love. "He seems a noble, wonderful man. Dedicated. Heroic. And very handsome," Zoe said.

Julia blushed. "It would be a terrible shock to the family, though, if I wanted to be a doctor's wife."

"Julia, you have to marry for love. I won't allow you to accept anything less," Zoe vowed. "No matter what your family thinks."

ON SUNDAY, ZOE and the Hazeltons walked to church. She watched Langford walk with his mother into the churchyard before the service. His slender mother, who always walked ramrod straight because of her corset, leaned heavily on his arm. He led her to a white stone mausoleum. The duchess carried a bouquet of spring flowers and they disappeared inside. *For Langford's young brother?* Zoe wondered. When they came out and walked back toward the church, the duchess was pale. She didn't cry, but she looked older. And filled with sorrow.

After the service, Langford walked with his mother on the return to Brideswell. Sebastian was supposed to walk with her, but he'd begged off. She saw him slip into the village pub, furtively looking around before he went in.

Since the day was beautiful, Zoe strolled around the house. She was just about to go into the drawing room by the terrace doors when her mother's voice reached her from inside.

"It should be a mother's job to help arrange her own daughter's engagement party," Mother complained.

"But we do want an occasion befitting Brideswell, not an amusement park," the dowager snapped. "I have handled several engagement balls and each one has been elegant and a success."

"Well, I know what my Zoe would want. And I want to see my daughter happy."

Oh, God. An engagement ball. As to her happiness,

Mother rarely asked her what she wanted. After Billy's death, Mother became more determined to guide Zoe's life than ever.

She walked away from the drawing room. She had no intention of getting into the middle of *that*. Bathed in sunlight, the water on the lake sparkled in the distance. New leaves glimmered on the trees. The formal gardens glowed with new color. She walked toward the folly, a stone temple built on a hill.

She'd have to go through with an engagement ball. But the thought of lying so publicly made her stomach ache. She might be bold, but she was not thoughtless or without a conscience.

As she walked along the path that wound up the hill, she saw Langford standing by the door of another small stone building with a steep roof, delicate stained-glass windows and a pointed door. A cross hung above the door. It was a little chapel.

Zoe walked up to it, and Langford saw her from the end of the vestry. He came up to her.

"Your own chapel? It's lovely." She saw inside to an altar, with a red-and-gold cloth laid on it. Jewel-colored light spilled in from the stained-glass windows. Langford's mother was on her knees before the altar, her head bowed.

"My father had it built for my mother, so she could come here and pray. Sometimes she has a priest come and give her mass. On Sunday, she comes in and says prayers for us all. Today, she is probably saying prayers for you, too."

"She is very devoted to her faith."

"She relied on it when my father made her unhappy." Langford bent toward her and Zoe lost her breath. He was close enough to kiss her. She wanted it, even here in a chapel.

His lips almost brushed her ear. "I won't let her be hurt."

"I don't want to hurt her," Zoe said. And she turned and left. Before she did something sinful and kissed her fiancé's brother in front of a house of God.

ALL THE CHANDELIERS blazed and hundreds of people filled Brideswell's huge ballroom.

Zoe fanned herself. She wore a light dress in soft pink, with small straps and a short skirt, but she was still melting, at her own engagement party. Mother had spent a week crowing that it was the most anticipated event in England.

Zoe had doubted it, but as she stood on the receiving line with Sebastian, she could tell quite a few members of the British peerage were here out of curiosity.

After the long line of guests were inside, Sebastian made the formal announcement of his engagement, kissed her hand, and the orchestra started up. Sebastian swirled her into a waltz. He hadn't attempted to woo her for days. A friend of his had arrived at Brideswell—a young former army captain, John Ransome. Captain Ransome was a beautiful man with high cheekbones, large brown eyes and full lips. And Zoe had noticed that the two men spent a lot of time together.

As the music faded after the first dance, Sebastian bowed to her. Then he disappeared. She saw him and Ransome near the terrace door. Ransome went out first, and then Sebastian followed.

She wouldn't mind fleeing this thing, too. Zoe snatched two glasses of champagne from a passing footman. She gave one to Julia, who had come up to her side.

"Typical Sebastian, making himself scarce at his own party," Julia said. "And he's taken Captain Ransome. Isobel has been staring at Captain Ransome all night. I think she has a crush."

Zoe looked where Julia gestured. The dowager—standing with Sir Raynard, who spent any evening he was at Brideswell at the dowager's side—whispered a few words to Isobel, who flushed and looked at her feet. The girl had probably gotten in trouble for merely looking. Zoe went over. "What's wrong, Isobel?"

The dark-haired girl blushed. "Oh, nothing, Miss Gifford."

"You must call me Zoe, my dear, if we're to be sisters."

Isobel sighed. At fourteen, she wore a youthful lavender dress with a hemline below her midcalf. "Zoe, there is someone I love, but he doesn't even see me."

"Then you must live your life and do exciting things. He would notice you then. You can do anything you want. Have a career, go to university, become a scientist, an author, a painter, an actress."

"I am going to do exciting things. Then everyone won't ignore me anymore." Isobel tipped up her chin, looking happy and determined.

Zoe nodded approvingly, then looked around the room for Langford. He had been on the receiving line, but had disappeared right after that. She moved near the terrace doors. She didn't want to have to pretend she was a glowing bride-to-be.

And she couldn't stop remembering...

Richmond slipping the ring on her finger the morn-

ing of his flight. She remembered the roar of his airplane, the wash of sunlight as the sun rose on the
horizon. Her happiness as she promised to wait for him.

She couldn't stand it anymore. The oppressive heat
of the ballroom. The stares—some quick and furtive,
some bold and unflinching. The whispers and titters.
Those she really hated. But she couldn't bear even one
more jovial word of congratulations. She had to escape.

On her way out the door, she took a bottle of champagne and she slipped through the terrace doors. For
once the night was sultry and warm. She had to put
some distance between her and the crowd at the house.

Moonlight sparkled on the lake, down the sloped hill
of the lawns. She made her way there.

ZOE SET DOWN her bottle of champagne on the small
wooden jetty that stuck out into Brideswell's lake. She
took off her shoes, rolled her stockings off, splashed her
feet and squealed. The lake was frigid after the stifling
heat of the ballroom.

If she didn't do something thrilling, she would burst
into tears.

Zoe stood and pulled off her dress, looking over her
shoulder to ensure the partygoers couldn't see her. She
unhooked her bra, slipped it off and pulled off her silk
knickers. She walked to the end of the dock, then dived
in. Her muffled cry of "golly" echoed over the water
when she came up for air.

She ducked under the water. When she surfaced, she
gasped. Moonlight fell on a man standing at the end of
the dock. Langford. His tie was loose, his collar open,
and he carried a champagne bottle by its neck.

"You are escaping, too," she called.

He stared at her dress and her bra, the cups pointing upward on the dock. "You are not wearing clothes."

"I could hardly swim in my evening clothes."

"You are going to freeze in there. It is dangerous, Miss Gifford. Come out."

She flashed a saucy smile in response to his fussing. "I know a lot of girls who wouldn't be afraid to walk out of the water right in front of you."

She said it to challenge him. But he picked up her dress and held it out toward her, the pink beads sparkling under the moonlight. "And you are not one of them. Otherwise, I believe you would have done it."

"Are you sure you don't want to join me? The water is very…refreshing."

"Freezing cold. I should know, Miss Gifford. I used to swim unclothed in here all the time when I was a boy."

"I don't believe you. I think you acted like a duke from the moment you were born." She was teasing him—and it was fun. She was laughing now, laughing instead of crying.

"That is not true. No infant in nappies can act ducal."

She giggled. "Come in for a swim. I dare you."

He would probably stalk away.

He didn't—he tipped up the champagne bottle to his lips. It looked decidedly unducal. She squirmed a bit in the water, watching his lips part. Langford had a very beautiful mouth. He drained the bottle and set it down. His jacket followed. He opened his white shirt, undid the cuffs, let it fall. Moonlight spilled over broad shoulders, his muscled back and arms. She gaped—she'd never seen a man built like this. All hard, strong muscle.

Bending his head to focus downward, he undid the

fastening of his trousers. At that point, Zoe realized what was happening. The Duke of Langford really was taking off his clothes. He had called her bluff. A lady would turn away. Or surrender and tell him to stop.

But she wanted to see him without a stitch of clothing. She couldn't resist. Besides, she never turned down a dare.

Slowly, his trousers came down. He kicked them off. He wore white underclothes. She let out a long breath at his lengthy, well-shaped legs that bulged with muscle. Even in cold water, she whimpered, hit with a surge of wild, hot desire.

Langford dived in off the end of the dock, slicing into the cold water. He surfaced several yards from her. Kicking to stay above the surface, he slicked back his wet hair.

She licked her tongue over her lips. How she loved watching his long body move. Even though he bore scars, he was…sexy. She heard the word a lot. Everyone used it when they wanted to be provocative. But when she looked at Langford, soaking wet, grinning, she *felt* it.

She took two strokes over to him.

"Stay over there, Miss Gifford. It would not be proper for us to be close."

"We're swimming naked. We've left proper behind, Langford." She stayed where she was. She was engaged—falsely—to Sebastian, but she yearned to swim to the duke. What would it be like to press against him, wrap her arms and legs around him?

She shouldn't have dared him. She was going to burst.

"I overheard you tell Lady Julia she looks pretty, on the receiving line," she said.

He was treading water. "She does. She looks happy and lovely. That is thanks to you."

The softness of his voice as he said that…made her quiver. "It was very honorable of you. You are a deeply caring man, aren't you? I never would have guessed it from your cold behavior with me. Though I also never dreamed you would come swimming. You're quite surprising, Langford."

"The problem, Miss Gifford, is that I do not want to be cold to you. Even when I'm up to my neck in freezing water."

There was a long pause.

Then Zoe swam a little closer to him. "What exactly are you saying?"

His wet hair gleamed blue-black in the moonlight. "I am saying that you need to get out of the lake now. Put your dress on and use my jacket and go back to the house. I will not watch as you get out."

"But I'm not—"

"Go now," he barked, all laughter forgotten. "You have been drinking. I will not have your drowning on my conscience."

He sounded icier than the water. But she didn't believe it. And she didn't believe he was worried about her drowning. "Admit it. It was fun, though, wasn't it?"

"Good night, Miss Gifford."

She was tempted to wait until he gave up and got out of the water first. But cold was seeping into her bones. She swam to the dock and climbed out. She turned around, but Langford was swimming with his back to her.

His words tumbled around inside her head. He had all but admitted he wanted her.

It was impossible. Crazy. They didn't even like each other. But as she pulled her dress over her wet body, then slipped his dress dinner coat on, she wished he had turned around and taken a good long look at her.

Then invited her back in the water for a kiss.

"I WANT TO go to university and learn how to perform surgery like Dr. Campbell and become a woman physician," Isobel declared at dinner the following night.

The dowager gasped, "Good heavens, why would you want to do something like that?"

Zoe paused in cutting her slice of stuffed veal roast. She said, "That is wonderful, Isobel."

"Miss Gifford said I could go to university if I wanted, Grandmama. I want to do it to help people. Women do become surgeons and doctors. I met Dr. Campbell with Julia, and he told us the most fascinating stories. He has held a human heart in his hands. He has seen the human brain. In slices, even, so it can be studied. He showed me—"

"Isobel!" the dowager cried. "Julia, you allowed this doctor to show these shocking things to Isobel? She is not yet fifteen." The dowager's gaze also narrowed on Zoe.

Langford cleared his throat. He set down his cutlery. Zoe rolled her eyes. He would tell Isobel off, be stiff and cold and annoying. She prepared to defend Isobel as Langford's deep baritone flowed over the table.

"Grandmama," he said, "it appears young women don't find these things shocking anymore."

Zoe's fork fell to her plate. The clatter could barely

be heard over the dowager's sputtering shock. Langford was defending his sister's interest in medicine?

"I see no reason why Isobel shouldn't go to university," he went on.

"Isobel should marry. It is what ladies of our class do," the dowager countered.

"I believed that once myself," Nigel said.

The dowager arched her brows. "It is your duty to barricade the door to these ridiculous notions. And answer me this—if Isobel is up to her elbows in blood, cutting open cadavers, what gentleman will marry her?"

Sebastian groaned. "This conversation is making it hard for me to enjoy my dinner."

"I agree," Maria declared, sounding unusually forceful. "I do not want you dabbling and discussing these things, Isobel. Many of the ideas held by these physicians are not godly and they are not proper."

Isobel gazed around at her family.

Langford said quietly, "Do not worry about fighting battles for the cause of women tonight, Isobel. There will be plenty of time."

"But you agree with them, don't you?"

"In my heart and soul, I probably do. But in my head, I know I cannot keep Brideswell—or you—living in the past. I do not want you to please me and be unhappy. Now let us eat dinner." Nigel turned to Julia. "What of the summer fete? What plans do you have for this year, Julia?"

"Same as every year," Julia answered smoothly. "Coconut shies. Rides. And a tug-of-war between Brideswell's men and the villagers."

Zoe gazed toward the duke. She couldn't quite believe what he'd just said.

He lifted his head. Held her eyes.

Later, in the drawing room, when the men joined them after brandies, Zoe walked up to him. Quietly, she said, "Let me take you flying tomorrow. I dare you." Then she turned and walked away.

HAVING SEEN SO many planes crash, he did not want to go up in one. They looked to be made of fabric and balsa wood. Fragile and filled with fuel to ensure they burst into a fireball on impact.

However, Nigel refused to lose face in front of Miss Gifford.

As he approached her aeroplane, parked in the lower meadow near the house, she climbed out of the cockpit and stood on the wing, holding one of the struts. Her bottom was round and shapely in her trousers. Her scarf whipped around her neck.

He'd had a hellish time for the past few days. One of his closest friends, Rupert Willington, was close to dying. And he'd received several letters from the sister of a young man who had been in his regiment. The girl's name was Lily Bell, and her brother was dead.

Lily Bell's words—her pain and anger—had grabbed him by the throat and wouldn't let go.

Perhaps part of the reason he'd agreed to Miss Gifford's dare was to see if "grasping life" really could save you from pain.

Miss Gifford let her body lean back in a long, slender line as she gripped the strut. "Are you ready to put your life in my hands, Langford?"

He knew she was goading him, teasing him. "Unless you are willing to let me fly your plane, Miss Gifford. And since I do not know how to fly, I doubt that would be wise."

Seeing her plane made him think of fields in France, where the planes were lined up, ready to fly into battle. He clenched his fists. There would be no Baron von Richthofen trying to shoot them down today. But even though the War was over, good men were still dying—

He had to stay in control. "It's a warplane."

She nodded. "Repaired and rebuilt." She crouched and ran her hand up and down a strut, then leaned her cheek against the gleaming metal piece.

Damn, the woman exuded sexuality with her every movement. She tossed a leather flying helmet and a pair of goggles to him. "I want to show you how to have fun."

"Why?"

That caught her by surprise. She cocked her head as she placed her goggles over her eyes. "You're unhappy and I want to prove that you have to grasp life with both hands and live it."

That was why he was here, but he said, "In the air, you are risking your life."

"Which makes you feel more alive. Climb aboard, Langford, and buckle yourself in."

He climbed into the front seat, fastened himself in as she instructed. The aeroplane roared to life, vibrating around him. The plane began to move and Miss Gifford guided it toward the lawns. Once on the smooth grass, the plane moved faster and faster. Suddenly the earth seemed to drop away. His stomach lurched. They rose higher and the trees grew smaller.

What held this damned thing in the air? He looked back. Her red-painted lips curved in a confident smile.

"Hang on for the ride of your life," she shouted over the roar of the engine, the sound of the wind. They were racing toward the clouds and the sun.

Nigel looked around him, able to see forever. Never had he experienced anything like this. He could see the sea at the edge of the country and the glow of sunlight on the dark water. The earth below him looked like a patchwork quilt.

Then Miss Gifford sent the aeroplane hurtling higher, climbing faster and straighter. The sudden ascent left his stomach behind. He swallowed hard, fighting the fear.

She leveled off, then banked in a wide turn. She suddenly pointed the plane downward and he gripped the sides. The engine screamed as the plane tore toward the earth. Then, when he thought they were doomed to crash, they made an arc and climbed upward. She was making a loop in the sky. They were upside down, and Nigel gritted his teeth, expecting his harness to give out and to find himself plummeting to the ground.

She rolled the plane as if it were a barrel. He hung on to his rising nausea. Excitement and fear and horror coursed through him. All the sensations of battle— without the shooting. He felt a rush of emotion, a roar of excitement. This *was* damned thrilling.

Miss Gifford banked the plane again and brought it toward Brideswell.

He didn't want the ride to end. He turned and watched the concentration, confidence and intelligence on her face as she guided the plane down.

The plane jolted as the front wheels touched down, and then the tail wheel made contact. She slowed the plane, which shuddered violently as it rolled over the lawn.

"So, did I thrill you?" she demanded as the plane came to a stop.

"Yes, I loved every minute up there. I got a chance to touch the heavens. I have to admit it, Miss Gifford. I have never felt more alive and thrilled." God, he wanted to kiss her. He wanted to haul her against his body hard and kiss her until she melted in his arms.

She cocked her head. "I thought you would look less stiff when you're thrilled. I thought a flight might thaw you out. Even when you go swimming nude, you manage to act like an icy duke."

Thaw him out. He felt as if his body were on fire. "I assure you I do not feel icy right now. Thank you for this chance to fly." Then, because he knew he owed it to her, "You were right. When I was up there, I could not feel anything but excitement and joy."

"It was my pleasure," she said softly.

7
FAST DRIVING

SEBASTIAN CAME TO Zoe after dinner in the drawing room. In a low voice, he said, "You took Langy flying. And you were with him down at the lake on the night of our engagement party. He sneaked back into the house through his study, but he did so soaking wet and without his coat. Zoe, people are going to start talking." Sebastian's green eyes were filled with hurt. "You aren't falling for my brother, are you? I want you to fall in love with me. I know it's going to take time, and I'm willing to wait."

"Sebastian, I've told you, I can't fall in love with you."

"I won't lose you to Langy," he said darkly. "I've come second to him my whole life. I've always been the disappointment. I won't disappoint you, angel." Then his grandmother walked closer, so he left her and walked over to his friend Captain Ransome.

Zoe needed to go for a drive—because, while she knew she couldn't fall in love with Sebastian, she couldn't stop thinking about his brother. After everyone else retired to bed, she pulled on her raccoon coat and went outside, to the garage.

One of the large double doors stood slightly open at the end of the row, letting gold light spill out. The chauffeur must be there. She supposed she would have an argument about taking her car. Squaring her shoulders, she walked inside.

The hood of the Daimler was up. A candle burned, a sight she'd become accustomed to at Brideswell, since it had no electricity. A man straightened as she walked into the garage, her heels clicking on the flagstones.

Dark hair. High cheekbones. Brilliant blue eyes.

"Langford? What are you doing?"

His shirtsleeves were rolled up, revealing bare, muscular forearms. Grease coated his long fingers. He picked up a cloth and cleaned his hands. Zoe swallowed hard. She'd never felt a spurt of lust like this, watching a man do manual labor, watching a man wipe his hands on a rag.

She had been too close to it in her impoverished past. But as Langford walked toward her, she quivered with awareness.

His vivid blue gaze held her. "You told me you like to tinker on engines. I wondered what the appeal is."

The wildest ideas went through her head. They were alone in the garage. The Daimler had wide, soft leather seats—

She twirled her beads. "You got your hands all greasy because of me?"

She couldn't lie to herself, tell herself she didn't like him because he was icy and austere. She knew too much about him now—about his compassion and concern. She had seen the man inside who could blush, smile, grow embarrassed at compliments.

Langford tossed the rag to a tidy worktable. "I spent four years in trenches. I've been a lot dirtier than this,

Miss Gifford." He smiled, surprising her. "Engines are indeed fascinating."

"Controlled explosions," she said. "I wonder who first thought of the idea for the combustion engine. Sparking gasoline vapors."

She walked over to the side of the car. Letting her fingers trail over the body, she moved to take a look at the engine. Her actions were flirtatious. Would he notice?

She didn't love Sebastian, her engagement was a sham, and suddenly it all felt so empty.

All she'd wanted was love. She'd been given everything else, except the one thing she wanted. This close to Langford, she was aware of him, revved like an engine.

But he seemed unaware. He was looking at the Daimler's motor. "I think it's the men who can design these—and who can make them work—who hold the keys to the future. I wanted to come back to Brideswell and keep it the way it was. But I cannot do that, can I?"

Softly she said, "I don't think anyone can stop change."

"I saw what was left of France—a wasteland, ravaged. I came back to Brideswell after seeing that devastation, and I vowed I would let nothing touch this beautiful world. I have a duty to protect the people of Brideswell—"

She saw he meant more than just the house; he meant also the farmers, the villagers, the smith, the vicar, his family, everyone.

"But it's a promise I don't know if I can keep. The world's been redrawn and carved up into new countries, but it's more unstable now than when the War began.

Grandmama thinks money is all Brideswell needs. It might help us weather the storm, but it won't divert it. In the War, it was all about these." He pointed at the engine. "Newer machines, newer weapons. The old tactics didn't work, so they decided that whoever could build the best weapon first would win. Aeroplanes, chlorine gas, tanks. But when one side upped the ante, the other met his bet. No one got ahead. Does building engines end now that the War's ended? No, because this is where the world is going…. And I do not even know how to fix one of these damned things."

"That's why you have a chauffeur."

Langford leveled a serious look at her. "According to my grandmother, war did one thing that was irrevocable. It made people see that many men of our class are just not very bright. Someday my chauffeur will wonder why he's in the position he's in when he possesses knowledge that I don't."

Langford was truly no longer the man she'd met on that first day. But she couldn't resist asking him, "Isn't he supposed to know it's because he was born to one class and you to another?"

"We all bleed the same," he said softly. Then he straightened. "I am sorry. Did you come to the garage for your car?"

"I suppose I did. I can't really remember now."

If he read the blatant invitation to kiss her in those words, he wasn't taking it. He unhooked the rod that held up the hood and closed it.

Langford took the ignition keys from a hook over the worktable behind them. "I want to know how an automobile works. How to take it apart and put it back together. I know my horses. I should know my automobiles, not to mention electric lights, telegraphs and telephones. You have embraced all of these things."

"And you could, too."

"I accept that I have to. And perhaps you've made me see that I want to."

"Do you drive?" she asked.

"Yes, but not often."

She took the Daimler keys from his hand, put them back and grabbed the keys to her car.

"Come for a drive with me," she said. "I need air and speed. And if you're a good boy, I might let you take the wheel."

He lifted his brow, looking so ducal, she had to giggle. But he opened the garage door, then got into the car.

Within minutes, they were on the main highway, where Zoe could press her foot harder on the gas pedal and feel the exhilaration of speed. Her headlamps cut two beams through the inky blackness of the English countryside. She had the top down, and her scarf whipped and snapped in the wind as the speedometer surged higher. But she didn't drive fast for the feel of her hair streaming back or the slap of the breeze against her cheeks. She did it because at this moment, like in her airplane, she was utterly in control.

She knew when to give it the gas, when to shift gears, how to turn the wheel so the car hugged the turns of the road.

The faster she went, the more Langford shifted uneasily in the seat beside her. He didn't like fast driving—or at least her fast driving.

She couldn't forget his words. It was the first time he had opened up to her and said anything about the

War. She wanted to hear more. She wanted to understand him.

"The world has changed for me mostly in exciting ways," she said, over the engine's rumble. "I can vote, drive, fly, have a career, make and keep my own fortune, dance, even make love. The world has changed for you, too—but mainly for the worse. Your world has gone."

"True," he said drily. "Everyone wants to run blindly into change. Look at Russia. Germany is collapsing— their money is becoming worthless as fast as it is printed. Almost thirty ruling monarchies have been deposed or abdicated so they could escape before they were killed. The world is still reeling from the wounds left by the War."

So was Langford. And Brideswell. "What are you going to do about it?" she asked. "Other than marry a rich girl."

"I could sell off land, but that is a last resort. It would destroy Brideswell. So I need to make stellar investments—which means being clever or lucky in an unstable world. Maybe I can succeed, but I need capital with which to start. I am hoping the investments I have can generate it."

"So you do have a plan."

"Not much of one. No matter what, it means I have to upheave Brideswell. I have to rip people's lives apart. If I sell land, the people on it have nowhere to go, no means to feed and support themselves—"

He broke off as she rounded a tight turn, only to discover there was a farm's stone wall right in front of her. Her heart pounded as she quickly turned the wheel. Her bumper just cleared.

"You should slow down, Miss Gifford. You do not know the road."

"Compared to flying an airplane, Langford, this is moving slow. I'm in control every moment."

"You might believe you are in control, but anything could happen," he said sharply. "And you could end up in the ditch, in an overturned car, with a broken neck."

"Thank you," she gibed.

"Perhaps I just don't want to see you get hurt."

She didn't answer. But she did slow down.

"Pull over," he said abruptly. "There is something you need to know. But if I reveal it to you, I demand your silence."

"Then don't tell me. I despise secrets."

"It might change your plans, Miss Gifford."

She slowed down, then turned off the main road onto a smaller track that led to one of the farms. She cut the engine. They were surrounded by darkness. Dots of light identified the farmhouse, but it was several hundred yards away.

"All right, Your Grace," she asked, "what is it?"

SUDDENLY, NIGEL REALIZED he could not tell Miss Gifford the whole truth. It was his brother's secret and he could not reveal it. It might drive her away, but he couldn't betray Sebastian's trust—even though his brother didn't give a damn about anyone but himself.

"Sebastian is in love with someone he cannot have," he said carefully. "But he wants a marriage with you for financial reasons, and he intends to make you believe you've captured his heart. He wants to court you and coax you into forgoing the divorce. But regardless of what he claims, he will never love you."

She sat in silence, hands gripping the steering wheel. Then she said coolly, "Sebastian will play this my way or not at all." She reached for the key in the ignition. "So, do you want a driving lesson, Your Grace?"

This was the Zoe Gifford he expected. But now he saw the pain behind her cynical words. He had watched her almost give in to tears over Mrs. Billings's loss. Saw her delight when Julia looked happy, when Isobel had proclaimed proudly that she wanted to be a doctor.

Suddenly, he saw Miss Gifford was a lot like him. She kept a careful control on her emotions. The blunt, shocking things she said hid what she really felt.

"Not yet." He put his fingers on her forearm. She let go of the key.

"I didn't say those things to hurt you," he said.

"Sure you didn't."

"I am trying to help you. Trying to keep you from being scandalized or badly hurt."

"I can take care of myself," she said.

"Are you really doing this to get your money?"

She slapped her hands against the steering wheel. "Yes, because I need that money to rescue my mother. She's got herself in a heap of trouble, and that money is the only thing that can get her out. She had gambling debts and she did something desperate to pay them. And if I don't help her, she could end up arrested. I know she made a mistake, but she was devastated by Billy's death."

"William. Like my brother." He was watching her crack before his eyes, all her sangfroid slipping away.

"We got a letter, just like Mrs. Billings. That's why I don't know how she survived *that* much pain. I don't expect you to care, but I want you to know the truth.

I'm not doing this for a lark. I'm not wantonly trying to hurt anyone. I have to protect my mother—"

She stopped talking. Moonlight shimmered on tears in her eyes.

Nigel's heart broke. He knew how she felt. Loyal to her family, responsible to them, willing to sacrifice herself for them.

He shifted in his seat and pulled her into his arms. He intended to just cradle her. Soothe her, because he knew how lonely it was to feel the responsibility to family, to a way of life.

In her soft raccoon coat, she was a warm bundle. She cuddled against his chest, taking hiccuping breaths. Her tears came easily now.

"Damn tears. I hate crying." She looked up, her eyes huge and luminous. His mouth hovered close to hers, his lips tingling with the awareness of her lush, tempting, scarlet mouth.

His lips touched hers, and he caressed her mouth with his.

He kissed her the way he'd always dreamed of kissing a woman. He cupped her face to hold her while he ravished her mouth. His hand slid into her short, bouncy hair, holding her still to make her his.

Her hand closed on his free hand and she led it under her raccoon coat. She pressed his hand to her dress, his palm cupping her warm, curvaceous breast. His heart pounded. He'd lost his innocence a long time ago, long before the War—his father had insisted upon it, presenting him to an experienced courtesan. That had been nothing compared to this moment.

He kissed her soft, hot mouth and felt the weight of

her breast in his hand and the thump of her heart beneath. This moment was breathtaking.

She drew back long enough to whisper, "I want more," before kissing him hard.

ZOE GASPED. LANGFORD kissed her passionately. Steam must be rising from her skin.

She let her raccoon coat slide down her shoulders. The deeper he kissed her, the more she wanted. She crackled and sizzled like live wires. She would scream if he didn't touch her.

His hand stroked her, lightly squeezed her through the thin cup of her brassiere. She wriggled on the seat. His mouth moved from hers and nuzzled her ear, her jaw, her throat.

Her moans drifted into the night. She *ached* for him.

She turned in the seat and slid over to him. Then she got on him, straddling his lap. She cupped his face, her palms on his strong jaw, and kissed him deeply.

Langford pulled back. His face looked agonized. Moonlight glinted on the long scars that ran down the side of his face. "No, this has to stop." He slid to the driver's side, lifted her off his lap and placed her down so she was in the passenger seat.

He turned the key—the engine sputtered, then roared. "I cannot seem to resist you. But this isn't right."

Pressing the clutch and the gas, he turned the car and drove back out to the highway. Langford drove well, his right gloved hand on the leather-wrapped steering wheel, his left scrubbing his jaw or rubbing his temple.

When they reached Brideswell, he stopped in front of the house. "You can get out here. I will take your car back to the garage."

"I'll go with you."

His gorgeous blue eyes looked so haunted. "No, you will not. You do not like me, Miss Gifford. I would advise you to stay far away from me in the future."

"Langford, this is ridiculous. There's no harm in a little kissing." She was lying. When she was with him, she felt a hunger she never had before. She wanted a lot more than kissing.

She got out of the car, wrapped her coat tightly around her and walked back to the house. How could she want this man so much?

And after that, Langford did a good job of avoiding her, and she avoided him. Mother continually talked about plans for the wedding, but Zoe managed to avoid that, too. Whenever Mother brought it up, she managed to pit the dowager against Mother and distract them both.

She had never shied away from anything in her life. But right now she was avoiding her upcoming marriage to Sebastian. And avoiding Langford.

Until a few mornings later, when she came downstairs for breakfast. Over the past few days, Langford had always been finished eating when she arrived. This time he was seated at the head of the table, reading a telegram. His hand contracted fiercely, crumpling the telegram into a tight ball.

She couldn't just pretend he wasn't in the room. "Is it bad news?"

He jerked his head up. "Nothing," he said abruptly.

He looked badly shaken. When he sat for breakfast, he dropped the crumpled telegram beside him, picked up his newssheet. He didn't notice her take the telegram. She smoothed it out.

When he realized what she'd done, it was too late. She'd already read it.

Langford bolted out of his seat. "You had no right to read that, Miss Gifford."

Now she could see the raw grief in his eyes. "I wanted to know what had made you so upset. I would be happy to drive you to London."

"That is not necessary. I will take the train this morning."

"I'll at least drive you to the station."

"I'll have Carter drive me in the Daimler."

"No, you won't," she said. "The duchess already took the car. Let me give you a lift, please."

"ALL RIGHT." THEN Nigel said, hating that it sounded reluctant, "Thank you."

"I'm sorry," Miss Gifford said, "that your friend is dying."

The telegram had come from the sister of his friend Rupert Willington. After struggling for years to recover from his battle wounds, Rupert was dying, had only days left.

It would not be a good idea to be alone in a car with Miss Gifford. At this moment, he could understand what she'd meant when she'd said she wanted more. He didn't want to think about the death of a friend. The pain was crippling. He wanted to lose himself like he had in the seat of her car.

If he were to kiss Miss Gifford, he might be able to forget the pain—

No, he had no right to do that. Not to her. Not to Rupert, who deserved to be grieved. He arranged to meet her in an hour. He had his valet pack a small valise, met with his secretary to leave instructions for Brideswell.

He met Miss Gifford outside the garage. She waited for him behind the wheel, scarf fluttering behind her. She drove down the drive to the highway at breakneck speed. He was accustomed to her driving now, and he was glad of the speed. He wanted to get to Rupert's side as quickly as he could.

She pulled in at the station in the village. Plumes of smoke streamed over the roof of the depot, and the train to London puffed into the station as he said, "Thank you."

"What is wrong with your friend?" she asked, direct as always.

"Nothing should be wrong with him," he said bitterly. "He should have been healthy, happy, married, a father. But he was a tank commander on the Somme, in the first tank battle. A direct hit crippled his tank, killing all of the men inside except Rupert. He was so badly injured, surgeons had to put him back together as if they were assembling a jigsaw puzzle—" He broke off. "I am sorry—I should not have let you know about all of that."

"Don't be sorry."

"I don't do this with anyone but you. Talk of the War. I should not do it."

"Your friend survived, at least. For a while," she said softly.

"He's been bedridden, in continual pain. He's struggled for years to stay alive. Now his body is giving out."

"Is he in a hospital?"

He fought not to start shaking. "He has a married sister, but the family has no money. She wanted to look after him, but she couldn't take on such a task. To care for an invalid is backbreaking work, and he needed the care of efficient, competent nurses. After the War, I had him kept in a convalescent home and had the best physicians in London treat him. But that was four years ago, and as Brideswell's money ran out, I couldn't do that for him anymore. He's now in a London charity hospital."

"You are a very good man, Langford."

His heart was tight with pain. "No. No, I assure you I am not."

She didn't ask him any more questions and he exited the car silently. He felt empty and cold as he took the train into town, then took a taxi to the hospital in London. One of the nursing sisters opened the door to him, led him through the hushed hallways to Rupert Willington's room. The place smelled of antiseptic, but also a stale, shut-in smell.

The sister said brightly but gently, "Mr. Willington, you have an esteemed visitor. The Duke of Langford has come to see you today."

Nigel's heart lurched. Rupert didn't move in the bed. His face was turned to the side and pale where it wasn't scarred. He had lain in this bed since Nigel had him brought here from the home. Despite his condition, Rupert normally managed to smile, to talk. Today, he lay with his eyes closed.

The nurse approached, then turned to him. Nigel's heart tightened. Was he too late? She walked into the corner and Nigel followed. Her face was placid but serious.

"He is not asleep, Your Grace, but he is failing now. His sister, Lady Eveshire, has been with him day and night, but she was so exhausted, we prepared a room in which she could rest."

Nigel nodded. Rupert's younger sister, Madeline, had been beside herself when Rupert returned so badly injured. He had helped the family as long as he could after Eveshire had gone bankrupt and they'd sold the estates.

Nigel took a chair and put it beside the bed. He held Rupert's hand.

For hours, he stayed there. Once Rupert's eyes opened. He murmured, "Nigel."

He'd thought Rupert would slip away quietly, sleeping. It was nothing like that. Rupert began to convulse. His frail body shook.

"Nurse!" Nigel grasped Rupert's shoulders, then remembered how frail his friend was and held him gently. Rupert was having a seizure. His eyes rolled back. Blood frothed at his mouth. "Nurse, come at once!" Nigel bellowed.

Hurried footsteps sounded and a panting woman reached his side. "I must fetch the doctors." She raced away, looking frantic.

"Fight, Rupert. Fight to live," he begged. Why? This was a hell of a life. But he could not bear the thought of losing Rupert. Not one more friend dead. Not one more person he cared about.

Doctors rushed in and Nigel retreated to a corner. Rupert died, but it was a vicious fight.

Nigel looked up at the door. Rupert's sister, Madeline, stood there, white with shock. She pushed past him and looked down at Rupert. His eyes had been shut by one of the doctors, but he didn't look at peace. She broke down and sobbed.

Nigel went to Madeline, held her in his arms. "I'm so sorry. But he was a hero."

Her fists hammered against his chest. "I wish he hadn't been!"

He let her hit him and cry and sob. "Maddy, shh. He had to go. We all had to."

She collapsed against him. "I wish I could have kept him home and safe. Look at us all—we've lost so much. Rupert held on for me. He knew he was not going to get well. He never cried in front of me, but I know, at night, when he thought I had gone, he cried for his lost life."

Nigel embraced Madeline and he kept thinking of what Miss Gifford said—that if you were left alive, didn't you have an obligation to live the lives they were cheated out of?

Her husband walked in then. Eveshire caught his eyes. "I am so sorry, Langford."

Nigel turned Madeline over to her husband's arms. "I will give any assistance you need with arrangements," he said, then discreetly left to see his lawyer and man of affairs in London, Charles Fortescue, to see what could be done for them.

He was in pain, grieving, and Fortescue looked as bloody morose as he did. Fortescue had just informed him of how badly his investments were doing.

"So much for my bloody plan," Nigel muttered. In his gut, he knew he was facing his family's ruin. "Look, Fortescue, this is why I said it was a bad idea to invest so heavily in American companies that did not have solid grounding." There were companies who had indeed made a fortune with new developments in railroads, television, motorcars. But there were far more companies with high hopes and dreams and no real business acumen.

"British companies are not faring much better," Fortescue pointed out.

"True. But with British ones, I got a whiff of disaster early enough to get out the capital. Damn it, man."

Fortescue winced.

"I presume you are telling me," Nigel went on, "that Brideswell has to go?"

"Not yet, Your Grace. And it would be possible to save the estate, if you were to sell off some of the property."

This time Nigel winced. He'd said to Miss Gifford that war had created change, but it had been coming for a long time. He'd known Brideswell was going through financial crises in his grandfather's time and his father's time. He knew the old ways were struggling, but he'd thought they could survive. War had precipitated the change so fast no one could stop it.

"You mean if I turn Brideswell into nothing but a large house with a lawn, I can potentially save it. If I turn my back on the estate's tenants. I won't do that."

"You may not have a choice," Fortescue said.

"Brideswell has to survive."

"These large estates are no longer viable, Your Grace. Money is made elsewhere now—"

"I'm a duke. This is my job, Fortescue. To protect Brideswell and its people. I might fail in that job, but I won't give up on it."

A TELEGRAM CAME for Zoe the next morning.

Zoe took it with her heart pounding. What if it was

from her uncle Hiram about Mother's forged check? Maybe he'd returned to New York early....

Thank God, it wasn't that. But she read it in Brideswell's foyer and reeled backward, gripping one of the Queen Anne tables.

Her brother, Billy—before he'd been killed—had been in love with a young woman named Daisy, the daughter of a steel magnate. Zoe had last seen Daisy at Billy's memorial, where the girl had been practically inconsolable. Now Daisy was gone, too. She had taken a bunch of pills, had washed them down with bourbon, and she was now dead.

Daisy would have been twenty-three. And she had given up on living.

Numb, Zoe walked through Brideswell's salon, the vast space overlooked by the gallery. She went blindly through the library onto the terrace. Why had Daisy done it?

Zoe started running. She ran down the gravel path that cut across the lawns. Ran until she reached the edge of the meadow where her airplane was parked, among bluebells and violets.

Zoe wiped away tears. And saw another solitary figure standing in front of her airplane.

Langford. His head was bowed. His hand gripped a strut as if to hold himself up. She hadn't realized he'd returned. He must have taken a late-afternoon train.

If he was back, his friend must be gone.

Right now, her insides felt as if they'd been all twisted up. She should be alone—but she went toward him, running away from her emotions.

NIGEL LOOKED UP as Miss Gifford walked over to him. "I am sorry. I will not be good company now," he said. "Rupert is passed away this morning."

She wore her flying costume—the snug-fitting trousers and leather jacket. But her face was stricken. She was in deep pain, and it wasn't from his words.

"I've just lost someone, too," she said hoarsely.

"Who?" It came out more abruptly than he'd wanted.

Her story spilled out. Of her brother, Billy, and the girl he loved named Daisy. The girl had taken her own life.

"I wish I could have done something—something to help her," Miss Gifford whispered.

"There was nothing to do," he said. "Some people can take the loss and the grief and bear up to its weight. Some cannot. You can."

"I *don't know* if I can," she said desperately. "I thought the end of the War would be the end of loss. I remember dancing and drinking champagne at an extravagant party in New York on the night after peace was announced. I did it so I didn't have to think about Billy. I was so naive."

She knew—as he did—that the end of the War was not truly the end.

"I don't know what to do anymore, Langford. I don't want to be crushed by pain. I don't."

God, neither did he. He didn't know if he kissed her first or if she kissed him. All he knew was he had her up against the side of her aeroplane and his mouth was on hers.

He pulled back, breathing hard. "I have no right to do this. You've lost someone you cared about. I lost a man that I couldn't save. If I'd had enough money for a home for him… Damn, I should have done more—"

"You tried. How many men did you save in the War?"

"I don't know. Not enough."

Miss Gifford lifted her gloved hand and touched his face. He was wrapped in her subtle, rich flowered scent.

She touched his scars. Her fingers skimmed over the ridges, the long deep gouge and the puckered skin.

He flinched, drew back and put up his hand to stop her. "Don't touch me there."

Hell, even he didn't like to touch his scars.

"Why not?" She pursed her full lips, and his heart beat faster. He remembered the warmth of her body against his in the front seat of her car. The way she kissed him had made him forget he was a scarred man just for a little while.

"You won't believe me, but I think they're beautiful," she said. "They are like medals—a testament to your bravery, your goodness. I'm an American. I never believed in the idea of nobility. Now I understand what being noble truly means. It has nothing to do with a title. It's not even about sacrifice or duty. It's about a passion for your world, one that runs through your blood. It's about loving something so deeply you would never put yourself first."

He was speechless.

"That is who you are, Langford. The way you help Mrs. Billings and care about the farmers and the way you stood up for Isobel and were there for your friend at the end." Miss Gifford reached up and put her hands on his shoulders.

Desire forked through him like a streak of lightning.

Admittedly, that happened every time she touched him. It shouldn't damn well happen today.

"I've realized," she went on, "that you are the most passionate man I've ever known."

"Miss Gifford, any one of my acquaintances would say I'm the least passionate man—"

"Shows you how little they know," she interrupted. "I bet you want to kiss me again right now."

"Yes." God, he wanted to grasp some of her warmth and hold it against his heart.

"I want to kiss you, Nigel."

He jerked back. He was always called Langford and before that by his courtesy title. But when she said his Christian name, it made him ache.

"I can't kiss you right now, Miss Gifford. My friend has just died."

"You're in pain. I can't think of a better reason to give you a kiss."

Her hand skimmed up the side of his face, and he felt it everywhere. It tugged at his heart, punched him in the gut, sent a pulse to his groin that left his knees weak and his head reeling.

"Do it. Kiss me. I want this. Please. Make me forget."

He lowered his mouth toward hers, his lips soft, on fire, ready to melt in a kiss. He gripped the struts of the aeroplane's wing, leaned in the last inch and took her mouth with his.

8

SOARING IN AN AEROPLANE

NIGEL DEEPENED THE KISS, tilting his head, parting his lips, teasing her with his tongue.

Miss Gifford kissed him back, did it hungrily, making him feel as though he was melting slowly from his mouth down. He was burning hot, wanting to lift her up against the plane and make love to her until she screamed in pleasure.

He leaned her back against the side of her aeroplane, and she lay along the curve of the metal body. Bracing his arms on either side of her, he pressed his body to hers. His hips wedged between her legs; his chest crushed her breasts.

He'd fought this for too long.

What would she do? Slap him? Say this was far enough?

No, she lifted one leg and wrapped it around his hip.

She was so beautiful, so filled with life. And more than that—he'd never felt so close to anyone else in his life, not even Mary.

He nuzzled her neck, tasting her delectable skin, breathing in her sensual perfume. She wriggled as he gently nipped her earlobe.

She ran her hands all over his chest and whispered in a throaty voice, "More."

He kissed to her collarbone, bared because her leather jacket was open and her man's shirt had the first two buttons undone.

She made him forget he was a duke. She made him forget he was supposed to be as hard as steel, as unyielding as rock, as emotionless as a block of lead.

She made him feel alive.

He admired her bravery, her kindness, and he was dazzled by her sensuality. But he should not do this. He tried to pull back, but her arm was looped around his neck.

He gazed into her violet eyes, unusual and precious, fringed by painted lashes. As a boy, before he'd taken on the responsibility of being a duke, before he'd gone to war, he'd dreamed of traveling the world. Zoe Gifford was like climbing the Himalayas, exploring deepest Africa, charting India. She was a treasure—beautiful, exotic, intriguing, sensual. Making love to her would be an adventure.

But foremost he was a gentleman. He couldn't forget that. "Miss Gifford, I can't—"

"Shh…" She put her leather-clad finger to his lips. "Let's make each other forget."

She guided his hand to her breast, and he flicked open the next button of her shirt. And encountered straps, cups of a stiff white fabric and the band that ran around her chest below her breasts…along with nothing else but a stretch of smooth, ivory skin to the waistband of her trousers.

How did he get into a brassiere? He had no idea. His heart was slamming in his chest.

Then she broke away from him, and he meant to stop,

but she shrugged off her leather aviator jacket and let it fall to the grass by the plane.

She unbuttoned her shirt and let the soft, green cambric fall open. Her lashes fell over her violet eyes in a look that was clearly a dare.

ZOE CAUGHT HER breath as Nigel's clear blue eyes held hers. Would he stay? When he kissed her, she couldn't think.

She didn't want to think.

So she surged up and locked her mouth to his.

He bent his head, and she smelled the fresh, clean scent of his hair as it brushed her cheeks. He kissed her neck and she slumped back against the airplane and moaned in real desire. "Beautiful." His voice was a rough growl. It made her feel tingly and dizzy as if she'd tossed a cocktail back too fast.

His mouth went lower and she held his shoulders— broad, strong shoulders.

His lips lifted in a smile.

His lashes dropped over his eyes, a thick fringe of black. Cupping her bottom, his hand between her and the side of her plane, he drew her to him. She looked up into his eyes. Caught her breath.

Fire burned in his eyes. There was no iciness in him now. She hadn't melted him. She'd turned him right into steam.

Now she knew. The Duke of Langford, the archly correct gentleman who had been so annoying and disapproving...

Was completely naughty at heart.

She ached so much between her legs. But once she

did *this,* there was no going back. She was supposed to be wild. But she had never been this kind of wild.

Then she felt a tug of guilt and disloyalty. Daisy, Billy's beloved, was tragically dead. She couldn't bear to think about it. Not about one more person precious to her being gone.

And Langford... Nigel had hung his head and she saw him fighting tears. The man who showed nothing, who held in all emotion, was struggling against pain too great to hold in. They both hurt so badly. They both needed this.

She was never going to love anyone the way she'd loved Richmond. But she didn't want to live her whole life as a virgin. She wanted to fly.

"Get in the cockpit," she whispered.

"I cannot fly the—"

"That's not what I have in mind. And undo your trousers when you get in there."

Her heart thrummed like the drum in a jazz band. She watched the duke put his foot on the wing and swing into the seat of the cockpit. Before he sat down, he undid his trousers and pushed them down to his knees. Revealing his long, muscled legs and drawers that clung to lean hips. Holding her gaze, he pushed those down, too.

Grasp life, a voice in her brain urged. *Now.*

He was the most gorgeous man she'd ever seen. She'd never wanted anyone like this. As if she were going to fly into pieces if she didn't press herself tight to him and feel his arms around her.

When she took a risk, she did it fast. She got up on the wing and into the tight space of the seat with Nigel, facing him. He drew her on top of him.

Her hands splayed on his hard, broad chest and he pulled her forward to kiss her deeply. His mouth was hot, commanding. She fell into his kiss as if she were in a spin and couldn't pull out.

She undid the fastenings of *her* trousers and tried to tug them down. "Rest your knee on mine," he directed. When she did, he helped her draw her trousers down.

She managed to get them to her ankles. Then Nigel eased them off, along with her boots, first one leg and then the other. All the while he looked at her with fierce, intense desire.

She was used to feeling fear along with a sharp tug of excitement. Any pilot was. She'd just never really felt it with a man before. But she felt it all the time with Nigel. Not just when they had swum naked in Brideswell's lake or when they'd kissed in her car. She felt it whenever they were in the same room.

She'd also planned to be confident the very first time she made love. But now she was trembling.

Her breath left her when he lifted her gently. She balanced above him, knowing what he wanted.

She closed her eyes and sank down on him.

Sophisticated girls had warned her there was pain—she hadn't believed it. Not really. They'd said it was worth it.

God, was it?

But then all the pleasure of his hands caressing her made the pain go away. Now she knew—this felt perfect. The heat of the sun engulfed her, and Langford was boiling hot beneath her. This was decadent.

It was everything she wanted.

Then something happened inside her. She felt hotter, tenser. All coiled up. Her hands fisted and hit his shoulders. Desperate, throaty moans came from her. Then all her nerves burst like fireworks, and she gave a wild sob, hit his back and surrendered to something thrilling and sweet and wonderful.

HIS CHEST FELT like a vise. Nigel was dazzled. On fire.

Miss Gifford collapsed on him, gasping softly.

He loved having her touch him, having her pressed against him. He savored the pressure of her hands. The weight of her rounded bottom on his thighs. The heat of her breath on his skin.

He was in the tight padded seat in the cramped cockpit of an aeroplane with a wild, tempting, gorgeous woman who was turning his brains into pudding.

He had been damned nervous, making love to her.

Miss Gifford was modern. Bold. She would have expectations. And when it came down to it, what the hell did he know about sex? His father had sent him to a courtesan to lose his virginity. Since it was bad form to relieve oneself with one's hand, regular visits to a mistress were encouraged. They were willing and entertaining. But he wanted a hell of a lot more with Miss Gifford.

He had wanted to please her.

They were mad about that in America—the belief that women could enjoy sexual relations, too. Women expected it. But more than that, he'd wanted to make love to her knowing she was having fun, too.

But he couldn't hold on anymore. It was as if a white light exploded in his head. Pleasure hit him in one huge bolt of wild sensation and he gave in to it. Then he bent to kiss the top of her head.

Belatedly, Nigel took a look around. They were still alone in the field, thank God.

She straightened. Her cheeks were pink, her bobbed hair tangled around her. He couldn't think what to say, so he kissed her.

Then she drew back. He shifted her so they were apart and he gazed into her glowing violet eyes. This was a precious moment. He'd never felt so connected to a woman.

She confounded him in every way, but fascinated him so much he could not get enough of her.

A dog barked and Nigel heard voices—voices of men who worked on his estate calling to each other.

With lightning speed he lifted Miss Gifford off his lap, drew her knickers back up, then her trousers. In battle, he'd learned quick reflexes. They had to preserve her reputation. "There's someone coming," he murmured. "We've got to get dressed."

The crunching of grass and bracken sounded louder.

She hurried with the fastenings of her trousers. "You must hide. There's no time for you to do up your trousers. Duck down."

She fastened her jacket with her brassiere still undone, smoothed her trousers, and she pulled her pilot's helmet and goggles on over her disheveled hair. She put on an innocent expression.

Nothing fazed her. Most girls of his acquaintance would be blithering wrecks right now. Not Miss Gifford. Coolly, she swung out of the cockpit and onto the wing of the plane.

The voices and footsteps grew louder and Nigel ducked down.

Dukes did not hide. But for her sake, he had to. This was one time he could not stand on pride.

Miss Gifford waved and nonchalantly called, "Good afternoon."

The men returned her greeting, and a few minutes later, the men and the dogs were gone, having noticed nothing amiss.

Relieved, Nigel stood and pulled up his linens and his trousers. He got out of the cockpit, jumping to the ground. As he did, she crouched down on the wing, grabbed one of the struts, leaned over and put her lips against his.

He released her after a breathless moment. "You are beautiful."

It was not enough. Not enough to explain the tug in his heart as he looked at her.

"Thank you." Her lashes dipped over her eyes. "I never dreamed it felt like that," she said huskily. "Now I know why people talk of nothing but sex. When it hurt, I thought—goodness, why do people do this? But then—it was glorious."

She spoke breathily, and her eyes opened wide, glowing with wicked delight. "You know, at first I was too shy to look at you while we were doing it. But now it's all I want to do forever."

It was dangerous, but Nigel was getting aroused again. Perhaps they could do it again, here, propped against the side of the—

Then his wits clicked back in and he realized what she had just said. It had hurt her. She didn't have experience. Despite having been so bold, despite having acted so cool and collected when they were almost caught, she'd been...

A virgin.

Bloody, bloody hell.

He had assumed… He had thought… She was so open and confident and daring, he had made a hell of a wrong assumption. "Miss Gifford, there is something I must do—"

She put her finger over his lips. "You have to call me Zoe now. And you must get out of here while the getting's good. Almost getting caught was *exhilarating*—but I want to go flying now."

"Zoe, no. You must hear me out."

She jumped into the cockpit in one smooth motion. "I don't want to talk right now. I'm desperate to fly."

His words of protest were drowned by the sputter of the engine as she started it. She mouthed something at him, then gave him a signal where she stuck her thumb up in the air.

Nigel had no choice but to back away from the aeroplane and let her fly away.

9
AT THE GARAGE

DAMN ENGLISH DINNERS.

Nigel had no time to speak to Zoe alone.

He did, however, have time to meet a "charming" girl his grandmother had invited to dinner. During cocktails in the drawing room, Grandmama dragged the tall, graceful, dark-haired girl to him and made the introduction. "Miss Elizabeth Strutt. Of the shipping Strutts. Her mother and your mother were grand friends at school. Perhaps you might play for us later, Miss Strutt. It is so rare girls even play pianoforte so well. They all seem to think they should be going to university."

Nigel almost shook his head. In three sentences Grandmama had outlined the girl's attributes: wealth, noble bloodlines and the fact the girl had been raised to be an old-fashioned lady.

He bowed over Miss Strutt's hand. At least Grandmama had the decency to move away.

The girl was the same age as Zoe. Her hair was waved and drawn back into a chignon. She wore a fashionable dress, but one of dark blue, much more sedate than Zoe's short-skirted one of dramatic black, covered with thousands of beads. Or the beautiful rose silk dress that Julia wore. Come to think of it, she looked a lot like his former fiancée, Mary.

"Sorry," Elizabeth Strutt said, in a cool, jaded voice that reminded him of Zoe. "They're pushing me at you in hopes of an engagement. Sadly, I am one of those girls who wanted to go to university."

"What do you intend to study?" he inquired.

Her brows went up. He had just politely told her there was no chance of an engagement.

"What if I told you I am still open to the possibilities?"

Nigel glanced across the room. Sebastian was talking to Zoe, but his brother kept sneaking looks at his friend John Ransome. Standing with her mother, Zoe stole glances at where he and Elizabeth stood. Their gazes met, and then they both turned awkwardly away. Then he looked at her again almost instantly.

What was she thinking? That he was a cad for having ravished her and offered her nothing?

He'd done something unpardonable to her—he'd taken her innocence and not made it clear what he intended to do. There could be a child.

He would have damn well offered her marriage if she hadn't started her plane's engine and coasted away.

His hand almost shattered his glass. He needed to talk to her. He wanted to grab her and drag her from the room. He couldn't do that. Not in front of guests and his family.

"Who is she?" Miss Strutt drawled.

The woman he had to marry. "My brother's fiancée."

"I should have guessed she is the rich American. It is quite obvious she is not one of us."

No, she wasn't. Zoe was something different and

impossible to understand. She had upheaved his life from the moment she'd appeared in the road outside Brideswell.

Now he was going to be living with her night and day. He would look across from her at breakfast. Go to her bedroom at night. Join her for marital visits.

And he didn't understand anything about her. No woman he knew would have given up her innocence, not without securing a marriage proposal first.

He did not know what Zoe Gifford wanted from him. But he knew what he had to give her.

Miss Strutt was speaking to him, but he could not focus on a word. In the same way, he had no idea what he ate during dinner. After the women left the dining room, he waited ten frustrating minutes when he muttered answers to political questions he didn't even hear, then pushed back his chair. "I suggest we rejoin the women."

He saw surprised looks on the faces of his male guests. There hadn't been enough time to finish cigars. But he damn well didn't care. He almost sprinted to the drawing room. And when he burst in, he looked for Zoe. But she was gone.

Grandmama made a beeline for him, her walking stick hastily smacking the carpet.

"Where is—" he caught himself "—Miss Gifford?"

The dowager looked around, rather like an owl. "I have no idea. Why are you concerned about your brother's fiancée? You should be concerned about your own."

The problem was his brother's fiancée was the woman who must become *his* fiancée. Then he blinked. "What fiancée?"

"Miss Strutt will be your intended, as soon as you

ask her. I have been assured by her mother that she will accept. We can have the whole matter taken care of in mere days, Nigel."

Miss Strutt was across the room, with his mother and Julia.

"I just met the girl hours ago."

Grandmama hit him on the forearm with her lorgnette. "Nigel, in this day and age, this is the best we can hope to do. She is an heiress. She is granddaughter to an earl on her mother's side. The girl is pleasing to the eye and polite. For an entire dinner she didn't argue with you or insist on discussing the War or women's rights."

"She didn't?" He couldn't remember what the woman had talked about.

Grandmama rapped him on the forearm harder. "Duty is the only thing we have, Nigel. The only thing that will keep us safe."

"It's too late. I can't marry her."

His grandmother let her lorgnette fall to her side. "Nigel, what in heaven's name are you talking about?"

"You do not want to know. And I don't want to discuss it. Suffice to say, I am going to get married. But not to Elizabeth Strutt."

ZOE HAD BEEN dragged upstairs by a servant claiming her mother had fallen ill, but the minute she'd closed Mother's door, her mother whirled around. "That girl intends to grab the duke as quick as she can."

"What girl?"

"Miss Strutt! Who else?"

Zoe's stomach felt as if it had dropped off the Woolworth Building. Her mother couldn't possibly know what had happened between her and Nigel. She prayed Mother did not know.

"I can see you're changing your mind. I've watched you watch the duke. You couldn't take your eyes off him tonight at dinner. What we have to do is make sure you get in there first."

When Mother wanted to arrange her life, Mother left all her fluttering behind and became more forceful than a titan of business. "Mother, I'm engaged to Sebastian."

"That, Zoe, is irrelevant."

She hardly thought so. And what was she going to do? She couldn't marry Sebastian now. Mother was right. All through dinner, she'd stolen glances at Nigel. Each time she did it, he tilted his head toward her as if her gaze was a magnet. She had to fight to tear her gaze away.

All through dinner all she'd wanted to do was crawl across the table, jump on Nigel and get all sweaty and excited while she made him turn to steam all over again.

This was like having a fever. And it was close to making her delirious.

Was she in love with Nigel? Or was this just lust? And what if there was a baby? She'd been so busy grasping at life and excitement, she hadn't thought about that.

"Are you in love with the duke?"

Mother's words rang in her head like an accusation. But she wanted to be honest and blunt—it was what you should do now. Stop lying. Stop hiding. Just tell the truth. "I don't know, Mother. I think I might be."

Or I'm in lust with him. Really, really intense lust. The kind of lust that makes you do crazy, crazy things.

"Well, then you can't marry his brother. If you marry and divorce Sebastian Hazelton, you can *never* have the duke. It's unlawful for a man to marry the wife of his brother, if she's divorced his brother, during the lifetime of his brother. I sent a telegram to our lawyers to check." Zoe was startled. Mother had asked lawyers about this?

Nigel had changed. He had been awfully passionate with her. And she couldn't stop thinking about him. She'd felt happy when she'd loved Richmond. She didn't feel exactly happy about loving Nigel. She felt all mixed up. "Maybe I'm not in love with Nigel—I mean Langford."

"Zoe, please. I'm your mother and I know you love this man. You can't marry someone when you are in love with his brother." Mother shooed her toward the door. "I feel much better now, Zoe. Now, go downstairs and ensure that Strutt creature doesn't get her hooks into him."

Zoe rolled her eyes, but she returned to the drawing room. Nigel was in the corner, speaking in a low voice to Miss Strutt.

It made her heart ache to see them together.

In the opposite corner, Sebastian laughed at something Captain Ransome said. Then Ransome took Sebastian's coffee cup and went to the urn to refill it.

It would be easiest to just quietly say her piece now. But the dowager was within earshot. She might be standing with the Reverend Wesley, but her head was cocked toward Sebastian. At the same time, her gaze was fixed on Nigel and Miss Strutt. Elizabeth Strutt had been going on about the past—hunts and balls she remembered from before the War. Her strategy was apparently to win Nigel by implying she would act as if they were living in 1912, not 1922.

Zoe thought that should be a perfect strategy to snare

Nigel, that it was obvious they made the perfect couple, but he looked agitated by the conversation.

If she couldn't have Nigel—if he was falling under the spell of a woman from his world—why should she end her engagement?

But she walked up to Sebastian. He lifted her hand to his lips and gave her a smoldering look. Why didn't the man she'd made love with do this? Kiss her hand. Gaze at her as if she were the only thing in the world worth looking at.

Sebastian claimed he wanted a real marriage—and she knew she couldn't stand up with him in a church, even to go through with a fake one. "Sebastian, something has happened. Things have changed. I need to speak to you alone tonight."

"My darling, any other night, I would be delighted to slip away to meet you. But not tonight."

"Why not tonight?" She wanted this business dealt with. "You have other plans for the middle of the night?" She lifted her brow.

"Actually, I do. I'm…meeting a friend of mine at the pub in Brideswell-Upon-Lovey."

"It's about our engagement. Sebastian, I have to—"

"Zoe, we'll talk tonight. I won't be back late. We can meet at midnight. Outside, by the garage. It should be warm tonight."

With that much time maybe she could talk herself out of this crazy need she had to break off her engagement. Maybe she could convince herself she had to go through with it.

And as for the duke—engrossed in conversation with Miss Strutt—he could go jump in Brideswell's frosty lake.

Zoe noticed the dowager take a discreet step back to listen in. "All right," she said. "Midnight. Sharp."

BUT ONCE SEBASTIAN LEFT, Zoe had a better idea. She assumed he was walking to the garage. He must be intending to drive to the pub, then return to meet her. She would catch him there before he left and get this business sorted right away.

As she hurried down to the garage, she was haunted by her mother's warning. If she married Sebastian, she'd lose Nigel essentially forever.

She reached the garage. A wooden building, much more modern than the stone stables, had been put up for the automobiles.

Sometimes the chauffeur worked there at night, but tonight there was no light burning inside. A figure came out of the shadows beside the garage door. He quickly darted inside and closed the door behind him. It wasn't Sebastian—in moonlight, Sebastian's pale hair would glow like silver.

This man was dark. Nigel?

He was all alone in the garage and all she had to do was walk right in. They could do just what they'd done in the airplane, but this time stretched out in the backseat of a car.

A jolt of desire shot through her that almost brought her to her knees. Well, maybe they couldn't do that, since she'd been careless about pregnancy before. But they could do other things. She slid the door open a few inches. She was about to slip in when a masculine voice said, "I was worried you weren't going to come."

Sebastian's voice. It was soft and sensuous, as if he was sweet-talking someone. Had he seen her? But he didn't expect her yet. She was about to call out to him when she saw a glint of light and Sebastian stepped out from between the Daimler and her car, carrying a candle. "But I'm glad you did… John."

John?

John Ransome stepped forward, into the circle of light of the candle. The glow touched his high cheekbones and ran along the curve of his sulky mouth.

Sebastian's face was tight with—with something that looked like agony. He took the last step that brought him close to John Ransome, so close their chests almost touched. They were both breathing hard. Their mouths were soft and gilded by the light of the candle and just inches from each other.

Then Sebastian took the last step and he wrapped his arm around Ransome's neck, splayed his hand in the man's hair and put his lips against his friend's mouth.

Shock kept Zoe frozen there, her hand on the door latch. For a few wild moments, she knew she shouldn't be standing there, watching this, and she didn't want them to see her.

She turned away and pulled the garage door closed as quietly as she could.

Crossing her arms over her chest, she started walking. She didn't know where. She just didn't want to go back to the house.

There had been a play in New York. A jaded, popular Manhattan girl named Maisie had taken her to it. The most scandalous play in the city, she'd been told. Every young woman of good New York society seemed to think that just seeing the play would lead a woman down an intractable path of doom and corruption.

Maisie had been so wild and thrilling and dangerously fun. She had affairs with members of Harlem jazz bands and knew the secret passwords to every hot speakeasy in New York.

She didn't care what anyone thought of her, and Zoe had spent every moment she could with Maisie. She wanted to learn how you stopped caring so you could live life.

The first moment the two actresses had placed their mouths close enough to touch, the entire audience held their collective breaths, waiting for the forbidden. Then the two girls on stage had kissed.

Zoe had been paralyzed, though Maisie hadn't been shocked at all. Her large brown eyes had been bright, full of excitement. Her pupils were huge and black with the drugs that were sold in the shadowy back rooms of private parties and speakeasies.

Maisie had leaned back, hiking her skirt up to show her rolled-down stockings and her bare thigh. "In the modern world, a girl can experiment with sex however she wants. That's what my set is about. We try everything." Maisie's gaze had raked over her boldly. "You aren't going to be boring and old-fashioned, are you?"

In that moment, Zoe had known she couldn't do anything that daring. She *was* boring and old-fashioned after all. After that, she'd stopped seeing Maisie.

So she wasn't shocked to know Sebastian preferred men. But knowing he had tried to con her was different. That hurt.

"Miss Gifford."

She let out a cry of surprise. It was Nigel. Walking purposely toward her across the gravel drive.

He'd called her Miss Gifford. They'd made love this afternoon, and he was being correct again.

She couldn't understand him.

How could he have changed back to being icy after being so hot and steamy with her? It had awakened all kinds of delicious feelings inside her. He just looked… grim.

"I want to talk to you." He caught hold of her arm and led her back to the garage. "We'll go in here. We will not be disturbed." He passed her and went to the door. He pressed down the latch.

She grabbed his hand. "No."

Nigel arched a ducal brow. "No? Miss Gifford, we will talk and we will do so now."

Maybe it was his return to icy, autocratic behavior. She'd thought she was falling in love; he was behaving as if they were strangers. Zoe knew this feeling—to expose one's heart, only to have it stomped upon. Whatever it was—something made her want to shock him.

"Sebastian is in there," she said, exaggerating a jaded, careless tone, but keeping her voice very soft, "with his friend Captain Ransome. They kissed. I think it would be embarrassing to interrupt them. It would probably lead to a scene, and I know how you dislike scenes."

10
THE PROPOSAL

NIGEL STOOD THERE, like a stone statue with his hand on the door. After an age, there was a click of the latch falling back into place. Slowly he drew his hand from the handle. "Did you just say that—that they are—are—?"

Zoe realized he couldn't say it in front of her. She whispered, "I said they are kissing."

"How do you know this?"

She moved away from the garage to the edge of the gravel drive in front of it, near some trees, and he followed. "I wanted to speak to Sebastian alone—I wanted to break off our engagement. But when I went into the garage, he was with Captain Ransome. I was standing in the doorway and neither man noticed me. When Sebastian drew Ransome into a kiss, I slipped out."

The duke winced. "You shouldn't have seen that."

"I didn't mean to catch them at such a personal moment."

"You shouldn't have seen anything so scandalous."

"I do know it happens. I've known men like that—there are many in fashionable New York. I've even seen plays in which women kiss."

If his jaw could have fallen off and hit the gravel, it would have. "You are—you are very sophisticated." He made it sound scandalous.

"I'm not. But I'm not shocked." She crossed her arms over her chest and thrust her hip forward. "What hurts is that when he was courting me, he was conning me. I didn't mean a damn thing to him. But he thought I was naive enough to believe him. And that hurts."

Nigel winced. "I am sorry you were hurt. And I am sorry, but you are correct."

Then she realized the truth. It was cool on the drive, but she began to feel awfully hot. And angry. "You knew all along about him. You knew *why* he was not in love with me. That was what you were trying to tell me in my car."

"He believed marriage would protect him from rumors. A long-term marriage would accomplish that better. A marriage that dissolved shortly after the supposed wedding night might only feed rumors."

"And you went along. For the sake of the family, of course." She let the last words ripple out in careless tones, but rage now made her shake. "Okay, you did try to warn me. But why didn't you tell me the *truth?*"

"I couldn't. It is Sebastian's secret. I had no right to tell you. Do you now see why I have disapproved of this from the beginning? That time you saw Sebastian punch me? That was why. He'd outlined his plan and I was furious. I knew you had lost your fiancé. You were vulnerable. But you were so stubborn, you refused to listen."

"So that is why you hit your brother over me?"

"Yes." And he turned red. Then he frowned. "Why are you ending the engagement, if the marriage was just to end in divorce?"

God, why did he think? Did he feel anything for her at all? Did the fact he'd punched Sebastian mean anything? She couldn't see any desire for her in his grim expression.

"I couldn't go through with a marriage with him when I was making love with you," she said softly. "I don't understand you. I thought after—after what happened, things would be different. Tell me, Nigel, why did you get into that airplane with me?"

"Because I did not think."

She drew back. "What a damned answer." She whirled and stalked away.

She had been falling in love with him, and he didn't care two bits about her. She'd thought his passion meant something—meant that he was dazzled by her, that he wanted her.... She'd thought it meant more than that. She'd thought if she could get the Duke of Langford to do something wild like that with her, he had to be falling in love with her.

She'd been wrong.

His footsteps crunched behind her. "I am sorry, Miss Gifford. Zoe. I expressed that badly. Please, let me walk you back."

She turned. "Don't bother. If you think following me will get you under my skirt this time, you're wrong." She threw out the words, full of anger. And not just at him. She didn't care what she said. She wanted to hurt him, even if her words physically hurt her, too.

Visible pain showed on Nigel's face, but she kept walking. Fast. He ran after her—she heard his steps on the gravel. He caught her arm and stopped her. He raked his hand through his hair, making it stick out. "As to what happened in the—the aeroplane, that is what we have to discuss."

"Discuss?"

"Yes. You see, Zoe, I owe you—"

"So this is where you disappeared to. Grandmama is having a fit, Nigel. She was hoping to attach you to Miss Strutt." Julia came walking toward them, emerging from the shadows, and she screwed up her face in an exaggerated expression of pain. "They never leave us alone until we marry. Were you going to escape by going for a drive?"

Julia gazed innocently at them both, then looked toward the garage. Nigel jumped in front of her view, grasped his sister's arm and turned her to face the house. Zoe saw the panic in his eyes. "No," he said quickly, "we were going back to the house."

"Are you up to something? You look nervous." Her gaze flicked from him to Zoe. Her eyes widened. "Oh," she said.

"What do you mean 'oh'?" Nigel demanded. "We are not up to anything. There's no reason for an 'oh,' Julia. Now, let's take you back to the house." He put his hand to Julia's back and forced her to walk swiftly away from the garage.

It was awkward, but funny, too. He was trying to protect Julia and Sebastian, Zoe supposed. It was very sweet how worried he was.

He was an irritating man, but in many ways a good one.

Maybe she could understand why he hadn't told her about Sebastian. Besides, could she really imagine Nigel telling her that Sebastian preferred men? He wouldn't have got the words out of his mouth. But he'd tried to warn her, in his own way.

Zoe glanced back to the closed wooden door. The anger she'd felt was still there, but Nigel's apologies had taken the edge off it. She supposed Sebastian was desperate. He was afraid. He was also in love with someone he could not have—at least not publicly.

Now she understood the bitterness and anger seething in him. His devil-may-care attitude must be hiding a great deal of pain.

Marriage would still help save Sebastian from rumors. And it would save her, too.

Could she go through with it? A good businesswoman would do it. Was she going to throw her mother into risk of prosecution by Uncle Hiram just because she couldn't forget Nigel—a man who obviously would never love her back?

JULIA STAYED WITH them as they walked to the house and accompanied them upstairs. At the door to the corridor that led to the women's bedrooms, Nigel said good-night to both of them, went to his bedroom and paced the floor. After twenty minutes, he gambled on returning.

At Zoe's door, Nigel looked up and down the hallway. All was quiet, and no sound came from inside her room. He knocked as discreetly as he could.

The door started to open. At that moment Nigel recognized his error—this was likely Zoe's maid, there to undress her. Panic rose. He took a step in retreat—

The hand that slipped around the door was slender, graceful, the nails glossy with red polish, the very tips unadorned. That was definitely Zoe. Her face appeared in the small space between door and frame. She was freshly washed. He hadn't seen her without makeup since the night in the Savoy. Her lips were full and lush but a pale pink. Her lashes were long and golden.

She looked younger.

Of course, she was only twenty.

He felt a spurt of guilt, but he was used to the feeling. "Miss Gifford, I need to talk to you."

"What about?"

"Let me in before someone sees me. Please."

"You have to answer one question first. Close your eyes."

Nigel did what she asked, confused. Anyone could catch him out here. There was no time for games. Did she not understand that?

"I'm wearing a silk robe and nothing else. Imagine taking my robe off me. Sliding it down my shoulders and letting it fall, leaving me completely...exposed to you. If you think about that, what do you want to call me? Zoe or Miss Gifford?"

God, he was in pain picturing that image. "I do not have the right to call you Zoe. Not anymore. Not unless I have the chance to make things right." He opened his eyes.

She frowned. "That wasn't the answer I expected." But she opened the door wide and stepped back, letting him enter her room and close the door behind him.

She wore a pink silk robe that clung to her slender figure.

Was there really nothing underneath?

Damn, he had no right to wonder.

She had one of Brideswell's best rooms, but before Zoe had come into it, it had looked a bit shabby. Furniture had been sold, the carpet was worn, bed hangings faded. Now it sparkled—gold brushes on the vanity, dozens of faceted glass bottles, jewels cast over the table, glittering dresses lying over the remaining chairs, the end of the bed. As if she was so busy grasping life that she had no time to care about anything.

"I dismissed my maid early tonight," she said. "I never guessed you'd come to see me, though." She stopped and turned around. "There's something I have to know."

Next thing he knew, her arms were around his neck and her mouth was wildly, passionately setting fire to his.

He caught hold of her arms and gently pushed her back. His breath came as fast as hers—in quick, shallow pants. "Nothing more can happen now, Zoe. I should behave respectfully, because I know you were innocent before this afternoon, in the aeroplane."

"Shouldn't the way you treat a girl depend on how you feel about her? Do you want to kiss me or not?"

"I have to behave like a gentleman. That is why I came to your room tonight."

"Really?" She sat on the edge of the small writing desk and crossed her legs. The silk fell away, revealing their beautiful length. Making it hard for him to think.

He couldn't understand her. He had taken her innocence. But she hadn't demanded anything from him.

He didn't know what to make of her. He understood the rules of Englishwomen. Zoe did not seem to be bound by any rules.

What did it mean for a marriage when he didn't understand her?

But he did desire her like mad. That was going to have to be enough to make the marriage work.

He cleared his throat. "Zoe, there is something I must say to you."

"You look so serious I feel like I've been hauled in

front of a judge." She dragged a silver case off the writing desk and took out a cigarette.

Nigel cleared his throat. "Given what has happened between us, it is my duty to marry you."

HE WAS USING the stuffiest, most pompous tones she had ever heard him use. He didn't bend down onto one knee. Instead, he raked back his hair, then paced in front of her.

After trying to kiss him, to find his passion again, Zoe felt as if she'd landed on earth with a hard thud. "It's your duty to marry me? Why, exactly?"

"I owe you marriage, Zoe. You were…innocent. I didn't realize you were. Now I pay the price —"

"Pay the price?" she repeated, getting angry. "I get it. You deserve to be punished, and marriage to me would punish you nicely?"

"A gentleman doesn't ravish a young woman and walk away."

"What if the woman in question wishes he would right now?"

"I don't understand. Surely you expect marriage, Zoe?"

"You haven't changed a bit," she snapped. "The only time you act like a living, breathing human man is when you're having sex. The rest of the time you're a block of ice."

"Be that as it may, we must be wed."

"I thought I might have thawed you out. Permanently. But all you have in your heart is cold, hard duty. I don't want to be sentenced to a lifetime with a man who resents being with me. So get out of my room, Your Grace. You're off the hook."

"Zoe—"

She scuttled away from him, putting the writing desk between them. How crazy she'd been to even dream he might be falling in love with her. And it hurt so much. "Get out. I don't care what you think you owe me. I refuse to marry a man who is buried in a deeper layer of ice than the North Pole."

A KNOCK ON the door woke Zoe early. Her eyes ached and felt puffy.

The door opened, and Mother swept in. "Zoe, I want to know exactly what is going on. I saw Lady Julia leave last night to take a walk outside, and I saw her come back with both you and the duke. Did His Grace arrange to meet you last night?"

She did not even want to think about last night. She sat up, her bedclothes falling away. "No, I arranged to meet Sebastian. I was going to break off my engagement with him."

Mother had been pouring tea on the tea tray. She jerked the teapot and a stream poured all over the tray. "You are going to do what?"

"End my engagement with Sebastian."

She could almost see gears spinning in Mother's head. "Why are you going to do that?" A delighted glow came into Mother's eyes. "It's because of the duke, isn't it?"

"I found out Sebastian is in love with someone else."

"He is? Good gracious, who?"

Zoe shrugged. She had been quite willing to shock Nigel. She wasn't willing to shock her mother. There might be fainting. Or Mother might end up taking to her bed ill, hoping to use Zoe's worry to coax her in the direction Mother wanted her to take. "Someone at the house party."

Mother frowned. "Who? Other than you, the only eligible girl was Miss Strutt." Mother smiled wickedly. "How delicious. So the girl brought in by the dowager to snare the duke is the sweetheart of his brother? Won't she be disappointed? And this is absolutely perfect—"

"If you are about to plot a way to get the duke to propose to me, don't bother." Perhaps shocking was in order. She wanted the conversation to end. "Nigel asked me last night and I said no."

"Nigel?" Mother repeated, in a strange, cracking voice.

"The duke. That is his first name."

"The Duke of Langford proposed. And you turned him *down?*"

"Yes. So you have no need to plot schemes. The duke and I beat you to it. And I may have changed my mind about ending my engagement with Sebastian—after all, we planned all along that the marriage would end in a divorce. It doesn't matter who he's in love with."

THE NEXT MORNING, Nigel received a telegram, and he took the train to London, then a taxi to an address in Whitechapel. The row house in front of him was one of a Victorian tenement, with blackened and crumbling brick. He went up to the front door and knocked. He saw faces peering at him through the first-floor window. Finally, the door opened.

It had taken a year for his investigators to hunt down Lily Bell. He stood face-to-face with a thin girl with her hair chopped in an untidy bob. A blue dress hung on her. She held a small child on her hip—one of her siblings.

"Are you Miss Lily Bell?" he asked. "I am the Duke of Langford."

"You! What do you want? What're you going to do—set the law on me over the letters I wrote? It was all true. You killed my brother."

She was the twin sister of a young man who had been in his division. "May I come inside, Miss Bell? I want to speak to you. I have come—" To apologize? How could he express his sorrow and regret and anger over what had happened to her brother? "I have come to try to help your family. To make things right."

"Right? Me brother is gone for good. He was a good lad. And he was no coward! There's not a thing you can do to make things right."

"Lily, what is the to-do about?" The door opened wide. A woman stood on the threshold, glaring. She was an older version of Lily, wearing a dirty flowered pinafore and a brown dress.

"I am the Duke of Langford. I came to speak to Miss Bell. She has been writing me letters about her brother. I was Ernie Bell's commanding officer in the War."

"You were," Mrs. Bell said. She went pale. *"You."*

"And I am very sorry for the tragedy that took place." Since Mrs. Bell showed no sign of moving back and allowing him inside, Nigel continued, "Ernie was a good boy. He was young and he was frightened—"

"Our Ernie was a brave lad. He volunteered to fight for king and country. The rest of what they say… That was lies. I don't believe a word of it. I won't—"

"I have come here with the aim of helping you and your family. I would like to give you an amount to help you with your expenses. Paid each month—"

"We don't want your charity," Lily Bell said. "We

don't want nothing from you. You killed Ernie. That's what you did. I'll never forgive you for that! That's why I sent the letters. How are we supposed to live without Ernie?"

"Quiet, Lily! You can't say such things to a duke." Mrs. Bell gave Lily a gentle push back into the house. She turned back to him, anguish on her face. "I don't want charity. But there's five of them—so many mouths. And there's no work now. The eldest boys can't find anything. The girls were in service, but they were told to come home. There wasn't money to pay them."

"I want to help you, Mrs. Bell. Ernie gave the ultimate sacrifice for his country."

The woman opened the door so he could come inside.

He stepped into a house with sagging walls and tilted floors. A stale smell of sour milk, cabbage and strong lye soap made him struggle for breath. Lily Bell stood in the shadow of a narrow hallway. The look she gave him was filled with venom.

For it was true— no matter what he did, he could not bring her brother back.

After taking leave of the Bells with more promises of help, he went to his man of business with a heavy heart to make the arrangements. And learned Charles Fortescue had shot himself because he had been embezzling from Brideswell's accounts.

There was nothing left. Nigel was facing complete ruination.

THE ROWBOAT GLIDED across the rippling water of Brideswell's decorative lake, the surface gilded by the low afternoon sun as Zoe watched from shore.

Zoe shaded her eyes. Captain Ransome was rowing

and Sebastian leaned back in the boat, his hand trailing in the water. He looked casual, careless, but his gaze was locked on Ransome's handsome face.

An ache wrapped around her heart. They looked so happy. They were obviously in love. At a moment like this, when they were alone, they could be a little more open about it.

She wanted love. And Nigel saw marrying her as a *punishment* for making love.

That horrible marriage proposal had made it plain that he didn't love her. He wanted to wed her for duty. She would never do that—never trap herself for a lifetime with a man who saw her as an obligation.

And if she married Sebastian, she could not wed Nigel, not for a long, long time.

Sebastian lifted his hand and shouted, "Zoe, hello! Wait there." He leaned to Captain Ransome, who was arching back as he rowed, murmured something, and Ransome looked over his shoulder and directed the boat toward her.

As they got closer, she picked her way down to the water's edge, where reeds grew and ducks paddled in the shallows. "I need to talk to you." She guessed there wasn't any need to be circumspect in front of Ransome. "It's about the engagement. Sebastian, it's off."

Now she knew what she was going to do. Because she couldn't go through with it. That was the crazy thing. Despite his attitude, she couldn't lose Nigel forever.

The oars splashed and the boat rocked as Sebastian half rose to his feet. He sat abruptly, hands on the gunwales. "Zoe, you cannot do that. My heart is torn in two and will never mend."

"Oh, stuff it," she called, using one of Julia's expressions. "I know the truth."

Sebastian pried the oars from Ransome, who was staring at her over his shoulder, and rowed hard, hauling the boat to shore. He jumped out, misjudged and sank up to his knees in murky water, ruining his light-colored trousers.

But he sloshed out as fast as he could. He clasped her hands, staring deeply into her eyes. "But I'm madly in love with you."

"Do you really think I'm that gullible?" Lowering her voice, she said, "I know you're in love with Captain Ransome."

"Let me give you my side first," Sebastian pleaded. "We'll go somewhere and talk about this. I need a bloody drink. Have you got your motorcar about?"

"In the garage. But I'd rather just talk here."

"They don't serve drinks here and I've emptied my flask." Sebastian took a silver flask from the breast pocket of his jacket, opened it and turned it upside down with a mournful air. "If you are going to dash all my romantic hopes, I need to be on my way to getting foxed first."

"You never give up, do you? We both know I'm not dashing your romantic hopes."

Like Father had taught her to do, she was looking at the cold, hard facts. Sebastian would be set up for life with his settlement from his marriage to her, and then he could pursue a love affair with Ransome. Of course, he had been planning to do that while *still* married to her. That made her mad. If he'd been honest with her and had wanted to go along with a sham marriage, she could forgive him.

But she couldn't forgive him for being so damn selfish he didn't care about breaking her heart.

Sebastian looked like a boy caught with his hand in the cookie jar, and she said coolly, "Okay, Sebastian, we'll go and talk."

She collected her car from the garage. With Sebastian in the passenger seat, she took off through the Brideswell gates, spewing gravel. She took the winding road at top speed, swerving around sheep, and she was satisfied to see Sebastian go pale.

"There! Stop there, Zoe!"

She slowed. Sebastian had the door swinging open before she parked, and she had to swerve so he didn't lose the door to a light pole. He ran around and opened her door jauntily, sweeping her a bow. Then he offered her arm. People were watching.

Sebastian had tried to break her heart—and Nigel was succeeding in doing it. She'd been right all along. Being independent was the best thing.

But she didn't want a scandal. Not that she cared about it, but now she thought of how it would hurt Julia, and Isobel and Sebastian's frail mother, Maria.

Sebastian led her to a Tudor house—she recognized it since there were many rambling, fake Tudor mansions housing American millionaires. A sign creaked overhead.

She lifted her brow at Sebastian. "You want to talk privately in the village pub?" Then she realized she was arching her brow, just like Nigel did.

Sebastian didn't seem to notice. "We had many a private conversation in New York speakeasies."

"That's different. Even when you're shouting over the

music, most people are too drunk to understand what you're saying. No one remembers a thing."

Sebastian led her to a table in the corner, then went up to the bar and ordered a pint and two gin and tonics. It was obvious why he'd ordered three drinks when he drained one gin himself, then sipped the beer. "Why would you want to break our engagement, Zoe?"

She had better get talking fast, before he was hammered. "The fact that you've been lying to me? Trying to make me fall in love with you, when you don't care about me?"

Sebastian squirmed and took another drink. "It wasn't my intention to hurt you."

"No, just to use me." She had intended to be tough and pragmatic. But to her shock, a tear welled in her eye and dripped to her cheek. She brushed it away. She'd come to Brideswell looking to obtain freedom— control of her finances and her life. Why was she now wishing she could have love?

"I am sorry, Zoe. I've hurt you badly—"

"You aren't making me cry," she declared with pride. "It's just…"

"What?" Sebastian's green eyes held hers. "You spent a lot of time with Langy. He hasn't put you up to this, has he? Breaking off the engagement. Is he the one who told you—?"

"No, he's not. I saw you. In the garage."

Sebastian went beet-red and drained his beer. "Zoe, is—is there something between you and Langy?"

She laughed bitterly. "Yes, Sebastian. Something happened between your brother and me."

"What kind of something? He didn't hurt you, did

he?" In two long sips, half of Sebastian's pint disappeared.

"Of course not," she said impatiently. Then remembered he knew his brother a lot better than she did. "Has he ever hurt a woman before?"

Sebastian took another long sip. He watched her from under his long lashes. As if he were considering what he should say. "Not that I know of," he said noncommittally.

"If there is something I should know," she said, "I'd like to hear it."

"The War changed Langy. Changed him a lot." Sebastian put his hand to his jaw and winced. "Still hurts, even now, with the bruising gone. Before the War, he never would have punched me. I would push his control to its breaking point and he never lost it. Right now, I would liken him to an unexploded shell on a battlefield. Looks inert, but it's waiting to go off."

She pushed him all the time. The only way he'd gone off with her was sexually.

"What happened between you and my brother?" Sebastian asked.

"Something that means I shouldn't marry you, if we were going to have a real marriage."

His brows shot up. "I can think of one thing, but I can't picture it of Langy. Not without clergyman and vows first."

"It doesn't matter what happened," she said brusquely. "I should throw this pint in your face over the con you tried to pull on me. You wanted me to be trapped and unhappy because you wanted to get at all my money. More than just the *very* generous settlement I offered."

He held up his hand. "Not true. It wasn't about the money. I need a wife. All I have to do is find a blushing bride and produce one child, and I've scotched the rumors for good."

"God, you're selfish."

"So I've been told. Nanny noticed it first. Thought it was one of those vices that should be smacked out of a lad. Never did a thing for me, though I did learn the joy of a good spanking."

She rolled her eyes. Sebastian liked to shock. "I'm not going to marry you, Sebastian."

He leaned back in his chair, looking grim. In a low voice, he asked, "You're not planning to marry Langy, are you?"

"He asked me." She saw Sebastian jolt back and his chair legs scraped the floor. "I said no."

"You're not willing to marry and divorce him?"

That hadn't been what she had in mind at all. Not when she'd thought she was in love...

But was this the answer to her problems? And Langford's? She would get her money. He would be able to still call himself a gentleman.

"He wouldn't do it," she said. "He doesn't believe in divorce."

Could she do it? Could she marry the Duke of Langford and then walk away? She could fly airplanes, drive fast. Was she tough enough to leave Nigel?

"I would have said no weeks ago," Sebastian said. "But when Langy got back from London, he told me Brideswell is now absolutely teetering on the brink of ruin. We won't last more than a few months before it will have to be sold. This is the modern world—and apparently a family's fortunes can go from ruin to worse ruin in a little less than a day."

"It's gotten worse? How?"

"Father lost most of the money between taxes, gambling and the panic after the War. His death duties almost finished off the estate. Langy struggled with what little capital he could raise. Invested it to try to bring us back. That's the modest income we've limped along on. These estates don't pull in any money anymore. Most of the farms aren't pulling their weight. They need modernization. Langy won't change, of course. He wouldn't throw out old widowed Mrs. Billings, the one who lost all her sons."

"I'm surprised you know this much about the estate."

"Every now and again I'm sober enough to pay attention."

Beneath every one of Sebastian's cavalier statements, she heard the brittle undercurrent. She knew Sebastian was unhappy. Just as everyone was at Brideswell.

"What happened was that Langy's man of business, Charles Fortescue, was embezzling. Speculating. The companies he invested in went bankrupt, so he couldn't pay back what he stole. He shot himself a few days ago, leaving the Brideswell coffers empty." Sebastian got up. "Fortunately, this establishment still extends me credit."

He bought another pint, and her another gin, because in the time it took him to go to the bar, she'd drained the first. It must have been strong. Her head already felt light. She looked up at the man who had charmed her in New York, who had told her, on the first night they'd met, that all was fair when it came to survival.

"Do you think Langford asked me to marry him because of Brideswell's situation? He said it was about duty because—because of what happened between us. But it was probably because he wants my money." When had he known?

Sebastian shook his head. "If Langy said it was about duty, that's what it was. He only knew about our state of ruin yesterday. You know, Zoe, you could still marry me. I'd be more than happy to turn a blind eye to your love affairs. You could do whatever you wanted. We could live on separate continents, if you like. Half the fashionable set do it."

"No, Sebastian."

"Can't blame a bloke for trying." Half of his second pint disappeared. "You know what I think, Zoe? I think you don't want to marry me because you're falling for my brother."

"I'm not." How did Sebastian do this? Now she saw the strange truth about him. The more he drank, the better perception he developed.

"What are you going to do?" she asked. She needed to change the subject. "Look for another bride?"

"My dear Zoe, at this point I fear my conscience would not allow it. Alas, all I wanted to do was save my family." He looked down at his hands. "I tried to change, Zoe. Tried to cure myself. It didn't work. Duty could not force me to fall in love with someone else. Someone female."

"Then don't change."

He frowned. "I have to make it look like I delight in women. For the sake of the family."

"I just realized: you and Langford are exactly alike. You love your family. You believe in duty. And that belief is killing both of you."

Sebastian lifted his pint to his lips to catch the last drops. "That is what duty is about."

"Why don't you go away? No one can spread rumors if you aren't here. What if you and Captain Ransome went to America?"

"Where they are just as unforgiving. I know of only one place in the world where Ransome and I would be drawn to the collective bosom of kindred sinners." Sebastian drew out a gold case, took out two cigarettes.

"Where's that?"

He lit both cigarettes, offered one to her. She took it, but let it smolder between her fingers.

"Capri." He tapped his cigarette on the rim of the glass, sending a shower of ash inside. "It's the place to go for the sexually ambiguous—and the sexually voracious, the ones looking for a partner of any gender, color or creed."

"Go there."

"The family would have a collective apoplexy."

"If you're discreet, no one has to know that you're not there for the sunshine."

"I don't have the funds to get there. Nor to support Ransome there. I can paint passably, so I would fit into the bohemian lifestyle. But even I know we cannot live on love alone."

She knew what it was to not be accepted. It must be so much harder for Sebastian. "If I had my capital, I could give you a loan. Enough to set you and Ransome up in Capri, I'm sure."

"Why would you do that for me?"

She couldn't really explain it. "Happiness is an elusive thing. I like to see people find it."

"If my brother were willing to wed you, then give

you the divorce you want, I could go in search of happiness." Sebastian grinned. "So what I need to do is get you and Langy married as fast as possible."

THE HONKING STARTLED BEELZEBUB, making him shy and rear, but Nigel got his mount under control. He turned the horse. Zoe's car was roaring toward him—right in the center of the road—a cloud of dust flying behind it.

What in the bloody hell—?

As it got closer, Nigel saw Julia at the wheel, her gloved hands gripping the steering wheel tightly. She shouted something that he couldn't hear. But her face glowed with exhilaration.

At her side sat Zoe with her long white scarf flapping behind her. Despite Julia's erratic steering, Zoe looked utterly self-possessed. But she was waving at him, indicating he had better get off the road. He lightly tapped his horse with his heels and trotted off the side of the road as far as he could go.

Suddenly Zoe put her hand on the wheel, helped Julia steer toward the right, and the car zipped by him with several feet to spare. It slowed down, pulled onto the side of the road and rattled and bumped to a stop.

He cantered over just as Julia let out a whoop of excitement. "Goodness, I love driving. It's so exciting and exhilarating. I feel so very much in charge!" She threw her arms around Zoe.

Nigel looked down from Beelzebub. Zoe gazed up at him. "I am giving Julia driving lessons."

"And teaching her to drive too fast."

"She isn't," Julia declared. "She told me to slow down. But my heel got stuck and I couldn't work the brake. It's not Zoe's fault I came at you too fast. And I insisted upon having lessons!"

"I want Julia to learn how to control a car." Zoe opened the passenger door and got out. "How to drive safely. But I think I will drive back to Brideswell and we can practice more on the quiet driveway."

He frowned. "Julia does not need to know how to drive. That is why we employ a chauffeur."

When he looked at the car, he thought of that night when he'd gone driving with Zoe and they'd ended up kissing by moonlight.

Zoe marched around her car to him. "Well, she *should* know how to drive. Every woman should. It will give her freedom. And she loves it. You aren't going to spoil her fun, Langford." Eyes snapping with challenge and fire, Zoe faced him.

He had to admit—once again, Zoe knew what Julia needed. He looked back to Zoe as Julia slid over to the passenger seat and Zoe took her place behind the steering wheel.

The truth was, he couldn't take his eyes off her. God, she was beautiful.

Softly, he admitted, "You are an excellent driver—I would trust no one else to teach my sister."

Zoe's eyes widened in surprise.

"All right, Julia. I won't forbid it," he continued.

"As if you even could, Langford." Zoe smiled at Julia. "Now, let's return to Brideswell." She started the car, reversing smoothly. And he watched them drive away.

Zoe was the answer to Brideswell's prayers. Her fortune could save it.

But he would not marry her for her money.

He wanted to marry her, and he knew it wasn't out
of duty or any desire to save Brideswell. He *wanted* her.
Somehow he had to convince her of it.

11
PICNIC ON A SPRING AFTERNOON

"THIS HAS ARRIVED for you, Miss Gifford."

The morning after her driving lesson with Julia, the butler presented a telegram on a silver salver. She looked at it and shivered. The last one had brought such terrible news. But she coolly said, "Thank you, Bartlet," and picked it up. This one wasn't about a tragedy, but it still made her sick to her stomach. It was from her uncle Hiram Gifford.

know about check *stop* telephone at once *stop*

The jig was up. He knew Mother had forged a check. Thank God there wasn't a telephone at Brideswell. For once it was a good thing they were so determined to fight change. This was a conversation she did not want to have.

Hiram was not like her father at all, despite being Father's younger brother. He was ambitious without any real talent or acumen, and he resented the millions that had been shunted aside and preserved in Zoe's name.

Half her fortune was tied up in shares in Father's company. Hiram was now the director of that company. He wanted a controlling interest, and he didn't have it.

With some of her shares, he could get it, and he couldn't afford to buy her out.

But armed with this scandal, he could try to blackmail her to take control.

She was not going to let him do that. She'd wanted to run a business as Father had done. But when Billy had died, Father brought Hiram in to act as president if anything happened to him. That had hurt. She could have run a company just as well as Hiram or her brother. But Father had never seen that.

"Zoe, is it bad news?" Julia took a seat across from her.

She crumpled the telegram. It was a disaster, but she'd learned a thing or two about hiding behind a cool mask from Nigel. "No. Dull stuff to do with financial matters."

"At least you are considered worthy of consultation. No one speaks to me about money. I'm expected to learn what's going on from reading facial expressions and listening to rumors." Julia sighed. "That's how I've learned my dowry has completely gone up in smoke."

"Oh, heavens, no." Zoe thought of what Sebastian had told her. "I'm so sorry."

"You knew, didn't you? You don't look shocked at all."

"Sebastian told me there was some trouble. But wasn't your dowry somehow protected?"

"It was invested, along with everything else. I don't understand—people in America seem to be making scads of money. How did we choose the companies run by idiots? And then, on top of that, a gentleman we'd trusted for decades embezzled our money and lost it all."

Zoe shook her head. She thought of her uncle. "It's

not easy to run a successful company. It takes something more than brains. It takes daring, common sense, ruthlessness and incredible foresight." Uncle Hiram did not understand the one thing Father had always explained to her. A company that went stagnant would die. A company had to be constantly growing and evolving.

All the more reason for her to have her money under *her* control.

"Goodness, how many people possess all that?" Julia asked.

"Very few," Zoe said ruefully.

"Of course, my dowry evaporated right at the moment when I jolly well need it."

Zoe jerked up. "You mean Dr. Campbell?"

Julia smiled. Glowed. Blushed. Then studied her teacup.

"Of course, he hasn't said anything yet, exactly… but I think—I think he might admire me. He even likes my bobbed hair."

"And so he should." Zoe was delighted to see Julia in love, but it made her think—she hadn't looked so dreamy and delighted over Nigel, had she? She had been more…agitated.

"He is different than any other man I've met, Zoe. He is an outsider here, not to mention Scottish. He believes Scotland should be independent, though he tempers his opinions around here. In truth, he's very passionate about it. He went to the Royal College of Surgeons of Edinburgh before the War. There were female students. He believes women are capable of being quite a lot more than house mistresses."

"Good. It is about time there was a man here who displayed some modern thinking." She sipped her cof-

fee. "Do you think you will marry? Surely he does not
care about something like a dowry when he is a surgeon.
And, if you are happy, do you really care?"

"I would live with him in a field if I had to," Julia
said. "But for all he doesn't agree with division by class,
and for all he believes a man—or woman—should be
able to succeed on merit rather than birth, he refuses to
marry me if he cannot support me." Julia clasped her
hands. "He is a good man. Once—once I went to the
hospital and I refused to leave even though he sent me
away. A child had been badly injured and I saw him
save the wee boy's life."

"He sounds wonderful. A man deserving of your
heart."

"The family would disapprove."

Zoe thought of the telegram, crumpled in her pocket.
The answer to her desperate situation was marriage. It
was the answer to Nigel's problems. And Sebastian's.
And Julia's. Her fortune could help them all. And no one
could disapprove of Julia or Sebastian finding happiness in the way they desired if she was responsible for it.

"You should follow your heart," she said.

Julia set down her coffee cup. "I will, if you will."

And that afternoon Zoe sent a telegram to her uncle:

no telephones at home of Duke of Langford *stop* will
be married soon *stop* debts will be paid *stop* advise
discretion *stop*

There. She had carefully said nothing. And hinted at
a lot. Hiram might just leap to the conclusion she was
going to marry an English duke—he knew she was
engaged to an Englishman of an autocratic family but

nothing more. He didn't know her engagement was off, so it should keep him quiet.

At least for a while.

THREE DAYS AFTER his failed marriage proposal, Nigel stood on the front step of Brideswell to welcome his cousin Adelaide, her husband, the Earl of Carleton, and their five boisterous boys. It was now late May and the weather was warmer.

Within an hour, Brideswell rang with the sounds of locomotive engines, automobile engines and aeroplane engines.

"Watch out, Uncle Nigel—I am on your tail!"

He was playing fighter pilots using a small biplane fashioned from wood with his youngest nephew, six-year-old Robert, when Julia opened the door to his study. She leaned against the door frame and smiled at them both.

"There you both are! You must come quickly. We are having a picnic."

"Hurrah!" Robert shouted. "I'm starving!"

"A picnic?" There hadn't been one of those since before the War.

"Mother's idea. Well, Zoe's, actually. Grandmama is beside herself with the noise the boys are making. She offered a pound note to whichever boy would stay quiet the longest. Three dropped out after one minute, and the victor lasted a few seconds more." A wicked grin lifted Julia's lips. "The nephews outwitted Grandmama."

Julia smiled so much more, Nigel had to admit, since Zoe had come into their lives.

"When Zoe mentioned taking the boys outdoors, Mother reminisced fondly about the picnics of the old days. So Zoe convinced Mother to arrange one—and helped with all the work, as did I. This way Mother felt she accomplished something wonderful without being overwhelmed."

"You are wonderful."

"And so is Zoe, of course. She is a very good person, you know," Julia said. "I wish you would stop arguing with her all the time."

"I do not argue with her all the time," he protested. Then blushed. He turned away quickly and was saved because Julia herded Robert out of the study, toward the waiting cars.

Watching his young nephews as he walked outside, Nigel felt another sense of longing. Having children— heirs—was a duke's duty. He had avoided Adelaide's children after the War, afraid his scars would frighten them. But children had a ghoulish streak, he'd learned, and the boys found his war wounds fascinating.

But they also asked too many questions about battle.

They drove up to a ridge, the sky clear and blue and the sun beaming down. Servants laid out trestle tables, covered with cloths, and set out chairs. Beneath the ridge ran the winding river, and the height of the ridge meant a cooling breeze washed over it all summer. Footmen spread a blanket for children and younger members of the families, helped the dowager, his mother and cousin Adelaide settle into chairs. Wine was poured into goblets and food brought out from baskets. Roasted meats, cold collations, cheeses and breads were set on silver trays and warming dishes—though the wind put the flames out.

The boys raced through the grass of the meadow,

tumbling and rolling. The three eldest ran back to the table, grabbed food and stuffed it into their mouths.

Adelaide gave a sigh. "They are like wild animals. Nannies are useless creatures these days. They refuse to discipline the children, they want more money and fewer working hours, and they still up and leave for a job in London with hardly any notice."

"Mother, we want to go down to the river," the eldest shouted.

Adelaide looked stricken. She was very thin, with brown hair pulled in a bun, and she looked exhausted. "Not on your own. You will all drown, I am certain, and then where will we be?"

"I will watch them, Cousin Adelaide," Julia offered. She looked to Isobel, but his youngest sister was sitting on the blanket, reading a book. Nigel squinted. A book on anatomy.

He had seen that book lying around in the library and had glanced at it. "Isobel, put that book down."

She looked at him over its edge. "Why?"

"Yes, why, Langford?" Zoe asked. "Isobel is interested in medicine. I thought you had already realized Isobel is going to be much more than a drawing-room ornament?"

"Yes, I am aware of Isobel's ambitions." He was aware of everyone looking at them.

"And of course, you encountered nurses in the War—"

"Of course I did. I was wounded. Several times." He took a step closer to Zoe. "It is a picnic. I just thought it maybe was not the most appropriate choice of reading."

"I think it shows how strong and how committed Isobel is," Zoe countered.

The woman was determined to point out he was wrong. They had moments of complete accord—and others where all she seemed to want was discord. Now they stood there, gazing at each other, breathing hard as if they had just run across the meadow.

"Let's go down to the river," Julia declared brightly, herding the boys away.

"She is a very smart girl, Langford," Zoe said softly. "You have to support her, you know. And you will have to support Julia when she chooses to marry."

With that, she turned and walked away, joining Julia. What in hell did she mean?

Nigel followed. Behind him he heard the dowager declare, "This is the book you are reading? Good heavens, there are pictures of bodies without skin. Do put this away while we eat."

He guessed Isobel wouldn't. Not now that she had Zoe's approval.

He admired men who pursued knowledge. His dream had been to travel to Persia and Egypt. Look for tombs and pharaohs. Search for the beginnings of civilization. But he was a duke and then war broke out. Duty had kept him from fulfilling his dream. And he knew how it felt.

Taking long strides along the narrow track that led down from the ridge of the river, Nigel caught up to Zoe. "I have no intention of denying Isobel her dream."

Zoe slowed her pace, allowing Julia and the children to surge on ahead. "Really? The man I first met would not have said that."

That startled him. He probably wouldn't have, back then. A few weeks ago. "What do you mean about Julia marrying?"

She gave him her direct American look. "Julia has fallen in love with Dr. Dougal Campbell."

"The young surgeon?" Now he understood Isobel's interest. "Julia—she's been raised to be a lady, to manage an estate—" He broke off. He was willing to accept university. But this—

"Anyway, you'll be happy to know the engagement between Sebastian and me is off," she said. "I can't do *my* duty and marry Sebastian. There won't be a divorce."

"I'm only concerned about one engagement." He stopped and caught her arm. Her violet eyes captivated him every time he looked in them. Half the time he couldn't remember what he wanted to say. This time, he couldn't forget. "Marry me, damn it. I'll agree to whatever terms you propose. You can have the same arrangement that you had with my brother. I agree to give you your freedom. Or you can be duchess for the rest of your life. Whatever you want."

That came out much harsher than he'd intended.

Her unusual purple eyes flicked over his. "Langford, are you...groveling? I assume it's not because you are so hopelessly in love with me, you'll do anything for me."

"I am on the brink of losing Brideswell," he said. "You probably do not care about that. But the settlement you promised my brother would save us all. Having your trust would save your mother. I do not like divorce. I do not agree with it. I think a gentleman and a lady should soldier on. But I cannot stand on pride when the ground below me is crumbling away. I will agree to whatever terms you want. We will marry. You will be my duchess for as long as you wish. If you want it to be five minutes or forty years, I will agree."

"Do you even like me, Langford?" she asked bluntly.

The question took him off guard. "I believe I do."

"You believe you do? You could sound a little happier. You could attempt to sweep me off my feet. When a man proposes marriage, shouldn't he say he's in love with you? Shouldn't he be in love?"

What English girl would ask a question like that? Under his collar he was hot with embarrassment. He was madly, passionately in love with her, but he couldn't begin to guess what she felt for him. "Are you in love with *me?*"

"That is a good strategy, Nigel. Turning the tables on me. The truth is, I don't yet know. But I think you have to love me or this won't work." She lifted her brow. "And I don't know if you do. I feel that every time you look at me, you see every way in which I am not duchess material."

"Not duchess material?" he echoed. Confused. He'd expected to deal with a yes or a no.

"You see all my flaws. Each time you look at me."

"God, no. I am the one who is flawed, Zoe." He raked his hand through his hair. "You know the truth about me. I am a bl— I am a mess."

"Your scars?"

"The scars. The shell shock. The shaking. The lack of control. Zoe, I'm not good enough for any woman as I am. Least of all you. But I do love you. You are the most exciting woman I have ever met. When I am with you, I feel like I am alive. You have a joie de vivre that I adore."

"I thought that drove you crazy."

"It makes you impossible to resist, Zoe. You make me laugh. You make my heart soar. When I held you in my arms, I had never experienced a more magical moment. Damn it, I just told you I love you."

She stared at him, and he swallowed hard and went on. "I want to spend my life with you. I know that may not be what you want. But it is what I dream of."

He cleared his throat. His speech felt awkward, and he felt stiff and embarrassed. He had not explained everything to her—he hadn't told her the complete truth about himself. "Any terms you give, I will agree to," he said. "Do I have your acceptance of my proposal?"

Her lips twitched. "Is my word going to be enough, or would you prefer it handwritten and submitted to your secretary?"

"Of course your word will be enough."

"Then I will marry you, Langford."

"Good. I will apply for a special license forthwith. We will be married as soon as possible."

His nephews ran back to him them. Already their trouser legs were soaked. "Hurry up, Uncle Nigel. We need help to make boats."

BOATS MADE OF tree bark, twigs and leaves bobbed on the lake. Sebastian strolled down, carrying a bottle of champagne and flutes. Standing on the dock that jutted into the water with him and Julia, Zoe drank champagne.

"Uncle Nigel, we are going to sink your armada," warned Robert.

All the boys threw rocks and shouted, "Boom! Bang!" The oldest had deadly aim and destroyed most of Nigel's boats in seconds.

Zoe couldn't take her eyes off Nigel. The man who had used the word *forthwith* in a marriage proposal was crouched in the reeds by the edge of the lake, shirt-sleeves rolled to his elbows, launching boats to amuse five young boys—their father, the earl, had stayed up on the ridge, enjoying a cigar. She had never dreamed Nigel would enjoy playing like this. Mud stained his trousers and he didn't seem to care.

Julia moved close. "Is it really true? Nigel just told me you accepted his proposal."

Zoe nodded.

Julia touched her arm, faced her with serious eyes. "You are following your heart?"

"Yes, I am."

"Even though I saw it with my own eyes, I never dreamed the two of you would fall in love. But I saw him after you took him driving and flying, and he looked like a different man. So much happier, so much more alive. I had begun to think he was very predictable and then he surprised me completely by falling for you. It restored my hope for his happiness."

Zoe blushed. She wanted to think they would be happy, but he had not sounded entirely happy when he proposed to her. She understood—for weeks she had thought falling in love with him was madness. But she couldn't stop herself. "I don't know if I make him happy."

"Of course you do!"

"He can be as starchy as an old shirt with me. He tries to hide everything he feels behind a mask of ice." He could be wild and wicked, too, when he made love, but she couldn't say that to his sister. "One moment I think I've genuinely made him smile, but then, the next moment, he is arguing with me. It makes me wonder if we aren't both crazy."

He said he behaved so awkwardly with her because he believed *he* had flaws. She liked him best when he was out of control. But he hated to be that way. Yet that was when his heart opened and she saw the man she desired.

"Crazy?" Julia frowned. "Are you sure you are in love with him?"

"This is the most complicated thing I've ever felt," Zoe admitted. "But I think it's love."

"Well, I am so happy you are going to be my sister," Julia said.

"I am happy, too. I've always wanted a sister."

What was she going to do? Stay married to him just long enough to get her money? Or make it last?

It was strange—she didn't know the answer. She wanted him with pure, raw hunger. But could a marriage between them work? She didn't want to reveal her uncertainty to Julia. Not when she'd encouraged Julia to follow her heart.

"Uncle Nigel, were you hit by a shell?" The question came from the middle boy of the five, but all the other lads perked up their ears, too.

"It must have been exciting to be in battle," Robert declared. "I would love to be a soldier. I would've killed the Huns."

"Battle is not as glorious as we think before we are there," Nigel said gently.

Zoe's heart lurched as she saw the sadness touching his face.

"How many Huns did you kill, Uncle Nigel?"

"I do not know how many. War is a strange thing. They were just young men—with families and hopes and dreams. Many of them were scared. I learned one thing from war. It's a tremendous waste. But what would have happened if we did not fight? That, I do not want to imagine."

The boys stared at him, confused. Zoe hung on his every word. Sunlight bathed him, but he looked as if he could see the mud-filled front.

"Wasn't it exciting and thrilling?" Robert asked.

"We always romance that—the adventure of battle. It's not a reason to wage war. There are better adventures you could have. You could travel the world on a ship or a train when you grow up, Robert. That is what I want. For war to be behind us, for you to grow up in peace. I only hope, as the world changes, that people remember what it cost."

This man…this man she could love. This man she wanted to be with. For a lifetime.

Nigel straightened. "But now it is time to pack up and go back to Brideswell. If you run back up to the ridge you might get some food before it is all put away."

The young boys gave whoops, splashed out of the water and charged up the path.

With Julia and Sebastian, Zoe picked her way over the uneven dirt path to Nigel. She wished she was here alone with him. She ached to kiss him.

She loved him when he was like this—when he spoke from his heart, and she got a glimpse inside it.

"Will you be married in London?" Julia asked, her voice bubbly as they walked up to the ridge.

She and Nigel hadn't talked about that. But she had to be married in New York.

Her home. Where she knew the rules.

When they reached the top of the hill, Sebastian took her empty glass and came back with one filled with the last of the champagne. He clinked his glass against hers. "I wish you every happiness, Zoe. And if my brother does not make you happy, I will return from Capri and have serious words with him."

"So you have decided to go? I'm glad," Zoe said. "I'd like you to be happy."

Sebastian glanced toward Nigel, who was brushing mud off his trousers. "I haven't told Langy yet. I doubt he'll be pleased."

"Nigel might surprise you. At heart, he is a very good man."

Sebastian's brows rose. "Proof that he loves you, if that's the way he behaves around you."

Zoe felt her cheeks go warm. "He loves you, too, you know."

Footmen began to pack the picnic away. She saw Nigel take a seat next to his grandmother. The dowager sat looking out over the ridge, looking away from the setting sun at the river valley bathed in light.

"There is something I have to tell you, Grandmama," he said.

To Zoe's surprise, Nigel was as direct as she would have been. He took a leaf from Zoe's book and said bluntly, "Zoe has broken her engagement to Sebastian, and I have proposed to her."

The dowager blinked. "It is like a game of musical chairs—but one where everyone's seat is pulled out from underneath them."

12
A VISIT TO THE CHURCH

As the sun set and the picnic was packed away, Zoe watched while the children were herded into their seats in the vehicles; doors were closed so they could not run out and disappear.

She was engaged. She would be married. If she wanted, she and Nigel could have children of their own. She could watch him sail boats with their boys. Would he play tea parties, too, with the girls? She intended to ensure daughters would strive to do anything the sons did—

"Well," said the dowager beside Zoe. "It appears Brideswell is to have an American duchess."

Zoe held out her elbow. "Would you like me to help you to the car?" Her emotions were in too much of a tangle to argue with Nigel's grandmother.

She had thought she would never love anyone but Richmond. But everything had changed....

Julia came forward, and the dowager took her granddaughter's arm, ignoring Zoe's offer.

"It's the beginning of summer," the dowager said. She was reminiscing to Julia as Julia helped her to the car. Zoe walked beside them.

"At my first picnic at Brideswell, I knew I was to marry the duke," the dowager continued. "Our mothers

had their hearts set on it. But by the end of the day, I
had fallen in love—with someone else. An earl's eldest
son. But he died. A duel, of all things. He was a charming man, a thorough rogue and a terrible shot. Two days
after, I accepted the Duke of Langford's proposal. I
cried all the way to the wedding. I stifled my tears for
the ceremony and the wedding night, for Mother insisted my marriage would be a disaster unless I held in
my tears until after that particular event."

Julia blushed and Zoe felt her cheeks heat up. The
dowager could be so surprisingly blunt.

She thought of Nigel, of course. Her wedding night
would not be filled with tears.

"But you did fall in love with the duke eventually,"
Julia said. She offered her arm to help the dowager to
the Daimler.

"I never did. It was for the best, of course. He was
as much a scoundrel. Just far better at avoiding being
caught."

"Do you think a woman should only marry for love
now?" Julia asked.

"I think a woman in this modern age can finally
choose to do what makes her happy. I am rather envi-
ous of you. And a lifetime of a marriage for duty is…a
lifetime."

Perhaps she understood the dowager more. A lifetime wed to a man you didn't like? It would be torture.

Zoe was doing what made her happy—she knew,
after seeing Nigel with his nephews, that she wanted
her marriage to last.

The dowager touched her arm. The older woman
studied her appraisingly. "You would never be satisfied with a sacrifice to make others happy, dear. Keep

that in mind. Do not marry Nigel simply to become a duchess, my dear."

"I'm not."

Of course the dowager thought Nigel would not be happy with her. The dowager believed Nigel wanted a woman like Miss Strutt—even though that woman was the logical choice for a duty marriage, not a passionate marriage.

"I am marrying for love," Zoe declared. "And we will be happy. I will make Nigel happy."

"My dear, you cannot make someone else happy. The other person must find happiness in themselves."

MIST ROLLED OVER the lawns, winding around Zoe's legs, tumbling in front of her as she walked down to the stables the next morning. Her mare was already saddled with a gentleman's saddle, the groom leading her out as she arrived. On his huge black stallion, Nigel waited for her. When he rode, he looked gorgeous. Romantic.

Last night, Nigel had sent her a note by footman. Folded, on cream writing paper, with a ducal seal embossed in wax to keep it closed. It had been so formal....

My dear Zoe, please ride with me tomorrow morning before breakfast. It is about the wedding and there's something rather important I must ask you.

That was who he was on the surface—restrained, reserved, formal. But yesterday he had told her what was in his heart. And she had captured his heart.

She knew what she had told the dowager was true—

she could help him recover from his wounds. She could make him happy. She had changed him already.

"Good morning," she said as she swung up. "What did you want to ask?"

"Good morning to you, Miss Gifford." He lifted his hat. "Let us ride first. But please take care in the fog. Stay close to me."

Once she would have been goaded to tease him due to his formality. But now she knew what he could be like beneath it—passionate, and playful and sweet as he was with his nephews. It made his ducal behavior even more enticing.

He was an elegant rider. His body rose and fell in a smooth rhythm. He looked as if he'd been born to ride. They crossed the lawns, took the track through the meadow past her airplane—the first place she'd ever made love.

They hadn't talked about the wedding.

"Nigel, let's stop and talk," she called. "What did you want to ask me?"

"Ride with me a little farther, Zoe."

She had to keep her mare close enough to him to keep him in sight. What did he want? He hadn't listened to the dowager, had he? Finally she couldn't stand it anymore. "Do you want to back out?"

With a barely perceptible tug on the reins, Nigel halted his enormous horse and walked the beast around to face her. "No. Do you?"

"No. But you're the one who sent a mysterious letter and now won't tell me anything."

"I want to ask if you would accept the sort of wedding I want, Zoe."

"Usually the bride gets to choose—"

She broke off. The softness in his clear blue eyes took her breath away. She'd never seen this expression on his face.

"Zoe, I know you want to marry in New York. Your mother told me. Then declared she wanted a lavish wedding in London, preferably in the most impressive church. But I would like to marry here, at Brideswell. I know you may not wish to stay here, but I want to offer it to you as your home."

But it wasn't her home. It was a different world. "I don't know. I had my heart set on New York for the wedding."

Their horses trotted side by side, down the track that wound through the fields of the estate and took them to the village. They passed townspeople and Nigel acknowledged greetings from each one. He knew everyone, of course, and had a polite word for many. She saw the look on so many faces—it was like watching a group of girls meet Rudolph Valentino.

She followed him to the church, the one they had gone to for Sunday services. With easy grace, Nigel swung off his huge horse. She watched the play of his muscles under his coat.

Once they were wed, they could make love whenever they wanted.

Did she want to wait until they traveled to New York?

She tensed on the saddle, causing her mare to skitter on the spot. Quickly she stroked the silky white neck. "Easy, easy."

What did she want to do? It had been so easy before, with Sebastian. Make a marriage in name only, free Mother from worry, then return to her life in New York, return to flying as fast as she could.

Now she wanted her marriage to last. But she was scared, too—she didn't know England and English law. Was she willing to relinquish control? "If I insist on marrying in New York, will you do it?" she asked.

She expected him to refuse.

"If it is what you really want, I'll do it."

He was willing to bend for her? "Then why are we here?"

"Just give me this one chance." He held out his hand to her.

She would do this, but she had no intention of marrying in Brideswell. Taking his hand, she dismounted. He led her into the old stone church.

Reverend Wesley came forward, hands outstretched. Zoe put out her hand to shake his, but he clasped both her hands and held them warmly. His was a kindly face, the smile bright and welcoming, his eyes brilliant blue. Wrinkles led out from his eyes and surrounded his mouth, as if he smiled often.

"Miss Gifford, I am so delighted to learn that you are to be His Grace's bride. The entire village is filled with great cheer at the news. His Grace has told me to sing the praises of my little church. He tells me I am to tempt you away from returning to America to be married. I would not be so bold, I assure you, if His Grace had not assured me I have his full approval when I say I would be most honored if you do hold the ceremony here."

She looked to Nigel.

"The whole village loves a wedding," he said softly.

She didn't want to offend the reverend. She was annoyed with Nigel. He was trying to back her into a corner. Well, Giffords didn't allow themselves to be—

She had been already backed into a corner by her mother's mistake.

But she didn't want to be railroaded by her husband. Why had he not just talked to her?

"His Grace was christened here, by me," the reverend continued, smiling kindly at her. "Many years ago, of course. But I have watched him and all his family grow from infancy. It would be a great honor for me to perform the ceremony."

The reverend led her up the aisle, toward the altar.

"I promise, Miss Gifford, we will make the church look grand. It would be filled with flowers—we have some of the most spectacular roses in the country here, and if you were to wed in June, they will be blooming."

He let her go and shuffled along the aisle. "We would have a choir, of course. And our organist is most skilled, as you no doubt observed in Sunday services. I know we are but a modest church, but the building dates from the Tudor period. Many great gentlemen and ladies have sat in our pews."

Nigel had stood in the background. He stepped forward and cleared his throat. "Reverend Wesley, do not pressure Miss Gifford too strongly. I wanted her to see the church through your eyes and learn of its history. But I am not going to, as they say, use strong-arm tactics. I came to Sunday services here, as did my father. We've come for generations."

"Your church is lovely, Reverend," she said. But this was not her world. "Let's walk around outside, Langford."

Outside she wheeled on Nigel. "You brought me here because you thought I couldn't say no to that kindly old man."

"I don't want to trick you, Zoe. I want to marry you here because I want to be married to you as fast as I can."

"For Brideswell."

"For me. I want to save my home, but I want you to be part of my life. I want you to stay with me."

That took her breath away. A smart dame always had a perfect response. But nothing came to her lips. Nigel stepped close to her—tall and dark with stunning eyes.

"Zoe." Just her name, and in his husky, tender voice, it made her melt.

In an old-world, gentlemanly gesture, he lifted her gloved fingers to his lips. She'd believed herself modern, but at this moment she felt like a princess being courted by the most wonderful prince.

"You touched my scars and told me you didn't despise them. You've eased my fears about how wretched they look. But I feel I have not been honest with you."

"What have you lied to me about?"

He winced at that. "I do not believe I've lied. But I have not told you the truth. Zoe, I am haunted at night by nightmares of battle. I wake shouting, drenched in sweat. That is why I use a bedroom in Brideswell that is away from my family's rooms. Sometimes, the images I see in my head—sometimes I think I could lose my mind, Zoe. It has been four years, and I am still a wreck. Do you still want to marry me even knowing all that?"

"Yes," she breathed. "That hasn't changed my mind at all." She thought of the dowager's words. "I can make you happy."

"I want to believe marriage will give us both a glorious future."

She gazed into his clear blue eyes. "Do they really care about this wedding—all the people in the village?"

"It will be a grand fete. The entire village will come out to see you pass in the carriage on your way to the church. There will be cheering and joy."

She could marry in New York, and there would not be crowds on the street. New York might be her home, but she felt a tug in her belly. Nigel had something she had never known—a true sense of belonging. "If we were to marry here, what would we do for a reception?"

A soft smile touched his lips. At her hint she might change her mind, he looked as if the sun had shone on him.

"Brideswell," he said. "Tents would be set up on the lawns and the wedding breakfast would be served outdoors."

"This is England. It will probably pour rain."

"Then we would have it in the ballroom."

"I don't know."

"Give me the chance to make you want to stay. I do not want to lose you to America, Zoe. I want a lifetime with you."

"I—I wanted to marry for love, Nigel. I think it is time I was honest with you. You know that I lost my fiancé. I was deeply in love with him. I know you think it was a scandal. I am sure you think I was bold and shocking and wrong. But I was not the reason for his divorce. I loved him with all my heart and I lost him. I thought I would never fall in love again. But I was wrong—I think I am falling in love with you."

"I won't push you to do anything you are not ready to do, Zoe. I do love you." He cupped her cheek and his palm caressed her skin. She turned her face into his hand.

Nigel kissed her in the churchyard. Not a sensual kiss, but a warm one. It sang of love.

She'd never kissed anyone like this before. She'd never shared a moment like this with anyone, even Richmond. The very air felt filled with lightning. Full of love and tenderness. But also of heat and such sensuality it made her weak in the knees.

Strong and firm, his hand splayed on her back and drew her tight to him.

Children's squeals broke in on their kiss and she pulled back. A group of village children ran into the churchyard, chasing each other in play. Nigel didn't pull back from the kiss—he leaned in and gave her one last quick one. Even though she'd thought a proper, staid gentleman would stop kissing her in front of children. He was changing.

"I will marry you here," she whispered. "At Brideswell."

MOTHER AND THE dowager had scrapped like two terriers over the engagement ball. That was nothing compared to the arguments over the wedding.

Zoe hurried down the stairs, pulling on her coat. She stalked up to her mother and the dowager. "Stop arguing, both of you. This is my wedding and it will be done exactly as I want it."

As she turned and left, she heard Mother declare, "Well, really, when I am trying to ease some of her burden. Heaven knows a wedding is such a lot of work."

"I agree." The dowager sniffed. "I know very well what a wedding reception at Brideswell requires. And

someone must ensure Reverend Wesley does not me-
ander when he does the service."

"I know. Our pastor used to wander off in his ser-
mons something fierce," said Mother. "My Zoe is a capable girl, but a wedding requires experience."

"I could not agree more," declared the dowager.

Zoe grinned. She'd known there was one thing that
would give those two women common ground—the
threat of someone else taking charge. She intended to
have exactly the wedding she wanted. To do it, she
would have to know when to negotiate, when to do
things secretly and when to stand her ground.

And having her wedding her way was the reason she
was driving down to the village church.

Isobel caught up with her at the garage and slipped
into the passenger seat of her car. "I'm going to the
hospital," Isobel said. "Would you give me a lift, Zoe,
please?"

"All right," Zoe said. "I have to see Reverend Wesley. About the vows."

Isobel frowned. "What about the vows?"

"There's a change I want to make in them."

Isobel proved to be so curious she followed Zoe to
the manse beside the church, instead of walking on to
the hospital. With her young sister-to-be at her side, Zoe
waited in the doorway of the reverend's study, hands
clasped in front of her, as Wesley got to his feet and
came to her.

"May I help you, my dear?" he asked kindly.

She held out a folded piece of white paper. "At the
wedding tomorrow, these are the vows I want you to
read."

The elderly man frowned. "I don't understand. I intend to use the traditional vows of the Church of England."

"These are the ones I want."

"But, my dear young lady—"

"It's only a slight change, Reverend. Nothing to be upset about. All I've done is taken out the word *obey* from my vows. This is the nineteen twenties. I'm to be a wife, not a serf."

"The word *obey* is part of the vows. I have no authority to remove words."

"I won't say it. You can go with the standard vows, but you won't get that word out of me."

Isobel let out a small squeak and clapped her hand over her mouth. But a smile blossomed behind Isobel's hand and her eyes glowed with excitement.

Reverend Wesley spluttered. "A woman obeys her husband, Miss Gifford."

"A woman is her own person, Reverend."

"My dear, these vows have been used in this church for centuries! Even if I had such authority, I would not stand before God and tinker with what has been ordained for his pleasure."

"You aren't marrying the duke. And neither is God. I am," Zoe said. "These are the vows I'm willing to make, so I'd advise you to say them."

13
WEDDING AT BRIDESWELL

ZOE TURNED SLOWLY in front of the cheval mirror. This dress would surprise Nigel, she was sure. She bit her lip. Modern girls were fearless. But her heart hammered and her hands trembled as she drew the material of the train into her hands so she could step off the stool.

Mother had always spun fantasies about what her wedding day would be like. At least she had when Father made millions. Mother wanted something to set New York society back on its collective heel. Girls worried more about one-upping each other on weddings than they did about their futures with their husbands.

Zoe wanted her wedding to be about love. And not an old-fashioned love. Not marriage as a social triumph. But two equal people who belonged together. She had been the one to sit down and sort out how her dowry would be dealt with—she'd set out her rules to Nigel and his lawyer. Instead of turning over her entire fortune of four million dollars to Nigel and Brideswell, she was giving half to the estate. The rest was to stay in her name. Nigel's lawyer had looked shocked that she wasn't giving everything to her husband.

Nigel had said, "If it is what Zoe wants, I accept. She is turning a substantial fortune over to my care. Enough to take care of the estate."

She'd gathered, though, it was not the way it was done. She couldn't tell exactly how Nigel really felt about that.

The door to her bedroom opened, and Julia and Isobel rushed in.

"Golly!" cried Isobel, who had adopted the expression.

"You look lovely, Zoe," Julia exclaimed.

It was Nigel's expression she wished to see, but that would not be until they were in the tiny church. The church in which he'd been christened. This was his world. Julia made her feel she belonged. But did she?

Hadn't that been her vow, after all those rejections by staid, old New York society? She would make her own world where she belonged.

"So do you both." Zoe hugged both her soon-to-be sisters-in-law. "You have been so good to me."

Julia held out the bouquet. White roses and delicate, white baby's breath in a small, tight group, tied with long satin ribbons. "Are you nervous?"

"I've had times in the air when I thought I was a goner. Yet for this, I am nervous." And excited. And filled with wicked, exhilarating anticipation.

"What do you think Reverend Wesley will do about the vows?" Isobel took her turn in front of the mirror, holding out her rose-colored skirts. Her hair was in curls, tied with ribbon.

"The vows?" Julia was adjusting Zoe's train. Zoe twisted to see it in the mirror. Mother had wanted yards of lace—and a train long enough to stretch from the upper landing of Brideswell's stairs to the bottom—had wanted feathers and diamonds. The dowager had wanted a demure dress—high neck, long sleeves, floor length. *This* dress was what Zoe wanted. It had slender lines and no sleeves. No diamonds or pearls. It was white satin and soft flowing tulle. It felt as if she'd wrapped a cloud around her. She had allowed a small train of satin, embroidered with delicate petal shapes—silver on white.

She adjusted her veil. It was a cap of lace on her bobbed hair, trimmed with soft yellow roses, and a length of lace that skimmed down her back.

Isobel had grabbed a biscuit off Zoe's tea tray—she had too many flutters in her tummy to eat anything.

"What about the vows?" Julia asked again. "Do stop eating biscuits, Isobel. You'll make yourself sick."

How would Julia react to her request? Julia had embraced being modern but also loved her brother. Would she understand why Zoe could not agree to "obey" Nigel? She had to be her own person. She simply had to be. "I wanted the reverend to make a small change to the vows. Of course, he said he could not do it."

Still chewing, Isobel said, "Zoe asked old Wesley to take out the part about her obeying Nigel."

"It's being removed from vows in America," Zoe pointed out. "Reverend Wesley refused, of course. Now I'll simply have to skip that part."

"It's being removed from vows? I didn't know that," Julia breathed.

"Because women aren't chattel. We don't need to obey a husband."

"Goodness," Julia said. Then she giggled. "Poor Reverend Wesley. I am surprised he didn't swoon."

"He went pale as a ghost." Isobel grinned. "Zoe said that the reverend wasn't marrying Nigel, nor was God. She was and she would only say the vows she wanted.

And I think she's right! Most of the boys I know don't know as much about things as me. I doubt they know more just because they've grown up to be gentlemen. And my boy cousins insist that women are useless at science, when obviously there have been brilliant women scientists. They also say women can't understand how engines work, but you do, Zoe."

Zoe smiled at the girl's look of admiration. "You're right, Isobel. It has nothing to do with whether you're a man or a woman. It depends on whether you have smarts—and if you're willing to use them."

"If you don't have to obey Nigel," Isobel said thoughtfully, "can I say I don't have to either?"

"That is different," Julia said. "Now hurry, Isobel. We must get Zoe to the church."

Julia and Isobel went downstairs first. Zoe followed, holding up her modest train herself. Carefully, she negotiated the front steps, but she stopped halfway down. Uncle Hiram stood by the drive—he had arrived three days ago to see the wedding. He was to give her away in place of Father.

Fortunately, Hiram had ambitions. The thought of being related to a duke had made him promise he wouldn't do a thing or say a word about the check.

Mother stood beside him, wearing a hat bearing more feathers than an albatross. Half of them dipped into Mother's face.

Uncle Hiram turned in a circle and whistled. "This sure is some place." He'd said that many times since his arrival. A grin split his fleshy lips. He was not as handsome as Father had been. Father had always looked strong and smart and elegant. "You've done well for yourself, Zoe. A duchess in the family. A duke for a nephew-in-law."

She knew she couldn't antagonize her uncle, even though she and Mother were almost safe. "You look very charming, Uncle, in your morning coat."

"The duke loaned it to me. Belonged to his father. I cut a fine figure, don't I?"

Since he could still cause trouble for Mother, Zoe smiled sweetly. "You do indeed."

"We should get going to the church, missy. Don't want to miss the big event."

She walked down the rest of the front steps to the carriage that waited for her. Parked behind the cars, it was a huge, Cinderella-style thing, complete with two snow-white horses. Suddenly Zoe felt as if the stairs were shifting under her feet.

She was leaving Mother. Leaving Uncle Hiram's guardianship. Leaving New York.

Women always went away with their husbands. They went to a new life, a new world.

She sure was. And she intended to make it hers— that was why she wouldn't agree to obey anyone. Not even the man she loved. She squared her shoulders and stepped into the carriage.

"You look nervous, Langy."

At the altar, Nigel ran his finger around his collar. Morning sunlight poured in the windows. He'd never felt so hot in church before. He glanced at Sebastian— standing at his side as his best man. His brother looked effortlessly elegant in his morning coat, appeared completely cool and unruffled. "I keep wondering if I've been mad to have asked her to marry me."

"I'm the irresponsible one. Now is not the time for second thoughts. Besides, if my tastes ran in that direction, I'd be champing at the bit right now. Zoe is a spectacular woman. Beautiful and thrilling. Every moment with her will be an adventure."

Nigel swallowed hard. "She is a remarkable woman. When I'm with her, I feel alive. Even when she argues with me. And she has a tender heart."

"Then you are a lucky man, Nigel."

It was the first time his brother hadn't used the irritating nickname. "I keep feeling guilty. As if I've claimed her under false pretenses," he muttered.

"I don't understand." Concern showed in Sebastian's face.

His brother had changed. Since Zoe had told him to find happiness and Sebastian decided to do it, he had lost his sulky anger. Nigel saw that his brother had tried to fit into their world out of a sense of duty. But it had eaten at him.

It took a certain kind of person to put duty above everything.

He had broken his vow of stoicism over the War—which he'd made as he limped home to Brideswell, recovering from his wounds. He had told Zoe what the War had left him with. He'd been honest with her—as much as he could be. There were some things he had to keep locked inside forever.

He needed to talk to someone about his fears. "Nightmares plague me. The damn shaking that comes on me without warning. What kind of husband will I be? When I look at Zoe, I picture her with a man like her. An outgoing man, an adventurer, a man who lives for each moment—a man who is not like me." His hand started to tremble. *Not now, damn it.* "The memories from battle get worse, not better." He had been thinking about Ernie Bell last night and woke from a horrific nightmare at 3:00 a.m. and couldn't even attempt to sleep afterward.

"She loves you, you know," Sebastian said softly. "I saw that on the first night she came to Brideswell. She was falling in love with you at dinner. Why do you think I punched you? You were ruining my plans with your nobility and strength and strong-and-silent behavior. You had her captivated."

"She is not certain yet. Not certain if she loves me." He fought for control by clenching his fists. Nerves and tension set him off. He was not going to let anything ruin this moment.

"She will. I want to see you happy. And you have to go through with your marriage now," Sebastian said. "Think of the scandal if you don't."

And he owed Zoe marriage. But more than that, he loved her.

He could be the man she deserved to have, damn it. He could hide the broken parts of him from her. "You are correct," he said. "I will keep my problems under control so they do not touch or hurt Zoe."

"One thing I've learned about problems," Sebastian said. "You can't control them." Sebastian shuffled his feet. "On that note, I wanted to thank you. For understanding why I have to go to Capri. For covering up with Mama and Grandmama—telling them I just wanted to paint."

"I am sorry it took me so long to understand what you need to be happy."

The church doors opened then, filling the doorway

with light. White fabric fluttered, and all heads turned and craned toward the entrance. Mrs. Dobbs, the organist, lifted her hands, and suddenly the first strains of the wedding march swelled through the church.

Her uncle Hiram Gifford brought Zoe forward, her hand resting in his crooked elbow.

Her bobbed hair was a cap of gold, her face almost bare of makeup, her eyes large and violet, her lips full and soft pink. A veil of some white gauzy fabric floated around her, held in place by a spray of diamond roses. She wore a simple white dress that seemed lighter than air. The hem swirled around her midcalves and a train glided behind her. A bouquet of white flowers was clutched in her hand and white ribbon streamers flowed out of the bouquet

Nigel had to take a step back. He almost lost his balance.

"She is the most beautiful woman I've ever seen."

"She is," Sebastian agreed, under his breath.

Nigel hadn't realized he'd spoken out loud.

Walking toward him, Zoe smiled. An ache wrapped around his heart. He had no right to be so happy.

A querulous female voice sounded over the strains of music from the organ. "Was it not the duke's brother she was supposed to marry? They've changed places, you say?"

He knew the voice—it was the dowager's sister, his great-aunt Alicia.

"It's a new world," his grandmother's firm voice answered.

But Great-Aunt Alicia was the only one to openly voice the thing everyone else was thinking. The village must be rife with gossip. He hadn't looked at a newspaper for over a week, because he didn't want to bloody well know. It was his duty to protect Brideswell. And now to protect Zoe. From everything—including from scandal.

"Hello," she said when she reached the altar.

"Hello," he murmured.

Reverend Wesley cleared his throat.

The words rolled together in a blur. Nigel had witnessed weddings of friends. Now that it was his own, Reverend Wesley's words seemed to come from miles away. "We are gathered here…in sight of God…"

A ray of rose-tinted sunshine spilled from the stained-glass window. Zoe stood in its pink-and-gold glow.

The gold touched crosses on the altar, making them gleam. It slanted over a plaque on the wall, placed there by his family. A list of the village men who had not come home from the Great War.

He didn't want to think of it now, but seeing the plaque, the crosses, made it impossible to forget.

Grasp life and live it as much as I can, so I can do his living for him as well as mine.

That was what she had said. But what right did he have to get a life when so many men didn't? Better men than he. He had sent men over the top. Sent them into the path of machine-gun fire. Many of those men had never had the chance to have a sweetheart, to be in love, to marry.

All that was left of them were crosses. And the memories Nigel still held of their deaths—at least those he remembered. Ragged, painful memories of bursting shells and mud and screams and fear—

The reverend cleared his throat. "I, Nigel Arthur William Hazelton, take thee, Zoe Anastasia Gifford——"

He was supposed to repeat his vows. But the laughter of doomed men echoed in his ears. Those moments when they traded jokes, seeking to live with normalcy in the middle of hell——

Beneath the sunlight streaming through the window, Nigel's skin perspired. Shirt, waistcoat and morning coat felt vise-tight. Sweat rolled down his back.

The reverend cleared his throat softly. "Your Grace," he intoned with discretion. "Would you repeat your vows?"

"Yes. Yes, of course." Nigel tugged at his collar. *Damned hot in here.* "I, Nigel Arthur William——" His voice cracked. Sebastian nudged him.

This was for Zoe. He owed her this—a beautiful wedding day.

He looked to her. What did she think of his clumsy words, his nerves?

He saw how her forehead was furrowed. Hell, if he wanted to believe their marriage could work, he had to get through this.

He cleared his throat, louder than the reverend had done. People shuffled on pews. His collar choked him. He'd faced battle. He could confront a wedding.

"I, Nigel Arthur William Hazelton, take thee, Zoe——"

On the words "take thee," a soft smile came to her lips. A shared smile. He looked at her face, and she filled his every thought. Moments now and she would truly be his. The words suddenly came easier.

Then it was her turn. The reverend fumbled with his prayer book and cleared his throat again.

"Do you, Zoe Anastasia Gifford…" Then inexplicably, the reverend stuttered, saying, "To love, ch-cherish and—and—" The man's voice dropped to a hushed whisper. "What is the meaning of this? Someone's altered my book!"

Nigel stared at Wesley, who tipped his book of scripture down. Some of the words in the man's book had been blacked out with a pencil. The reverend cast a shocked glance at Zoe.

With his tone of voice like the hissing sound of a leaky tire, Wesley said, "Your Grace, I apologize. I do not understand. Miss Gifford wished to make a change in the vows."

Nigel turned to her. Murmurs rose through the congregation, but they hadn't heard what Wesley had whispered.

Zoe met his gaze. "I didn't do anything to the book. I told him just what I wanted to say. I wanted my vows to you to be exactly the same as the ones you say to me, Nigel. Without *obey.* Someone was just having a joke with the book." She gave Wesley a gentle, beautiful smile. "Why don't you continue, dear reverend? It's been so very lovely so far."

With that, Zoe managed to win over the reverend Red in the face, Wesley took a deep breath and continued. Out popped the word *obey.*

She wasn't going to repeat it. Nigel was sure of it. Once he would have been shocked. Now he could see Zoe was correct—what did it matter? His father hadn't done a lot of loving and cherishing during his marriage. A vow was not what you said, but what you did.

"I, Zoe Anastasia Gifford, take thee, Nigel Arthur William Hazelton, to be my wedded husband," Zoe repeated, her voice ringing out in the church. "To have and to hold from this day forward, for better for worse, for richer for poorer, in sickness and in health, to love, cherish and to obey, till death us do part, according to God's holy ordinance."

She had said the word she objected to. And he knew she'd done it for him—to spare him embarrassment.

Suddenly Nigel realized something else. Zoe was now his.

The responsibility almost overwhelmed him. She was bold and honest and more filled with life than anyone he'd ever known. And he was a damned mess.

The rings were presented on Sebastian's gloved palm. Nigel shakily slid one onto Zoe's slender finger. His voice was equally shaky as he said, "With this ring, I thee wed."

RICE RAINED OVER THEM. Zoe clasped the hand of her husband and let him lead her out of the church to the guests and the villagers.

"Three cheers!" shouted one of the villagers.

Hurrahs followed. Caps flew into the air. Children squealed, scampering around the legs of adults. In the crowd, Zoe saw the simplest laborers, the merchants and all the local gentry. Every soul in Brideswell had gathered to wish them well. The elderly farmer who she had encountered on the road the first day she'd arrived was there, looking on with his familiar dour expression. Mrs. Billings leaned heavily on a cane, helped by Julia's sweetheart, Dr. Campbell.

Joy surrounded them.

But Nigel had looked anything but happy in the church. He had looked exactly as he had when she'd found him outside Murray's jazz club, suffering from shell shock.

"A kiss!"

A cry started over the crowd for a kiss.

Was Nigel going to kiss her? He had looked so upset in the church. When she saw him at the altar, he had looked stricken and in agony. He had been tugging at his collar. At that moment, he looked as if he were going to shake to pieces or explode in anger.

Then he'd looked at her. His blue eyes went wide as he drank in the sight of her in her dress. His lips had softened and she saw him suck in a deep, long breath. He had looked…as if he'd been struck by lightning.

He had been nervous, stumbling over his vows. But he had not looked outraged over the word scribbled out in the book, and she'd thought he would. She knew who had done it. She had looked at the guests and Isobel had flushed with guilt.

Now, at the happy demand for a display of affection, Nigel looked blank. As if he had no understanding of the meaning of the word *kiss*.

"We shouldn't disappoint them, should we?" she said to Nigel. "They're happy for you."

He drew off his hat with a nervous gesture. From his towering height, he bent to her lips. Without saying a word. She went up on tiptoe and their mouths touched.

It was the softest kiss. Not passionate, but very gentle.

"Huzzah!" several people shouted. "Hurray to the duke and his new duchess!"

"Long lives to them both!" cried others.

Nigel broke the kiss first, moving back and wearing a light blush. Laughter and more cheers sounded among the villagers. Zoe laughed up at her new husband. Softly she teased, "That wasn't a kiss to sweep me off my feet."

"That is not the kind of thing I can do in front of an audience," he said stiffly.

More rice was thrown at them, and then a girl cried out, "Do toss the bouquet! Oh, please!"

Laughing, Zoe turned her back to the crowd. She knew just where Julia was standing. And she threw her bunch of roses over her shoulder. A feminine squeak sounded and Zoe whirled around to see a chunky young woman elbow Julia out of the way and snatch the flowers out of the air. She shared a rueful look with Julia.

Then Zoe turned to Nigel. She felt she was glowing from the inside out. He wasn't smiling—he was watching her, a poignant expression on his handsome face.

"We should go to the carriage, Zoe. To return to Brideswell."

He said it in far too cool a way. "Good," she answered. "I want to get you alone."

"We won't be alone."

"Nigel!" she cried in protest. Why didn't he get it? But she soon saw he was right. A footman waited at the carriage, holding the door open. There was the driver, of course. And the carriage was open, so everyone could see the newly married duke and duchess. It was sweet. But not good when she ached to kiss him hard.

Nigel lifted her train and she slid along the smooth seat. He held the train to her, and she bustled all the fabric around her.

She had insisted all the villagers be able to attend the wedding breakfast. Mother had been shocked. Mother had had her heart set on an exclusive guest list, bursting with dukes, earls and possibly—gasp—a prince or princess.

Mother and the dowager had been in agreement in their shock. Tents for the reception? The farm tenants touring the grounds and piling food on plates? Horrifying.

But it was going to be done.

The coachman flicked his reins and they were off. Zoe didn't quite know what to say. Why had Nigel been so nervous in the ceremony? Why was he so stiff and quiet now? They both sat awkwardly. They'd been married for just a few minutes. Before, she would have said something to annoy him. But she didn't want to do that now.

No, she was going to be honest. "Are you having second thoughts?"

Nigel jolted in surprise. "Of course not."

"Then what was wrong in the church? You were pulling at your collar and sweating. You looked like you wanted to run."

There was a silence. At the picnic, in the churchyard, Nigel had actually talked about what he felt—he'd talked about love. But now he was acting cold and austere, the way he'd been when she'd first met him.

"Have we just made a colossal mistake?" Zoe asked.

"COLOSSAL MISTAKE?" NIGEL repeated, startled. Was that what she felt?

"I wanted this to be the happiest day of your life. I intend to make it that."

"It is." Hell, he'd said that too curtly. He had been fighting to control his shaking through the wedding.

Deep in his heart, he was afraid she had made a mistake in marrying him.

Once he would have been unable to find the words. Now he had to try to explain. For her. "Zoe, ever since I returned from the War, wounded, I've avoided large events. Standing up there, on display, I feared I would embarrass you in some way. I feared I would start shaking—or worse. I was afraid of doing something that would shock or horrify people."

"They are your friends and family," she said.

"True, but who can criticize you more or hurt you deeper?"

"I suppose only people whose opinion you care about can hurt you. But don't you see you have nothing to fear?"

He had everything to fear. This should have been the happiest day of his life. But the guilt in his heart churned harder today. Because he was having joys denied to so many men who had entrusted their lives to him. Because when he stood in front of all the villagers, people he had known for his entire life, he had felt conscious of his scars. Conscious of the tremors in his hands, brought on by nerves.

"I know," he said. He wanted to change the subject. "We have the breakfast. Then the honeymoon. Then the financial business will have to be taken care of. I have a schedule to put in place—improvements to the farm buildings, purchases of new farming equipment—"

"We've just married, and you're thinking about farming equipment."

He flushed. "You are correct, Zoe. We have other things to think about." He frowned. "What happened with the vows? I looked out over the guests and I saw

Isobel go red. That usually means she is guilty of something."

"I think it was Isobel," she admitted. "She was with me when I talked to Reverend Wesley about the vows."

"She scribbled in a book of scripture."

"She doesn't agree that women are property of men. She's a modern girl." Zoe cocked her head. "You had better not punish her. I won't allow it."

"Ah, you want me to obey you."

She was about to protest, but he held up his hand. "I am teasing, Zoe. I will not punish her."

"Thank you."

"But I will talk to her," he continued. "It was still wrong to deface the reverend's property."

Zoe giggled. That, he hadn't expected. Then she laughed. "Nigel, I love you. When you talk like that it makes me want to—"

She slid across the seat and pressed against him, crushing the yards of tulle in her dress, and she kissed him. As passionately as she could.

Hungrily, he kissed her back. He wanted to give her the kiss of a lifetime.

He heard applause from the people lining the road and he drew back. He could not do this—kiss with abandon so publicly.

Zoe waved, bubbling with joy. To him, she said, happily, "I can't wait until our honeymoon. The time at our wedding breakfast is going to be agony, you know, waiting until we can get away. I am so excited to see Monte Carlo."

Nigel cleared his throat. Guilt was surging again, and he couldn't seem to forget all the young men he'd known who had died—who had wives and sweethearts and had given up their chances for love. "Zoe, I cannot go to Monte Carlo. I cannot face traveling across France. It is too filled with memories for me. I will not leave Britain, Zoe. I cannot. Instead, we will go north, to my hunting seat."

"WHERE WILL YOU be taking your honeymoon? The south of France is a popular choice. Hot, of course, but to be on the coast of the Mediterranean—quite lovely." Knocking back champagne, the tall, thin countess had cornered Zoe. Zoe wanted to find Nigel, and this irritating woman wanted to find her soft underbelly and stick a fork in it.

Julia looked panicked. A lot of people had heard the countess's carrying voice. "There are lots of lovely places one would want to go."

"Nothing compares to the south of France. I adore Monte. Anywhere else would be uncivilized."

Mother had told her to go to Monte Carlo or Nice for their honeymoon and she'd thought it would be fun. But Nigel refused to leave Britain and hadn't told her until they were already wed.

It hurt to have a decision made without including her. But she wasn't going to give Lady Chawley-Lampkin, or Crawfish-Lumpy—whatever her name was—the satisfaction of knowing she was unhappy. "His Grace did not want to return to France," Zoe said coolly. "Not so soon after the War. He feared it would dredge up unpleasant memories and he chose to remain on British soil."

"Pshaw. You should have insisted, my dear."

"I didn't want to make the duke unhappy." And what business was it of this woman's?

Was it really true that Nigel had been afraid his shell

shock would affect him at the wedding? And why would it—if the day really was a happy one?

She'd never dreamed she would feel unsure on her wedding day.

Nigel said he loved her. She loved him. It was *enough*.

Lady Lumpfish was still speaking. "I thought perhaps the arrangements would have *already* been made," she said in a cutting tone. "The duke's *brother* is a frequent visitor to Nice and Monte—it's well-known Lord Sebastian loves the tables."

So that was what this was about. A chance to claw at her about shifting from Sebastian to Nigel.

"I wondered if the duke simply decided to pick up where his brother left off," the countess continued. "Though I suppose you felt you could do better."

"Who cares where you go?" Zoe said coldly. "I thought honeymoons were supposed to be spent indoors. Even in the south of France, we'd never see more than the bedroom."

Food slid off Lady Chawley-Sourpuss's plate and landed with a squish on the woman's shoes.

Zoe smiled and walked away. Couldn't they leave yet? Toasts had been made. The good wishes had long vanished, and now, fuelled by Brideswell's champagne, the women were showing their claws.

A hand touched her arm. Zoe hoped it was Nigel's, but Julia stood there, lovely in her pale blue bridesmaid's dress, the scalloped hem dancing around her slim legs.

"Can I hug you?" Julia breathed.

Zoe felt her nerves ease their grip. "Of course."

They embraced. "You should have caught the bouquet," Zoe said. "I tried to make sure you got it. Since I'm quite sure you are going to be the next one to wed."

Julia blushed. "I wouldn't have dreamed of such a thing if it wasn't for you. I would have been locked away in Brideswell, still deeply unhappy. Anyway, I did try for the bouquet, but Lady Chawley-Lampkin's daughter elbowed me out of the way. Look—there is Nigel."

Julia pointed down the lawn. Zoe saw Nigel with his nephews. He saw her and began to run toward her.

Zoe's heart stuttered. Nigel wore a smile—a brilliant smile of joy. Seeing her had made him smile.

"I haven't seen him this happy since before the War," Julia said. "You have changed him, and I wouldn't have thought it was possible."

It was proof a modern, determined American girl could accomplish anything. Including winning the man she loved.

14
WEDDING NIGHT

Near Berwick-Upon-Tweed

"My LITTLE GIRL, a duchess!"

Zoe had barely got into her mother's room when she was snared in Mother's perfumed embrace. Mother beamed. Zoe wasn't sure if it was happiness—or the champagne at the reception.

"Well, we did it, dear. I'm so very happy."

"Happy for me for marrying the man I love."

Mother rolled her large violet-blue eyes. "Happy for you for securing your future." She lowered her voice to a determined whisper. "I remember what it was like to have an empty larder, a dirt floor and the despair of not knowing where the next meal would come from. I vowed you would have so much more."

"Mother, I grew up that way."

Mother waved logic away. "You must barely remember it. Your children will never know that kind of a life, Zoe. And neither will you or I. Ever again." Mother's expressive eyes narrowed. "And you must keep our past quiet, Zoe."

"We don't have anything to be ashamed of."

"You remember what things were like when we first

came to New York. Do not give anyone anything that can be used as ammunition."

Mother let her go and strode back to the door that led to her dressing room. From the doorway, she wagged her finger at someone in the room. "Now, be careful with those dinner gowns. Have you no idea how to pack a trunk? Those things are the height of fashion in New York and I don't want them ruined."

Zoe peeked around the corner. Two trunks stood open, and Mary, Mother's maid, was rushing to and fro, trying to transfer Mother's dozens of outfits to the cases.

"Mother, are you leaving already?" Of course she would be, Zoe realized. She must be returning to New York. Silly, but she'd expected her mother to be here when she returned.

Homesickness washed over her with such strength she could barely stand.

She was twenty. For all her bravado, she'd never been on her own before.

She was married. She was crazy about Nigel, but when she thought about it, she really barely knew him. Her husband was still a stranger.

"Of course we are leaving, dear. I have been told the train leaves at three o'clock. Now, darling, I'd love to talk, but my maid has packed my trunks all wrong and they have to be redone in the next hour, and that's not going to happen unless I'm standing over them."

"Your train leaves at the same time as mine?" It meant she could have one very last hug with Mother before they went separate ways: Mother to Southampton to sail home, and her to the north with Nigel.

"It's the same train, darling. Of course it leaves at the same time."

Then she understood. "Mother! You are *not* thinking to come on our honeymoon?"

"Zoe, a lady does not raise her voice."

"Stop trying to act like the dowager." Was the dowager still the dowager now that she was the duchess? Zoe had no idea. And it didn't matter. "Mothers do not accompany daughters on their honeymoons."

"They do." Her mother lifted her fingers to count the instances.

"No! I've heard the stories. Every single time the bride was miserable."

Mother's expression was pained. "Then where am I to go? I doubt I'll be welcome here, if you aren't here."

"Go back to New York. With Uncle Hiram."

Mother looked obstinate. "If I'm alone with Hiram, he will harp on that check. Endlessly. I can't face a transatlantic voyage with Hiram."

Now she could understand Mother's fear. While Mother had caused her own disaster, she understood. But she could not have Annabelle Gifford on her honeymoon. She couldn't do the things she wanted to do with Nigel with Mother hanging around.

"I will speak to Nigel's mother. I see no reason you couldn't stay longer and let Hiram travel ahead of you. Remember, Mother, if you go back, you can crow to every leader of Manhattan society that I am now a duchess. Brag about the wedding. Rub it in a little."

Mother did look happier. But she feigned shock. "We do not brag, Zoe."

"You brag all the time."

"That is not bragging. There is nothing wrong with informing people of our family's accomplishments."

Zoe rolled her eyes.

"But if I go back to New York, what will you do? You're going to the ends of the earth for this honeymoon. You'll be bored stiff, honey."

"Mother, I really don't think so."

ON THE TRAIN, Nigel read the newspaper while Zoe watched the countryside go by. It was warm in the compartment. Rain started outside, making the sky dark, and Zoe fell asleep, curled up against Nigel. She awoke as the train pulled into a station—gray clouds and showers made it almost like night. They hurried to a car and set off north.

"Finally," Zoe murmured. "I can kiss you."

Nigel gave her one kiss—a quick, proper one. Then he drew back with a quick glance toward the chauffeur. "Wait until we arrive," he said softly.

Zoe pressed up against the glass, but couldn't see into the dark of early evening and the windswept sheets of rain. Finally, the car stopped before a house. She could barely make out stone walls, a tall roof and pinpoint spots of lights burning here and there behind windows. They had passed tall, craggy hills and black lakes. Lightning forked through the sky now and thunder boomed so loud it seemed to rock the car.

"Are we in Transylvania?" Pressing her face to the window of the car, she peered out.

"Still in England," Nigel said. "We are near Berwick-Upon-Tweed, the northernmost village in the country."

The northernmost place? It was even more rain drenched than anywhere else she'd seen in England. Zoe pushed down a sense of disappointment. If Nigel feared he would remember the War if he stepped on French soil, she didn't want him to go through such pain.

The car door opened and a footman in livery stood by the door, holding an enormous black umbrella. Zoe slid out, and as Nigel joined her, she turned to him, got on her tiptoes and whispered, "Why don't we go right upstairs to bed?"

She said it quietly so only he would hear.

"Now?" Nigel frowned. "It's dinnertime."

"You're joking, right?" She was so frustrated. She rested her hands on his broad shoulder. She moved so close her lips brushed his ear and said, "Isn't it glorious to think we can make love whenever we want? It's no sin. No scandal. And I'd like to start now."

His footman stared impassively ahead.

"That would be impossible," Nigel said in a low voice.

"How can it be *impossible?*" How could she be the only one eager to go to bed?

"Quiet, Zoe. We cannot just run in the door and run upstairs to bed." He gazed at her as if it were obvious.

"I don't see why not."

"The staff will be presented to you. We will be required to change for dinner. Cook will want to display her prowess to you tonight. After dinner—after coffee in the drawing room—we will be able to slip away."

He was being staid and annoying. She felt a funny kind of panic. She'd thought once they were married and the wedding was over, and they were free of duty, he would be that man who'd made love to her in an airplane again.

"I don't care about any of that. Can't we just go upstairs then get something sent up if we get hungry later? Like room service?"

"The staff would be offended," he said softly. "And Cook does not do…room service."

"Have you forgotten what you bargained for when you married me? Remember the airplane?" Nigel really could drive her mad. No man had ever annoyed her like this.

Zoe slipped out of her coat and stepped out from the shelter of the umbrella. In only a few moments, she was soaked. Her dress clung to her. It stuck to her bosom, held up by her bra, stuck to her stomach, her bottom and her legs.

"What in blazes?" Nigel growled. He grabbed the umbrella from his footman. Zoe giggled as she saw that both Nigel and the servant's sangfroid had shattered like glass.

Nigel stormed toward her and held the umbrella over her head. She brushed her wet bob back from her face and gazed innocently at him.

"What are you doing?" he demanded, but quietly, so the footman wouldn't hear.

"Now I have to go up to my bedroom and take off all my clothes to change into dry ones for dinner." It was summer, June, but the rain was cold. Still, she would be damned before she'd shiver. "It's up to you if you want to join me."

The footman took the umbrella from Nigel. Her husband put his coat around her. "I will never forget the aeroplane, Zoe," he said softly. "Both times we were in it together."

HE DIDN'T COME UPSTAIRS. So Zoe gave in, changed into a silk dress of pale blue, with strings of beads and a feathered headpiece.

She'd dreamed of a honeymoon spent in bed. Of waking up with Nigel, utterly naked between tangled sheets. Of nibbling strawberries and cream from a tray, drinking champagne, then rolling on the bed and making love all over again.

But at this moment, she didn't know where her husband was.

In his deep, gorgeous voice, he'd told her he would never forget the time they'd flown in her airplane. And the time they made love. She had quivered with desire as his husky voice flowed over her. As she breathed in his scent imbued in his warm coat.

But he hadn't taken up her invitation!

He wasn't in his bedroom—she'd checked. He'd dressed for dinner apparently after she'd given up on him and decided to have a warm bath. There was no plumbing at this house either. Buckets of steaming water had been brought up from the kitchen. She'd felt sympathy and had them stop with just enough water to make herself wet and wash her hair.

She ended up wandering down the same large corridor twice. Even though this house wasn't as large as Brideswell, it was still enormous. When he had called it a "hunting seat" she had pictured something small. This was a mansion. And with the rain and few lamps lit, it was a dark and rather gloomy one.

"Are you lost, Your Grace?" A woman materialized from the shadows. "I am the housekeeper here, Mrs. Folliat."

"I am looking for the drawing room. And my husband," Zoe said. She was certain there was already talk about her downstairs. She had waved at the servants gathered in the foyer and announced, "Lovely to see you all gathered here. I've gotten wet and I would love a bath." She'd swept upstairs—and paused at the landing. "Would someone show me which bedroom is mine?"

No doubt she had scandalized the staff. But they would be, no matter what. She wasn't going to be what they would expect in a proper duchess. So she might as well get them accustomed to it.

Mrs. Folliat looked as if she'd sunk her teeth right into a lemon. But she gave directions and Zoe sashayed into the drawing room moments later.

Nigel was already there. Along with a tray of drinks—and a footman.

"You should have brought a wrap," Nigel said. "It gets chilly in the dining room."

"I wouldn't have expected anything else." She sipped a gin cocktail. "How many houses do you have?" She'd known true poverty in her childhood. And she couldn't help but point out, "Funny what passes for hard times in different parts of the world."

"We keep it for shooting. It and the London house are the last of our houses besides Brideswell. The others are long gone. I know I really should have sold this house, but my mother loves it dearly. As does Grandmama. After my brother's passing, I did not have the heart to get rid of this house."

She had been flip. But she saw pain in his eyes and felt guilty. He did that to her—goaded her to say something sharp, and then he showed vulnerability, made her heart ache and made her feel terrible for teasing him.

"You don't have to worry about that anymore."

"No. Thank you, Zoe."

"Don't thank me." She smiled wickedly. "But how about you show your gratitude after dinner?"

He ran his finger around his collar and a blush washed over his high cheekbones.

The gong rang then, summoning them into dinner. Two places were set—at the ends of a long table. Zoe sighed. They could have dinner, but not a conversation unless they shouted.

Tomorrow, she intended to change that.

So as not to offend Cook, Zoe went through course after course, watching Nigel along the length of the table. Watching him drink wine and eat was terribly erotic. A voice kept whispering in her head: *This is your wedding night.*

Dessert came—a charlotte russe, large enough to feed a whole house party.

That had to be it.

No, trays of cheeses were brought out. One of the footmen stepped forward. "Coffee in the drawing room, Your Grace?"

"Very good," Nigel said.

She was bouncing on her seat in irritation. He didn't look perturbed at all. How could he want *coffee?* Didn't he want to get up to bed? She didn't get it. She thought the *groom* was supposed to be even more eager than the bride.

He had been pretty eager in her airplane—

They retired to the drawing room. There was no fire—apparently one was never lit during the summer. Her shoulders jerked involuntarily. Cold seemed to whisper through the house like ghosts. She faced Nigel, who had settled in a wing chair. "Don't you want to go up to—?"

She had to break off as coffee came in, a huge silver urn of it, carried on a large silver salver. It was a procession: first the urn, then the cups, then cutlery, then trays of delicate cakes.

Of course, again, they weren't alone. A footman remained, to cater to their every wish. Everyone in England talked in front of the servants. She supposed it helped force them to engage in proper, polite conversations and keep ladies from raising their voices.

"The drive was good," Nigel remarked. "From the station."

She was not going to make small talk on her wedding night. "Sure it was. But I think I'm ready for *bed*."

Nigel got to his feet. "Good night," he said.

Good night? Bugger that, to use one of Sebastian's expressions. "I'll see you soon," she said jauntily.

ZOE FLOPPED BACK on her bed. She yawned. Her body wanted to fall into sleep, but she was fighting to stay awake. This was her *wedding* night and Nigel *had* to come to her sometime. She'd been upstairs for an hour. Where was her husband? A discreet rap sounded on the white paneled door that connected from her room to Nigel's bedroom. Their bedrooms were side by side, and on the opposite sides, they each had apartments consisting of a combined bathing and dressing room, and one small parlor each. All in a smaller scale than Brideswell, of course.

It probably wasn't even Nigel, Zoe thought, annoyed. Probably her maid or another servant. "Oh, come in," she called.

It was Nigel. In a robe of dark blue, belted at the waist.

Her heart pounded and her breath came fast. He could do this to her—make it almost impossible to ap-

SHARON PAGE

pear jaded and sophisticated. It made her feel vulnerable, exposed.

She rolled onto her side, propped up so her body made a sensuous line. Her white satin nightgown spilled over her thigh and poured onto the bed, revealing almost all of her bare legs.

She lifted a brow at her husband. "It took you long enough."

"My apologies." His hands gripped the belt of his robe. But he wasn't taking it off. "Should we get into bed?"

"Get into bed?" Zoe jumped off her bed, stalked over to him, and then she wrapped her arms around his neck, her legs around his waist.

He was strong, but she must have startled him because he fell over, landing on her mattress.

"We're not going to do something as boring as that," she said.

She stretched out on top of him in her formfitting nightdress and wriggled suggestively over him.

It worked. His erection swelled beneath his robe. Even beneath the thick velvet she could feel it. Planting her hands on his chest, she kissed him.

He responded. His mouth opened and he kissed her hungrily. Their tongues dueled. Their lips crushed together, hot and hard. Nigel tore his belt open, then his robe.

Pajamas. He wore a set of pajamas.

Zoe slid her hands all over him to torment him for wearing pajamas when this was their wedding night. She caressed him over his chest under the fabric. Then slid her hands into his trousers.

He groaned in surprise against her mouth.

But he drew back from her kiss—he always did that. He would stop when she was raring to go. His large hand wrapped around her wrist. He stilled her hand. "Zoe, no."

"Why not?" Nerves hit her. And doubts. She might be bold but she had no experience. And dukes—rich, autocratic men—were supposed to keep strings of mistresses before they married. Had Nigel done that? Before the War, before he was injured and scarred? He had seemed to know what he was doing in her airplane.

Gathering courage, she stared boldly in his blue eyes. "Don't you like it?"

"Yes, but you shouldn't—"

"Shouldn't what? Touch you? Don't you remember what we did in the airplane? I'm not going to lie on back and shut my eyes and do my duty. Sex is supposed to be fun. I intend to have fun. A lot of it."

She wriggled down his body. His trousers had a drawstring waist, so it wasn't hard to tug them down.

One quick glance up at Nigel's face showed he looked shocked.

Did he really think she planned to be proper now they were married? That afternoon in the airplane—or when they'd kissed in her car—she'd felt connected to him. Closer to him than she'd felt to anyone.

She wanted that feeling on her wedding night.

"I'm not going to be proper," she warned. "I bet most ladies are only proper in bed because they don't feel any desire for their husbands."

Pursing her lips—which she'd painted with lipstick while waiting for him, to look as alluring and pretty as she could—she bent down a planted a kiss to the most intimate part of his body.

"Zoe—" Her name came out terse, and before he could say more, she parted her lips and took him in her mouth. She knew girls did this—girls in New York talked about it. Young men had even asked for it in the backs of cars, though she would never have done it with them.

But she wanted this with Nigel. She wanted to shock him right down to his toes.

And she wanted to delight him. He was her husband. This was what marriage and intimacy was all about, wasn't it?

He started moaning and groaning, and his head tipped back as if he were in severe agony.

She loved seeing him like that. So out of control. His feet were bare because his slippers had fallen off, and his toes were stretched out straight.

He groaned, "Zoe, you have to stop."

No, she wasn't going to do that. Not even at a duke's command.

Nigel's hips jerked right off the bed and his fist slammed against the mattress and he howled.

Zoe was stunned. She'd made him yell.

Suddenly she was lifted. Lifted by his strong arms and he kissed her.

He rolled her onto her back. He pushed at the thick counterpane and the bedcovers, trying to get them down underneath her. She helped him by shimmying them under her. Finally she was lying on soft, cool sheets— her experience in England was that the beds were *always* cool or cold.

He got over top of her, his arms braced on either side of her shoulders, his legs open over hers. She gazed up at him, aware of his size. He was so much taller, his

legs incredibly long. Supporting himself on his strong
arms, he bent to her. His lips brushed her collarbone.

Skimmed lower and touched the swells of her breasts.

She trembled underneath him. Yes, this was what
she'd dreamed her wedding night would be.

He kissed her breasts through her nightdress, kissed
his way down her abdomen. Watching her from beneath his thick, black lashes, he took hold of her satin
skirt and lifted it.

Higher. Higher.

He bared her to him. She caught her breath, thrilled
to be so exposed, but nervous, too. Her heart beat faster
with anticipation than it had ever done.

His mouth lowered to her most intimate place.

And his kisses there made her moan, shiver, then
scream with sheer pleasure. She climaxed, her eyes shut
tight, her hands gripping the sheets.

Gasping in the aftermath of ecstasy, she giggled,
squealed and wriggled on her bed.

This was glorious. Just what she'd dreamed of. She
felt she could fly without an airplane. She felt filled
with power, naughty, wicked and so very happy she
wanted to sob with joy.

Stupidly, she felt a bit shy. Even after all they'd done
together. She fought that—she was not going to be a
wilting flower.

ZOE PULLED UP her nightgown and drew it over her head,
tossing it off the bed. She rolled onto her tummy, wig-
gled her bottom, and Nigel felt all the blood drain out
of his head as he covered her. God, she was beautiful.
Naked. Exquisite. Luscious.

This wasn't what Nigel had imagined his wedding

night would be. His father had told him to expect a nervous bride, trapped by ignorance, frigid and afraid.

Of course, Zoe had never been like that.

He took off the top of his pajamas, kicked off his trousers.

He wanted to give Zoe pleasure. He'd sensed her unhappiness. If he gave her pleasure here, maybe she would forgive him. For his awkwardness on their trip here.

She moved with him, wild and wanton.

He fought to hold on. All the sounds she made, the words she gasped in her lovely voice, were the most erotic things he'd ever heard.

She screamed, "Nigel! Nigel, oh, goodness!"

At that instant, his control snapped and he climaxed. A bright light burst in his head, and exquisite pleasure shot through him. He almost collapsed, consumed by ecstasy and exhaustion.

He leaned over her and captured Zoe's mouth in a series of quick, frantic kisses as they drew in deep breaths.

Zoe was his *wife*. How had he ended up such a lucky man?

Gently he moved away from her, collapsed on the bed and drew her down with him. He took ragged breaths. His heart still hammered.

Zoe sat up getting off him, and she fumbled through the evening bag she'd tossed on the bedside table. From her gold cigarette case, she took out two and held one out to him. He took it, his fingers brushing hers. Even after the wildest, most intimate sex, just that touch sent sparks through him.

With her manual strike lighter, she lit her cigarette, then his.

She sat up. Her naked, slender legs stretched out and crossed at the ankle. Her lipstick was mostly gone, some still smeared on her lips. Her bobbed hair was a tangle.

She looked indescribably sensual.

Nigel rolled onto his stomach to be closer to her. He brushed his knuckles along her thigh.

"You know, I was starting to worry," she said.

His heart lodged in his throat. "Worry about what?" he asked cautiously.

"I told Lady Chawley-Sourpuss that it didn't matter what was outdoors on a honeymoon since all the fun is indoors."

He sucked in a lungful of smoke and coughed. "Good God, Zoe. You did not say that to Lady Chawley-Lampkin."

She tipped back her head and blew a smoke ring. "I did. She was trying to pry into why we weren't going to Nice or Monte Carlo." She gave him a bold gaze. "Anyway, I was telling the truth. That's what I expected out of a honeymoon."

He blushed. They weren't going because he couldn't face crowds and couldn't face the memories that would surge when he traveled. He didn't know what it would do to him.

"But when we got here, you didn't seem too anxious to come to bed."

"I was, but it would not have been proper to rush upstairs, Zoe." Not entirely untrue. Nigel took a draw on the cigarette. "I hope it was worth the wait."

"It was." A silver tray sat on the side table. Zoe stubbed the cigarette in it. "But I'd like to spend as much time in bed as we can. This is our honeymoon."

MAKING LOVE TO Nigel had been sexy and naughty and erotic. Zoe lay down beside him and pressed her body tight to him. She felt dizzy and glorious.

She knew people who had to smoke all the time. They got irritable and nervy when they didn't have a cigarette in their hands. She never wanted to be addicted to anything. For the same reason, she didn't use cocaine or morphine. She drank, but not to excess.

But making love to Nigel? She could get addicted to that.

"Good night, Zoe." Nigel kissed the top of her head, and then he sat up. "Breakfast will be served downstairs. Your maid will bring you your tea in the morning. I'll see you at breakfast. Unless you prefer your breakfast in your bed now that you are married."

The covers rustled and he slid out of bed.

She bolted up. Gaping in disbelief. "What do you mean, 'at breakfast'? Aren't you going to sleep with me?"

"It isn't done, Zoe."

"Of course it is. People do it all the time."

But her husband shrugged on his robe. At the connecting door, Nigel bowed to her. Bowed! Then he was gone.

15
NIGEL'S MEMORIES

"GET YOUR HEAD DOWN. Goddamn it, get your bloody head down!"

The shouts wrenched her out of sleep. Confused, Zoe opened her eyes wide and sat up, groggy. Who was yelling? The cries were muted, but they sounded so desperate and awful.

"Dear God, what in hell are you doing? Get back, Cromwell! Get back before you get your head blown—" A loud yell of horror and agony pierced her right through to her heart.

Oh, Lord, it was Nigel.

Zoe jumped out of bed, let out a scream herself as the cold grabbed her and hugged her tight with its icy arms.

"Nigel!" She ran toward his door. What was wrong? He sounded as if he were dying.

She wrenched the old ornate doorknob and ran into his bedroom. It took her moments to understand the scene before her eyes.

One of his curtains was open, throwing moonlight into the room and casting silver-blue light over Nigel.

He wasn't in the bed. Naked, he thrashed to and fro on the hardwood floor. Garbled words came out of his mouth. He shouted names and incoherent sentences. She recognized one word. *Blood.*

She stood, gripping the doorknob, looking down in shock.

She must stop this. He could hurt himself. His face was a mask of tortured agony.

"They're coming. They're coming. Get out. Save yourself." He didn't shout that. It was a fervent, desperate demand.

How did you snap a man out of a nightmare? She got on her knees at his side. She must snap him out of this as quickly as she could. He could hurt himself. He was suffering terrible pain. And it was terrifying to watch him. He acted as though this were real.

She was trembling. But she grabbed his shoulders to shake him, sure it would wake him—

He let out an unearthly yell and he threw her. Now she knew his strength, for she slid back along the floor until her back stopped by hitting something hard. Pain exploded in her shoulder. She'd slammed into the front of a leather chair.

Should she get away from him?

She couldn't leave him like this.

Zoe struggled up onto her knees. She put so much pressure on her shoulder to do it, she cried out. It was a fight, but she got to her feet. Then she gathered her strength and shouted, "Nigel, wake up! You're having a nightmare!"

But this was like no bad dream she'd ever had. He seemed to be living it.

She needed to make some sort of loud sound to shock him awake. She grasped the fire poker and the shovel and struck them together.

The explosive crack of sound didn't do what she'd

hoped. Nigel threw his body, outstretched on the rug, hands trying to gouge into the floorboards.

This was what he would have done when something exploded. She saw it with cold, harsh clarity. He would throw himself into the muck to avoid the explosion, the shrapnel.

"Nigel. It's Zoe." She knew it was a risk, but she'd always declared she wasn't afraid of anything.

She went to him again. Touched his face. She flinched, expecting him to strike her again. But he didn't move. His body heaved with his deep, ragged breaths, as if he'd exhausted himself. As if he had no more strength inside him.

Even though she knew he had shell shock, she hadn't really understood what it meant. She'd thought it was awkward shaking—which surely he could fight. She hadn't dreamed it was this.

Was he plunged back into hell every night?

He hadn't escaped war at all. He wasn't being shot at, but his mind thought he was. It was as real for him at night as it had been for four horrible years.

Her hand on his face seemed to soothe him. She tried shaking him again gently. He mumbled in protest, but finally his lids flickered.

Deep blue eyes gazed up at her. Eyes filled with agony.

He rolled onto his back, and she got on top of him. She hugged him, her satin nightdress pressing to his bare skin, tangled around both their legs.

"Zoe," he whispered. "What happened?" He sucked in a deep breath. "I was having a nightmare, wasn't I?"

"Yes. I heard you and I came in to wake you."

He lifted her off him, horror and disgust written on his face. "I didn't want you to see that."

"I know you suffer from shell shock."

He didn't say anything. He sat up, arms dangling off his knees.

"Where are your servants? You can't tell me they didn't hear you scream."

"I have forbidden them from coming in when I am having one of the fits."

"Nigel, what if you'd hurt yourself? They should have ignored you and come to help you."

"Good servants do not do that."

"Then I'll have to take care of you." She got to her feet. She came back carrying his robe and settled it around his shoulders. She overlapped it in front of him so it warmed him.

He touched her hand. "What are you doing?"

"You're cold. You need whiskey—or brandy or whatever you prefer to drink."

"Why are you doing this? I thought you would be horrified."

"Haven't you learned yet that it takes a lot to shock me?"

"Go back to bed, Zoe. Once I've woken, I cannot get back to sleep."

She looked to his mantel clock. "But it is four o'clock. You will be exhausted if you don't get any sleep."

He shook his head, sending stray locks of dark hair to dust across his eyes. "Even tired, I won't sleep. I don't fight it anymore. But now you know why I cannot sleep with you."

She saw his pain in admitting it.

"If you're going to be awake, why not come back

to bed with me. We could make love again. Make love until the sun comes up." She took his hand and put it against her breast. Then she bent over so her lips touched his right ear. "I don't usually fall into bed until dawn," she whispered. "So I can make love until morning...if you want."

He lifted her, picking her up easily in his arms. His lips touched her forehead and he cradled her against his chest.

"Or we could use your bed," she suggested.

Effortlessly, he carried her to his bed and he placed her gently on it.

She got onto her knees. "Your bed is even bigger than mine." She touched the bed curtains, tied to the ornate columns of the bed canopy. "These are lovely. I think this bed is very old—am I right?"

"Two hundred and fifty years old. Used by many Dukes of Langford."

She giggled, and then her soft laugh caught in her throat. "Let's use it together. Please come to bed with me."

Crooking her finger in invitation, she fell back onto the soft mattress. Nigel followed.

He made love to her so slowly it was exquisite. After, she snuggled against him, put her arm over his chest and her leg over his. She intended to keep him with her.

"You have so many terrible memories of the War. You must have good memories. I don't know any of those. There's so much I don't know about you. What's your happiest memory?"

His lips touched the top of her head; his fingers caressed her bare shoulder. "The moment you walked into the church this morning."

She loved being constantly caressed by him. And that was what he kept doing. Skimming his fingertips over her arms, her shoulder, her neck, collarbone. Making her skin tingle everywhere. "Is that really true?"

"Yes. The second-best memory I have is of being in your aeroplane and looking up at you as we made love."

Her heart pattered wildly, aching with love. "I want to know about your past. What were you like as a little boy?"

"A holy terror."

"I can't believe that." She didn't want to yawn, but she couldn't help it. Making love left her sleepy and lazy and so relaxed she felt she floated on a cloud.

"It's true."

She was aware of Nigel gently kissing her temple. Of cradling her even closer, lifting her onto his chest to lie on him. His arms were strong, muscular, and wrapped around her.

Struggling to subdue another yawn, Zoe opened her eyes wide. She was going to stay *awake*. Nigel needed her. "What's the naughtiest thing you did as a boy?" she murmured, her cheek pressed to his firm, broad chest.

She never heard the answer.

ZOE WOKE UP ALONE, of course. Her maid had come in and was opening the tall velvet curtains. But even as Callie tugged the heavy drapes back, revealing the window, only gray light filtered in. It wasn't raining, but thick iron-gray clouds blotted out the sky.

This wasn't supposed to matter because she was supposed to be waking up with Nigel and she would reach for him, and they would make love all morning. All day.

But he had put her back in her own bed while she slept. She didn't even know where he was.

"His Grace wished to tell you he has gone walking on the moor, Miss—Your Grace." Callie blushed. "That's a strange title, isn't it? What's it supposed to mean?"

"I don't know," Zoe said, ruffling her hair. "A king is a 'highness.' I guess 'grace' was supposed to be the next best thing."

"I'll try hard to get it right, Miss Zoe. I mean—"

"Never mind now. We'll work on it." She thought of the mean, snobby girls in New York having to curtsy to her and call her that. For a moment, she felt like her mother. A wicked sense of satisfaction flared in her heart.

Then it fizzled.

It seemed a silly and insignificant thing. Compared to the pain Nigel was going through.

"What does one wear to walk on a moor?" She thought of the sensible shoes worn by women at Brideswell, and the tweed skirts, the shapeless things they called jumpers, the heavy coats.

"They wanted to know if you wanted your breakfast in bed, Your Grace." Callie said her title carefully.

She could have breakfast in bed. She supposed ladies did that to fill time. Then they went through the rigors of getting dressed. "Don't bother. I'll go down for my breakfast."

Zoe dressed in trousers and boots, a shirt open at her throat and the leather jacket of her flying ensemble. Breakfast awaited her in the dining room, like at Brideswell. Places were set at one end of the long table. She ate quickly.

She was walking out the front door, pulling on her leather flying gloves—in June, for heaven's sake, because the wind off the ocean was cold—when the butler materialized out of nowhere. "Might I inquire as to your destination, Your Grace?"

He asked politely, but he was prying into where she was going.

What did the staff think? This was England. It was normal, probably, for a husband and his brand-new bride to have separate breakfasts, and for him to go for a walk instead of going back to his wife's bed on their honeymoon.

"I'm going to walk and catch up to my husband." She deliberately called him that—instead of "the duke." Mother would have called him "the duke," but she wasn't going to. He wasn't His Grace to her; he was her husband. And they could stuff their shock.

A brisk wind whirled around the house and threw Zoe's bobbed hair around her face. She heard barking and followed the sound, rounding the stone house. Nigel, wearing tweeds and tall leather boots, playfully fought a stick from the mouth of a white hound, while two brown ones barked and jumped around him. Freeing the stick from the dog's jaws, he put his arm back, then threw the stick with power and ease. It hurtled high and the dogs streaked off after it. He threw like a New York ballplayer.

He saw her, and she saw a guilty expression come over his face. He shook it off, but it was there. "Good morning, Zoe. Did you sleep well?"

She walked to him. "I take it you didn't get back to sleep."

The hounds were running back to him. The white

dog had the stick and was in the lead, the other two hard on his heels.

"I had a better night than I've had in a long time."

"But you didn't sleep, did you?"

The dogs arrived then, and Nigel put his attention to tossing the stick again. She watched him—the broad shoulders moving under tweed as he wrestled the stick away. The soft, controlled command he gave that made the dogs sit.

Small things took her breath away. The pure blackness of his hair brushing his white collar. The length of his eyelashes and the curl of them. He must have been absolutely beautiful as a child. He was gorgeous now with his piercing blue eyes, his sharp cheekbones, his mouth that rarely smiled, but when he did, she was so tempted to kiss him.

When he straightened and threw the stick, she asked softly, "What happened to you in the War? What haunts you in those terrible dreams?"

His shoulders stiffened. "I do not know. I never remember the dreams."

His gaze stayed on the dogs. Which meant he was lying. "I am sorry I woke you, Zoe. That is why, when I returned to Brideswell after the War, I had a room in the south wing of the house. It's rarely used and far enough away that I don't disturb anyone. Here, the servants made up the room adjoining yours. I will move to another—"

"Don't! Please, don't. I don't want you to feel you have to run away from me." She folded her arms over her chest. "Can't you forget what happened in the War? You're safe now."

"I know. That's the madness of it. I got through. I

survived. I was graced with life, when so many died. But it's a tainted gift. I do not believe I'll ever be free of the War."

She hurried to him and touched his arm. "There has to be a way. Treatments—"

"I have learned about the treatments used. Cold baths to shock, for example. It's torture, and half the time it leaves the man a worse wreck than when he started— no good for anything. I will not do that."

"If you don't, we will never share a bed. Sleeping with you, curled up against you all night. That is what I want to do. But you're telling me I'll never experience that, if you don't try to find a cure for this."

"Zoe—I'm sorry. I should have been honest with you."

"There must be a way."

"It's been four years. I know there is no way."

They were alive, they were married and they could make love whenever they wished. Zoe knew that should be enough. It wasn't so terrible if they didn't sleep together. But it was something she had wanted from marriage. "Nigel, have you finished your walk or are you willing to give me a tour?"

He offered his arm. "I would be delighted. I didn't want to disturb you this morning, and I always walk early when I'm here."

"How often do you come here?" There were so many things about him, about his life, she didn't know. And she felt bad about having spoken bluntly about his condition. For once, she believed she shouldn't have been honest.

"Usually once a season. I come for hunting in

the autumn. In the summer, it is cool here and hot at Brideswell, so the family usually comes in August."

"How about London—how often do you visit there?"

"We avoid town in the summer. Go for the opening of Parliament. We avoid the winters there now—too expensive to fully open the house."

"How many houses did you once have?"

"Six. I sold off three to cover Father's death duties. We kept Brideswell, the London house and this one." He was leading her up a hill. "We can see the ocean from up here."

They stood at the top, and she could see the vast horizon, the rolling waves. She thought of something else they hadn't discussed. "When will you want to make trips to New York?"

"New York? A transatlantic journey." He shook his head.

Her heart tightened. "That's where my family is—my mother and my uncle, my cousins."

"I would never stand in the way of your visiting your family, Zoe."

"But you won't go."

"I'm uncomfortable with that sort of travel. People are put off by the scars."

She realized what he was saying—that he would travel only in his small world, where he felt safe. If she wanted to go home, she would have to go alone. "I want to take the weight from your shoulders. I want to help you."

"I will not talk about the War, Zoe. These things would horrify you. I refuse to do that to you. It's my duty to protect you from such things."

"Nigel, I've been touched by war. I lost my brother."

"No, Zoe. I will not speak of it."

"I'm a strong girl."

"I know, but I don't know if I am strong enough to tell you the mistakes I made, Zoe. I can barely live with them myself."

THAT NIGHT, ZOE made love with him in her bed, kissed him passionately and slept alone.

As she settled into her bed and drew up her covers, she still knew eventually she would have her husband in her bed.

Americans possessed drive, energy, conviction, and they had a great deal of faith in themselves—that was what Father had always told her. It was what made them successful.

Nigel had told her he could not reveal the mistakes he'd made to her. She took his no as a temporary situation. But like Father when he'd taken over a company, she recognized she needed a longer, more careful campaign.

She wanted her husband to open his heart to her. She'd been honest all along with him.

The next morning, he tapped on her door, surprising her—and buoying her faith. He wore his riding clothes—breeches, a jacket, hat and tie. "Would you like to ride with me this morning?"

"Of course," she said.

When he left her room, she pulled on trousers and a tweed hacking jacket, then followed him downstairs.

They went for the ride before breakfast. It was early morning, and the sea breezes had cleared away most of the fog that had gathered overnight. Patches still filled the valleys, and wisps of fog streamed around the horses' legs on the tracks. As the last of the mist evaporated, Zoe galloped after Nigel across fields until they reached a ridge that overlooked the sea. The air tasted of salt. Waves rolled up on a beach of pebbles, far below them.

Nigel brought his mount close to hers. He leaned over and kissed her. They controlled their horses, while they kissed and kissed. She loved it—the heat of their mouths, his hot, impulsive passion, the brisk coolness of the whipping breeze.

She knew he wouldn't talk to her yet, but she was determined that someday he would. Nowadays, husbands and wives were supposed to be partners. They were supposed to be together for more than just the economic advantage of sharing a household or holding to some idea about their duty to procreate. She put her gloved hand to his face and caressed him. To let him know she cared so much about him. Her fingers grazed over his scars.

He didn't pull away from her hand.

In the afternoon, he took her tramping all over the property. Through meadows filled with daisies and buttercups, beneath the leafy canopy of the woods.

"This is my favorite spot," he told her. He led her along a narrow path that wound through slender trees and dipped into a valley filled with wild roses. She breathed in the glorious scent. The dogs ran with them, charging away to follow scents, then returning with tongues lolling and tails wagging.

"It is beautiful."

He turned and smiled—a dazzling flash of white teeth and dimples. "Come here." He stood her in front of him and covered her eyes with his hands. "Let me lead you," he said, his voice a soft, deep growl by her ear.

She obeyed, letting him gently guide her. She smelled the brine of the ocean. Nigel took his hands away. They stood on a sand beach—the sand was wet and firm—in a small cove. Waves broke in foamy white on the beach. On each side rose the gray, rugged rock face of the ridge.

"It's beautiful."

"The beach is submerged late in the day, when the tide comes in. It comes in fast here, because of the shape of the cove."

He held her hand and they scrambled over rocks, walking the length of the cove. Together, they threw sticks for the dogs. When Zoe noticed the water lapping at her shoes, Nigel said, "We should go up."

They did, and the next days followed the same pattern. She had tea outside with Nigel, on the back lawn, beneath the large branches of an oak. He read his newspapers and she read hers. They ate sandwiches and sipped tea, then walked, or rode until it was time to dress for dinner. They had moments where they laughed together—like at the moment when the housekeeper came in with ten letters. All from Zoe's mother, and all written in the two extra days Mother had stayed on at Brideswell.

Each night, after dinner, she would join Nigel in the drawing room for sherry and brandy. At eleven o'clock regularly, they retired to bed.

In bed, Nigel was a different man. He focused on her, giving her pleasure. When she suggested daring things, he was always a little shocked, and then he agreed.

Afterward, he would kiss her, wish her good-night,

and he would leave her bed. When all Zoe wanted to do was fall asleep with him in a decadent tangle of arms and legs.

She worried about Nigel. She was frustrated he wouldn't speak more to her, but he refused. He had secrets locked inside.

She loved the quiet moments they shared. The companionship she felt even when they were reading their own newspapers. Or when he shared stories about past years at the hunting seat as they walked.

But those moments didn't help her forget how much he was suffering or ignore the wall it created between them. If anything, it was worse to feel her heart soar as they walked hand in hand and know he wouldn't sleep with her. That he never intended to sleep with her.

One night, when she couldn't sleep, she walked through the house. Rain pattered against the window-panes. She carried a candle, for there was no electricity here, of course. In a drawing room, she saw the glow of another candle's flame. She padded into the room.

Nigel stood by the window. He leaned against the glass. He started, whirling around when her foot made a floorboard creak. "What are you doing up? Did I wake you?" An intense look of guilt burned in his eyes.

"I think the rain woke me." She shivered. "It's cold in here."

"You are going to take me to bed, aren't you?"

"Oh, yes," she said.

The anguish lightened on his face and he held his hand to her. As they walked through the room, Zoe bumped a hard object under a white dustcover. A small pile of records slipped to the floor.

When she lay in her bed alone later that night, after

sex, the records gave her an idea. She bet that object under the dustcover was a gramophone.

And she was right.

The next afternoon, after tea on the lawn, she took her husband to the drawing room. Per her instructions, a footman had set the gramophone on a small table, with the stack of records in their paper sleeves beside it. "I found that in here." She picked the first sleeve off the top, drew out a record and put it on, gently placing the needle.

The music and first words came out, and Nigel strode over and lifted the needle. He did it with such a fast, efficient motion he didn't even scratch the recording. "Not that one, Zoe. Not 'Keep the Home Fires Burning.' Too many memories. They listened to that while I was at war."

Her cheeks were hot, her body cold. She'd wanted to bury his memories, not provoke them. Desperate, she went through the pile. Two records slipped off, fell to the parquet floor. The word *waltz* caught her eye and she quickly put the record on.

Soft notes and gentle music filled the room. She wanted to be danced around the room. But she'd never seen Nigel dance. Not even at her engagement ball.

He came to her and he held out his hand. "I have not waltzed in a long time. I would very much like to dance with you, Zoe."

Gently holding her hand, he drew her to him. He put his arm around her waist, pressed his hand lightly to her back. So close, she had to tip back her head to look up at him.

He whirled her into a waltz. He guided her expertly, and he moved so gracefully she felt she floated across the room. She had no idea he danced so well. She circled with him, her heart soaring just as it did when she flew. Around the room, they spun. This dance could last forever, couldn't it?

But it couldn't. The music died away and Nigel brought her to a stop.

She wanted to tell him he was a good dancer or say how beautiful it had been, but the moment her lips parted, he kissed her.

The whirring sound of the end of the record filled the room. But she didn't care. She melted in Nigel's arms, in his kiss.

When he stopped kissing her, he said huskily, "You have tried so hard to make me forget my memories. To help me. You have walked all over the countryside to accompany me. You have played with three wet dogs. You have invented the strangest cocktails I have ever tasted. All to make me forget. You—you touch me so deeply, Zoe. I love you. I love you so very much."

"Doesn't that mean you can trust me and talk about what happened to you?"

He hesitated. His deep blue gaze burned into her. Then he shook his head. "I can't do it, Zoe."

THEIR WALTZ CHANGED EVERYTHING—and Zoe didn't know why.

That night, Zoe snuggled up to Nigel in his bed. "Are you sure you don't want to try sleeping together?"

He kissed her and got out of bed. First he poured some brandy from the decanter kept in his room, and he downed the drink in one swallow. Then he paced. Naked, he walked back and forth in front of the fireplace. Finally he said, "Zoe, this is harder for me than I thought."

"What is? Do you mean our marriage?"

He looked so sad. "Even when we make love, I cannot forget the memories that haunt me. For some reason, it makes me feel guiltier. And that makes my memory get sharper."

"Then I'll work harder to make you forget."

"It will not work. I need time to prepare myself to see you. I need time to quell my memories and to try to control the way my body betrays me."

"But that never happens when we make love," she cried. "You never show any signs of having shell shock then."

"I am struggling, though, Zoe. That is when I fight hardest to control it. I do not want to hurt you." He paced again and he didn't look at her. "It takes me a long time to prepare to see you. Hours of ensuring I am in control. That I've pushed any memory that could trigger an incident far back in my brain."

"An incident?" What was he saying?

"What you saw during my nightmare. What I need to do when I am going to see you is prepare for you. Dukes in the past visited their duchesses on a schedule. I'd like to set aside nights and times for lovemaking."

"Like appointments?"

"Exactly like that." He looked at her, his mouth taut and grim.

What could she do? He couldn't give her more. Not yet. She thought this was wrong—but it was what he needed. At least for now.

"All right, I guess," Zoe said.

16
THE ANNOUNCEMENT

AT THE END of the fortnight, it was time to return to Brideswell. The car drove to the train station, and she and Nigel caught a late-morning train to the south. They had a first-class compartment and Zoe wished she could lift up her skirts right there and seduce him. But she had agreed to appointments for lovemaking.

She asked him his plans for Brideswell and Nigel told her about improvements to farms, and cottages in need of roofs. His excitement was sweet. He truly cared about his tenants.

She had a few changes to Brideswell she intended to make. But she wanted those to be a surprise.

"We're coming into the station." Nigel leaned back from the window. To her surprise, he gently kissed her. "Returning to Brideswell with you is the most special moment I've had." Then he blushed. "Other than our wedding. And when we were in the aeroplane—"

He could be so sweet he made her want to cry. She kissed him back, in a long, loving union of their lips.

They disembarked and porters brought their cases. The Daimler whisked them to Brideswell, where Nigel's mother—her mother-in-law—and Julia waited on the drive. Zoe got out and Julia came forward at once to kiss her cheek.

His mother came to him. "Did you have a lovely time? Take many walks?"

Only a mother would ask her son that when he returned from his honeymoon. "Several, once the rain ceased." He offered his arm to his mother. "I must go inside and speak with our steward. Now that we've returned, there's much work to be done. Work that can now be done."

Zoe followed him inside with Julia. He left for his study, and she went with the other women to the drawing room, where the dowager sat, in front of a large silver tea tray.

The dowager's lips were pursed with disapproval. She sipped her tea. "Sebastian has gone to Capri. He left shortly after your wedding."

Nigel's mother, Maria, sighed. "He has gone so far. I fear I won't see him again. That I have lost another of my children—"

"He isn't lost just because he is making his own life," Zoe insisted.

"Living like a bohemian." The dowager sniffed. "An artist—he wants to be an artist."

"What else is a duke's younger brother supposed to do? He is going to be happy. Isn't that what matters?"

"I had thought perhaps he might settle down and wish to enter the church," Maria said. "I wanted that for one of my children. It would not be my church, but it would have been in service to God."

Zoe's brows shot up. "Sebastian? Goodness, the church wouldn't have made him happy. Sebastian loves dancing, music and parties."

"That is true," the dowager said thoughtfully. She looked at Zoe a long time. "But Capri?"

Zoe faced her grandmother by marriage. "I know he will be happy."

"An American would say that is the most important thing."

"And we would be right," Zoe said cheekily.

THE HOUSEKEEPER, MRS. HALL, led Zoe upstairs later that day. "At the duke's instruction, we prepared apartments in the south wing. The wing has not been used for several years. It has been aired, repairs have been made, and decorating has been done per His Grace's request. I trust you will find it satisfactory."

Zoe sensed the housekeeper's tension. Tall and thin, with iron-gray hair pulled back in a no-nonsense style, Mrs. Hall could have been Mrs. Folliat's grumpy sister.

Zoe had watched Father deal with workers, so she knew to take charge. "I will review it now," she said, "and see if anything needs to be changed."

She was led through two corridors. The housekeeper stood respectfully by the door, her hands clasped while Zoe toured her bedchamber and the attached rooms. Her bedroom had large French doors that opened onto a balcony. This view was off the meadows and fields, stretching toward farmland dotted with sheep. She could see a bright yellow spot—her airplane.

A room filled with wardrobes and drawers was attached to hers, decorated with old paneled wood and fading wallpaper. There was a sitting room with a writing desk. She opened a door she expected would lead to Nigel's room. Instead there was another parlor, more sparsely furnished.

Mrs. Hall came up to her from behind as she stood staring.

"His Grace did not want the connecting bedroom prepared for him," the housekeeper intoned. "He insisted you should use it as a sitting room, Your Grace. He chose the next suitable bedroom, farther down the hall."

For one moment the woman betrayed herself. She stared at Zoe with avid curiosity, waiting for her response. Of course the servants wondered why a newly married man would not want the convenience of being beside his wife's bedroom.

In front of the servants, she could not talk about Nigel's nightmares or his shell shock. To do so would be to betray him—she knew he wanted to hide it. "Perfect," Zoe said calmly. "That is exactly what I wanted him to do. I do need heaps of space.

"Everything will be fine for now." She closed the door. "I'll redo that dressing area when I have the bathroom installed."

"Bathroom?" Mrs. Hall stared now, her jaw dropping.

"Yes," Zoe said. "Brideswell is about to get plumbing and electricity."

And a week later, workmen were pouring into Brideswell. The house filled with the sounds of hammers and saws and men shouting to each other.

"Zoe, what is going on?" Nigel came into the morning room while she was writing correspondence.

"I've hired men to put in electric lights." She smiled seductively at him. "And we will now have taps. You're going to be able to take a real bath. We could even take one together."

He looked so stunned, then so pained, her heart

lurched. And she leaped to comfort him. "Of course, I'm only teasing, darling. When you're ready."

THEY STAYED TO their schedule of lovemaking—Nigel came to her room on Wednesday and Friday nights. Each time was exquisite, though the waiting between felt like forever. Until late August, when the entire family traveled north to the hunting box for a shooting party. Twenty additional guests were to arrive, including the Earl of Carleton's family, other cousins of the Hazeltons and friends. Mother sent letters, telegrams and constantly telephoned Zoe, advising her that she had to put the Gifford family on the map. She had to carve out her place as the premier hostess in England.

When they arrived at the house in Berwick-Upon-Tweed, Zoe made a tour of the house and Julia came with her.

"I want to do something more meaningful with life than being a good hostess," Zoe confided to Julia as they walked together through the bedrooms. Zoe was checking to ensure they were ready—she trusted her housekeeper, but knew to make clear that the final approval was hers.

"But I know this house party is important," she added. "It will be the first time Nigel has had so many people in the house for such a long period of time. I know he's nervous—nervous of people seeing his scars." She knew he was afraid of having an episode of his shell shock in front of them. "I need this to go well."

"It will," Julia promised.

Zoe went over the house from top to bottom, ensuring every room looked perfect. She reviewed every menu with Mrs. Folliat. For two days, she spent most of her time outdoors on the drive, greeting guests as they came. Nigel stood with her. She saw his tension in the hard set of his shoulders, the stiff way he stood, the way his hand clenched and unclenched.

Her nerves were on edge.

The first dinner with the house full was a success. But the next morning, when Zoe woke up, she was terribly sick. She grabbed the chamber pot, thankful for once that she had the archaic porcelain pot in her room, and she threw up. Except for when she'd lost Billy, she'd never done that. She was so nervous it was chewing her up inside.

For those first two days she felt brittle every moment.

The afternoon of the second day, the men went out to the shoot in a vehicle called a "hunting brake," the likes of which Zoe'd never seen before. Traditionally the women stayed at the house. Several played bridge. At tea, in the drawing room, Zoe poured, the vision of the perfect hostess.

The dowager took her cup. Zoe felt that horrible spurt of nausea. Why now? Her stomach gnawed with hunger and she picked up a biscuit and nibbled at it. She wanted to eat, but the thought of doing it was awful.

In a group of women, talk inevitably turned to children. Zoe relaxed—in this she had nothing to say.

"Girls these days are so flighty. It is the duty of every bride to ensure there is an heir. Really, some of these girls are more worried about their slender figures than they are about duty!" The speaker was Lady Chawley-Sourpuss, of course. Zoe felt the woman's gaze drop to Zoe's belly. "Of course, it would be *early* for signs of a child on the way."

Zoe opened her mouth to say something sharp—the

woman was determined to find fault with her. Either she was not pregnant and not doing her duty. Or she was expecting and had probably got married because she was pregnant.

But the dowager jumped in before Zoe could say anything. "When a duke marries, there is one question that consumes everyone," the dowager said, lifting her teacup to her lips. "And that is: Is the duchess expecting yet? Of course, no one but the duchess will know—until she is ready to make an announcement."

Every woman in the room—her mother-in-law, Julia, Lady Sourpuss and all the others—all paused. They didn't peer at her, as that would be gauche. But everyone was holding their breath.

"I'm not," Zoe said. "But it isn't because we aren't trying."

Every woman in the room gasped in shock. Zoe felt defiant. They'd wanted her to say something scandalous—and she had.

The dowager's brow rose. She leaned over and whispered so only Zoe could hear, "I am afraid you might be mistaken, my dear."

"I think I would know," Zoe said. "Just as you said."

Zoe poured more tea. She knew she wasn't pregnant, for she'd had light spotting from her courses yesterday. The problem was she and Nigel weren't trying *enough*. She wanted to make love to him every day. Damn this blasted schedule.

At that moment, horns were heard outside. The women rose all at once, for the men had returned from the shoot.

Zoe made a decision—enough of this tension and

empty chatter. She wasn't going to sit with the women tomorrow. She was going to go shooting.

And tomorrow night—the second night of the week he was scheduled to come to her—she was going to convince Nigel to make love to her more often. When they were in bed, and he was kissing her and being intimate with her, she felt closer to him than at any other time. She needed that closeness—especially here, where she felt surrounded by people who didn't like her just because they didn't like watching an American girl take one of their dukes. She was done with the walls between them.

IN THE MORNING, they loaded into several shooting brakes, with shotguns and a picnic luncheon loaded in the backs of the vehicles. Nigel hadn't been pleased with her decision, but recognized she was going to come no matter what he said.

They rattled up a rough, rocky track. Zoe wore trousers and her slim-fitting tweed coat. When the cars could travel no farther, they got out and tramped up a path, carrying the shotguns. The hunting group set up by a pile of boulders. Beaters went ahead, flushing out the birds—thousands were raised on the estate by the gamekeepers for shooting parties. The whir of wings filled the air, followed by shotgun blasts.

In her poor days, Zoe had learned a thing or two about hunting.

She dropped in her cartridges, flicked the shotgun closed and took aim. Two quick blasts brought down two grouse.

She became aware of murmurs among the gentlemen as they watched her shoot. Her skill surprised them.

They admired it, but she felt that snobby tension developing. She shouldered her gun and found Nigel. For several moments she watched him shoot.

"You have very good aim," she said to him when he took a break.

His eyes wore the haunted look. "I have had too much practice with shooting. I find I do not have the taste for it anymore, but grouse shooting is tradition."

She walked up to him. Impulsively, she slipped her arms around his waist and kissed him.

"Langford," shouted his cousin, the earl. "There are birds to be bagged. This is why women should not be on the shoot. Too distracting."

"I've come to challenge him," she called out. "To see who can shoot the most." She threw a bold glance at Nigel.

They continued to hunt, each bagging several birds. She was going to be beaten—which she didn't mind because she didn't want to show up Nigel in front of his friends. But then her husband deliberately missed two shots, making their score even. That, she hadn't expected.

Nigel opened his shotgun. His loader—a young local boy—reached for it, but Nigel shook his head. "I think I will stop now."

Zoe did the same. The sun was dropping in the sky. "We're even," she said. "You could beat me with one more shot—and I do know that you missed on purpose."

"Yes, we are even. There are no winners or losers in a marriage, Zoe. There are no wagers. You made me understand that I am not to shoulder responsibility for you. We are a partnership. Now let's go back to the house for dinner."

"Yes." She smiled at him. "And you do know what tonight is? Our scheduled night for sex."

"Shh," he warned. He actually looked around nervously.

"You do know that making love to me is your duty?" she whispered teasingly. "So you are doing what you are obligated to do—because you are the duke."

She left him then, walking ahead to the vehicles as the servants gathered up the food, the shotguns and the bagged birds.

But he caught up with her, his voice grave when he said, "It's not a duty, Zoe. It's my greatest pleasure."

Thinking of those words, she could barely stand waiting through dinner—with almost thirty people in the dining room. She waited until Nigel rapped on the connecting door to her bedroom.

Zoe sat up as he walked in, letting the covers tumble off her naked body. "I want you to come more often, Nigel," she said.

"Zoe—I cannot."

"We've been together since June. Surely you don't need to find that much control with me now. And why should you—I know the truth. You have nothing to hide from me."

"It's more than that," he said. He undid the belt of his robe. "The summer and fall will be extremely busy. There are improvements to the tenant farms and cottages that have to be finished before winter. I want work to proceed as quickly as possible."

"But we're here, where you can't worry about any of that. There's nothing keeping you out of my bed."

He flushed. "Zoe, I am doing what I can. I am sorry if I'm not as passionate a man as you need." To her shock, he began to retie his belt. "Maybe tonight I should leave—"

"No, you don't." She got out of bed naked and she undid his belt and opened his robe. "I think you are just as passionate as I want."

She led him into bed, but as he got into it with her, he extinguished the lamp. They were plunged into darkness. The bed creaked as he settled beside her.

He could be so scorching with her. So tender, too— sweet and romantic and utterly unlike a cold, autocratic man. But she still felt a distance between them. A wall between them.

She wanted to tear it down.

AFTER THAT NIGHT, Zoe went out on the rest of the shooting days. There was the challenge of gauging the shot, the excitement of finding if her aim was true. She enjoying the shoot, but each day was the same routine. Nigel refused to change their schedule for lovemaking. She knew he was tense from having a house filled with guests, so she conceded.

She yearned for the wild passion he had shown in her airplane. But having people around seemed to make him withdraw more. Now not only did they have standing appointments for sex, but Nigel wanted the lights off.

Their lives were routine; sex had become routine.

When they returned to Brideswell, she was going to make changes—the first one would be that she wanted him to sleep in a room close to hers.

But back at Brideswell, when she woke the morning after they'd returned, she felt sicker than ever.

After a knock on the door, her tray was brought in by her maid, Callie. "It's a lovely fall day, Your Grace, and I've brought your breakfast and your morning papers—" Callie broke off and stopped, clutching the tray. "What's wrong? You look so ill—"

Zoe tried not to breathe. But she couldn't avoid it. One breath sucked in the heavy, intense smell of food—bacon, kidneys, eggs. It smelled of fat and salt and spices. Oh, golly. She clamped her hand over her mouth.

Zoe got out of bed, dropped to her knees on the rug—two hundred years old, the dowager had said—and she grabbed her chamber pot and threw up in it. Once she'd drunk too many cocktails and she'd been sick. She'd hated that feeling. This was worse. There was nothing inside her to come up. And it hurt. Worse, as she sat up and leaned back against her bed, she still felt queasy.

Callie was on her knees, fear in her huge blue eyes. "Are you all right, miss? I mean, Your Grace?"

"I keep feeling nauseous," she muttered.

Callie said, "Oh." Then "Oh! You know what that means, Your Grace. My mother told me that when you're expecting a baby, you can be awfully sick. That's why you don't want any boy getting you in the family way."

Her stomach felt it was sloshing from side to side, and she struggled to follow Callie's flow of speech.

"Maybe you're expecting, Your Grace?"

Zoe wiped her mouth with the back of her hand. Then she wondered if duchesses did that.

"I can't be. I had my monthly flow last week."

"Not very much, Your Grace," Callie said pragmatically. "And it's not unusual to have light courses at the beginning when you're expecting."

Apparently, Callie knew more than she did. But then,

Mother wanted her to act like a lady, and ladies didn't talk about throwing up when you were pregnant.

Zoe groaned and pushed her tangled hair back with both hands. "Maybe I *am* pregnant." Or knocked up, as some of the boys at home—her original home—used to say.

The dowager had been right after all. Zoe looked at the chamber pot. Had the dowager vomited into one of these every morning when she'd given birth to the previous duke? That thought almost made her giggle. "Do I have to go through nine months of this?"

Callie looked startled. "Oh, no, Your Grace. This morning sickness usually only lasts three months. My mother had twelve of us, and eight came after I was seven years old."

"So you know what happens. That's going to be helpful."

"His Grace will be very happy." Callie blushed a little.

"I guess he will be," Zoe said. This was what everyone had been waiting for. This was supposed to be her job, giving the duke an heir.

If it was a girl, they'd probably all be disappointed. Well, if it was a girl, she was going to bring her daughter up to be courageous and strong.

Zoe put her hands on her tummy. Still flat. It was so impossible to believe there was a life growing inside her. She was going to be a mother. Thrilling. Frightening. Exciting.

But at the same time, what would it be like to be pregnant? Mother had worried her whole life about feeding her and Billy when they were poor, and once they had money, what she'd wanted was for Zoe to move up the social scale and marry well.

Zoe refused to be a controlling, dictating mother. She wanted her child to have choices. To have the whole world.

But all the things she loved to do—dancing, flying, driving—she was determined to do them. Being pregnant, becoming a mother, wasn't going to change her.

"Get me dressed quickly," she said to Callie. "I have to tell my husband."

SHE HAD TO go in *search* of her husband.

Nigel had breakfasted early and was somewhere on the estate, but no one knew where. Zoe tried his study and the estate office, then the stables. The groom thought His Grace had ridden to Ashbury Park, one of the neighboring estates.

Armed with directions to Ashbury Park, Zoe drove out of the gate at Brideswell and turned onto the main road, anxious to tell him the news right away. Her car swallowed up the miles to the other house quickly, and she turned in that gate, followed a curving drive. Unlike Brideswell, where a straight drive brought you closer and closer to a huge house, the lane curved around masses of bushes.

She drew up to the house—a regimented house, with a Grecian-style pediment and columns. Not as old as Brideswell, she would guess. Nigel was walking out of the house. He turned back to a tall, slender woman who had bobbed black hair.

For a moment, she thought the woman was Julia.

No, it wasn't. It must be Lady Mary, Nigel's former fiancée.

Lady Mary Denby walked up to Zoe's husband, and he clasped her hands. Lady Mary smiled at him, laughed at something he said. Zoe saw the closeness between them—they had known each other since they were children. They stood there, on the front step, wrapped up in each other.

They had common ground, he and Mary. Probably Mary would let him be the husband he had been raised to be.

Or was there more? Was he still in love with Mary? Was this why Nigel was withdrawing from her?

Her healthy American sense of competition was sparked. She wasn't giving up without a fight.

Zoe smacked the heel of her hand against her horn and sent out a loud blaring sound. Nigel jumped and turned. Lady Mary Denby was the one to pull her hands away, Zoe noted. What did that mean? That he didn't feel guilty?

He saw her, and his lips parted in a brilliant smile.

She rolled her car to a stop by the step. Instead of opening the door, she stood, put her shoe, heel and all, on her leather seat and vaulted over the door. *Like to see you do that, Lady Mary.*

Zoe leaned against her car. "I've got some important news, Nigel." She probably should call him Langford in front of Lady Mary. Too bad she didn't care. "I thought I'd come here to tell you." She glanced toward Lady Mary. "Good afternoon. Did you invite my husband to come and talk about old times?"

"I suggested my husband speak with Langford," Lady Mary said, her placid, cool ladylike smile on her lips. "Running an estate is a new business to him, and I thought he might appreciate some advice."

"Well, I need a few minutes with my husband. Then your husband can have him back."

"Actually, I was leaving to ride home, Zoe," Nigel said.

She realized he was looking only at her. His gaze didn't leave her and go back to Mary.

She suddenly felt terrible for feeling jealous, for feeling…inadequate. "I'll walk with you to the stables." She hadn't planned to give him her news on another woman's turf, but maybe this would be good. Nigel wasn't looking at Mary, but her ladyship couldn't keep her eyes off him. Zoe could see the blatant hunger in Mary's eyes. Apparently she regretted letting him go.

But the next time he came to Ashbury Park, he would remember this was where he'd learned he was going to be a father.

They walked down a gravel path together and she got to the point just as they reached the stable. "Nigel, I haven't yet seen a doctor, but I'm pretty sure that I'm pregnant."

He didn't say a word.

Why not? Suddenly, Zoe realized he was not keeping step with her. She stopped and turned. He was rooted to the path, looking utterly stunned.

"Is it such a surprise?" she asked teasingly. "You Englishmen do know how girls get pregnant, don't you—"

He clasped her waist, lifted her in the air, and she gasped as he dazzled her with the largest grin he'd ever given her.

Then he gently but quickly set her down. "I shouldn't have done that—"

"I'm fine. I'm not going to break, Nigel."

He gathered her in his arms. He held her tightly. "I am so happy, Zoe."

In front of the grooms, Nigel pulled her into a kiss that could have boiled the North Sea. Zoe closed her eyes as she caressed his lips with hers. Tears fell down her cheeks—tears of joy. She was so happy. A baby! And Nigel was so happy, he didn't care about kissing her passionately in public.

This was the most wonderful, wonderful thing.

THE NEXT DAY, Zoe went up to the nursery to assess how it would need to be redecorated.

It was a sunny morning—sunlight spilled in through the paned windows. In the doorway, she stopped.

Nigel was there. Even in the house, he dressed formally—in his suit, waistcoat, tie. But he had taken off his coat and he stood in the light in his shirtsleeves. In his hands, he held a doll, of all things—one with a painted porcelain face. On a small table stood a jumble of toys.

"Have you been searching for toys for our baby?" she asked softly.

He turned and gently put down the doll on one of the cots. There were six of them in two columns, running along the walls. "Yes. I have not been up here for years. It brings back many memories. But you must change the room as you want, Zoe."

"I won't change anything that is filled with good memories for you," she said softly.

"Soon our baby will be in here. We will be making new and wonderful memories of our own." He came over to her and embraced her. "Zoe, thank you for making me so happy."

"It's not all due to me," she said. "You had a very big part in this, too."

"I am nervous about becoming a father. My own father was a typical duke—he cared only about his own pleasures, left us in the hands of nurses and governesses. Then, when Sebastian and I were getting old enough to be sent away to school, my father decided to toughen us up with punishments."

"I'm sorry. I loved my father very much. I love Mother, too, though she drives me crazy."

Nigel smiled at her. "You were very lucky. Your mother obviously adores you. I wish I could have had the chance to meet your father."

"Thaddeus would have liked you very much. He would have admired your sense of responsibility, your bravery in war, the way you care so much for family."

"You make me sound like a very noble man, Zoe."

She giggled. He was blushing. "That's what you are."

"You make my heart soar every time I am with you," he said. She kissed him. His hand touched her hip, lightly brushed her stomach.

"There's nothing to feel yet," she told him. "But there will be soon."

"There are bassinets over there," he said.

She walked over to them—three, with ivory satin lining and delicate lace trim. She couldn't picture Nigel—over six feet tall, strong, grizzled, so very handsome and ducal—in a tiny bassinet. "I will need clothes for the baby."

"We have a christening gown in the family," he said. "Used by all the children, since my grandfather's day."

Laughing, she kissed him again, ready to burst with joy.

She was excited—but over the next two months, her life changed. Nigel wanted her to take care of herself. She attended balls with Nigel, though as a married woman she was expected to just sit and gossip. He didn't want her to fly. He didn't want her to drive. Or ride. He fussed over her. He was not at all austere, but he drove her just a bit mad. He treated her like an invalid and brought her stools to prop her feet on.

But Zoe still wanted to live—whether her husband approved or not, she still rode, drove her car, took Julia to London—just largely in secret.

The worst change of all? For fear of hurting the baby, Nigel wouldn't make love to her.

LIKE EVERY MORNING so far in November, Zoe woke to somber light. But there was something different today. She woke to a house filled with exotic, spicy scents.

Callie came in with her tray, which she could now face without nausea, thank goodness.

Callie put the tray over Zoe's knees. "They're cooking something downstairs, Your Grace. It's a big production. Two kitchen maids are chopping dried fruit, and Mrs. Creedy, the cook, is making something mixing flour and preparing suet. I asked if it was something from India, like when she made curry, but Mrs. Creedy told me off. Said it was the most English thing she could imagine."

It was Sunday, so after breakfast, Zoe dressed for church. Zoe wore tweeds, but not as an Englishwoman would wear them. Her skirt reached just below her knees—modest for her—but it fit trimly to her curves. She wore a tight-fitting jacket with a neckline that plunged and a man's shirt underneath, with the neck open. She wrapped a long fringed scarf around her neck. The country gentry liked to see what the American duchess was wearing, so she liked to dress the part.

In church, Zoe sat beside Nigel, in the Hazelton family pew at the very front. Of course, he sat looking proper and respectful, and though she let her fingers stray and gently touch his thigh, he didn't acknowledge her touch. Which made it all the more fun to do.

After church, she wandered through the aromatic house until she found Nigel at his desk, in his study. Ever since she had announced her pregnancy, he smiled whenever he saw her. But she knew he was restless and wakeful at night.

A week after she'd told him the good news, she had got up to use the chamber pot. She'd heard gruff sobs from Nigel's room. She'd tried the door. It had been locked.

She'd heard the sounds night after night. It had to be over the War. Why couldn't he put it behind him? There was no point asking him—he continued to refuse to speak of it. But she was always aware of it.

She walked up to his desk. "What is Mrs. Creedy cooking that smells so wonderful?"

Nigel looked up. "It's Stir-Up Sunday."

"What is that? It sounds naughty."

"It isn't. This is the day the Christmas puddings are made, on the Sunday before Advent, so they have time to mature for Christmas Day. The reverend spoke of it in his sermon this morning."

She hadn't noticed the sermon since she had been touching Nigel's leg.

"You'll stir it, too," Nigel said.

"The pudding? In the kitchen?"

She didn't believe him. But soon he led her downstairs, where they joined the rest of the family, including the dowager, Nigel's mother, Julia and Isobel.

Zoe had never been in the kitchen before. The walls were stone, the ceiling low. There was the servants' dining room, then an arched opening that led to the kitchen. Along one wall stood an enormous metal oven and stove that gleamed like a mirror. A huge ornate buffet was opposite, filled with china dishes. The two new kitchen maids hurried around—with the money from her inheritance, they had been able to acquire more staff.

A huge metal bowl rested on one of the large wooden tables in the kitchen.

As the duke, Nigel had the privilege of stirring first. He winked at her, took the wooden spoon and stirred. He shut his eyes, and his lips moved, but she couldn't hear what he said.

When he returned, she cornered him. "Did you say a magic incantation?"

"I made a wish. Every member of the family takes a turn to stir the pudding. You make a wish while you do it. Stir only clockwise. Stirring anticlockwise invokes the work of the devil."

"You don't really believe that."

"It's tradition. And no one has ever put it to the test."

She liked this, teasing Nigel. "What did you wish for?"

"Telling you would spoil the wish," he said at first. Then he murmured, "But maybe it was for a healthy, happy baby. And an easy birth."

"I know what I'm going to wish for," she said.

His gaze was wary.

She waited until she had walked up to the large mixing bowl, picked up the spoon and stirred the batter, studded with chopped candied fruit, nuts and raisins. Then she rejoined Nigel. "Maybe," she whispered by his ear, "I wished for you to come to my bed every night and let me exhaust you with pleasure. You could come to me tonight and find out."

He drew her aside as his mother went in to stir next. Maria looked incongruous stirring a pot while wearing a beautiful dress, her hair elaborately marcelled.

Nigel bent close to her. "I shouldn't. In your condition, I shouldn't make you submit to my attentions. And I cannot sleep with you, Zoe. Most definitely not now. If I was in one of my fits and I caused harm to you or our child, I could not forgive myself."

"Nigel, you aren't making me submit. I want you. I miss holding you in my arms." Her voice cracked.

His brows drew together. "All right. I will come to you tonight," he said softly.

A sudden cramping pain went through her belly. "Oh!" Zoe put her hand on her tummy.

"Is something wrong, Zoe?"

"No. I—I don't know. I felt a cramp. I think my skirt is too tight. I will need larger clothes."

He put his arm around her.

"I'm fine, Nigel," she assured him.

"No, you are going upstairs to rest. I insist."

She let him escort her—at least this way she would have him in her bedroom. When they reached her room, she ran her fingers up his chest. "And it is perfectly fine to do it, you know. I asked Dr. Drury," she said.

Shock turned Nigel's face blank. "You spoke to the doctor about—"

"Sex? Yes. Why shouldn't I?" She put her fists on

her hips. "He's a doctor. He assured me, with a lot of embarrassment, we could have 'normal marital relations' during the pregnancy. He was so uncomfortable, I asked, 'What about abnormal ones?' I thought he was going to faint."

Nigel looked just as shocked as the doctor.

"But you can make love to me without harming the baby." She could see on his face he didn't believe her. She sighed. He was so stubborn.

Nigel kissed her hand, apparently not aware the tender, sensual gesture made her ache with desire. "You must rest, Zoe," he insisted. And he took her into her room and tucked her into bed.

SHE STAYED IN bed all afternoon, but more pains came through dinner. Zoe wore a loose, waistless dress of red silk, and she fought to get through the meal, believing the cramps would stop. Then a stab of pain shot through her so sharp and fast, she struggled to push back her heavy chair. She could barely move it—that was why the footmen drew them out—but she stood anyway.

"I'm sorry," she said. "I've just had a sudden pain."

"Oh, my dear." The dowager looked up swiftly and set down her fork. "Have you had these for very long?"

"I had a few just after we stirred the pudding. They are getting worse—" She broke off as one forked through her again and she clutched the back of the chair.

She saw it—the dowager's face, fighting to disguise sorrow.

"What is it?" Zoe gasped. "It's the baby, isn't it?"

"Langford, send for the doctor," the dowager said quickly. "Though I fear there is nothing he can do now. We must take Her Grace upstairs."

There is nothing he can do now. Zoe met the dowager's blue eyes—the same deep clear blue as Nigel's. She didn't need the words. Everything was written in the sympathy on the older woman's face. But she whispered, "I am going to lose the baby, aren't I?"

As the question left her lips, she felt a strange gushing sensation. Her underclothes were wet. It was if she'd let go and wet herself. Another cramp came and her legs almost collapsed.

"What can I do?" she gasped to the dowager. She looked down. A large wet spot showed on the skirt of her dress.

The dowager's chair had been drawn out. Nigel pushed his own chair back without waiting for help.

Zoe felt the dowager's gloved hands on her shoulders. "You must go upstairs, my dear. I do not think there is much we can do until Dr. Drury arrives. And then—"

"Has this happened to you before?"

The dowager looked prim. She lowered her voice, but said crisply, "Not to me, but to the duchess, Langford's mother. She lost three of her babies this way."

"She lost her babies?" Zoe whispered.

More spasms came. They lasted so long Zoe clutched the chair—

Nigel swept her into his arms. Long strides took him to the stairs, and he carried her up as if she were weightless. All the while, the cramps came. Held in his arms, she went through agony.

"Nigel—oh, please, you must stop. Put me down. Oh—"

"No, let me get you to your bed." As though she weighed nothing, he raced up the steps with her, took her to her room. Her sheets flew back—someone tore them out of the way. Nigel laid her gently on her bed.

Another cramp took her. She curled up with it, a sob escaping her. "I can't stand it!"

The dowager came forward and touched Zoe.

"It's too late, isn't it?" Zoe asked her. She knew the dowager would be honest. Blunt.

"I believe once you feel these pains, the poor wee child is gone. That is what we were told. Nothing can be done."

All her life she'd flung herself into risk—when she was the only one who would be harmed.

"What did I do wrong?" She was helpless. She'd always feared being helpless. She had felt this when she'd learned of her brother's death. He had been at war, so far away, and there had been nothing she could do.

Fury flared in Zoe. This wasn't fair. She had to stop it.

NIGEL PRESSED HIS knee into the mattress and leaned over Zoe. He clasped her hand. Brushed her hair back. Her skin was clammy. "It's all right, love. Hold on, love. The doctor will be here soon."

What could he do? He ached to make this stop for her. He couldn't bear seeing her writhe in pain. God, he had been in battle, lost young men to bullets and disease—nothing was as terrifying as this.

"I want it to stop," Zoe begged. "Make it stop. I don't want to lose my baby. Please make these pains stop. They're pushing him *out*."

Her plea fractured Nigel's heart. He had never seen her like this. Zoe was trying to get off the bed. He had to hold her on one side, and his mother held her on the other, to keep her down. She had managed to pull her aeroplane up when the engine stalled—she'd done it with stunning calm.

Now she dissolved into pain, fear, horror. It made his heart almost stop.

He had to do something.

"Where is Dr. Drury?" Nigel demanded, shouting to one of the footmen who stood near the doorway. "Has he arrived yet? Go downstairs and see if he's come. Make sure the bloody car was sent for him. We need him *now*."

17
THE LOSS

MASCULINE VOICES ROSE and fell, and when they grew hushed, Zoe fought terror. Maids rushed in and out, flustered and gasping. When Zoe's eyes opened, between bouts of pain, she saw desperate faces, piles of linen and Nigel—his dark hair in a disheveled mess, his eyes stark with worry, his skin as pale and deathly white as a ghost.

Sweat coated Zoe's chest. Her short hair was wet and stuck to her head. The pains came, and her stomach—her womb—went hard as rock. She kept pushing. She couldn't help it. She didn't want to. She didn't want to push her baby out. It wasn't time.

But she couldn't stop her body.

She clutched at a hand. Nigel's hand clasped hers, firm and strong. "I can't stop pushing," she cried.

Someone took her other hand—it was her mother-in-law, who tried to soothe her. "You must relax, *ma petite.*"

Nigel's mother had also seemed so fragile and ghost-like. But now her grip was strong, and her voice was filled with passion and command. She clutched her mother-in-law's hand.

"You went through this," Zoe gasped. "I'm so sorry.

But it can't be true. There can't be no hope—" She broke off and cried out.

Voices babbled at her. Nigel tried to soothe her. A deep voice said, "You must breathe, Your Grace. Please try to relax, Your Grace."

It was Dr. Drury. As he leaned over her other side, Nigel's mother moved aside, and Zoe reached for him desperately.

"I don't want to lose my baby," she begged. "Please, can't something be done? *Please*."

"Stay calm, Your Grace," the doctor said, sounding terribly stern and so concerned it made Zoe sob.

"I can't. I can't," she cried. "Won't you listen? Make this stop."

"Your Grace, we cannot make it stop now. We have to see it through."

"I have a fortune. A *fortune*." Her shrill tones hurt her own ears, but she was desperate. "I'll pay anything. Give you anything if you can save my baby."

"Your Grace, I am afraid it is not a matter of money."

"Then what's the point?" she cried. "What's the point of millions if they can't save a child?"

"Zoe, calm yourself." Nigel stroked her hand, gently, lovingly.

"No! I am not going to be ladylike now. I don't care if I'm a damned duchess. To hell with that!"

"Can you save the child?" That was Nigel, his voice raw and strained. Then his voice cracked. "Will Zoe be all right?"

The doctor drew Nigel back, and she tried to cling to her husband's hand, but he was forced to let her go.

"Yes," Drury said. "There should be no danger to

Her Grace. But the baby cannot be saved. She is miscarrying. I am afraid it means the baby is already dead."

Already dead? Perhaps he thought she couldn't hear over her own cries and screams, but she could.

Nothing could be done, as the dowager had said. She had clung desperately to hope but now it all dissolved and rushed out of her heart. She felt weak, drained, empty. "Why?" she cried. She screamed as her womb tightened again, and she doubled up with pain. "Why does my body do this if my baby is gone?"

The doctor leaned over her. "Your water has broken, Your Grace. Now your body will deliver the child naturally."

"The baby is going to be born? I don't understand. You said the baby was gone."

Dr. Drury turned to Nigel. Lamplight glinted on his round spectacles. He spoke low again, but she heard him. "Her body has to expel the deceased fetus, Your Grace. There will be less pain than a normal birth. She will have strong contractions, but I assure you it will not last long."

Through a haze of agony, she saw Nigel's face. Saw the slash of pain at Drury's words.

"What can I do, Doctor?" he asked.

"Support her through it. I would normally send you away, Your Grace. But for this, perhaps your presence is helping."

What could help? She clung to Nigel's hand, but there was nothing that would help her.

She sobbed. Her body had betrayed her. She was going through with a birth that was hopeless.

Crying out, she arched up. Pain racked her. All this, all this, and her precious darling baby would not live.

"Why did it happen?" Nigel implored Drury. "Have we done something wrong?"

Had *she* done something wrong? That was what Nigel must mean. That had to be it, wasn't it? She drove too fast. Rode too much.

"It could be many reasons," Drury said, in his brusque manner. "The most likely one is that the infant was not developing properly. There was some defect, something so severe that the child would not have survived anyway. No one did anything wrong." Then Drury seemed to remember where he was and he added, "Your Grace."

She arched on the bed, screamed. She squeezed Nigel's hand.

Pure panic showed in Nigel's eyes. "Zoe, Zoe."

Would their baby have had blue eyes? Tears streamed down her face. She felt them pour over her lips.

"Soothe her, Your Grace. Try to distract her from the contractions."

His hand caressed her cheek. He took a cloth and wiped at her tears.

The strongest urge to push overtook her. Her muscles all worked together. A slippery, gushing sensation came from her.

"There. We have the wee mite now," the doctor said. "The rest will follow after."

Dimly, Zoe saw the doctor do something on the bed, between her legs. He held a small bundle in a piece of white cloth.

She was tired. So tired. But she held out her arms. "Let me see the child."

"No, Your Grace—" Drury began.

"Please. I must see him." She was so certain it was a boy.

The doctor hesitated.

"I have to see him. I have to know. I have to say goodbye." Tears spilled down her face again, hot and sticky.

Dr. Drury looked to Nigel. "I don't advise it, Your Grace."

He would side with the doctor. After all, she was a wild, brash American with no ideas of what was proper.

"If Zoe wishes to see the child to say goodbye," Nigel said, "I will have to insist on it."

Zoe couldn't quite believe it—that Nigel had agreed with her. "Thank you," she whispered.

The blanket was held in front of her, wrapped around a small bundle. With all the swaddling, it was slightly bigger than her hand. She supported it, opening the folds of the blankets with weak, shaking hands.

A tiny little creature, wet and mottled red with blood, lay in the hollow of the stained white sheet. Her child. Smaller than the palm of her hand. The size of a pea pod. But there was a tiny head. Small, curled-up hands. Little legs folded together. Oh, God—a tiny nose and delicate closed eyelashes. Little fingers.

A perfect little child who had no chance to know life. She gazed down through a veil of blurring tears. "Hello, little one," she whispered, the words croaking and catching.

She gazed up at Nigel. "We will wrap him up—I want him to be comfortable. I want to have him buried. With a marker. So I can go and see him—"

The tears were too strong. They strangled her voice,

cut off her words and her breath. She had to give in to them.

Sobs racked her; tears streamed down her face. Nigel's hands took their baby and his blanket out of hers.

She looked at him again. Nigel stared down at their child. His face was blank, utterly without expression. He looked as though he was carved from stone.

Then he said, "We had a son. He was so beautiful. So precious and small."

Was he angry? He must feel rage, as she did. But his face showed nothing.

She was so furious with herself. She hated her body. How could it have done this? She didn't believe the doctor. Look at their tiny child. He was so perfect. There could not have been anything wrong with him. Her body had done this terrible thing.

"...must rest," Dr. Drury said. "The remaining placenta will be delivered. It could be hours. Bleeding could be heavy for several days, then turn to a spottier discharge..."

Numbly, she fought to listen to Dr. Drury.

"Drury, this is not the time. Zoe has had a great shock. We will discuss later what is to be done."

She looked up at Nigel. He looked ducal as he spoke to the doctor—cold, collected, in control.

They had lost their child!

It was as if ice had formed over him. But she knew what it meant—it wasn't that he didn't feel anything. Nigel withdrew to avoid pain. She shivered at his frostiness. If he was this cold, his heart must be completely broken.

She saw surprise in Drury's eyes. "You are bearing

up admirably, Your Grace," the doctor said quietly. "Her Grace will need your strength."

Drury had no idea. Inside, Nigel had to be crumbling apart. Just as she was.

She hadn't meant to lose their child.

Then Nigel looked down at her. Suddenly he lifted her in his arms. "Have the bed stripped and remade at once. The duchess must rest."

He held her in his arms while the servants bustled. Her dress had been pulled off her, but she wore a white shift, soaked with red blood. Her thighs were streaked with it. The red splotches seemed to whirl in front of her eyes.

She fought to not faint.

Maids rushed to tear off old sheets, replace them with clean ones. Nigel sat her on the edge of her bed, and the doctor withdrew as Callie changed her. Zoe wiped listlessly at her legs with a wet cloth, taking off some of the blood. But she didn't care.

Her legs shook, but she grasped her bed column and tried to stand. "Where is our baby?"

"He's been taken away, Zoe." Nigel's large body was in front of her, so she could not get off the bed.

"Where? Where has he gone?"

"Drury has taken him. We have to…arrange for the burial. But you must rest, Zoe."

"There are things I must do. I want—I want to wrap our poor son in a blanket. I want to know he's warm. We must name him. We should give him a name. I don't want a grave marker that has no name. It isn't right."

"Shh. We will think of all that in the morning. For now, you must sleep."

"What is the point of that? It won't make things go away."

Tenderly, he kissed her forehead. He gently arranged her so she was lying on her fresh bed, and he pulled the covers up. "Please rest. Just rest. For me."

She kept arguing; Nigel kept insisting. She felt weaker and weaker. Soon she didn't have the strength to talk anymore. She closed her eyes.

Her last realization was that she was still crying. Tears still trickled to her cheeks, even as she drifted off to sleep.

ZOE WOKE TO one blessed moment of confusion. Then her memory of the evening flooded her. She jerked up in bed. It was still dark—there was no hint of light around her curtains. The swift movement hurt her belly, and she put her hand there. There had been only the smallest thickening of her middle. It was still there, but inside she was empty.

Rest. They—Drury, Nigel—had told her to sleep. But she couldn't sleep away pain. She had never been able to do that.

Gingerly, she got out of bed. Her bare feet sank into the softness of the rug beside her bed. Tomorrow she would use the telephone and tell Mother her little grandson was gone.

Everyone who had known about the baby, who had greeted the announcement of her pregnancy with joy, would have to be told the news.

This hurt so much. How did people survive losing a child after they had held their babies, or who had watched a child learn to walk, or speak, or had seen their precious child begin to grow?

There was no forgetting, was there? It would be terrible to forget. Just as with her brother, she must do her duty and never forget.

She needed a goal, for when she had a goal, she rushed onward and had no time to look back.

Zoe pulled open the drapes. Moonlight illuminated the grounds of Brideswell. It was late November—the trees now looked skeletal; the gardens had gone dormant. Condensation ran down the windowpanes like tears.

On her vanity sat a decanter of sherry. Someone had put it there. She sipped some, letting it heat her dry, aching throat.

She heard a muffled sound. Or thought she did. Lifting her head, she faced the open door that led to her parlor. Nigel's room was on the other side. Zoe heard another soft sound. He must be awake.

Did she want to see him? He must be angry and in pain. But she had to face him sometime.

She pulled on her robe, tied a lackluster knot with heavy hands and walked into her dressing room. The door was open to his bedroom and she stood on the threshold of his room, in the darkness. Moonlight spilled into Nigel's room.

The sight before her hurt her deeply.

He sat at his writing desk, elbows on the blotter, his head resting in his hands. "Oh, my God," he muttered. "My child. My little boy."

He was sobbing. Great, shuddering sobs that racked his shoulders.

That was why he'd shown no expression. He had been fighting to hold in his pain and grief. Fighting not to cry.

She couldn't go to him. How could she? Dr. Drury had insisted it was not her fault; it was not Nigel's. That the baby had died because he simply could not survive. But when she had seen the baby, he had looked…perfect.

She didn't know how to offer any comfort or solace to Nigel. What could she give?

She drew back and walked back into her room.

Slowly, she sank to the edge of her bed. Her body felt both heavy and empty. She stared at her bare feet. She swung them, for her bed was so high, her feet didn't touch the ground.

A little boy would have loved to do this—swing his feet, play on a bed.

She put her hand to her mouth to smother the sound of her tears, but a cramp shot through her stomach. Then another. And another.

Oh, God.

She cried out with them. Nigel burst through from the door to her dressing room. Her bedroom door flew open and Nigel's mother rushed in, along with maids. Drury followed, rolling up his sleeves. In another bout of pain and shock, she got rid of the placenta.

Nigel wiped her forehead with a wet, cool cloth. And this time they listened to Drury as he explained what would follow. She would have more bleeding. It could last for days, but eventually it would stop.

Zoe couldn't speak for the pain in her throat, the tightness. In a few weeks, all trace of their lost little boy would be gone.

She awoke again in the morning, woke to another gray day. She woke knowing the pain of grief. The dry, raw throat. The listless, heavy beat of her heart. The weight of pain shoving down on her shoulders.

It would kill her, this grief. Kill her unless she fought it.

18
BRIDESWELL AT CHRISTMAS

THE HOUSE SMELLED of the tart, fresh scent of pine. Preparations for Christmas at Brideswell had begun.

Zoe went downstairs, wearing a long tweed skirt, a cardigan, a scarf around her bobbed hair. She had thrown herself into Christmas decorating. The busywork ensured she had less time to think.

It had been more than three weeks since her miscarriage. She believed she'd stopped bleeding—it was two days since she'd seen spots. She no longer felt physical pain. But every moment she wished it hadn't happened. Wished she was having Christmas with the gift of a baby growing inside her.

Nigel had insisted she be treated like a delicate patient, but she could not stand lying in bed any longer. If she behaved like an invalid, she had nothing to do but *think*.

Arms crossed over her chest, Zoe walked from room to room, watching dark green garlands of pine boughs and holly be hoisted up by the maids and footmen and secured over doorways and windows. Maids giggled as they saw mistletoe go up over doorways in the drawing room.

An enormous tree had been brought into the main hallway—the top of it stood higher than the railings of the gallery, so it could be reached from there to be decorated. In a vast flurry of movement, servants hurried about with ribbons and garlands and wreaths and boxes of ornaments wrapped in tissue.

Every moment Zoe was filled with a yearning to smile and cry. She walked to the window and traced the condensation running down the panes.

Outside the windows, snow blanketed the lawns and the gardens. Snow had fallen heavily all week. It made the trees look as if they'd been iced in white marzipan.

If only she could be standing here hoping to one day look out and see their son playing in the snow.

She thought of Nigel launching boats for his nephews. She could imagine him laughing as his son tossed snow at him.

Her heart twisted in her chest and tears came, as if they'd been wrung out of her heart. Quickly she brushed them away. The ache in her heart was terrible—she couldn't stand it anymore. Once she was sure she could control her tears, she turned away from the window.

She walked around the tree, assessing it. Since electric lighting had been installed at her direction, the tree would be decorated with lights that could be plugged in. No doubt it would shock the dowager and her mother-in-law, but it would be beautiful.

Planning the tree had felt good. Productive. Maids began to hang the glass balls on the tree—Zoe took some and helped, pointing where some should be moved.

But the moment she pictured her son holding up an ornament, wanting to put it on the tree "by self," as she used to demand, she knew she must do something else.

She left the maids to the tree and hurried away. She

found Julia in the dining room, giving directions. One of the maids squealed and Zoe turned. A garland of evergreen boughs tumbled from the doorway and fell to the floor. The girl was covering her hair and her cap with her hands, trembling on the top of a step stool.

She got down with shaky legs.

Zoe scooped up the end of the garland, held it above her head and began to march up the steps. The maid gasped and grasped the side of the stool. "No, Your Grace. You mustn't do that."

Julia rushed over and reached for the garland. "We'll have the footmen put these up. Zoe, you shouldn't be up there."

"Please don't fuss over me." Zoe sighed. "I really don't want it. It's not that I've not appreciated everyone's kindness and concern. It's just that I do not want to be considered fragile any longer."

"But, Zoe, Nigel will have my head if I don't take care of you," Julia protested.

"Nigel refuses to see that I need to do something other than lie in a bed." Though she might want to lie in a bed if she could do it in Nigel's arms. But that did not happen. He hadn't come to her and held—just simply held—her since she'd lost the baby.

Frustrated, she tramped down the steps, her heels clattering on them. She handed the garland to one of the young footmen—Ben, a local farmer's son. Zoe waved it away and remained standing, but still the new young parlor maid, Gladys, brought the silver tea tray for her.

Obviously she was supposed to sit and drink tea and watch the world, not take part in it. These were Nigel's instructions to the staff.

She couldn't *stand* doing that.

She knew Nigel had been the one to insist she be fussed over. Why didn't he listen to her?

"You really should sit and rest." Julia removed the lid off a box, took out a delicate glass-ball ornament and began to thread a ribbon through the loop to hang it. "When is your mother to arrive?"

"In two days." Zoe held in a shudder. She wasn't ready for Mother's visit. When she had telephoned to tell Mother about the miscarriage, Mother had howled over the phone. It hadn't helped. But to take care of Zoe, Annabelle Gifford was determined to come and be with her over Christmas. Mother was sailing on a more southerly route, then traveling by train.

"Are you all right, Zoe?"

"No. I know it is going to be terrible with Mother. She will fuss. She will talk about it all the time. I want to move on."

"We will keep her occupied. There are so many things to do at Christmas—collecting the Yule log, caroling, games, exchanging gifts...."

Again that awful thought came to Zoe: it would have been so sweet to have welcomed Christmas knowing that for the next one, they would have a baby.

Her heart squeezed so tight she couldn't draw breath. She didn't want anyone to know. Zoe couldn't bear being ushered up to her room. She couldn't bear Nigel insisting that she rest. She couldn't argue with him— that was the problem. She couldn't have sharp words with him, because he looked so grim and haunted and unhappy.

But if he kept pushing her—if he kept insisting she do nothing, she was going to snap and she was going to fight with him.

And she didn't want that. The thought of it was like a fifty-pound weight crushing her heart.

Julia frowned at Zoe's silence. "I've been trying to think of a gift for Nigel. I can't think of one."

No one knew enough of what was in Nigel's heart, Zoe saw, to know what kind of present he would like.

But she shook her head. "Perhaps something light-hearted. A jazz recording. Something that will make him forget, even for a little while; something to make him smile. When I look at him, I know he's remembering. All the time—" She broke off.

That, she hadn't meant to say out loud. She couldn't even bear to think it.

"Zoe, I—"

"He can't forget the War. I know he won't be able to—to put this behind him. He barely speaks to me...." She took a deep breath. "But I know when I look at him that is what he is thinking of."

"Oh, Zoe, I'm so sorry."

That was what tormented her. They had been slowly building happiness between them—the joy of the baby, the time they had waltzed on their honeymoon, their intimacy. When he looked at her now, he wasn't thinking of kissing her, of being intimate, of learning to fly. He must be thinking of how much he'd lost.

It was what she thought of when she looked at him—she thought of how she wanted to be happy with him, how she wished they were celebrating a baby coming, how she wished there wasn't so much pain in his eyes. When their eyes met, that was what they shared now—deep, hard pain.

IN THE LATE AFTERNOON, as the sun dipped and long blue shadows fell over the snow, Zoe put on heavier walking shoes, a wool cloche hat, a long coat, a long skirt and woolen stockings—Julia had insisted she needed all these things to walk outdoors in the winter.

She was going to slip out through the French doors onto the west terrace when she heard someone clear his throat behind her and she jumped. "Where are you going?" asked a commanding, masculine voice. "It is freezing outside and the walks are slippery. *You* are not to go outdoors."

Zoe spun around. Her husband stood there. "I have to go outdoors. I want to see—to go to our son's grave. I haven't even seen it yet. I've rested and rested and I can't stand it anymore."

He didn't come closer to her. Instead, he paced on the rug, near the fireplace and its roaring fire. But despite fires, Brideswell always felt as if the walls were breathing cold on her.

"I know you have not seen it yet, but now is not the right time. It's the coldest day of December so far, and we've had snow, then rain, and now everything has frozen solid." Nigel raked back his hair. "Zoe, you look pale and tired. It is too early for you to be up and about."

"I'm pale because I've been kept in my room like the madwoman in *Jane Eyre*. Every time I've tried to do anything, someone stops me."

"Everyone is worried about you."

"I am worried about me most of all. I feel so different. It is as if I barely remember the woman I was only one month ago."

He flinched. She saw how different he looked. That was one thing with him avoiding her—the changes she saw in him were not incremental to her. "I feel empty and lost," she said. *I'm sure you do, too. I know you do.*

I hear you cry, even though you lock your door to me now. "I'm afraid to feel like this. I don't want to be this empty, sorrowful person. I don't want to look at you and think only of our loss. I keep thinking there must be a way to go back."

"There is not, Zoe. I know."

"I can't erase what happened, but I can't live as if I'm dead. And I can't fight the emptiness and pain unless I begin to do things. Deep inside, I feel too tired to try to do anything. My body feels heavy and weak. But I don't want to become a listless, useless female who does nothing but drape her body on the couch. If I have nothing but my thoughts and my pain, I will go mad."

He jerked his head up. "All right. But I do not want you walking on your own. I will take you to our son's—our son's marker."

She waited while he dressed in a long wool coat, a scarf—his "muffler"—a tall hat and leather gloves. They went out the front door, and Nigel took her hand and tucked it in the crook of his arm.

They were going to see the grave of their baby and she couldn't talk about it. "You collect the Yule log tomorrow, don't you?" she asked. "On Christmas Eve day. Julia told me you light the log and it is supposed to burn all through Christmas. And at night, there is caroling and the midnight mass. I intend to do all these things tomorrow."

"No, you will not. It will be too tiring."

"I am fine, Nigel. I'm strong. And I want to be a part of your traditions." *I want to be a part of your life.* They walked to the quaint stone chapel that had been built for Nigel's mother. Beyond it was a little churchyard, covered in a blanket of shiny, frozen snow. Dollops of snow sat on the ornate stone marker.

Flowers sat in a stone vase at the headstone—a bouquet of roses from Brideswell's greenhouses in spring colors of yellow and pink and unique gold. They were fresh, and a white ribbon held them together.

She hurried forward and almost lost her balance. But Nigel was there and he caught her, putting his arm around her waist, and when she skidded again, he had to draw her against his chest to keep her upright. Her cheek brushed the wool of his coat. He smelled of Brideswell—pine, smoke, eternity—and he also smelled like Nigel.

His touch left her breathless. She had longed for this—just to touch him and hold him. Zoe didn't straighten and regain her balance. She let her body relax against his, and she let her cheek feel the beat of his heart, muffled by his coat.

If only—

Sorrow welled up, and she couldn't turn and look at the piece of cold stone that marked the little boy who had never had a chance to live.

What was she going to do? Drown in pain? She was so afraid—losing her brother and losing Richmond had been awful. But this was a pain that seemed to have seeped even deeper into her heart and her soul.

"I want to do Christmas things," she said defiantly. "I want to walk through the village and sing carols and drink rum punch and mulled wine and get drunk so I can't think. But, oh, God, Nigel, I can't think of Christmas without thinking of a little boy who would one day be excited to have a stocking and to open his presents."

"I know."

"I feel so trapped—trapped between wanting to do nothing but hurt and wanting to break free. I can't stand feeling so *trapped*."

"I know, Zoe. Look at you—you're freezing and you're shivering."

It wasn't the winter air making her cold. "I can't hide in bed forever. Whether you like it or not."

"No. In battle, there were so many men I couldn't save. And I couldn't save our son. But I *will* take care of you."

She was about to protest again, but then she did the worst thing possible—she sniffled and sneezed.

NIGEL PICKED ZOE up into his arms, against her protests, and carried her back toward the house. She felt so light in his arms. She'd lost weight. She had been so slender before; she'd had no weight to lose. It was proof the loss had hurt her, and she did need his protection and care.

The day had been cloudy after rain, and the small amount of sunlight was fading. The dampness in the air shot through his skin. It must be freezing her.

Zoe. Darling Zoe.

He'd dreamed of a good Christmas—his first Christmas with Zoe, looking forward to the birth of their baby. He'd pictured taking her caroling, walking at her side and singing. He'd imagined rolling up his shirtsleeves to help fetch the Yule log. He'd imagined Christmas Eve with the tree twinkling and a roaring blaze in the fireplace and Zoe in his arms. Both of them talking of the things their child would grow to enjoy—the excitement of gifts, crackers, sweets.

This was pain like he had never known. The only

way he could survive it was to think of Zoe—to help her, take care of her.

Now when he looked at the tree, the decorations, he felt stabbing grief.

He had been afraid to touch her—she'd looked so ill after the miscarriage. He had been afraid to kiss her, because she had to be so heartbroken. He had wanted to both leave her alone and give her privacy, but also hover over her and give her everything she needed.

He loved holding her in his arms. Cradling her.

She was determined to push herself—she'd told him she had to grasp life to survive grief.

But she wasn't ready yet. He was sure of it.

"Nigel, I don't need to be carried right up to my bed," she argued as they crossed the threshold into the house.

He did not answer. He just took her there. She was his responsibility.

He tucked her into bed in her shift so she could warm up, rang for her maid and summoned tea to be brought to her room, taking leave of her so she could rest. As he reached the foyer, Nigel saw the glitter of the tree, the sparkle of the electric lights on the tinsel garlands. Zoe had orchestrated its decoration—it glowed and sparkled as if it had been made by angels.

Close to him hung one of his favorite ornaments—a sugar mouse of icing sugar and egg white, colored pink, with a yarn tail. He'd loved them as a young boy and he knew his son would have adored them, too.

His heart wrenched so hard in his chest he staggered.

"Nigel, oh, my dear, you look terrible." The soft voice belonged to his mother. She came forward into the salon.

She looked frail—Zoe had been thin and pale, but

he saw now the inner strength that Zoe exuded. Even downtrodden, Zoe fairly sparkled with verve.

"It is very hard, isn't it?" Mama said.

"Yes." It came out gruff, choked.

"For Isobel, I had to take great care, Nigel. I had to lie in bed for my last three months with my feet elevated. I was afraid I would lose her. I lost three children. You were away at Eton when those losses happened." She sighed. "Zoe is so spirited. I wonder if that is what happened."

"You think Zoe lost the baby because she is spirited? I don't understand."

His mother's sad green eyes gazed at him. "Well, I just mean that Zoe may be one of those women who must take care and do absolutely nothing while she is expecting a child." Gently, his mother said, "You will try again. For another baby."

He hadn't even thought about that. He was wrapped up in the loss. "Yes. Eventually."

"You must take great care then. To make certain she does not lose another baby."

He nodded. He would do whatever it took to take care of Zoe.

THE DAIMLER DROVE UP the driveway and pulled up at the front door. Zoe looked out from a window. Nigel had forbidden her from going outside merely because last evening she had sneezed and he was sure she was too delicate to take any risks.

Nigel was outside to greet her mother, as was his mother and Julia, Bartlet and Mrs. Hall, the housekeeper. Mother rushed out, draped in furs. Annabelle

Gifford blew kisses to everyone and embraced Nigel's mother, then Nigel.

Oh, no, she was not ready for Mother. Tallulah Bankhead had nothing on Mother for theatrics. She didn't have long before her mother found her, of course.

She was in the morning room, which tradition dictated was not supposed to be used in the afternoon. But Zoe had said, "Damn that," and she ordered a fire in it every day because she preferred it to the parlor.

Mother burst into the room like a twister. "Zoe! Zoe, my darling, how you have suffered!" Of course, Mother did not stop there. She went on, "The duke must be disappointed."

Tears welled. If Zoe stayed angry and cool and sarcastic, she didn't cry. "Disappointed? Mother, it's broken his heart. It's broken mine."

"Well, what you must do is become pregnant again. As quickly as you can."

"Pregnant *again?*"

"Yes. Give the duke an heir and he will surely forget this—"

"How can you say that? I can't replace my son. I can't erase him either." Fury and pain swamped her. Zoe grabbed her cigarette case and pulled one out. She lit it with shaking fingers—she rarely smoked. But she wanted to break *something,* so a cigarette would have to do.

"I didn't break a vase, Mother, and can't go and buy another. I don't want to! And Nigel certainly doesn't touch me. Unless you can have an audience with God and suggest an immaculate conception, I am not going to have another pregnancy for quite a while. And it's been only *a month.* Maybe you think that's enough time before I plot how I'm going to conceive another heir, but I don't."

She spoke coldly, but she hurt inside. Duty. Position. Brinkmanship. She didn't care about any of that. She wanted a child because she wanted a child. Not a future duke, not insurance for her position, not someone that Mother could show off.

"Zoe, this is coming between you and the duke."

"Everything is always coming between Nigel and me." The War. His nightmares. His refusal to tell her anything. His desire to order her around. This loss…

"He doesn't have any reason to—to blame you, Zoe? You did eat properly, didn't you? You weren't trying to stay too thin? You didn't drink too much? Or behave too wildly?"

"I was being the perfect duchess, Mother. I didn't do *anything* wrong." But she had gone flying, driving. And she had barely eaten for the first three months. Had she done things wrong?

Mother embraced her. "I am not being heartless when I tell you to have another child. Your heart is broken, and there is nothing that helps heal a broken heart as having a child to love."

"You—you aren't suggesting it because I'm supposed to produce an heir—because you just want a grandchild to be a duke?" At her mother's expression, Zoe ached with guilt. "I'm so sorry. That was what I thought. That you were worried about social position—" She broke off. Her throat seemed to be closing shut, filled with tears. "Oh, Mother, I don't know. I am afraid. What if I try again and the same thing happens?" she asked desperately.

"It won't, Zoe. Of course it won't."

Christmas Day

CALLIE CAME INTO her room with a silver tray—with tea and something that smelled spicy, rich and delicious. "Cook sent up mince pies this morning, Your Grace. She said it was a hearty treat for Christmas."

"You have it, Callie. I can't face more than a cup of tea." Zoe hadn't thought Christmas Day would hurt so much. It was supposed to be a time of joy—

But so many people faced it with sorrow in their hearts. And they survived.

Zoe knew she could survive. But she hated the pain.

Callie popped a small mince pie in her mouth—the entire thing. Zoe poured tea, cupped it with both hands and sipped it. Not a ladylike way to drink it. She shivered. "The room is freezing. I should have insisted upon installing central heating as well as the telephone and electric light."

"This house is dreadful cold, Your Grace," Callie agreed. "The servants insist that in January I'll have to crack the ice of your washing basins in the morning. That can't be true!"

Ice coated her windowpanes, water ran down the inside, and every small movement put her skin in contact with sheets cold despite her body's warmth.

This was one of the reasons she wanted to share a bed. She should be waking on Christmas morning curled up in a bed made warm by Nigel.

She closed her eyes and thought of doing that, with a baby still inside her, with his hand caressing the bump of the baby beneath her nightdress.

God, it hurt.

"I suspect it is true, Callie." She finished her tea,

slipped out of the chilly bed. The cold of the floor seeped into her feet even though she stood on a rug. But she suspected most of the cold she felt was on the inside.

She dressed quickly in a skirt and long-sleeved blouse, slipped on a cardigan and went downstairs.

Nigel was there, in front of the Christmas tree. They had no houseguests besides Mother—Nigel had insisted that no additional relatives or friends come while she was recovering. He stood immediately.

She wished she could run to him and kiss him.

"Good morning," he said, very stiffly.

"Merry Christmas, Nigel." Her greeting sounded just as awkward.

"Merry Christmas, Zoe."

"I wanted—I so wanted to be thinking of a future with a child today," she whispered. "A child who would be so excited by Christmas—"

"Zoe, don't. Please. We should not do this today—not today of all days."

She needed to talk about it—it was like a live thing inside her, this pain. He looked haunted and vulnerable. She smiled at him. It was a forced smile, but she tried. "After breakfast, we exchange gifts, I think. That's what Julia told me. I have the perfect gift for you, you know."

Good Lord, Nigel's eyes looked haunted.

"If you didn't get a gift for me, it doesn't matter," she said lightly. "You look so worried. But I am just so excited for you to see what I got you."

"Zoe—I am sorry. This is not going to be a very happy Christmas for you. I cannot do that—I cannot forget about the loss. I cannot grasp this day as you can."

"Try," she said. "We can't change things." She wanted to speak to him of having another child. Mother was right—she did have room in her heart to share grief and joy.

But she knew she had to wait. He looked as if pain was strangling him.

"Merry Christmas, my darling," a voice gushed, and the scent of gardenias whirled around both her and Nigel.

It was Mother. Mother put a small amount of food on her plate and secured a chair beside Nigel. Mother wore a slim-fitting long skirt of satin and an intricate velvet top, along with jewels around her neck. She wished Nigel a merry Christmas, then said to him, "The best tonic for your sorrow would be to bring joy into your life. You must try for another."

Zoe gaped. "Mother!"

"This is what I must do? Thank you, Mrs. Gifford, for giving me so painful a direct order." With that, Nigel stood, bowed and left.

"Mother." Zoe glared. "Don't push him."

But watching him go, she realized she did want another baby. His baby. She wanted one dearly. Intensely. Just like the way she wanted to fly—it was a yearning in her soul.

She had to make Nigel see it was what they needed to do.

After breakfast, the family grouped in the drawing room: herself and Nigel; the dowager; Nigel's mother, Maria; Julia; and Isobel. The huge Yule log burned in the enormous fireplace. Zoe was about to suggest they open presents—anything so she wouldn't think about Nigel's sorrow and their loss.

But the dowager set down her tea. With a sigh. "This is the first Christmas I have ever had without Sebastian. Of course, I had four without you, Nigel, but you were at war."

Oh, golly, she didn't want him to think about the War today. "Let's open gifts," Zoe declared. She grasped one from under the tree. It was Nigel's gift from her. She handed it to him and watched as he opened it. He lifted the leather flying helmet, then the goggles.

"There's more," she said.

He lifted up a photograph and frowned at it. "It's a picture of an aeroplane."

Zoe met his blue gaze. "I'm going to buy you that airplane and teach you how to fly."

"No, you are not," Nigel said shortly. "You are supposed to take care of yourself."

"I have done. Now I am ready to do things again."

"I forbid it."

Zoe's stomach felt as if it had dropped away. Julia, his mother, his grandmother and Mother stared back and forth between them.

"Flying again would make me happy."

"The thought of you flying does not make *me* happy, Zoe." He looked at her, and the autocratic expression vanished. His eyes softened. "Please."

She feared he would do this every time she wished to do something. But her heart lurched at the look in his eyes. It was love. Despite their loss, he still did love her. "All right."

"Open your gift," he said.

He gave her a slim gold-covered box. She opened it. A necklace of sapphires glittered. "I had no idea what to get you," he said awkwardly. "My jeweler suggested this piece."

"It's lovely." But if he didn't know, why hadn't he

asked her? The necklace was beautiful, she had to admit. He'd wanted to surprise her and it was very sweet.

Mother came over to her side and gushed, of course.

But she would have wanted something he'd thought over himself. Had he not been able to do that because he was so filled with pain?

She wanted to feel close to him again—like the time they'd danced to the gramophone, the wonderful times when they'd made love. She knew now what she truly wanted for Christmas—

The rest of the presents were torn open in a flurry. Zoe had bought Isobel a book on anatomy. The dowager took one look and had to be restored with sherry. She'd got the dowager a diamond brooch of an owl, for the dowager reminded her of an owl, sitting erect on a branch, blinking, turning its head around to watch. The dowager had bought her silk handkerchiefs and a tweed suit with a much longer skirt. Zoe held it up. "It will be perfect when I've had it shortened a few inches," she said teasingly.

She had bought her mother-in-law perfume, sent from Paris. The room was strewn with bright colored paper and ribbon—

A child would love to play in it all.

Then two footmen entered, carrying a miniature house on a board. The house looked like a country cottage with tiny windows and an open door. Figures represented a village scene. There was a small pond with ice-skaters that were barely taller than her thumbnail.

"It's a snow house," Julia said. "It's one of our traditions. Nigel, why don't you tell Zoe what it is?"

"It's a cardboard house, filled with silly little gifts and made to look as if it's covered in snow."

Nigel took the roof off the house. Zoe reached in and drew out a small silver charm of a pixie. She had to swallow tears.

Nigel pulled out a kazoo and Zoe insisted he try to play a tune. That made everyone laugh.

She touched his hand and he didn't pull away. They shared a look, a poignant one.

She needed this. To touch him.

Later in the afternoon, Dr. Drury and Reverend and Mrs. Wesley arrived. To Nigel, she whispered, "I heard it was tradition and I didn't want them to be hurt or think I'd snubbed them. So I extended invitations."

"I had said no guests." He frowned. "Why didn't you discuss it with me?"

"What would you have said? A flat-out no?"

Footmen came in then, so Nigel couldn't argue more. On silver trays sat small, hot sausage rolls. Glasses of sherry were served and everyone toasted Christmas.

Zoe lifted her glass to her lips just as the gong summoned them to the dining room. Nigel led her in, without saying a word. She smiled—a wobbly smile—at the sight of the table. Candles stood in a display of holly as the centerpiece. Christmas crackers—tubes of colored crepe paper—sat by every place.

Zoe pulled crackers with Reverend Wesley, and she put on her paper hat. Nigel set his beside his plate. Then the dishes came out: a first course of smoked salmon, followed by parsnip soup. Then turkeys—three of them—expertly carved, beautifully browned. Chestnut stuffing spilled out. Potatoes, brussels sprouts, carrots, baked parsnips, gravy.

Finally a Christmas pudding came out, flaming, with a sprig of holly upon it.

Exhausted and full, everyone else went to bed early. Zoe caught Nigel in the foyer. He stood by the tree, illuminated by the twinkling electric lights. He held an ornament of a tiny angel, stroking it thoughtfully with his thumb.

Their little angel…now in heaven…

The sherry and the wine at dinner made it much easier to walk right up to him and say, "Nigel. You've kept away from my bedroom because of…because of the bleeding. But I believe it is finally done. It has been a few days. Please come back to my bed. At night, I feel so alone."

He let go of the angel and it swung slightly on its gold cord. "If it has been only a month, I do not think we should."

"Oh, why not? We could think of having another child. I *would* like that. Perhaps my mother is right. Some of this pain would go away if we have another child to love."

But Nigel looked as if she'd punched him in his gut. "God, Zoe. I cannot do that yet."

She had hoped for one special gift today—she had hoped to be held in his arms, to be kissed by him, to make love to him and wrap her arms around him. She was ready to be intimate with him again. She *needed* it. It wasn't just about being a modern girl and being free to be sexual. She ached for the closeness, the intimacy and the comfort that came with it. She needed to share love, instead of pain.

"I feel—I feel you are angry with me," she said despairingly. "That you blame me for losing our child."

He clasped her elbow and drew her to him. "Zoe, no. No—it wasn't your fault."

He spoke hesitatingly. But she believed his words. She had to. "Then why do you cry at night and keep your door locked? I feel like you are keeping your distance from me. We run into each other by accident. I feel like you avoid me because you can't stand to see me. Nigel, I can't live like this."

"I did not want to hurt you. I will change—I will not keep away from you, if that is what you want."

"What do *you* want, Nigel?" Zoe begged. "I don't know."

"I want this," he said gruffly. With his hand on her elbow, he brought her one step closer. He touched her cheek, brushed his hand along her bobbed hair, then cupped his hand gently around her neck and brought her lips to his.

By the glittering light of the tree, he kissed her.

19
THREE O'CLOCK IN THE MORNING

NIGEL SWEPT HER off her feet, into his arms, and Zoe's heeled shoe almost knocked a glass ball from the tree.

His left hand was splayed to support her back; his right hand cradled her bottom. He had her clasped to him, so she could hear the hard, fast beat of his heart. He carried her easily, crossing the marble tiles toward the sweeping, ornate staircase.

"Nigel, what are you doing?"

"Taking you to bed. To *my* bed."

She wrapped her arms around his strong neck and held on while he carried her upstairs.

This was what she ached for. Passion and love. Closeness instead of distance. She buried her face in his neck. With her lips brushing his throat, she felt the smoothness of his freshly shaved skin—he must have been shaved before he dressed for dinner. He smelled of witch hazel, and his skin was so warm.

Tears prickled in her eyes. But she didn't dare let them free. If she began crying she feared she wouldn't stop. Closing her eyes tight, she kissed Nigel's neck. She nibbled his jawline, then his earlobe—tugging on it. He breathed heavily as he carried her. She felt his heat through his elegant white-tie dinner jacket.

Nigel pushed open his door with his foot. Zoe caught

a glimpse of his ancient valet. Without a word, the valet beat a retreat through the connecting door to Nigel's dressing room.

Nigel lowered her to his bed. The mattress sank slightly under her, and Nigel got on top, his arms braced on either side. He lowered his mouth to hers in a long, slow, steamy kiss.

She remembered the moment when Nigel had held their tiny son. The love and agony in his eyes. The slight tic of his jaw, which was the only gesture he made to release the shock and pain—

She hadn't meant to remember. But with her eyes closed, it was all she could see. Zoe opened her eyes wide. As Nigel kissed her, she caressed his shoulders and back desperately, trying to fall into his glorious kiss.

This was what she wanted. What she'd begged for.

So why did she feel so wrong inside? So unhappy? How could she celebrate life and passion now, when her son had not even drawn one breath?

She couldn't think that way. People moved on. They survived. They did. She had to.

There could be another child.

Nigel lifted off her and tugged off his white bow tie, his jacket. She squirmed under him. He began to fight with the buttons of his shirt, and she breathed, "I can't wait. Just take your trousers off."

He managed a smile, a slight one. But it didn't reach his eyes. Still, he undid his trousers and pushed them down. Followed that by shoving down his linens.

But then—

They couldn't. They weren't able. He wasn't fully

aroused, and she was tense. It hurt when they tried, and she gasped and whimpered with the pain.

Breathing hard, Nigel moved off her and lay beside her. He stroked her shoulder awkwardly. Sweat beaded on his forehead. "I am sorry. I couldn't— I never thought. All I could think— No, never mind. I'm sorry, Zoe."

Out of his garbled words, she knew what he wanted to say. "I—I—" She wanted to tell him she couldn't either. But the minute she tried to explain that she hurt too much, tears came out.

A flood of them.

She tried to hold them back. She even sat up and put her face in her hands, as if that would somehow keep them inside.

He sat up, too.

"I couldn't do it either," she finally mumbled into her wet palms. "I'm still—I'm still sore."

"I hurt you."

Zoe dropped her hands from her face, wiped tears from her eyes and cheeks with the satin of her nightdress. "You didn't *mean* to, and that's what matters. That's not why I'm crying. I don't know why I'm blubbering like this. Crying won't fix anything. Crying won't make anything right. I don't know what will."

His strong arms held her and he let her cry. She rolled on her side, curled up in a ball, buried her face into his shirtfront and bawled.

It felt as if she cried for hours. She stopped only because her chest ached and she didn't have any tears left. Then Nigel got off the bed and drew his covers over her.

"Come into bed. Please." The bed felt so large, so

empty. She felt small, and the only time she liked feeling small was when she was in his arms.

Nigel hesitated. "I shouldn't. I will sleep elsewhere tonight."

"Don't. Please. I don't want to be on my own anymore."

"You know I cannot stay. What if I have a nightmare? I fight and lash out in those dreams. What if I hurt you?"

"But maybe you won't. If we don't try, we will never change things." She couldn't reveal he had hit her during his nightmare once.

He frowned. "We cannot change things."

Oh, God. He'd never intended to change or heal or try to break free of his memories. "I think the only thing that can help with pain is having someone to help you through it." When he held her, she felt that she had someone else to bear the weight of grief. Maybe that was the secret. "Maybe holding each other and going into the future hand in hand can help us. Maybe that way, we can put the past behind us."

"I can't."

"But all this pain is coming between us."

"I am sorry. There is nothing I can do about that, Zoe."

Then he left her. On her own.

She couldn't sleep, of course. For one glorious moment, when he'd carried her upstairs, she'd tried to believe they could snatch at happiness.

Was Nigel right and they never could?

In the morning, she walked in on him in his study. Nigel had his back to her. He was staring out of the window and he had a letter in his hand.

To his back, she said, "I want to go to London. I

want to do something. Go dancing. Go to clubs or the theater. I want to take you dancing, Nigel. I have to believe we can find a way to heal and I think we would both feel better if we—"

She broke off. She thought he would turn while she spoke, but he hadn't. She approached him. From the side, she saw his eyes were shut and his shoulders were moving with grief. "What is it? What's happened?" She went right up to his side. She reached for the letter—

But he crumpled it and moved away from her. His eyes had opened.

"It's about the War," he said brusquely. "Not something I want to talk about."

"You look terrible, Nigel. You look so haggard. Won't you come with me to London? Come and listen to a jazz band and dance with me."

"Zoe, don't you understand that I can't do that?"

"Then tell me what is hurting you so much." She pointed at the letter. "It's more than just our baby. Why has the War followed you for four years?"

"There are things I have to bear alone."

"But you don't!"

"Maybe in America, husbands and wives are expected to be friends and share everything," he snapped. "Though, have you noticed that in your home country, almost twenty percent of marriages are being dissolved by divorce?"

She reeled back.

He stopped. "God, I'm sorry. Zoe, you don't want to know my secrets. If you want to go to London, why not take Julia? Do some shopping. Go to the theater. Enjoy yourself."

He was pushing her away.

She was tired of it. Tired of being told by her husband that she had no right to share his sadness or to try to help him. "All right. I'll go to London. I would prefer to go with you. In New York—" She broke off. She had never told him how hurt she was to be cast out by New York's upper crust. She'd never wanted him to know she used to be poor. But just the thought brought the same swirling anger. The same piercing hurt. She tossed her head. "Back at home, I made my own way. If I have to, I'll do it here."

THE LETTER HAD been stained and dirty, the printing down in smeared lead pencil, and it had shocked Nigel to his soul.

It had come from Mrs. Bell. It read:

Our Ernie's birthday were at the beginning of the month. It made Lily sad and angry as it always does. She said she wanted to do something about it. "Make the buggers finally pay" is what she said. I told her off for that kind of talk.

She walked out in a huff. And she hasn't come back. She were stepping out with the draper's lad. But he don't know where she's gone off to.

I'm afraid she's gone off with a man, even though she was raised better than that.

But I hoped maybe in her temper she'd come to you and you might know where she is.

What had she meant: *make the buggers pay?* Lily had been filled with rage and pain. God, he understood. Nigel went to his desk. He could not let Zoe know his secrets. He took up his own pen, dipped it in his inkwell and wrote carefully.

> My dear Mrs. Bell,
> I have not seen Lily. But I am concerned, as I do not believe she is the type of young woman to leave without giving word to you. I will undertake a search for Lily to ensure she is safe.

If Lily had done something foolish, it was because she had lost her brother. And he was responsible for that. At least this, he could make right.

ONE GLOOMY JANUARY MORNING, a week after New Year's, when they had toasted 1923 with champagne at midnight, Zoe drove to London with Julia. She tried to focus on the road. Nigel hadn't come to her at night since Christmas Day and their failed attempt to be intimate. Her mood was edgy and tense, urging her to drive fast, her foot heavy on the pedal, her hands working as the car hugged the curves of the road. Julia looked a bit green by the time they pulled up at the front entrance of the Savoy.

Zoe checked them into two enormous suites. As she joined Julia in her room, leaped onto the edge of the bed and flung off her hat, she announced to her sister-in-law, "I haven't come to town only to buy clothes. We can do that in the day, but tonight we are going dancing."

Julia looked startled. "Dancing? Do you think you should?"

"Because Nigel wouldn't like it?"

Julia bit her lip. "Zoe, it is not my business, I know. But I have seen you and Nigel together since…since your loss. What has happened between you? You both seem so unhappy. Is it more than grief? You aren't— you aren't falling out of love with my brother, are you?"

"Your brother is wounded and troubled and he refuses to share anything with me. He told me to come to London—without him. He told me he didn't want to try to forget his pain—and if it came between us, there was nothing he could do about that."

He had rejected her. He had told her he didn't care that she needed him. But, oh, heaven, she still loved him.

Zoe jumped off the bed. "Let's get dressed. We'll have dinner, then go to this club—it's supposed to be one of the wildest clubs in London. For one night, I want to dance frantically and enjoy music and simply not think!"

She was trying to act much more cavalier than she felt, but she had to try something.

In the Savoy's restaurant, she and Julia had a decadent dinner and drank wickedly potent cocktails, and then she took Julia to the exclusive jazz club. Bottled Joy was the best jazz club in London and she had the password to gain entrance.

Zoe drove them there and parked her car at the side of the road. She jumped out of the car, but Julia got out cautiously.

Bottled Joy was in the basement of a Victorian-era house in Soho, where even the light from street lamps scooted past, afraid to hang around. A narrow stair led down into a well of darkness.

"Are you certain we should have come here?" Julia gazed around apprehensively. "This is not one of the better parts of London."

"It's like a New York speakeasy," Zoe said. "The best ones are in church basements and warehouses. They're dark and secretive."

Julia shivered in her coat. "That's because America has prohibition. This club doesn't have to be secret."

"But that's what makes it deliciously fun. We'll try it, but we'll leave if you don't like it."

Zoe rapped on the door. A small sliding door opened and a large eye that looked like a boiled egg peered out. The muffled sound of loud, bold music poured through the opening.

Zoe leaned her cheek close to the door. "The bobby's knickers."

The door opened. The primitive drumbeat, the soulful blare of clarinets and trumpets poured out. So did a cloud of thick smoke from the dozens of cigarettes that dangled between fingers. Dresses and jewels sparkled and the men wore black ties and dinner jackets. Silver trays were whisked around the room by waiters. Atop the trays stood tall glasses, short tumblers, champagne flutes, martini glasses filled with drinks of every color. When a waiter passed one of the few lamps in the place, the cocktails glowed like a stained-glass window in a new kind of church.

The band was made up of young black musicians and a gorgeous, large black woman who crooned into a microphone.

A man in black tie with hair as fair as Sebastian's bowed to her. Then he grabbed her hand and tugged her onto the dance floor. Zoe danced wildly with him, then moved on to the next partner.

She danced with viscounts and earls and common men. Several men asked her name, but she didn't bother to give it. Julia was danced over to her, her cheeks pink with excitement and exhaustion as she was dancing through one song after another.

Then some gentlemen recognized Julia—and began to realize who Zoe was. Murmurs rushed through the crowd. People whispered, "It's the American duchess."

She saw scathing looks. She got a hell of a lot of attention. But she wasn't doing anything wilder than anyone else in the room.

Besides, she didn't care what anyone thought or what they said. For one glorious night, she could laugh and dance and feel alive and young again, instead of old and cold and despairing.

Now that she was in this glittering, brash, exciting contrast to Brideswell, she realized that was exactly how she'd felt. Old. All of her felt empty—her heart and her soul, not just her womb.

She danced as fast as she could to the jaunty music of "Toot, Toot, Tootsie (Goo' Bye)."

"Enjoying yourself?" her current dance partner shouted.

"This is how I want to feel," she declared to him—he might be the Earl of Morland or Viscount Sawfield or some man named Mr. Smythe-Williams, but she didn't really care.

"This is what *I* want to feel." Her dance partner's hand slid down to her bottom and he gave a hard, fast squeeze. "I was feeling that I might fancy a bit of a tussle."

She hauled his wayward hand back up. "I want to dance. I want to enjoy the music. But that's *all* I want."

"Nothing wrong with some horizontal dancing. A bit of the rumpy-pumpy, what?"

His hand strayed down again. She moved it back up, then tried to pull away. But his meaty hand was clamped around her wrist and she couldn't break free.

A silver tray soared past, carried by a waiter in black tie. Zoe grabbed a bright green drink that sloshed in a martini glass. In one neat motion, she threw it in her dance partner's face.

Shock made him recoil and shut his eyes, but the strength of his fingers didn't change. If anything, his hand clamped harder into her skin.

"You little bitch." Roughly, he pulled her with him and pushed her up against the wall in a shadowy corner, near an abandoned table and a limp potted palm. He shoved her so her head rebounded into the wall. Pain exploded in her skull.

He was huge. A hulk of a man and he had her pinned against the wall.

She spat at him. "I'm not a bitch. I'm a duchess."

His hand was raised to strike her. At the word *duchess,* his hand sank down. "Well, I'm a duke," he sneered and leaned in toward her, fleshy lips smacking.

"Goddamn you, get off!" she shouted.

The wild music was winding down at that moment and her shout pierced the room. Julia let out a cry and was rushing toward Zoe, followed by her dance partner—

Suddenly the brute was pulled off Zoe. He was shoved roughly aside and another man stepped forward. Equally tall, but his size came from muscle. He had black hair, as dark as Nigel's, and piercing black eyes. A small mustache graced his thin upper lip and a scar forked down his right cheek. "The lady has made it clear she's not interested," the man growled.

The obnoxious duke staggered toward him, but suddenly halted, then shrugged. "Frigid woman. Not worth my time." He stalked off.

Julia reached her. "Zoe, goodness, what happened?"

"Nothing bad." The dark-haired man's eyes sparkled at Zoe. "Safe and sound. I'll take my leave, Your Grace. Unless I could interest you in a dance. I keep my hands to myself."

Julia's eyes were wide.

Zoe knew it was time to leave. There was always that moment when the night changed from fun to dangerous. Even though she liked risk, she had never been completely stupid. She knew this was the moment to leave.

But what was she running to? A hotel room with a vast empty bed. Or back to Brideswell, to another vast empty bed. She would be running to pain—the sheer agony of wanting to be with Nigel, when, ever since Christmas night, he had been even more distant from her.

She had no intention of letting any other man than Nigel in her bed. But she just couldn't face going back to a room that was empty save for herself yet.

"I'd love to dance," Zoe said. To Julia, she instructed, "Why don't you dance some more?"

Julia's partner needed no further encouragement. And Zoe's dark-haired man whirled her onto the floor. The band started up again, this time straining to soar over the babble of voices with "Aggravatin' Papa." Her run-in with the disgusting, groping duke was the gossip of the night.

"So who are you?" she asked as she had to stop and catch her breath once the song finished. Plucking a feather from a table setting, she fanned herself with it. The dark-haired man took out two cigarettes and lit them both. She took one. "You came to my rescue, and I don't even know who you are." She took a long draw on the cigarette and blew a floating smoke ring.

She knew she had better not sound and act too flirtatious. If only she could be here with Nigel. She could flirt all she liked with him. She could dance daringly. She could be seducing him with every move she made right here in the club.

But he would never come here with her. He'd made that clear.

Her partner gently touched the middle of her back and led her to a table. He seated her, then bowed. "British Army Major Lanceton Quigley. You probably don't know that name yet. But you will—when I've flown around the world."

"You're planning to fly around the world?" Her heart sped up.

Quigley took a seat beside her. "Aye. Two more blokes and I are going to do it in May. The last lot had to abandon their attempt last year, but we know we can prevail."

"I take it you were an ace in the War?"

"Twenty-five confirmed," he said. He waved his hand to summon a waiter. Zoe ordered the club's special drink, the Bottled Sin, and Quigley ordered Scotch.

"That's very impressive." Zoe had hung on to Richmond's tales of duels in the air. She found it thrilling enough to fly a plane—filled with excitement and danger—but she'd never have the courage to do it while getting shot at.

"I lost a friend when he attempted to fly across the Atlantic," she said softly. "Richmond DeVille."

"DeVille? I know him. American ace. Forty victories, though he claimed forty-two. Tragic loss, that was."

"Yes." She felt sorrow thinking about Richmond. But not that aching pang she used to feel, the one that declared she had lost the love of her life. Richmond was not that love anymore. He was a man she had once loved and he was thoroughly in her past now.

She remembered Julia admitting she felt guilty for falling in love again, when the man she'd lost had been cheated of so much.

Zoe did understand that feeling. But she now saw she could never have preserved her heart for Richmond forever. Now when she let her eyes close, it was clear California-sky blue eyes she saw. Eyes filled with mysterious memories and pain; eyes that haunted her. A handsome face that bore more scars than the British Army major and was simply stunning to look at. Once you really let yourself look at the Duke of Langford, you couldn't stop.

A drink in a champagne flute was set in front of her—it was peacock-blue and bubbling. It was sweet and tart and decadent and she downed half of it. "How are you planning to do it? Crossing the ocean is dangerous. Pretty much suicide." She swallowed hard. If only Richmond could have seen into the future. But then, would he have looked? Would he have wanted to know he was going to fail? She doubted that, even if he'd seen it, he would have believed it.

If she had known she was going to miscarry a child, would she have wanted to never be pregnant at all?

She pushed those thoughts away. "What's your airplane?"

Quigley took a sip of his Scotch. "I am probably going to bore you to tears."

"No, I'm on the edge of my seat. This is so exciting."

"We're planning to fly a modified Airco DH-9. Known now as the de Havilland DH-9." His dark eyes lit up as if a fire burned inside him. "That's the plane used by the three men who had to abandon their attempt, but we're confident we can do it. That leg will take us from England to Calcutta. From there, we're crossing the Pacific, so we'll use a floatplane to get us to Vancouver, Canada. Then we'll use another DH-9 to get us to Montreal. After that, we broach the Atlantic, back to England. We'll cover about twenty-three thousand miles."

His passion was addictive. More so than sweet cocktails.

She yearned to feel the same excitement. To have a reason to leap out of bed. To have a real goal. Not a dream, but something tangible and real that she could grasp in her hands.

One of the musicians struck a bell slowly, and then the band began to play the strains of "Three O'Clock in the Morning."

"This is my favorite." Quigley got to his feet and bowed. "Dance with me, Your Grace?"

She liked this man, the joy that radiated from him, the passionate fire that burned inside him. He had been through war, but it hadn't broken him inside.

Nigel was broken. She saw that. She wanted to fix him—just the same way she knew a broken airplane engine could be fixed. But he wouldn't let her.

Quigley led her in a graceful waltz. She'd danced

to this song with Richmond. It had seemed beautiful then. Now it brought tears into her eyes and her throat.

If only—

No, she had to go *forward*. Go forward or she would go mad.

He whirled her around as the tempo rose in the middle of the song, and as the speakeasy spun around her, she saw a tall, black-haired man in white tie. She came to an abrupt stop.

Nigel stalked up to her. He tapped Quigley on the shoulder. "You will unhand my duchess." Pure fury radiated from him. He stepped between her and the army major.

Zoe began to laugh. It must have been the potent liquor in the cocktail. "For heaven's sake, Nigel. You're rescuing me from the wrong man."

Nigel turned abruptly and a fire glowed behind his eyes. The passion and anger in his face took her breath away.

"I don't bloody well care," he said. Then he pulled her onto the floor and waltzed with her. Electricity seemed to crackle around his body. His hand was firm on her lower back. "You will not dance with anyone else but me."

"That's all I ever wanted to do," she threw back at him.

Before he could answer, Julia rushed up. Zoe's sister-in-law pointed to the opposite end of the room. The band had struck up the next tune, a primitive, grinding beat. Curtains rustled and a woman with bleached blond hair fought her way through them. She moved awkwardly on high heels. And as the drummer hit his cymbals, the woman pulled her skirt apart and let it fly.

Julia's eyes were huge with shock. "Zoe, that woman is taking off her clothing!"

"HERE WE ARE AGAIN: back at the Savoy and you're annoyed with me."

Nigel watched his wife as she lay on the large bed on her tummy, heels kicked up in the air. She lifted the white-and-gold telephone receiver and ordered champagne to be brought to the room.

"What in God's name were you doing in a place like that?"

"Dancing and enjoying the music. I had no idea it was a strip club. The waiter in the restaurant downstairs didn't mention that. Anyway—both Julia and I are females. That girl didn't possess anything both of us haven't seen before. She just had more of it."

"Zoe, for God's sake—" Nigel stopped talking. He would say something he would regret. "You could have been in danger. That place is filled with vice. There were people taking cocaine. Half the rest of them were saturated with alcohol. Stinking drunk. As for that man—"

"I told you that British Army Major Quigley was the perfect gentleman. He rescued me from a duke with groping hands. Apparently a position on the British peerage doesn't guarantee class." She rolled on her side, playing with her beads. "Present company excepted, of course."

"Zoe, did you really need to go dancing so much you would end up in such a hellish, dangerous place?"

She sat up. Her lighthearted expression vanished. "You pushed me away, Nigel. You told me to come here without you. Where did you think I would go? And since you shoved me away, why do you care?"

"I do not mean to push you away—"

"It is what you do every time I try to be close to you. The only times you didn't push me away were the times when we made love. I thought that proved you had passion for me. Maybe I was wrong." She launched up and paced, twirling her beads like bold flappers did in silent films. "Was that just about duty, too?"

"That was *not* about duty." He couldn't talk to her. Where could he start?

But he had been too short and abrupt with her the other day. He had to make it up to her. That was why he'd come to London at all. Knowing Zoe'd go back to the Savoy, he went to the restaurant for dinner. A very helpful waiter had informed him where to find his wife and sister.

"I danced with Major Quigley and he told me he is going to attempt to fly around the world. He and two other men are planning it for May. It was so thrilling to listen to him."

"Wonderful," he said sourly. "There was a failed attempt last year. I doubt it is possible."

"But we won't know unless someone tries it—and succeeds."

"They won't succeed, Zoe. I saw those flimsy aircraft in battle. It would be impossible to cross the—" Nigel broke off.

Now he understood.

Zoe's violet eyes glowed with excitement. She had been in love with aviator Richmond DeVille. Quigley must have reminded her of all the things she had loved in the daring aviator and flying ace.

DeVille represented the glamour of the War. He was a hero.

Nigel knew he represented the hell of it—the muck of trench life, the futility of sending thousands of young men out to be cannon fodder.

Who would Zoe rather be in love with? The answer was obvious. But he was tired. He had come here because the dowager had smacked her cane into his back until he had taken the train after Zoe had left.

"Go in pursuit of her," Grandmama had said. "You cannot allow the girl to run amok in London. There will be scandal. I'm sure everyone assumes she is already having affairs."

"Why?" he'd demanded. "Because I'm scarred and half-mad?"

His grandmother had recoiled. But she had answered, "Because she is American and she wears short skirts and flies an aeroplane. We are British, Nigel. She is different, and to an Englishman that is akin to being in league with the devil."

"Rubbish," he'd snapped. "People are saying it because I am a mess."

"You are not. But this is the modern world, Nigel. She may go to London and not come back."

That had stunned him. When he thought of losing her—

Hell, he'd known at that moment he couldn't bear life without her. He had run for the damned train and had come to London as fast as he could.

He had to be contrite. "Can we stop allowing the War to come between us? It changed me and I am sorry about that, Zoe. But I—I love you."

The champagne arrived at that very moment.

ZOE LET HER cigarette burn down to her fingers as she stared at her husband's back while he opened the hotel-room door to the waiter carrying the bucket of champagne. Nigel had stripped off his coat. He wore his white waistcoat, his white tie, and his white shirt stretched over broad shoulders.

As Nigel opened the door, she heard the strains of the waltz from the ballroom on the first floor. Of course it was "Three O'Clock in the Morning." Now it sounded sweet and poignant and full of promise.

Excitement flooded her. She walked to Nigel and she took the champagne from him. She took the wrapper off the cork with one fast tug, then began to work at the wire that held the cork in place.

"I'll open this. You take off your clothes," she said.

He raised a brow at her, but undid his bow tie, then his waistcoat. She wriggled the cork, easing it from the bottle. She didn't like to watch good champagne rush out in a whoosh. Watching it spurt over the floor would break her heart, even though she could just pick up the phone again and order another bottle. It was too many years of having nothing, she supposed.

Nigel undid his cuffs and drew off his shirt. At the sight of his muscular chest, she tugged hard on the cork. It flew out with a pop and the champagne rushed up the neck of the bottle. Quick as she could, she let it flow into the glasses, filling them until they overflowed.

She took a sip of champagne.

He played with his glass, not drinking. She turned on a bedside light, then turned off the overhead light. Gold light caressed the wide V of his torso, his bare shoulders. "Are you ready for my attentions, Zoe? It has only been just over a week since we last tried."

"I know I'm ready." She felt ready. She ached inside. "Besides, the past few days, I've touched myself while thinking of you."

He was lifting his champagne to his lips and he coughed and sputtered. She grinned wickedly.

Then he said, "God, Zoe, I love you. Want you. Adore you."

When they made love, he muttered her name desperately, even as he carefully, attentively brought her to her peak. She gasped and cried out. He shuddered over her, and she held him tight. Then he fell on the bed beside her.

And she smiled and closed her eyes.

THE SHOUTING WOKE HER.

There was no one beside her, but there were grunts, muffled shouts, muttering coming from somewhere in the room. Zoe swallowed her heart down from where it had lodged in her throat.

He was on the couch. Nigel had draped himself over a too short sofa to go to sleep. All because he was too afraid to sleep with her.

She pulled on her robe. And she hurried to him.

She knelt by the couch.

Sweat covered his forehead. Every once in a while, he would thrash or hit out with his hand. She strained to hear what he was saying. Like the first time she'd witnessed his nightmare, on their honeymoon, she couldn't understand the words.

Maybe if she could, she would know what kept haunting him. Was it one thing—one terrible, traumatic event? Was it many things?

She didn't care about the danger of touching him, even while his strong arms flailed.

One word came to her, agonized and distinct. "Boy." Then "Too young...wrong... God, no!" His body racked and heaved, and his shoulders jerked, as if he were being held down and fighting to break free.

She stroked his face. "Nigel, it's all right. You're with me. Zoe. The war is over."

Gently, she spoke to him. It took... Well, it felt like forever. Finally, he stopped moving. He groaned. His eyes flickered open.

"Zoe... God, I'm sorry. I woke you with my nightmares."

"I don't mind. I really don't. I love you." She gazed into sleepy, troubled blue eyes. "You spoke of a boy. Who was he? What happened to him?"

Nigel's hand passed over his mouth. "I don't know," he muttered. "I don't remember the dream. I don't know anything."

"Was it you?"

He shook his head. "No. No, it was not me." He wrapped his bare arms around her.

And she was lost—hungry to be touched. His certainty meant he'd lied—he *did* remember his dream. But she didn't want to fight.

Could she accept him as he was? Filled with secrets and memories he would never share?

She pressed tight to him and hugged him back. They stayed that way as dawn spread over the London sky, creeping around the window blinds. For all that time, he stroked her, and she pressed kisses to his naked chest.

Nigel might hug her so her cheek rested over his

heart, but he would never let her closer to his heart than that.

But it didn't matter.

She'd needed something to wipe away pain. Zoe knew she had it—a goal that had taken root in her heart.

She was going to be the first woman to fly around the world.

20
WINTER AT BRIDESWELL

THROUGH JANUARY, SNOW blanketed Brideswell. Ice coated the panes of the windows. The house was heated entirely by fireplaces, and while they had wonderful blazes, cold wrapped around the house and squeezed tighter with each day. Like the other women at Brideswell, Zoe grew accustomed to wearing a heavy shawl. At first she thought she would never survive the months of cold, but Nigel revealed the beauty of Brideswell in the winter to her.

And she was smitten—almost from the first moment he led her outside to a horse-drawn sleigh.

Nigel wore a long wool coat that made his shoulders look impossibly broad. With leather-glove-clad hands, he lifted her into the front seat, wrapped a fur throw around her. He climbed in beside her and picked up the reins. Snow had just fallen, frosting everything in glistening white, and they almost flew over the fields.

This was something new and thrilling. She had been the one to take him flying. He gave her something just as exciting.

She laughed. "There were horse-drawn sleighs in Central Park in New York, but I've never been in one. This is wonderful!" She loved the crispness of the air, the unique quiet created by the snow, broken by the jingle of bells.

Nigel turned to her, his eyes soft. "Tell me about your life in New York."

That startled Zoe. She watched the snow sparkle. "You've never asked me about it before."

His voice was husky. "I should have. I have been too wrapped up in my own problems. Tell me everything."

She had to be careful—she didn't want to tell him how poor she had once been. She told him about Broadway and Central Park, the galleries and the snobbish women who ruled Manhattan society. "In the winter, we would go to parties and dinners. But I loved to go ice-skating."

"I can give you that," he promised.

That afternoon, he took her ice-skating on the frozen part of the pond. Just to tease him, she pelted him with snowballs.

Through winter, there were dinners, balls—endless entertaining. She began to feel less like a strange outsider and more as if she were visiting friends.

And she and Nigel made love…often. Something had changed. Nigel would rap on her door on unexpected nights.

She loved being under the covers with him, making her bed warm, making them both hot and sweaty.

They would lie in her bed afterward and she would savor the precious time when he held her, stroked her. He would kiss, caress, cradle her until she fell asleep, and then he would leave.

Once she propped up on her elbows and asked, "Why don't you need your schedule anymore?"

He looked surprised. As if he had never considered

why. "Being with you, like this, makes me happy. Before, I was afraid and nervous—I had to gather strength to come to you. Now I see that being with you gives me strength."

She kissed him hungrily. Lovingly.

After that he made love to her again, leaving them both bathed in sweat and breathless and laughing with pleasure. Then he started to come to her every night. He seemed as if he couldn't get his fill of her. She didn't speak of the War. She didn't try to coax him to spend the night with her. She knew the exact moment he would get up to leave—she could tell by the way his arm stiffened around her, by the way he would let out a soft, sad sigh. It hurt him to leave her, but he still wouldn't change.

So she would kiss him good-night and let him go.

All through the winter, she made plans for her goal. To fly around the world, she needed an airplane. Finding the perfect one kept Zoe busy for the month of February—she finally purchased one at the end of the month. Nigel was busy with work on the estate—planning work and repairs for spring.

She hadn't told him her plan, because it would mean she would have to leave him for months.

On the first of March, her airplane was ready for her to bring to Brideswell. She had purchased an old DH-9, used in the Great War. She'd had it refurbished, with a new engine installed.

She took the train, hired a car and traveled to Croydon Airport. There she saw Major Quigley. "Your Grace," he shouted. He strode over to her, bowed.

For a long time they discussed the mechanics of airplanes, improvements to the engines that they wanted to try. Then she said, "In two months you will be making your attempt to circumnavigate the globe."

"Aye." Quigley grinned. "Wish us luck."

"I do. You'll have to wish me luck, too. I intend to be the first woman to fly around the world."

He gaped at her in shock. "Your husband is letting you do this?"

"I am my own person," she declared. And she knew right then she was going to have to be honest with Nigel. She was supposed to be brave. She'd argued about him keeping secrets. Now she was doing it, and it had to stop.

As SHE LANDED in the field the next morning, her plane rumbling over the rutted ground, rain began to spatter her. Zoe brought the craft to a halt beside her other airplane. She laughed victoriously and raised her hands in the air. She had beaten the rain—she had made the flight from Croydon to Brideswell a lot faster than she'd planned.

She felt damned proud. The engine she'd insisted on installing in the plane was everything she'd dreamed—powerful and elegant.

"Zoe!"

She swung out of the cockpit and Nigel ran across the ground to her. He pointed to the sky behind her. To the masses of black clouds that had pursued her here.

"I know! I beat them. I was certain I would, Nigel."

"You could have been wrong. You could have been caught by the storm. Damnation, why do you still have to take risks?"

"I've flown through storms before. It's tricky, but I've managed each one successfully." And she would need to know how to handle inclement weather. She might not be able to outrun a storm when she had nothing but ocean beneath her.

In the distance, thunder boomed.

Nigel looked thunderous. "Zoe, you are not to put yourself in danger again."

After taking her sleigh-riding and skating, after making love to her so tenderly and with so much joy, he was filled with anger again. He wasn't asking her to be careful. He was commanding her.

"I don't plan to put myself in danger." She caressed the side of her airplane. It was painted a bright, vivid red. "She's gorgeous, isn't she? I couldn't wait to bring her home." She turned to Nigel. "She's a de Havilland DH-9. British built. This one saw service in 1917 and 1918. A lucky plane—it flew several missions and came back from each one unscathed. I had it refitted with a newer Liberty engine that I had shipped from the States." Pride filled her heart. She had arranged the modifications herself and she had visited the airfield often to check on the work. She felt like her father—she had a goal, she had employed the right people to see it through, and she had been a stunning success.

She stroked the plane. "I am going to be the first female to fly around the world. I've begun working on it—charting out my route. And I'll have to think about my flight crew—"

"No."

"What?"

"I forbid this, Zoe." Nigel crossed his arms over his chest.

"But this is my dream—"

"You expect me to just accept this?" he barked. "How long would this flight take you?"

"Less than six months."

"I am supposed to let my wife fly away from me for six months?"

"I know it sounds like a long time, but it won't really be that long."

"This is ridiculous, Zoe."

He said it dismissively and his words twisted in her like a knife. "I intend to be the *first* female to circumnavigate the globe. I can do this. You need three things: guts, ability and money. I do have those things, Nigel. And I want to show the world that I do."

"You are my wife. There is nothing else you need to show the world."

He really believed that. She saw it in his eyes. "I am more than just a man's wife."

She wanted to be known for something she had done, something she'd accomplished.

"Zoe, you could be killed. You could be hit by a storm. Or get lost. The engine could give out. You could crash—" He rubbed his temple. "I've seen aeroplane crashes in the War. Seen the fuselage explode. Seen the charred remains. Isn't it enough that I still let you fly?"

"You do not 'let' me do anything. I am going to do this, Nigel. You can't stop me. I have my own rights."

"You had no right to plan this without telling me," he snapped.

"I knew what you would do. Start acting like a father and not like a husband. I'm expected to support your decisions. I turned half my money over to you for your home. I want you to support my chance to make my name in the world, to do something of value."

"I can't support this, Zoe. I won't." And he stalked away across the field.

21
THE CRASH

Zoe went to bed that night fuming. Nigel was not going to stop her. He couldn't take her dream away. She would never do that to him, and she wouldn't let him do it to her.

But when she woke up the next morning, she felt queasy. This was the third day, and she knew. She hadn't had her menstrual period since January, but Dr. Drury had warned her that after the miscarriage she might be irregular.

Beneath her hand, her tummy was still flat, but she knew with bone-deep certainty she was pregnant again. It was women's intuition, maybe. And as soon as she came to that conclusion, she felt a leap of excitement— and ice-cold fear.

Dr. Drury had told her miscarriages tended to happen in the first three months of a pregnancy. She couldn't raise Nigel's hopes only to see them dashed if something went wrong.

She couldn't bear it. It would devastate him.

They had found some fledgling happiness and she didn't want to lose that.

She would wait to tell him, wait until it should be safer to do it, when it was more likely she would actually carry the baby until the end. Or she would wait until she began to show—then she would have to tell him.

And she would pray nothing terrible happened.

She got out of bed and started pacing around the room, her hand on her stomach. She wanted to feel happy—and she did—but terror gripped her, too. If she lost the baby, she couldn't bear such a heartbreaking pain either.

"You also can't walk around your room, worrying, for months and months." There was nothing she could do. But wait. And hope. She wouldn't believe the baby was real until she had passed the first few months of pregnancy—until she was in the clear.

Zoe walked to the window and looked out at the rare and beautiful bright blue sky. "Well, your dream is over for now. You can't fly around the world now." It would take at least six months. She couldn't fly while eight months pregnant. That would be crazy.

She cupped her stomach. Her dream was gone. But—

She was *happy.* Closing her eyes, tears dripped to her cheeks. Another child. She had been blessed. But she looked up at the perfect sky—gorgeous for early March. She ached for just one last flight.

She'd lost her other child....

But she couldn't believe that flying had had anything to do with that. Her body had betrayed her and flying an airplane had had nothing to do with that. There were village women who worked on their farms until they practically had to give birth in the fields.

One last flight wouldn't hurt. One more—before she put her dream away and stopped flying for a very long time.

And after she got dressed and had a little breakfast to

try to settle her stomach, she went to do it. Julia caught up with her and they walked together along the gravel path. Snow clung in little patches to Brideswell's lawns.

"It's a beautiful day," Julia said.

"It's the perfect day." Zoe stretched her arms to the sky, as if she could grab it and climb into it. "Clear blue sky. Soft, puffy clouds kissed by sunlight. This is the kind of morning that begs you to fly."

"Does it?" Julia strode at her side, dressed in tweeds and sturdy brogues, with a black cloche hat and a peacock feather. "I can't imagine how you find the bravery to go up there."

Zoe used to say she did it because it was exciting. And if you never experienced danger, you had never really tasted life. But she knew it hadn't been bravery or a yearning to do something monumental that made her want to fly around the world. It was as much a desire to run away from sadness and regret and pain.

She kept trying to fly away from everything that hurt her.

Now she was going to stop running away. Nigel had reached out to her. And they were going to have happiness—when the baby was born.

After this one last flight, it would be a year until she could fly again.

She closed her eyes. This new life inside her made her think about the one she'd lost. Made her worry and feel fear. Soaring in the air one more time, feeling strong and in control, would help her push away the fear and the memories. She couldn't have memories when she was making split-second decisions in the air.

Zoe tipped her face up to the sun. "Once you're up, you are in such awe, you forget to be afraid. Though

I never felt fear in the air without being in a situation that warranted it." She was putting on a brave face, for her thoughts were on what she couldn't control. The health of her baby.

"That's not like me," Julia said softly. "I'm apprehensive about everything."

Zoe opened her eyes. "You are not. You *think* you should be."

Julia frowned, her plucked brows drawing down. "I never thought of it that way before."

"I hope you aren't apprehensive about your surgeon. Not about falling in love."

Julia turned to her. "I've made up my mind. I know I have to have him, or I'll never be happy. I cannot marry for duty. Both Mama and Grandmama are constantly drumming it into my head, but I remember what you said. That I should follow my heart." Julia looked pensive. "The problem is—I fear my surgeon feels as they do. I fear he will never ask me to marry him, because he believes it is out of the natural order of things." She sighed. "Why are there men who are so noble and stubborn, and some who have absolutely no morals at all? We should blend them all together and then they would be perfect."

Zoe sighed. "They might be. But then they would be bland. And we women wouldn't like that at all."

Julia laughed. Zoe smiled. They turned around the stables and ahead Zoe saw her brand-new plane. She felt the tingle of excitement to her toes.

"Don't worry about your surgeon. I'll convince Nigel to agree to the marriage."

"Thank you, Zoe. And your aeroplane is gorgeous."

"The red of my favorite lipstick," Zoe said, beaming. She didn't care what Nigel said. Flying around the world was what she'd been born to do. Someday she would do it.

And she was not going to let his family stand in the way of Julia's happiness.

JUST LIKE THE first time Zoe had brought her first plane to Brideswell, Nigel heard the cough and sputter of a motor in the air. But this time it sounded as if it were dying. It would go silent for seconds, roar briefly, then choke away again.

There was something wrong with the damned plane.

Nigel peered through the glass door of his study, but trees blocked his view of the sky. Cursing, he threw open the door and ran out onto the stone terrace.

Then he saw her: the sleek shape of her bright red biplane, emerging from beneath a thick white cloud. Just like the other time she flew in, she was dropping fast. Dropping toward the house. She must be trying to land on the smooth lawn, like she had done before. But as she neared the house, the sputtering ceased. The engine had cut out.

He began to run down the sloping lawn.

He heard the desperate sounds of Zoe trying to make the motor catch again.

But there had to be a point when it was too late.

He stared up at the sky. Wind buffeted the red wings, tossing the plane about. The craft seemed to jiggle through the air, as though held up by an invisible hand that would dash it to the ground. It wasn't gliding toward the ground; it was twisting and writhing, and there would be no way Zoe could land it safely—

Christ, she was going to clip Brideswell's roof. It would send her spinning into a crash.

"Zoe, pull up!" he shouted. "Pull up! You're too low." God, how could she pull up with no engine?

He was watching his wife slowly spiral into an aeroplane crash, powerless to help her.

By a miracle, the plane lifted a few inches as it soared over the house. Not a miracle, he realized. Somehow Zoe had caught an updraft, likely caused by the gusts of wind striking the stone face of Brideswell. His teeth ground so hard they almost snapped as he watched her landing wheels strike the battlements of the old part of the house.

He expected to see the wheels break off. But they didn't, thank God.

He heard the engine fire again, and his heart began to beat, but it was a last gasp, like a death rattle. After a moment, the engine went completely, eerily silent.

She was going to crash, goddamn it.

Nigel ran around the house, reaching the front to see the plane give one last writhing fight to stay aloft. Then the nose dropped and the plane streaked toward the lilac bushes massed on the lawn. It went into the group of them, propeller first.

He heard her scream. The fearful, agonized scream of his wife. The weight of the wings forced the plane to overturn.

"Zoe! Zoe!" he shouted.

He ran toward the plane. Realizing one thing—hitting the tree had kept the plane from slamming into the ground, kept the front end from crumpling into the fuselage, kept the fuel from igniting.

He had to get her out. The branches could have

ripped into the gas tank and the fuel could be leaking out.

God, had the branches hurt her? Had the crash hurt her?

He had hauled boys out of battle—boys with their legs gone, their faces torn off. He had gone to fallen lads to find them headless.

His brain felt as if it were exploding with horror as he feared what he was going to see when he found Zoe. His precious Zoe—

She was strapped into the cockpit, unconscious and upside down. The plane had been skewered by the strong green branches of the tree, but the weight of it falling had shoved most of them out of the way. She bore some scratches on her face, but she seemed miraculously all right.

She was strapped in, which had saved her life. But now he had to get the buckle undone. He had to do it fast. He could smell fuel. They were one hundred yards from the house. Shouting sounded around him—indistinct.

Goddamn belt. He couldn't get it free. He tore at it wildly—stupid thing to do. It got him nowhere. He had to work logically, carefully. He didn't care if the fuel exploded and took him. But he had to save Zoe. He loved her so much.

He pressed close to her, trying to ensure he didn't hurt her. He couldn't see where the belt fastened—he could do it only by feel. Forcing his brain to work fast, he remembered how he had done it up in the passenger seat of her other aeroplane.

It released.

He lifted her, drawing her out and putting her over his shoulder. Then he ran. Toward the house.

He waved the shocked, startled, curious, shouting people—his family, the servants—to go back. "The fuel is leaking. It will explode. Get back!"

There was a roar and a great wall of hot air shoved him forward. He fought not to let it throw him to the ground so he wouldn't hurt Zoe. He stumbled to his knees. There was another sound—of bursting glass as windows on the main floor of the house blew out in the shock wave.

Was anyone hurt in the house?

"Oh, my heavens, is she all right?" It was Julia, dropping to her knees at his side as he laid Zoe on the grass.

He didn't know. All along, he'd assumed she was unconscious. Gently, he put his hand to her throat. Nothing. Christ, no. No—

No, there. He felt the beat of her pulse.

He met Julia's terrified eyes. "She's alive. I don't know how badly she's injured. I have to get her inside." He turned finally to see the devastation behind him. The wood-and-canvas plane was being eaten by flame. The lilacs were on fire, their blackened leaves curling up and floating into the sky.

Men of the estate were running toward it. Some had buckets; others carried brooms and blankets to beat out the flames.

"I have to get her inside. Stay with her while I deal with the fire. We have to fetch the doctor."

It was then he heard the most beautiful sound he'd ever heard. Softly, Zoe's voice came from below. "Nigel?"

"Zoe. Dear God, Zoe." He was afraid to move her,

and when she struggled to sit up, he put his hand gently on her chest and bent close to her. "Lie still. I'll get you into the house. Do you hurt anywhere?"

"My face. It stings. My arm—I think I hit a branch as I shielded my face. And my stomach. My stomach hurts. I slammed forward into the controls—"

But the belt had held her in. It had to mean she wasn't badly hurt. Dear God, it had to.

"My stomach. Oh, God. Oh, Nigel. I forgot— Oh, God, the baby."

Baby? Was she confused? Delirious and thinking back to the awful night when they'd lost their son?

"I didn't tell you. You must tell the doctor. I was pregnant again. What if the baby is not okay?"

Her eyes closed, and she fainted with her hands clasped in his.

He'd never felt anything like it. She was pregnant again. She'd flown while pregnant—maybe she had been planning her trip around the world, ignoring his objections.

And so he wouldn't stop her. She just hadn't told him. He shook with fear and rage.

Christ, none of that mattered now. He lifted her carefully and carried her into the house.

ZOE SAT UP in her bed, propped up by a half dozen pillows in silk cases. Callie had fussed over her, dressing her in a satin nightgown with a feather-trimmed peignoir. It was two days after the crash and she didn't care what she wore.

Dr. Drury had come to check on her. "Feeling better, Your Grace?"

It was so hard to speak she had to shake her head

first. "I lost the baby, Dr. Drury. Today I felt the same gushing sensation. A lot of blood came out."

"Then I am afraid you probably have lost the child, Your Grace."

Drury was a direct man. There was no denying the truth. No trying to ease her guilt. "It was the crash, wasn't it?" she asked, her heart hollow.

"It may have been the shock. It might have been an injury you sustained during the crash. Or it may have been destined to happen anyway."

"I was so foolish. After the last time, I should have been more careful."

Tactfully, he said nothing, of course. Then he said, "It may have made no difference."

"Perhaps my body is not able to bear a child."

"It is far too early to say that yet. To reassure you, Your Grace, these miscarriages may have no bearing on your ability to have healthy babies—and many of them. I have known women to have several miscarriages, then go on to have three or four children. Or more."

"Thank you." She couldn't bear to hear any more. Nigel had left her alone after Drury's first examination of her when she was still in and out of consciousness. She had slept so much in the past two days. If Nigel had come to see her, it was while she had been sleeping—

"Dr. Drury, can I speak with you before you leave?"

Husky, raw, it was Nigel's voice. He stepped into her room. His face was so pale it was stark white and his eyes were dark wells of shadow. "How is the duchess faring?" Nigel asked.

"Much better, I believe." Drury looked to her. He closed his leather bag and looked at her. "What I recommend is rest. I am sure you want to protest, Your

Grace. I know you did not like to stay abed last time, but you have been through an ordeal and you need to give your body and your mind time to heal."

"Last time." Nigel's jaw hardened before Zoe's eyes. A pulse beat in his temple. She saw the twitch.

The doctor left and Zoe heard feminine voices in the hall—Julia, the dowager and Nigel's mother all speaking to him. She looked into her husband's ice-cold blue eyes and she felt a spurt of fear. She didn't fear that he would strike her. Something far worse was going to happen.

"You lost a child again," he said.

His voice was flat. Devoid of emotion. Once she hated it when he was icy. Now she knew she was to blame for his cold, hard iciness. She felt such crippling guilt it made her nauseous.

"I need to speak to Drury before he leaves. Then I'll return," he said.

Her husband closed the door behind him. She dropped her face into her hands.

He was back in moments. Raking his hands through his blue-black hair, he stalked back and forth at the foot of the bed. "Why, Zoe? Why fly when you knew you were with child? After losing our first child, how could you have put the second at risk?"

"I didn't think there would be any risk—"

"You didn't care if there would be risk. I know why you did it." His face looked as if it were carved from stone. But his jaw twitched. "I looked at the notes in your writing desk. The letters you put in there, the notes you made in your journal. Your plans for your attempt to fly around the world. I told you to stop and you didn't. You were planning to do it while pregnant. What did you plan to do—hide this all from me? Damn it, Zoe, how could you do this to me?"

"I wasn't going to fly around the world. As soon as I knew I was pregnant, I realized I couldn't do it. And once the child was born... I knew I wouldn't want to leave for months to fly. I would want to be here for every minute with our daughter or son. But I wanted to make one last flight. I had planned the changes to the plane and I was so proud of them, and I wanted to fly it one last time before putting it away for months. Then the engine failed. Yes, I did continue my planning, but I had made the choice to stop today. And you—you read my letters and my journal. You pried into my private things."

"I am your husband."

"You act like my jailer more than my husband. I am sorry I crashed my plane. Sorry I lost our child. Sorry! Sorry! Sorry!" She was shrieking at him.

The more shrill and desperate she became, the icier and more withdrawn Nigel looked. "Then I'm sorry, too, Zoe. I'll leave you to rest, as the doctor said." He turned toward the door.

"No! You've hurt me and upset me and you have to stay and have this fight with me. You can't hide from emotion this time, Nigel. I won't let you—"

But he walked through the door. She was going to slip out of bed and chase him, but her legs felt too shaky.

She flopped on the bed. They had been rebuilding a tenuous relationship again after losing one child. What would happen now that they'd lost two?

He blamed her for losing this child. Yes, she'd been rash to fly. Yes, she'd been consumed by her yearning to do something remarkable. But it wasn't wrong for her to want to achieve something. It wasn't.

HE HADN'T FELT like this for a long time. Not since he had first been on the battlefields on the Western Front and had seen the carnage. Not since his brain had almost imploded from the insanity of sending young men out to run at machine gunners.

The hot rage he'd felt at the beginning of the War quickly froze over into a cold, empty sense of loss. With each day, he'd grown icier. But now the pain coursing through him was hot. Fiery hot and burning him on the inside.

Nigel poured a tumbler half-full of brandy. He threw the full contents down his throat. It was like using gasoline to quench a fire.

God, how could she have taken such a chance? Why hadn't she told him about the baby? Why had she kept it a secret from him?

You have kept secrets from her—when she begged you to reveal them.

He poured another drink and tried to use it to silence the voice in his head. But it didn't work. He had to keep his secrets from her.

But she had not wanted to share the news of a baby with him.

God, why had she flown that blasted plane? He'd had the windows repaired the day before and the wreckage of the aeroplane cleared away. The burned lilacs had been cut down. But he would never forget. Never...

God—

"Your Grace."

He spun and snapped at Bartlet, "What in hell is it?"

He tasted brandy in his mouth—it tasted sour now. Instant contrition hit him. "I apologize, Bartlet. My nerves are— I am on edge."

"I understand, Your Grace. I apologize for the interruption, but there is a gentleman on the telephone. Lord Steward. He asked to speak to you at once."

Steward was a friend of Nigel's former superior in the War, Brigadier Arthur Stanley, who had since inherited his family title and had become Lord Durham.

Frowning, Nigel went out in the hallway and picked up the phone. "Langford here," he said quietly.

"Langford," shouted a loud, serious voice. "This is Steward. I am telephoning you about Durham. He's been shot and killed. By a female named Lily Bell. The girl had been writing him letters, blaming him for her brother's execution for cowardice. I believe you know something about this girl."

"Wait, Steward—" Nigel felt as if the floor had tipped. "Lily Bell murdered Durham? Are you certain of this?" The girl had been upset. She had written angry letters. She had disappeared. But this—

"It appears to be so."

Appears. "What happened to the girl?"

"She has vanished," Steward said. "She has not been home to her family for weeks—"

"I know that. I have had investigators searching for her. Is it certain she's the one who shot Durham?"

"Durham's secretary seems to believe it is," Steward answered. "He claims he heard the girl shouting at his lordship. Shrieking like a banshee with rage. He went in to get the girl out, and when he opened the door she was shouting that she would shoot Durham. Durham was sitting in his chair behind his desk, white as a sheet.

He tried to capture her, but she ran out. The secretary—
his name is Goodeve—heard a sound like a shot that
night. He was up late, attending to paperwork. Found
Durham again in his study, dead on the floor."

"Was there a witness to the actual shooting?"

"No, Langford, there was not. Has to have been the
girl, though. Had an argument, made threats, was on
the scene. And now she's done a bunk."

"That is not evidence, Steward." That was what Zoe
would say, with her American defiance over things she
felt were based on the English class system.

"There is a hunt on for the girl, of course," Steward
said. "Since you have been looking for her, you will be
of use. Can you come down to London?"

"Now? Hell, not now—" Nigel broke off. He had to
know what had happened. If Lily Bell had done this…
it was because he had not prevented her brother's execution.

This was his fault, damn it. He should have been able
to find her when she left her home. Stopped her from
doing this. Durham—a good man—was dead.

His hand shook. "I cannot come to London yet.
Damn it, I will come when I can." Christ, he needed
to help Lily. He should be here for Zoe. But he didn't
know what to do for Zoe. And he was filled with anger.
Maybe it would be best to be away from her.

THE QUIET OF the house pressed on her. Zoe couldn't
stand it anymore. The servants spoke in hushed whispers around her room. When Julia or Nigel's mother
came to see her, they used the tones you did with someone who was dying.

Zoe called her mother in New York and told her that

she had crashed her plane and had had another miscarriage. Mother had been furious, of course.

"If you keep pushing him, keep hurting him, you will lose him. You are a duchess, Zoe. It's your duty to give him a son. For God's sake, do that for him."

She had hung up. She was tired of fighting everyone.

She got up and put on a jumper of light gray wool and a plaid skirt. In front of her vanity mirror, she pulled her comb through her limp and lifeless hair. Hollow eyes stared back at her. The woman looking at her looked so much older. As if each loss—her unborn children, her brother, her father, Billy's beloved—had carved wrinkles in her face and washed the sparkle from her eyes.

She supposed that was exactly what had happened.

She walked through Brideswell and maids said, "Good morning, Your Grace," in sad and subdued voices. Warm sunlight spilled through the two-story-tall windows into the foyer, but Zoe shivered.

Once she would have thought of flying or driving to ease the pain in her heart, but she couldn't face flying. She walked into the drawing room. There was a decanter of sherry, favored by the dowager. She thought of using a glass to try to help her.

Then she saw something else. The perfect thing. The thing she needed.

She set it up as quickly as she could. Within seconds, the bright, vibrant tones of a song burst into the heavy silence of the room. She closed her eyes and twirled around the floor and let the music lift her heart. The song was fast and light and she bit her lip. Even though tears leaped to her eyes, she knew she needed more jazz. She plucked another recording from the stack.

"What in God's name are you doing?" The words

were barked at her from the doorway. "I was in my study when I heard this—this racket."

Zoe turned, the record balanced between her fingers and the cardboard sleeve. "I just wanted to put on some music. The silence in this place... I know everyone is being kind and concerned, Nigel, but it's like a tomb. I feel like I'm being crushed alive."

"You can't possibly want to listen to music."

"I do." She put the second record on the phonograph and dropped the needle on it. Music swelled. Nothing bright and sparkling this time. This song was gentle and sad and soft, and she moved to it.

Nigel stalked to the gramophone. She reached out to stop him, which only made him work faster. He wrenched the needle from the record, scratching it. Destroying it.

"This is wrong," he snapped. "How can you enjoy yourself now? How can you damn well want to dance?" He held the ruined music in his hand.

Zoe shook. Could he not even let her grieve as she wished? "I have to listen to music," she said, her voice cool. She was too tired for shouting, for passionate arguments. They had changed. Now he was filled with hot anger, and she could not express any emotion at all. She was drained of all emotion.

"I like to listen to music, even when I feel sad," she said. "It lets me touch every one of my memories and hold them close. It lets me cry."

She was tired of fighting over every little thing, of carrying the weight for the loss of their baby. For this one was her fault—she knew he thought that. He avoided her, after all.

She snatched the record from his hands and she broke

it in hers. She threw the pieces to the floor. "Fine. There won't be music. You've taken that from me. When will you have taken enough that you've evened the score?"

He walked away from her without a word. Without giving her an answer.

Two days later she discovered he had sold her airplane—her first one—while she'd been recuperating. And he had sold her motorcar.

Two footmen carried a trunk down the stairs.

"What is going on?" Nigel demanded of the servants who were quietly grunting while struggling to balance the load of the trunk.

The man carrying the back of the trunk, the newest footman, stared at him in confusion. "Her Grace. Wants the Daimler brought around. Mr. Bartlet told us to hurry up with her trunks."

Nigel took the stairs two at a time and found his wife in her bedroom. She wore a coat and skirt that reached far above her knee and a bright pink cloche hat.

"Where are you going?"

"I'm going home. Where I can listen to a recording if I want. Where I can drive a car without feeling that I'm a vile monster. I am going back to New York."

"To visit your mother—"

"I don't belong here. I make you unhappy. And you seem to want to make me unhappy. We've suffered loss. But you can't just stop living when that happens. I can't be in mourning until I die."

"I am not asking for that."

"Once you said you loved my spirit. My joie de vivre, you called it. But you don't love it. Ever since we've been married, you've fought my spirit. Sometimes I think you married me to crush my spirit. That it was a challenge to you to make me miserable. I've done nothing but make you miserable."

"Zoe, I don't want you to leave."

"You do. We will both be happier."

"Stay."

"Everything would have to change. And you hate change."

"Change…how?"

"You have to let me grieve in the ways I want to grieve. You attacked me for listening to music when I told you why I needed it. But you have to forgive me. And I need you to share with me the memories that haunt you."

He stared at her. "You want so much."

"No, I want *too* much. I accept that," Zoe said. "What I did was misunderstand the man I was falling in love with. I thought I could thaw you out. But I was wrong. I can't change you. I shouldn't want to change you. But I wanted you to be the man who laughed with me, who made love to me in an airplane—I wanted you to be that man all of the time. That's a part of you, but not all of you. I have to be married to all of you. But I can't be."

FOR SOME REASON, Nigel could take in her words, but his brain refused to understand them. "What do you mean by 'you can't be married to all of me'?"

"You wallow in guilt and grief, Nigel. I can't. You want me to surrender every joy in my life and I can't. I can't live like this for the rest of my life."

"What in God's name are you saying, Zoe?"

"I want a divorce."

"That's impossible."

"Don't you remember when you proposed? You said you would agree to my terms. If I wanted to be a duchess for five minutes or forty years, you would agree."

He had said that. He regretted the words now. "I was wrong."

"Well, I'm leaving. For good."

"That's ridiculous."

"I can't do this anymore. You lash out and then you're contrite. I'm tired of absorbing your anger, tired of my emotions being utterly controlled by yours. I'm tired of disappointing you. I am going home. Brideswell is secure and you have done your duty. If you want to marry and have a child, you will have to divorce me." She picked up her scarf, threw it around her shoulders. "One more thing. Your mother and the dowager won't accept a marriage between Julia and Dr. Campbell. Don't stand in the way of Julia's happiness."

"Julia has been raised to be a lady, to run a grand house, not to be a wife living above a doctor's surgery. She belongs in a house like this. Just as you belong here, because you are my wife."

Zoe leveled him a direct glare. "It doesn't matter what Julia was raised to do—what matters is what she *wants*."

Then she walked out of her room.

Nigel ran to the top of the stairs, leaned over the railing. All he had to do was call her name. Call to her to wait, to give him another chance. But she would stay only if he did the one thing he could not do.

It wasn't changing. That wasn't what scared him. She wanted the truth from him. Wanted him to admit what still haunted him from battle. He couldn't because if he told her he would lose her anyway.

It was better to let her go.

He released the smooth polished balustrade. Shoved himself back so he stood at the top of the stairs, where she wouldn't see him. He heard the murmured voice of Bartlet. He could not make out her answer, but the soft, rich tone of her voice wrapped around his heart.

Zoe was right. He had made her unhappy.

He loved her so damn much. It was why he had to let her go.

To where she could be happy.

He heard her walk away, heels echoing on the foyer floor. He saw shafts of sunshine spill into Brideswell as she opened the door. Then the door slammed shut and the loud *thud* echoed in his ears.

22
NEW YORK

Four months later
Early July, 1923

NIGEL POURED OVER newspapers and the society sheets. For four months, the closest he had been to Zoe was to see her face in grainy black-and-white print in the news. The American and British press loved to report every antic of the "American Duchess" as she cut a swath through New York. Every party she attended, every restaurant she frequented, the speakeasies where she was photographed leaving at dawn. She celebrated her twenty-first birthday in New York in April—and he hadn't even known it was her birthday.

The attempted flight around the world by Major Quigley never happened. But in early May, Zoe flew solo from New York to Florida. Nigel had felt a deep shot of fear and nerves as he read about it. She could have crashed. He could have lost her forever.

But when he saw the picture of her—her bright smile, her wave for her well-wishers—he'd experienced an intense surge of pride.

There was no woman equal to Zoe.

On this morning, the fourth day of July—America's

Independence Day—Nigel went through the papers, ignoring articles on the state of the world, searching for a story about Zoe.

Touching her photograph wasn't as good as touching her. But it was all he had.

There were two pictures in the paper. One was of Zoe sitting at a round table with a bald, bespectacled man. The caption read: "The American Duchess steals another heart. Rumor has it Hollywood director Theodore O. Drake (pictured) plans to make Her Grace, the Duchess of Langford, the star of his new picture."

In the second, Zoe stood in front of a ribbon. "The American Duchess opens new art exhibit of the works of modern artist Jack Donahue." A young man in bohemian clothes gazed adoringly at Zoe.

He was going to lose her.

The realization hit Nigel hard. Like a shell exploding in front of him.

"No, damn it," he muttered. It wasn't jealousy or possessiveness. He loved her. These past four months, he had thrown himself into his hunt for missing Lily Bell. But it hadn't worked—there wasn't a moment when he did not think of Zoe.

Bartlet moved soundlessly into the room. "There is a telephone call, Your Grace. It is Her Grace."

Nigel stared, stunned. Zoe had never called him on the telephone. He had never even tried to speak to her over the instrument.

He pushed his chair back and went out into the hall. There he picked up the receiver of the telephone, held it awkwardly against his ear. "Hello? Zoe, is that you?" Crackling filled his ear. He shouted, "Zoe? Are you there?"

"I'm here, Nigel."

She sounded different over the phone. Older. The softness to her voice was lost in the cables that spanned the ocean. God, there was so much to say. But he couldn't shout it over the telephone. "I want you to come home."

"What? I can't hear you, Nigel."

"Why have you called, Zoe?" His heart ached with hope. She was returning to Brideswell.

"Nigel, I need to have a divorce."

"Zoe, not a divorce. No." Could she even hear his hoarse voice, thousands of miles away?

Her voice came through clear. Sad, but determined. "Nigel, I don't want to be alone for the rest of my life. I am only twenty-one. I want to have love, and you won't give that to me. I've met men who would love me. Please let me go."

"Zoe, I can't."

"It's not fair, Nigel. You don't want me."

"God, Zoe, I *do* want you," he shouted. Across the foyer a maid gasped and dropped her duster. He looked at the young woman with agonized eyes. He did not care that she had heard his pain. Once he would have cared about appearances and scandal, but not anymore.

"I want you," he said loudly. "I have lived four months of hell."

"You want me only on your terms. I thought you would come after me. I really did. But you aren't coming, are you?"

"I cannot travel, Zoe. I am a scarred-up wreck of a man—"

"You aren't! And aren't I worth crossing an ocean?"

"I could ask the same of you. Why will you not return to Brideswell?"

"Because I would do that—in a heartbeat—for you.
But I have to know you've changed. So far from this
conversation, I don't think you have. Come after me or
let me go, Nigel. That's your choice. Tell me right now
what you are going to do."

"Zoe—" There was Lily, who was still missing.
There was the thought of crossing the ocean, stuck on
a ship with people shocked by his scars. "I don't know."

She hung up.

A telegram came the next day. Simple. Direct. It
read: Let me go *stop*

Nigel drove into the village the next day and sent
one of his own, addressing it formally since it was correspondence, and he could hardly be familiar when it
was being inputted into a machine.

dear madam *stop* the duke of langford does not divorce his wife *stop*

In response, the next day he received a telegram that
read:

my dear husband *stop* our marriage is a drafty and
leaky institution with sagging roof and no modern
plumbing *stop* we are not comfortable in it anymore
stop we have outgrown the edifice *stop*

So once again, he found himself at the telegraph office in the village:

speak for yourself madam *stop*

To which she replied:

there must be some scandal that would make you willing to let me go *stop* intend to cause embarrassment
in the extreme *stop*

"NIGEL, SOMETHING MUST CHANGE," Julia said.

He looked up. He stood at the edge of the small lake,
tossing in stones. Zoe had swum in here without any
clothes, lit up by moonlight.

"The weather has to," he said. The air pressed on
them like a hot, wet blanket. In some places the cloud
in the sky was black as night, as if it were stoking up
its anger before it stormed. "This heat has to break.
Have you seen the news from London? All this heat is
fomenting civil unrest."

His sister took off her hat and used it to fan her face.
"I am not talking about civil unrest. I came here to talk
about your *marriage*."

"I know what you want to talk about."

"You aren't any happier without her."

"I never expected to be," he said.

Julia waved her hat at a buzzing bee. "Then why did
you let her go?"

He'd spent months trying to answer that question. "I
was afraid to keep her, afraid to convince her to stay.
Afraid I would hurt her. Hell—" He had not meant to
curse in front of his sister. "I *had* hurt her."

He took a deep breath, watching the water ripple
under the sunlight. "When Zoe went back to America,"
he said softly, "I didn't go back to what I was before.
Neither did Brideswell. It became something new."

There were no strains of jazz music floating from

the drawing room. No cough and sputter of an aircraft engine. There was no woman who jauntily walked into breakfast, determined to challenge his every belief and defy his every command.

"I understand what it was like for you," he said. "I thought Brideswell would always be a refuge. I dreamed about home when I was in the trenches. This place seemed like heaven. But it isn't like that for me anymore. The house, the estate, they are filled with memories. Bad ones and good ones. I could fight to sweep them away, but I realize I don't want to lose them. After you lost—" He hesitated. Even now, five years later after the War, he didn't want to remind her of loss. After what Zoe'd said, he'd expected Campbell to come to him any day asking for Julia's hand. But the surgeon hadn't. He didn't understand why not.

He suspected Zoe would. If only she were here so he could ask her.

"You can say his name, Nigel. Anthony Carstairs."

"It's been five years. I suppose you are healed now that you care for someone else."

Julia picked up a stone from the pile he'd gathered. She skipped it. While his had splashed in the water and sunk, hers skipped four times.

"I will never forget him," she said. "I will always have memories. I suppose if I live to be very old, some of them may slip away, but I will keep them alive as long as I can. My first dance with Anthony was in the ballroom here. I remember it so vividly. I remember the very first time we stood in the foyer after everyone else had left, and I had a few precious unchaperoned moments. At first, living with those memories was like walking on glass. Every step was filled with stabbing pain. Now those memories are sweet. The pain is still there. His life was cut short. It was an awful loss, and I can't do anything about it."

"But you can embrace life," he said. "Zoe was right. But I've realized that too late. I drove her away because I couldn't embrace life, and I tried to stop her from doing it, too."

"Zoe is not gone forever, Nigel. She was in love with you."

"She wants a divorce, Julia."

He expected Julia to be surprised or shocked. She wasn't. But she said, "I don't think that is truly what she wants. She left because she was hurting terribly. She wouldn't have felt such pain if she didn't love you deeply."

"That doesn't make sense. How could the fact I drove her away prove she loves me?"

"Do you love her?"

Julia's abrupt question startled him. She sounded like Zoe.

"Yes."

"Isn't that enough reason to try to win her back?"

He turned away from his sister, from the question in her eyes. "I'm scared to try. I have too many sins in my past that she knows nothing about. I cannot be the man Zoe wants me to be. I would like to embrace life, live for the moment or even for the future, but I can't escape the past."

"Perhaps you don't have to. Perhaps what you must do is share your past. Tell her about the things that trouble you."

Ever since Zoe had gone and Lily Bell had gone

missing, his nightmares had got worse. He barely slept. Exhaustion dragged at him. "I cannot."

"I don't see what you have to lose," she said bluntly.

"Zoe has lost so much—her brother, her fiancé, two babies even before they were born. She needs her happiness. I don't know if I can give her that."

"Can I marry Dougal Campbell?"

The question threw him off balance. "Yes. I want to see you happy."

"There was a time when I don't think you would have agreed. You would have thought the marriage beneath me. You have changed, Nigel. It has happened little by little, so gradually you haven't noticed it happening. You accepted Sebastian's decision to live in Capri. You have accepted my relationship with Dougal."

"I listened to Zoe about those things."

"You changed for Zoe. You can do it again, Nigel. You love her."

"And I should go to America and fight to win her back."

Julia nodded. She brushed away a tear and threw her arms around his neck. "I am happy you've changed," she whispered. "I was afraid for you. I hated seeing your pain, hated knowing you had been through hell and it still haunted you."

"You knew all that?" he asked slowly.

"Of course. We all did. We've tried—Mother, Grandmama, myself—to be careful around you. If I could have turned back time for you, I would have done so."

Dear God, he had trapped them all, hadn't he, with his grief and guilt? He had not been protecting them. He had been hurting them. If it had not been for Zoe, he would not have let Julia blossom or Sebastian follow his heart. His mother had been locked up in grief over losing Will and probably over losing some of her babies before they were born.

He gave Julia a kiss on her cheek, but she waved him away. "Go and pack to sail to America."

Nigel ran back to Brideswell. He raced in through the drawing-room doors. His mother sat in a wing chair, pouring tea for his grandmother. Isobel was away at school—something he had been able to afford using the income from Zoe's settlement on Brideswell, now carefully invested.

"Nigel, what is going on?" Grandmama cried. "Are we being invaded?"

Panting from his sprint, he pushed back his sweat-soaked hair. "No, I am going to America. To bring Zoe back." He couldn't catch his breath but he declared, "I'm sorry. I've been a bloody fool. We have to change. We have to open our hearts to the future. I let Zoe go, and that was the damned stupidest thing I've ever done. I tried to build walls around Brideswell. Now I want to knock them down. I want to throw open the doors. I want to see my family happy. If you will excuse me, I have to pack and book a ticket on a steamer to New York to win back my wife."

He ran out of the room and heard his grandmother say, "Goodness, I think the heat of this summer has gone to his head."

"No," his mother answered softly, but in strong and happy tones. "I think, finally, my son is healing. I am so very glad."

NIGEL CURSED EVERY minute it took to travel. First by the Daimler to the train station. Then by train to Southampton. He took a moment to send out one final telegram: am coming to New York *stop* expect me on the 20th *stop*. The journey by ship was ten days of sheer frustration. He paced the decks as if his fast, tense strides could propel the liner faster. In the evenings he was invited to dine at various tables—everyone wanted to dine with a duke. People tried to ignore his scars, and he tried to ignore how hard they attempted to do it.

After the War, his scars and his shell shock had made him reclusive. Now none of that mattered as much to him as getting Zoe back.

Once he reached New York, a cab dropped him off at the front gate of Zoe's family home on Fifth Avenue.

He did something Zoe would do—he let out a whistle. His eyes bulged at the sight.

An ornate French château had been re-created, with turrets that soared to the sky. The house took up half the city block and was surrounded by a tall wrought iron fence, with a gate inset with a gold coat of arms.

An archly correct butler opened the door. "Good afternoon, sir. Is the mistress expecting you?"

"I am the Duke of Langford. The mistress of the house is my mother-in-law. At this point, I cannot speculate if she is anticipating my arrival."

"Your G-Grace." The butler bowed deeply. "Good afternoon. Please follow me."

Nigel was led to an enormous drawing room. Mirrors with heavy gilt frames ran the length of one side of the room, reflecting the arched windows on the other, along with gilt trim and the two enormous chandeliers.

He heard the clatter of heels on the floor and smelled gardenias by the bushel. Mrs. Gifford swept into the room like Marie Antoinette entering the Hall of Mirrors.

He bowed and she curtsied, rang a bell, then waved him to a large Queen Anne chair.

She took her seat. "Your Grace. I had no idea you were coming to America." She licked her lips, an anticipatory gleam in her eye.

"Zoe didn't tell you? I sent a telegram informing her I was coming."

"You did? Oh, dear." Now she looked at him with terror in her large eyes. She wore a dress of silk that swirled around her thin legs and a headdress with diamonds and three white feathers. It startled him, considering it was the afternoon.

He found he couldn't stop looking around the room. Light was reflected everywhere and kept dazzling him.

"I see you are admiring this drawing room. It's one of a half dozen in the house. It is far nicer than Alva's. Her house is so dark and gloomy and oppressive. I thought I should like a drawing room that looked just like the Hall of Mirrors in Versailles."

He shuddered. She'd achieved that. But then he realized she'd mentioned a name. "Alva?"

"Alva Vanderbilt. The one who married her Consuelo to a duke." She gave a smug smile. "Well, I did just as well."

"That marriage ended in divorce, I believe."

The smile vanished. "It did. I do not intend the same thing to happen to Zoe. The girl is being an absolute fool. I was pleased to see that you told her you wouldn't accept a divorce."

"No, I will not."

"Zoe is determined to have one, though. She can be stubborn."

"Then I shall have to reclaim her affections."

The teacup almost dropped from her fingers. Tea sloshed to the rug. "That is why you are here? To win my daughter back?"

"Yes."

"And Zoe knew you were coming? That girl! She's gone to California."

His heart stuttered. Why had she left? To avoid him?

"She said if anyone wanted to see her, that person was welcome to go to Hollywood and see her there. Looking back on it, I guess she meant you, Your Grace." Mrs. Gifford looked worried. "That girl is playing silly games."

"No, she is not," he said softly. "I hurt her." But it was hopeful, wasn't it, that she wanted him to come after her? "Mrs. Gifford, I want to repair my marriage. I made a great many mistakes, but mainly it is tragedy that came between Zoe and me. Zoe escapes tragedy with adventure and excitement. I can't do that. Losing the babies hurt me a great deal. I understand it also hurt her. But our pain built an impenetrable wall between us. I need to breach that wall, but I don't know how. I have to make amends to Zoe. What do I need to do to make her believe I can change?"

"You shouldn't have to do anything at all!" she declared. "Zoe needs to see sense. I have lectured the girl six times to Sunday that she had no right to leave you. She should have listened to you and done her duty."

"Mrs. Gifford, while I would love to agree with you, I recognize that lecturing Zoe, insisting she do her duty, won't work. I'm asking you now—what *will* work?"

"Zoe is unfortunately very wild." Annabelle Gifford heaved a great sigh. "We were not wealthy at the beginning. Um…not at all. When we came to New York, despite my husband's position in business and his success, the rulers of New York society snubbed us. They liked our new money—they were smart enough to know they needed it—but they didn't like us. The women were the worst, of course. There wasn't much they could do to me—poverty gives you a thick skin. But it hurt Zoe badly. She was young, impressionable. To be sneered at and ignored and mocked hurt Zoe very much. She said it didn't affect her. That she didn't care. But she did."

He had always thought Zoe was supremely confident. How else could she fly an aeroplane, drive so fast, grasp life with both hands if she didn't believe she had the right to?

"Tell me more," he said. "Tell me about Zoe."

Mrs. Gifford patted her hair. "Well, that's all said and done and in the past. We've come a long way since those days and I don't see any sense in raking them up—" She broke off, tugging the ropes of pearls around her neck.

He was about to speak, but he had to stop as a silver tea tray was brought in, and Mrs. Gifford served him carefully, obviously having studied how to do it.

He set down his cup. "I don't care about your past or Zoe's origins. I want to know more about her. To understand how to win her heart."

"No mother knows how her daughter's heart really works, Your Grace. If we did, we'd get the marriages we wanted out of them every time. And those marriages would stick."

23
CALIFORNIA

NIGEL HAD TRAVELED the Atlantic by boat and Manhattan in a hot, ripe-smelling taxicab. Now he had crossed the entire, vast, endless expanse of America in a Pullman sleeping car attached to a locomotive. After five days on a train, he was restless, frustrated and anxious.

The brilliant blue California sky stretched over him as he was driven to Zoe's rented mansion. He was driven down flat roads lined by palm trees. Open cars motored by him. They passed by sprawling mansions of white stucco. Behind the houses stretched the blue water and pounding surf of the ocean. The ocean around England was darker and fiercer. This ocean was an inviting blue, with rolling white-capped waves.

As they drove, his cabdriver rhymed off the names of the owners.

"Who are they?" Nigel inquired.

"Movie stars and directors!" The man twisted to stare at him as if he were crazy.

Zoe's house was white with a Spanish look, like most of the others. His driver opened the gate and pulled up in a circular drive by a fountain.

Zoe had found a very British butler for her rented California home. "Yes?" the man inquired.

"The Duke of Langford. Here to finally see my wife, the Duchess of Langford."

The butler's jaw dropped open. "No foolin'?" he gasped. Then he straightened and adopted his proper pose. "Her Grace is not in—"

"I am growing tired of hearing that. I will wait for her. She is still in California, is she not?"

"Indeed, Your Grace. Actually, Her Grace is outside, on the beach. I will show you where to go down to the sand."

He was taken to a long room, with a low timbered ceiling. The white stucco wall had a pattern of shells. There were ornate brown and blue tiles and masses of palm trees outside. But one thing grabbed Nigel's attention and kept it there.

It was a portrait of Zoe—an enormous painting with a heavy, ornate silver frame. It hung on the wall at the opposite end of the room. Nigel walked to it, staring at it.

Bold brushstrokes of wild, vibrant colors leaped out. It was a modern impressionist portrait fashioned of bold shapes. In the picture, Zoe was seated on a velvet stool in front of a vanity table. She had been painted in the nude.

Her long, slim back was rendered in pink, white, ivory, touches of blue and gold. Her face was turned away from the mirror, so her profile was shown to the observer and shown in the mirror. The mirror also reflected her bare breasts, done with loose, dashed brushstrokes.

This was Zoe being modern and daring. But she was also his—his precious treasure.

Her butler stopped and turned. "If you care to wait here, Your Grace—"

"What I care to do is to have that picture removed from this wall."

"I beg your pardon—"

Nigel pointed at the picture. "That portrait will come down."

Consternation showed on the man's face. "I have been given no instruction by Her—"

"You will have it moved now. You will rehang it in whatever bedroom you are having prepared for me. As for Her Grace, I will explain the change to her."

Two gardeners were summoned and had taken the portrait down when a thin young man with slicked-back dark hair strolled in, wiping paintbrushes with a rag.

Nigel stared at the man—he looked bohemian and disheveled. Black stubble clung to his cheeks and jaw. A cigarette dangled from his lips. A white shirt spattered with paint hung on him, the sleeves rolled up, the neck open, shirttails hanging out. He was the man from the photo in the newspaper.

"Hey, what're you doin' with my picture?" the painter asked.

Nigel gave an icy ducal stare. "You painted that portrait of my wife?"

"You must be the duke." The man stared insolently. "What did you take it down for?"

"I am having it moved to my room. It is only for a husband to see his wife in a state of undress."

The artist blinked. "She was right about you. You *are* a stuffed fish."

Nigel's heart hurt. That was how she saw him? Of course—how else had he behaved with her? He couldn't argue he had behaved badly because he loved her. The last time they had fought, after she'd lost the second baby, his anger had been selfish.

"What are you doing here, anyway? I thought she was getting a divorce."

"That is what I have come to discuss." He narrowed his eyes. "What are *you* doing here?"

"Zoe lets me use part of her garage as my studio." The artist smirked. He continued to clean his brush. "You're going to lose her, Duke. I intend to convince Zoe to marry me."

"I have no intention of losing her. You have an hour to pack up your belongings and leave. Now," Nigel growled. "And how in hell do I get down to the beach?"

The artist pointed to a row of French doors sullenly.

Nigel passed through them onto a sun-drenched concrete terrace. He took the stairs down to the sand, which was soft, pale and blazing hot. His boots sank into it as he trudged along, searching for Zoe.

Girls lay on towels or reclined on deck chairs. Skimpy, skintight bathing costumes revealed acres of skin.

Then he saw her—her lovely profile. Her eyes were closed, lashes touching her cheeks. Her face was tipped up to the sun. Her hair glowed like gold. She was wearing a beige robe of a light fabric, belted at her waist. She looked so young.

He'd forgotten how young she was. Only twenty when they got married. They both had so many bad memories behind them, acquired in so little time.

He walked around in front of her so his body blocked out the sun.

Finally, she opened her eyes and she squinted at him. "Nigel? You found me? You came all this way? Why?"

He'd had days to plan this moment—his journey to this point had taken him more than two weeks. But he didn't know what to say. *I want you back.* "I told the artist who is living in your house to leave."

"It's my house. I can collect any artists in it that I like. I think I'm going for a swim. I'd invite you but I don't think you are dressed for it."

She stood from her chair and fastened the strap of her flower-trimmed bathing cap.

"Zoe, stay here. Stop running from me. Talk to me."

"You don't want to talk. You want to issue commands." She undid her belt. Her robe fell to the sand.

Nigel gasped, choked, sputtered.

She was beautiful.

Zoe gazed at him, her face filled with defiance. Every instinct told him to forbid this. His brain warned he could prove he'd changed by letting her do this— letting her parade her bare midriff, her long legs, her curves on the beach.

Hell, he hadn't changed that much.

Snatching up her robe, Nigel hauled Zoe to him and wrapped the robe around her. "I don't give a damn how wild you need to be to blot out pain. I want you. I love you. You belong to me—"

"No, I don't. I'm nobody's chattel." Her eyes were blazing. "I have my own house. My own friends. I can do what I want. I can fly if I want. I bought myself a car. I might even start making movies. Why not? I could do it, you know. I don't want your world, and you don't want me, so let me go."

"I *do* want you. Do you no longer love me, Zoe?"

"I—" Her violet eyes flicked over his face. She met his gaze, then looked away.

"Zoe, I behaved badly. I hurt so much. You are right. I behaved like I was angry when you flew and your plane crashed—"

"I make you angry, Nigel. Can't you see it's no use between us?"

He reached for her hand. When she didn't snatch it away, he felt a flare of hope. He stroked her fingers. "This is what I should have done after you lost the child. I see that now."

His voice cracked and he tried again. "The truth was that I wasn't angry. I was afraid. In battle, there were so many times I was afraid. And sick with guilt, knowing most of the men under me wouldn't survive. I had to lie to them. Keep their spirits up. I was not allowed to show fear. I was so afraid I could have lost you. I reacted badly—I had no right to lash out at you, to sell your aeroplane and your car. It was fear, Zoe. I thought the only way I could fight that fear was to ensure I kept you safe. But I don't want to make you unhappy."

She turned toward the ocean. The crashing waves framed his view of her. His gaze went down, and when he looked at her bathing costume again, he got hard, aroused and shocked all at once. The bathing costume summed things up rather nicely, if he thought about it.

"We are two very different people, Zoe. You crave adventure. I had my fill of risk and daring. I want peace, comfort and happiness."

"Nigel—"

"Maybe you are right," he said, his voice low because his chest was so tight. "We don't belong together. Even now, I can't honestly tell you I want to see you fly again.

You want to do daring things. I wanted to think I had changed and had opened my mind. But in my soul, all I want to do is keep you safe. Maybe I should do the decent thing…and let you go."

Zoe stared up at him. "That's what you really want? You know, I never dreamed you would leave Brideswell and cross an ocean and a country to get to me. Nor did I ever expect you to reach the conclusion you should let me go. I thought I would have to fight and fight. I—"

"Ready, honey? Let's shake things up and go for a swim."

Nigel took a step back as a tall, dark-haired girl came up and linked her arm with his wife, interrupting them. He could not speak about their private relationship in front of others.

Then his eyes bulged as he took a good look at the young woman. She wore a brief bathing-costume top of a shiny gold fabric. Like Zoe's, it was twisted at the cleavage of her breasts, the fabric artfully arranged to cover her bosom—just barely. It looked like something a chorus girl would wear. A long, gold fringed skirt encased her legs. Then he realized it was a piece of fabric, tied at her waist. The dark-haired girl tugged the knot and the skirt fell down. She kicked it away. She wore a skimpy pair of gold underpants.

Nigel couldn't stop himself. He picked up the wraparound skirt and held it up to shield both the woman and his wife.

The dark-haired woman laughed. "Darling, you are too sweet."

"I am making you both respectable."

"Honey, this bathing costume is no briefer than the one I wore in the movie where I'm captured for a sheikh's harem. That's the point I want to make. I can wear this on-screen, but not out here on the beach. What's wrong with women showing a bit of healthy flesh? We're not hurting anyone. Come on, Zoe!" With that, the woman ran, laughing, toward the water's edge and she raced into the waves.

"Who is that woman?"

"That's Lily Leigh. The actress."

"You are consorting with actresses?"

Zoe glowered at him. "She is a friend. A good friend. And she is struggling to carve her way in the world. She started with absolutely nothing, but everything she's done she accomplished herself. I am in awe of her. And I promised to go swimming with her in this bathing costume to make a point."

He went to grab Zoe's arm, but she darted away. And raced out into the waves.

The next thing he knew, a policeman was running toward his wife and Lily Leigh, blowing a whistle and shouting something about indecent exposure. A bunch of men with cameras were coming from the other direction.

"That Lily. She's a genius," shouted a man who had suddenly materialized beside Nigel. "Lots of girls have been arrested for wearing shocking bathing costumes, but this publicity stunt will put her on every newspaper in the nation. Clever of her to convince that duchess to do it, too."

The actress had set up the whole thing. Only she wasn't the only female being locked up with shackles.

The sun beat down, making sweat drip into Nigel's eyes.

He was watching his wife get arrested. For being

indecently exposed. While flashbulbs went off and a bunch of lean, wolfish-looking reporters took photographs.

ZOE NEVER DREAMED she would be looking at Nigel with the bars of a jail cell between them.

Her husband was the most gorgeous man she'd ever seen. Her house had been filled with movie actors and producers and handsome young men hoping to become the next Valentino. But no man she'd seen took her breath away like Nigel. To her, his scars made him irresistible. They spoke of the danger he'd faced. They revealed on the outside what had forged the man on the inside. The man who respected his tenants, who had fought for his country, who was now willing to give her the one thing she'd claimed she wanted.

He was right. How could they live together? But in that moment, she knew she loved him. Not still. More than ever.

"Stop pacing, Nigel. You're making me nervous."

He stopped, growled and stalked to the bars. Gripping them, he faced her, a few inches from the iron. "Is this what you meant when you put in your telegram that there must be some scandal that would make me willing to let you go?"

"Not exactly. That wasn't why I did this." She swallowed hard. "Do you want to let me go like you said on the beach?" It was what she knew she needed. Her independence. She couldn't live, loving him, knowing there was even more than an ocean and a continent between them.

If she moved on, she could put their past behind her. Couldn't she?

When she looked at him, God, she didn't want to.

"I am getting you out of here," he said curtly.

"They'll fine me, I'll pay it and I'll be out. They will likely let me out on bail—"

"I am getting you out now," he broke in. His hard, cold tone sent a shiver down her back.

With that, her husband stalked out of the jail. She saw him a few hours later and he was accompanied by a police officer carrying a set of old-fashioned keys.

She had been behaving cool and sophisticated, but as the door to her cell swung open, she almost ran into Nigel's arms. Being locked up had been more frightening than she let on. She wasn't as wild as she pretended.

"I had a discussion with one of the magistrates," he said. "The charges have been dropped."

He had brought clothing from her house. In private, she stripped off her prison garb and put on a dress, a coat and fresh stockings that she fastened with garters.

Nigel waited for her. With his hand at her lower back, he propelled her outdoors onto the steps of the police station. Reporters had found them somehow.

"The press in America is as irritating as in England," Nigel growled. He pushed his way through. There was something about a tall, irate duke that made people move aside.

When they drove through the gates of her home, she looked to him and finally asked, "What are you going to do? Leave? I suppose you are furious again." She took a deep breath. "If we were divorced, you would not have to be scandalized by me being in jail."

"No, Zoe, I am not leaving."

What did that mean? Was he staying because he

wanted her? She couldn't believe that—she wanted to believe it, but she couldn't risk her heart for him again.

The front door opened to her, and she walked in—

Her foyer and living room were filled with white roses. And Jack, the artist, stood in entrance to her living room, with two battered suitcases. "Afternoon, Duke. I was just going." To her, Jack said, "A dozen deliverymen came with them. They poured in the house, dumped roses everywhere and marched out. Left a card. I put it over there."

Zoe picked up a white card.

"Who are these from?" Nigel stared, his face pale. He didn't look angry. He looked lost.

"Mr. Howard Cornelius Randolph," Jack said, looking glum. "Made millions in oil fields. Fills the house with roses every second day."

She had encouraged flirtations with Jack and with Howard. Flirting kept her from thinking.

But the pain in Nigel's eyes hit her like a knife in her heart.

"He's in love with you. I cannot blame him for that. But are you in love with *him?*" She saw his shoulders shake. His hands fisted as he fought it.

She'd thought he had closed his heart to her after they'd lost the babies. But maybe his heart had been raw and open—just like hers was.

"I'm not. But I am supposed to go to his party tonight." She had to know. She had to test Nigel. "His parties are wild and thrilling and exciting. There's jazz, dancing and wild and crazy games, and the liquor flows like water."

"May I escort you?" her husband asked, very formally.

"I don't think it's your kind of party. You won't enjoy yourself."

"I want to take you, Zoe. I want to experience one of your wild parties with you. Even just once." Nigel took her hand and lifted it to his lips.

His kiss made more shivers go down her spine. But good, exciting ones.

"Goodbye, Zoe. I can accept defeat gracefully."

She barely heard Jack's parting words. She had told Nigel she could collect all the artists she wanted, but she had done that to tease him. Her knees quaked as her husband kissed the palm of her hand.

MR. HOWARD CORNELIUS RANDOLPH's mansion was about half the size of Brideswell, built of gray stone to look as if it had been there for two hundred years, and it blazed with light like an amusement park. Vibrant jazz music poured out of it—Nigel could hear the music from blocks away. It looked as if the world and its brother had been invited to the party. Cars filled the circular drive. There had been a collision between a Model T and a flashy cream-colored car covered in gleaming chrome, and a fight had broken out between the drivers.

Zoe pulled her car up to the curb. "We'll get out here."

She swung her shapely legs out, her silver dress glittering, as a young man ran up and she tossed the keys to him. "Park it when that mess ahead is cleared up."

The party made the jazz club in London look like a church meeting. They passed through the crowd in the house to the gardens in the back. Fountains shot water into the sky, and a pool wound between them like an exotic lagoon, with lights glimmering on the water and turquoise-colored tiles. An entire orchestra was positioned on a stage near the house. Tables were set out under tents, laden with food. Waiters darted to and fro with trays of champagne. Over the terrace and the lawns, people drank, shrieked and danced in contorted rhythms.

At one white-cloth-covered table, a girl lay on her cheek, asleep and snoring. At another, a man darted under the tablecloth and the girl sitting there began to squirm and squeal.

Zoe came to places like this, alone. Without him there to protect her.

Anger coiled in him. Anger at himself.

Zoe was kissed and hugged by dozens of men and women—people Nigel did not know. The evidence of a life she led that had nothing to do with him stabbed his heart and his conscience like twin knives.

He never should have let her go.

He should have fought for her that day she walked out of Brideswell—he should have fought for her before she reached the stairs. She took out her lipstick and slowly glided the soft, red stick over her full lips. Nigel couldn't look away from the smooth, slow motion and the way a glossy layer of cream was left on her soft mouth.

In a heartbeat, both his tie and his trousers were too tight.

"Dance with me," she said. "It is a party, after all."

He hesitated for one moment. Then he took her hand. The memory of dancing with her hit him hard. It was one of their sweet, happy moments.

Julia said Zoe had changed him, and he hadn't even

seen it happen. If he wanted Zoe, he had to change even more—and do it himself.

He led her to the terrace. Under twinkling lights, her silver dress sparked as if she had bathed in stars.

She danced with him, her graceful hand on his shoulder, her other hand in his. They moved in a flowing foxtrot. Around them was an explosion of sound and light and wild people—like people in a riot—but he didn't see or hear any of it.

They went to the buffet after that, and a tall, handsome blond man in a pink suit suddenly materialized out of the crowd or the ether. He lifted Zoe's hand and kissed her gloved fingertips. "My darling. I thought you might wear one of my roses as a token. You're a pure white rose yourself."

Nigel stepped forward, but Zoe smiled. "Howard, this is my husband, the Duke of Langford. Unfortunately, I couldn't wear one of your roses. There were so many and they were so lovely, I had them all donated to local hospitals and convalescence homes."

Randolph looked startled. But then he said smoothly, "A very lovely gesture made by a very beautiful woman."

For all his good looks, Randolph had a ruthless, mean look about him. If Nigel had met him in London, he would peg him as a street tough—the type to slit your throat for your purse. The man stuck out his hand. "I should be honored, having a real live duke at my party."

"But you're not," Nigel muttered. He moved closer to Randolph. "Do not send flowers to my wife anymore," he said softly.

"You might be out of your league, Your Grace," Randolph sneered. "We do things differently in America. When you're passionate about something, you take it."

"I am passionate about my wife. And I spent four years in trenches in Europe. I know how to protect what I love."

Maybe something of the scorching-hot anger inside him showed on his face. Randolph stepped back. "All right. I concede. No hard feelings. Right?"

"Agreed—if you leave her alone." Nigel turned to find Zoe. She had moved away from them. She stood near a tent with her hand on the arm of a tall, thin, dark-haired man. She smiled at the man, a sweet smile one gave a good friend.

"That man," he said to Randolph. "Do you know him?"

Randolph had pulled out a long, thin cigar and was lighting it. "Lynton Bailey," he said through clenched teeth. "Bailey is an American flying ace. A very good friend of Zoe's."

She was in rapt conversation with the dark-haired, handsome Bailey. She had been in love with an aviator before—DeVille. And she had been entranced by Major Quigley's plan to fly around the world.

Nigel's heart stuttered. She had found another kindred spirit. Had he already lost her?

No—hell. He wasn't going to let her go that easily.

He walked up to them, stopping a few feet away. "Zoe, I came to ask if you wanted to dance."

"You want to dance again now?" She turned to him.

Then Nigel registered the music being played. A wild, flamboyant jazz tune. He had to try to change for her. It was the only way he was going to keep her.

He had to do what she did—forget about the past and look to the future. "Teach me how," he said.

Bailey took out a lighter, held it to his cigarette. The flame shook. Nigel hadn't noticed it before—the tremble in the pilot's hand.

Waving to Bailey, Zoe took Nigel's hand and led him into the crowd of flailing people. He tried to follow Zoe's movements—waving his arms and kicking his legs forward. Certain he looked like a fool, he laughed. At himself.

Zoe stopped for a moment, as if struck dumb. Then she shouted, "I dare you!"

Next thing he knew, she jumped into the fountain and began dancing in it.

Madness. But she'd dared him. And if he wanted to win her back, he couldn't refuse.

He strode to the fountain with ducal determination and hopped over the stone wall, submerging his shoes and half his trouser legs. Water flew around him as his legs flew up and his arms waved. Zoe put her hands in the water and splashed him. He splashed her right back, moving faster, drenching her from head to foot.

He was laughing so hard his chest hurt.

He got close to her, determined to get her completely soaked, when she leaped up, wrapped her arms around his neck and kissed him so hard and so passionately he was sure the water on his face and hair turned to steam.

Lifting her in his arms, he carried her out of the fountain, wove through the crowd and got her to the front door.

After he ordered her car brought round, he demanded a towel. A bevy of servants—men in livery of white tie and black tailcoats, along with maids in black with crisp white aprons and caps—brought armloads of them for her. Fluffy, folded and white.

He took a large one and wrapped it around Zoe, used a smaller one to dry her bobbed hair. He quickly rubbed his own hair.

Then they were alone, sitting on the front steps of the mansion, waiting for her car. He had danced with Zoe. Kissed her in a fountain. But what would he do if she was in love with someone else?

"He has shell shock. The aviator. Bailey," he said, watching her expression.

There had been a dreamy look in her eyes that dropped away. "Yes," she said. "That's why I've been talking to him. I wanted to know what affected him so badly. I thought it would help me understand what you went through. He said there were a lot of things that shocked him. He witnessed one horrible, gruesome thing after another. But there was one incident that affected him so badly he couldn't fly anymore. It was terribly sad."

She took a deep breath and Nigel held his. He began to understand. She hadn't been falling in love with Bailey—she had been searching for a connection to *him*.

"A young friend of his was also a pilot, and he was shot down." Her voice was soft with sorrow. "Lynton went to help, but the young man burned alive. He heard the screams—they still haunt him." Zoe looked at him, and her violet eyes glowed more than the acres of stars above them. "I know there was something for you. There is something that haunts you. Lynton could tell me, and look—it didn't horrify me. It didn't make me faint in shock. We cannot go forward unless you finally tell me what is holding you back to the past."

He never dreamed he would tell her here, sitting on a set of stairs in front of a California mansion, soaking wet.

He couldn't keep it from her anymore. If she hated him—if he lost her for good, he would have to accept it.

This was what he had traveled thousands of miles to do—put his sins in front of Zoe and find out if she could ever love him in spite of what he'd done.

He let out a hoarse groan. "The first man I saw die…a shell burst in front of him. I can't describe what it did to him, but I still see it in my mind—" His voice cracked. "But that was battle. I could understand loss there. What I couldn't understand was when we killed our own men. I was ordered to have men shot for cowardice. I objected, but my superiors insisted. They wanted to make examples. Dear God, one of them—he was wrapped head to foot so he could not move, before he was taken and shot."

He stopped, took a deep breath. "I have never spoken about this to anyone. I vowed I never would. They were just boys, Zoe. Not men. Boys who were shot for cowardice. They were young and frightened. And the soldiers holding the rifles were just boys. Shaking like leaves. My superiors were afraid they would be unable to pull the triggers. I was to ensure they did. I refused. I was threatened with court-martial. I doubted the commanders would have me shot—one of the privileges of being the son of a duke. But the order was carried out while I was on patrol. When I could do nothing to stop it. Then, when I returned from war, I began to receive letters from a young woman. She had learned that I was her brother's commanding officer. He was one of the young men shot. She wrote me letters filled with hatred, called me a murderer. It is the truth of it."

"That was the letter you would not let me see."

Looking ahead, Nigel nodded.

She moved closer to him, rested her hand on his arm. "But you tried to stop it happening—"

"I suspect you would have risked getting shot to stop something so wrong."

She frowned. "You think—you think I would be that noble a person?"

"Of course I do. It's in your heart."

"But you had to follow orders."

"Duty. Bloody duty." Nigel shot up from the step and paced in front of her. "When I finally realized how damned wrong it was to blindly follow duty, I was too late. One night we were in the trench—we'd been waiting there for days for something to happen. That night, the Germans started shelling. Suddenly, a man was shouting from out on the field. One of our men. He was the only living soul out there and the explosions of the shells illuminated him. He stood upright with his arms stretched out and yelled, 'Look at me! Do I look like a tree?'"

Her hand went to her mouth. A red stain formed on the fingertips of her glove.

Not blood. Just lipstick.

"I realized it was Private Long. He was twenty, and before he volunteered, he helped in his father's greengrocer business. He had lost his mind, and I went out to him to haul him to the ground and get him to crawl back. Then he was hit, so I scrambled to get to him. The next shell exploded close to me, threw my body back twenty feet—that gave me the scars I have on my face. I crawled back toward Long again. I was bloody fed up and willing to risk my own life—no one else's, just mine—for Long. But one of my other young men, an eighteen-year-old named Archie Cromwell, came out to help me. He was shot to pieces by machine-gun fire. He lingered in the mud for minutes, screaming in agony. I survived, but he died because I decided to do something bloody stupid. I went out to Long because I didn't care if I died—" He stopped and shook his head, as if he could shake off the emotions gripping him.

He had to go on. He had one more thing to tell her. "I don't know if I truly welcomed death, but I kept thinking it wouldn't be so bad. It would have to be quiet, for one thing. I wouldn't hear any more screams. After the executions of my boys, that's what I dreamed of every night. Their pleas and their screams. When I crawled out to Long, I was damned tired of worrying about survival, and I thought getting death over with might not be so bad."

He stopped. No doubt, she thought him insane.

Her voice came to him—soft, rich, filled with sorrow. "Nigel, you did what you could! You tried to stop the insanity of shooting frightened young men. You did not intend to hurt Cromwell. You must stop punishing yourself."

She still didn't understand. "When Will died from influenza," he said, "I thought I was going to lose my mind. *I* should have died, not him. I would have given anything to silence the voices in my head. The frightened young men pleading for their lives, terrified. Archie's screams. And then your brother and my friend Rupert…and our unborn children… Why in God's name were so many innocent lives taken?"

He broke then. He'd fought so long to be stoic. To keep it inside. He'd fought the shaking and the panic. He'd desperately fought the damn tears.

They came now. He stood there, not acting like a duke, not acting like a gentleman whom others could depend on. He cried. Like a child. His shoulders shook with it. His chest ached. His throat rasped down breaths—it felt as if he was pouring fire down his throat.

God, she would be horrified. Disgusted. She admired aviators, successful oilmen, film producers and brash painters. Obviously she liked brave and daring men—

Her arms came around him. And she held him.

"You must despise me," he growled.

"Despise you? Nigel, I love you."

He wrapped his arms around her slender body. His lips brushed her forehead. "Let me take you to bed. Zoe, I want to spend tonight with you—all night. I want to sleep with you and hold you in my arms. I don't know if I can do this, but I have to try. If I can't, I'll give you your freedom."

24
GOING HOME

ZOE PEELED OUT of the mansion's circular drive and sped along the winding road that hugged the rocky coastline. They passed mansions that overlooked the beach. Here and there, the road almost seemed to hang out over the ocean, and if you looked down, you looked right at the rolling silver-tipped waves of the vast, dark Pacific. The breeze flowed over them, chilling her bare arms and her slender chest beneath her damp, thin dress.

"Stop here," Nigel said abruptly. "You're cold."

She pulled the car onto the shoulder of the road. Here was a long distance between the houses. On one side— where she'd carefully parked—was a drop-off, which fell several yards to the beach and the dark, crashing ocean. On the other side were tree-dotted hills and rocky outcroppings. The movie business had left New York to capture good weather and cheap land, and only a few yards from palatial houses, she could hear howling coyotes.

Nigel took his jacket, which was dry since he had stripped it off to dance in the fountain. He draped it over her shoulders.

It smelled of him—of masculinity and sandalwood. And sexual promise.

"You opened your heart to me, Nigel. How could you

have ever thought I would despise you for it? If you'd told me a year ago, I could have shared it with you. I could have told you that I just see you as the noblest, most wonderful man I've ever known."

"I'm not a flying ace or a self-made millionaire or an artist—"

"You are a hero and an English duke." She wrapped her arms around his neck.

And kissed him.

She stopped only to breathe, "I intend to take you to my bed. And you're going to stay there." Then a wild thought came to her. "Do you remember the night when we necked in my car?"

"I remember every single moment I've spent with you. Each and every moment was unforgettable."

Her heart soared, and he asked, "Do you know what I would like to do?"

She shook her head.

"Make love to you on the hood of this car. I've heard one of the benefits of automobiles is that they are a convenient place for ravishing."

Next thing she knew, Nigel had sat her bottom on the smooth, silver-blue hood of her flashy, brand-new Chrysler. Wrapped in his coat, she was warm, and she *ached* with desire. As a car whizzed by, illuminating them with headlight beams, Nigel nuzzled her neck, her jaw, kissed his way to the sensitive place at the base of her ear.

Someone hollered at them, but Nigel didn't stop.

Zoe leaned back, pulling her husband with her by his broad shoulders. She drew her short skirt up. Nigel didn't require much persuasion. He positioned his hips between her spread legs, kissing her intensely. He slid his hand under her bottom, lifting her to him. He pushed down her panties while she fumbled with the buttons of his trousers. She drew her silk underpants off and tossed them behind her into the open car.

She'd never dreamed he would actually *do* this.

She wrapped her arms around him, lifting herself to him.

"Zoe, you are so beautiful."

"So are you," she added. She knew to say it was to challenge him, but she wanted him to know it was true.

He paused a moment. Behind her, she heard the thunder of the waves on the sand, the murmur of the wind through palm trees, the erotic, harsh breathing of her husband, the soft little moans she made. She waited for him to argue. Or to look away and touch his scars.

He didn't. Instead, he held her gaze, the moonlight making his eyes pale blue. He just made love to her more fiercely. The hood of the car flexed beneath her; the body of it rocked on its springs.

A delicious look of agony captured his gorgeous face. Oh, yes—

She exploded. Her legs wrapped right around his hips; her fingernails drove into his shoulders. She burst like Chinatown on their New Year's celebrations.

Zoe moaned, gasped, laughed with pure joy.

She liked him wild, rough and as much unlike a restrained duke as he could be.

When it was over, he lifted her off the hood. She didn't quite know what to say. She was still feeling her way. "I like you when you want to make love on cars, not when you're grumpy and austere."

"Unfortunately, British men are a blend of both," he

said softly. "We have dirty minds, but we believe a great deal in guilt, duty and torturing ourselves."

"So I've learned about you." Bundled in Nigel's coat, she looked up at him in the dark. The thrill of making love had filled her. But she wondered—what would they do next? What did he really want? What did she? "Thank you for telling me what happened to you in the War. Thank you for revealing that to me."

The beam of her headlights cast cool light over his face. The bliss of making love had faded from his expression and he looked grim again. But he forced a smile for her, as he held out his hand. "Let me drive."

"It's my car, but all right."

She tossed him the keys, opened the door to the driver's side and slid across. Carefully, Nigel drove off the shoulder—no mean feat since the sand was soft and the wheels had sunk in. Once they were back on the paved portion of the road, she gave directions and he floored the gas pedal.

Zoe gripped her door, and Nigel took the curves like a racing driver. He took his gaze from the road for one second. "I've been practicing over the past four months," he said. "I wanted you to have the experience of having your heart in your throat."

"Well, you do keep putting it there," she drawled.

What would happen tonight? Could they really sleep together as husband and wife? Would he leave if he couldn't?

Last time, he'd let her go. This time, would she let *him* go?

THEY REACHED HER HOUSE. Nigel turned to her and she couldn't help it. She lunged and captured his mouth in a kiss again. With lips locked, they slid out of the car.

Kissing, they stumbled up the white stone steps to her house. Nigel rapped on the door, and Zoe saw it open and a maid stand holding it, with her mouth gaping open.

She and her husband kissed their way up the stairs, clothes dropping on the marble foyer, the priceless rugs, the gleaming wood stairs. All the way up the stairs, they devoured each other.

"I've missed you for four months. I have a lot of wasted time to make up for," he murmured.

"You could have come at any time."

"I was too stupid to understand that," he said.

She was shocked. "The Duke of Langford just called himself stupid?"

"The Duke of Langford is smart enough to know when he is an idiot." He lifted her right off her feet.

He carried her to her bedroom, and they both tumbled onto her white, oval bed. She sat up and pulled her dress off, sent it to land in a wet heap on the floor. Then she got to work on Nigel. She loved helping him undress. She wanted to tear his elegant clothes off him. She'd just made love with him on her car, but she wanted him again.

She loved him, and loving him meant she hungered to be intimate with him.

He made love to her for literally hours. Until they were both gasping for breath, laughing with delight.

"I love making whoopee with you," Zoe whispered, and he laughed.

Stretched out on her silvery satin sheets, she ran her hand over Nigel's bare chest. "I never really thought you would come after me."

"You didn't? You were wrong, Zoe." His blue eyes

lost their post-sex haze and grew serious. "Are you sure you want me to share your bed for the whole night?"

"I'm not afraid if you have nightmares. I want to be with you to soothe you, to make them go away."

"I'd like to try."

She leaned up on her elbow. The haunted look was still there on his face—also guilt. "Have you told me everything, Nigel?"

"No. There is something I didn't tell you. About the young woman who wrote letters to me. It was not her letter that you saw me reading. It was a letter from her mother—the young woman had gone missing. Her mother assumed she ran away with a lover. In the spring, this young woman went to see the man who was my commanding officer, now Lord Durham. She shot him and escaped."

"Oh, my God." Her heart twisted. Now she understood the depth of his guilt. "You were worrying about this over Christmas—the girl going missing. And when I had the crash... That was when your former commander was shot. No wonder you were so deeply troubled. I wish—I just wish you had told me."

"I wish that, too. That's why I am telling you everything now. I have tried to find the girl. Lily Bell is her name. I've hired investigators and they searched all over the country for her with no success. She's disappeared without a trace."

"Why *are* you trying to find her? So she can face imprisonment?"

"She was angry, upset, and she threatened to make someone pay for her brother's death. If she is guilty, she will go to prison, but I want to help her as much as I can. And I want to ensure the truth comes out if she's innocent."

Her hand brushed over his heart. She felt how fast it pumped. "You don't think she is guilty?"

"It's hard to kill someone. Very hard. I don't know if she had it in her."

This was the man she truly loved. The one who believed in a young woman's innocence. "You must find her, then," Zoe said. "If she's innocent, that must be proved. Maybe there was someone else who wanted to kill this man."

"Lily went to his house and shouted at him. That's why she is the only suspect."

"Maybe someone else took advantage of that."

"I didn't think of that. I was so fixated on finding Lily Bell. If I can prove she is innocent, I will have accomplished something. I will have righted one wrong, at least."

"You are a noble man," she said. "It's late now. We can talk more in the morning. Right now, Your Grace, I want you to wrap your arms around me, sleep next to me."

She snuggled up to him, letting her fingers play over the bulge of his naked biceps. For an hour, she caressed his hair, stroked his arms and chest. He kissed the top of her head. Eventually she heard his soft, measured breathing.

He was asleep.

She closed her eyes. He would probably shout. Or start thrashing around. She would have to be ready for it.

But when she opened her eyes, sunlight was sneaking

in around the blinds, and Nigel still had his arm around her, holding her possessively. And he was still asleep.

Zoe leaned over and kissed her husband's forehead. Tenderly, she brushed back his now-dry blue-black hair.

When she gently put her lips to his long eyelashes, he woke up. For a moment, he looked shocked. Then his full lips curved into a smile and he rolled her onto her back.

FOR THE NEXT FORTNIGHT, Zoe worked with Nigel, making long-distance telephone calls to the police in London. Sending telegrams.

Zoe came down for breakfast one morning—she and Nigel took the meal outside on her sun-drenched terrace—and Nigel jumped out of his seat. His smile dazzled her.

"You were right." His voice caught and she had to wait in suspense while he took a breath and continued. "The police have arrested Lord Durham's secretary for his murder. It turns out the man had been embezzling from my former commander for years. Durham found out and his secretary took advantage of Lily's visit, setting her up as a scapegoat. None of this would have come out, Zoe, if it had not been for you."

"What of Lily?"

"Once the story hit the newspapers, she knew she was no longer wanted for arrest. My men put advertisements in the papers, asking her to come forward. She did and has been reunited with her family."

"We will help them, Nigel. There are so many people who were devastated by the War. I want to help the Lily Bells of the world."

Nigel came forward, lifted her hand and kissed it gently. "Now I have a surprise for you."

"What?" she asked.

But Nigel refused to give her a clue.

He drove her to the local aerodrome, where wind socks flapped and snapped the wind. Zoe smelled the grease and oil that came with engines, heard the sputter and roar of airplanes preparing to take flight.

"Why have you brought me here?" After her crash and the miscarriage—and the way Nigel had sold her airplane in secret while she was recovering—she'd never dreamed she would be at his side and near anything with wings again.

He drove across the tarmac and brought her car to a stop beside a deep blue airplane. "I brought you to see this."

"The airplane?"

"It's mine," he said.

"Pardon?"

"I bought it. Admittedly with the profit Brideswell has been making on the investments from your dowry."

When she'd asked for her divorce, she'd known she was leaving half her money tied up with Brideswell, though she could have demanded money paid for support. But she had her two million well invested and she was quite well-off on her own.

But she didn't want to be on her own anymore.

"I didn't buy it for you—I thought you would prefer to find your own." Nigel reached behind him and plucked a flying helmet and goggles out of the rumble seat. "I want to take you up for a flight. Over the past couple of weeks, I've taken flying lessons from the ace, Bailey."

"You learned how to fly?"

"I wanted to share your love. I was wrong to demand that you give up something that matters to you so much."

"All right, Your Grace. I'd love to fly with you."

He pulled on his leather flying helmet and did up the strap. He looked very handsome. A little unkempt, she noticed. He hadn't shaved this morning and he had a growth of stubble that made him look rakish, dangerous, bad.

He pulled down the goggles and drew on gloves. "There's a hat and goggles for you in the aeroplane," he said. "I didn't want to give away the surprise."

She hadn't sat in the passenger seat for a long time. Half turning, she watched him at the controls. "Do you love to fly or did you just do this to impress me?"

"It excites me, Zoe. I am falling in love with it. Now I understand why you said you have to grasp life and live it."

Zoe didn't say anything. She held her breath as Nigel picked up speed, as he adjusted the wings, and when they just about ran out of runway, he got the airplane off the ground. They flew upward, swaying like puppets suspended from string. Over the metal buildings of the aerodrome. Over trees. Over the white beach and out to the edge of the crashing waves.

Panic gripped her. Richmond had crashed into the sea.

"Don't! Turn back! Don't do this!" Fear writhed in her. She was screaming at him. After all the tragedy they'd had, this would be the final one. The plane would go down. They would both be lost. Nigel gone, lost to her forever.

"Don't fly out over the water! We'll probably die. We're fated—"

"I won't," he yelled back. "Just the water's edge."

He kept to his word, flying along edge of sand and water, where the waves washed over the sand. He flew with considerable skill. He was cautious, too. Then he banked a turn and made for the aerodrome.

Her fears had been irrational. But she couldn't take them back now.

After they landed, Nigel brought the plane to a stop at the end of the landing strip. He turned to her and lifted his goggles. "So, am I any good?"

"Yes, Nigel. You are."

"I didn't mean to frighten you when I flew along the ocean."

"It's just that I remembered Richmond. The last time I saw him, he was flying out over the Atlantic. I watched him until he disappeared from my view—a tiny speck over vast, heaving waves. I had a lot of nightmares after he was lost." She had never told him this. Why now? He had opened his heart to her because she'd demanded it. But she hadn't done so with him.

"I had nightmares after my brother's death. After Richmond's. After I—I lost the babies. That's why I understood your nightmares. I've been haunted by my own."

"We've known a lot of tragedy, Zoe. But I want to believe what you told me to believe. That we have to leave the past behind us and live."

She shook her head. "It hasn't worked. No amount of cutting loose filled the emptiness inside me. I ran back to New York and hoped parties and speakeasies would keep me so busy I wouldn't hurt anymore. Then

I ran to California—to see the movie business and the ocean. I thought I could escape pain by going to a part of the world that held no memories for me. But memories come with you, no matter where you go."

"I'm so sorry, Zoe." He got up and leaned over from the pilot's cockpit. Kissed her.

She moved back from his mouth. "When I came here, the memories that hurt the most weren't the ones I expected. It was the memories of you."

"I hurt you that much?"

"The memories didn't hurt. It was the thought that I'd lost you. You have done so much for me. You came across an ocean and a country for me. You learned to fly. Nigel, you are the most wonderful man." She smiled. "I've had my fill of California. I'd like to go back to New York."

THEY STAYED AT Mother's house, and Mother was beside herself with hope. "You make this work, honey," she said the moment Nigel was out of earshot, and she had a chance to grab Zoe's arm and pull her into a room alone. "What a feather in my cap if your marriage to the duke sticks."

Zoe rolled her eyes. She wanted it to stick. But that night she had to wonder if she would lose it all.

Nigel wanted to escort her to a genuine New York speakeasy. She took him to Chumleys, rapped on the door and gave her password.

They danced and shared cocktails, and she was having a wonderful time until she encountered two girls she knew from her first year in New York. The most spiteful girls, now women of twenty-two.

"Oh, it's the Barefoot Duchess," one of them said, in her high, tittering voice. "Too poor for shoes."

Oh, God. Zoe's heart plummeted. Now Nigel was going to know the truth.

"More like the Dirt Shack Duchess," squealed one of the girls. "When Zoe gets her divorce, she won't be a duchess anymore. Just a Dirt Shack Hus—"

"I beg your pardon."

Zoe had tried to ignore them, but Nigel, behind her, cleared his throat. "You will refer to my wife as Your Grace, if you please." He glared down, projecting enough icy cold to frost the entire Atlantic. Lowering his voice, he said, "It is irrelevant whether Zoe is a duchess or not—though she will be remaining a duchess for the rest of her life. You will show her respect because she is a far better woman than you could ever hope to be."

With that, he guided Zoe away, to the small section of floor where couples danced.

"Nigel, you just insulted daughters of the leading social hostesses in New York. We won't be invited to any parties."

"We will. We will choose not to go."

He whirled her around in a fast fox-trot. She laughed. "Do you know—there are times I love the icy duke in you." She thought. "No, I'm wrong. I *always* love the icy duke in you. I've only just realized that."

He danced them to a shadowy corner, let her go and pulled out a chair. Even in this crowded place, a lift of his brow brought a waiter and in seconds they had cocktails. Zoe played with her drink without taking a sip. "I should tell you why she called me a Dirt Shack Duchess."

"Your mother told me a little about your past, Zoe."

"Did she? I thought it would take the threat of death to drag that out of her." She looked down at her drink. "I was dirt poor. I only had one pair of shoes when I was growing up, and they had to be saved for church and times when I had to look respectable. I was probably lower than your lowest kitchen maid. At least she has a clean dress. You thought I was good enough to be a duchess. Even when you knew about me, you came after me. You, who can look down his nose at all the best New York families."

"Zoe, are you telling me you really didn't feel worthy of being a duchess?"

She couldn't answer.

"Zoe, you are more than a duchess to me. You are something extremely special. You are an American duchess."

Tears welled in her eyes.

"You've been hurting for a long time," he said softly.

"All my life," she admitted. "The insults and the nasty things other people said to me—those things hurt. When I came to New York, no matter how nice I tried to be, some people wanted to hurt me. So I decided I wouldn't let them. I just wouldn't care. I wasn't living life. It was all an empty blur of louder music, stronger cocktails. The more I hurt inside, the faster I ran."

"You don't have to run away anymore. I love you."

"But now, when you look at me, I bet you don't see a duchess. Don't you see a poor girl with unkempt hair and dirty feet?"

"I see the most wonderful, remarkable duchess in the world, my duchess and my wife. I love you. Don't forget it."

"I won't."

"Stop running, Zoe. I'll stop hiding from pain if you stop running from it."

She held out her hand to shake his. Tears threatened to spill and her throat was tight and raw. But with happiness. "It's a deal."

The sky over New York was rosy-pink when they emerged from the club. Nigel's tie was undone, the collar of his shirt open. Damp with sweat, his hair was a disheveled tangle from dancing until dawn.

"You're trying so hard to be the man I wanted. You don't have to do all this to win my heart. You already have it." She slipped her arm through Nigel's and leaned against his warm, strong body. "It's time again to go home."

"I'll call a cab."

"You'll need one that can drive on water. I'm talking about Brideswell."

EPILOGUE
THE BABY

Nine months later
April 1924

"ARE YOU REAL?" Zoe whispered. Spring sunlight poured through her window—along with a soft, warm breeze and the rich smells of Brideswell in the early spring. Birds chirped as if serenading the tiny bundle she held in her arms.

Ten tiny fingers felt their way out of the layers of blankets. They stretched out, as if feeling the air. Zoe laughed with delight, even as her throat was tight with the tears of pure joy.

She had come here in May of 1922, believing it was a cold, gloomy place. All her feelings had changed. Zoe now gloried in the promise of spring: the sight of leaf buds, snowdrops and new green shoots on the lawns.

Nigel pushed open the door. "Nurse said you were feeding our little boy. May I come in?"

"I've fed him, though he sucked himself to sleep before I could burp him. I should wake him, for he won't settle with a tummy filled with air. But I don't have the heart to do it. He looks so sweet."

Nigel walked over to the side of her bed. Their baby looked so much like him—with blue eyes and a shock of black hair. He was only two days old. So small with such delicate, inquisitive hands and feet that were wrinkled and curled up. The baby had a very serious face—when he was born he had looked like a very grumpy version of Nigel.

Her husband perched on the edge of the bed beside her, gazing down at their child. She smiled up at Nigel. How tired he looked. Her labor had taken a whole night, and Nigel had stayed with her every moment. Dr. Drury had been appalled. A delivery was no place for a husband, let alone a duke. But Nigel refused to leave her side.

He'd been with her last night when their baby needed feeding. He was the most devoted father and now his eyes were red-rimmed and he looked utterly dazed.

"He is gorgeous. And you still feel fine?" Worry crept into Nigel's deep voice.

"I feel wonderful. I can't believe it is really true. He is healthy. And perfect."

"Now he needs a name," Nigel said.

"Your grandmother has already told me what he must be called. She insisted there is a string of family names for males, and I must choose from those. Put together, they sound rather odd. William Nigel Arthur David Albert. I told her I had no intention of saddling any child with all of that. I told her I intended to name him for my father: Thaddeus Cecil Gifford. T. C. Gifford. She almost fainted."

"Thaddeus. It does suit him."

She giggled at that. "Nigel, I said that only to torment your grandmother! I thought of William, after our brothers."

"No," Nigel said. "I want him to have his own name.

He is not here to replace anyone. Not even here because I'm supposed to have an heir. He is here to have as much of his own life as he can. The world is his to grasp. Family names were to show where you came from. What will be important for this fellow is who he is going to be—and what marvels will unfold as he grows up. I realized it will be 1952 when he is my age. I expect the world will be a different place yet again."

"Nicholas," Zoe said suddenly. "It has a little of Nigel in it, but it is a name that is all his."

"And a name that begins with Z for his second name. The only one I can think of is Zachary."

"Do you think this will be the final straw for your grandmother?"

"I think when she holds him in her arms she will simply fall in love with him." Nigel leaned over and kissed her. "I love you, Zoe."

She was about to answer when there was a brisk rap on the door.

The door opened before Nigel could give permission, and a tall, blond, tanned man stood in the doorway.

"Sebastian!" she cried. "Oh, I am happy to see you."

Her brother-in-law came to her. His hair was pale blond, his skin a coppery-brown. He wore a yellow suit and tie. Bending over Zoe, Sebastian hugged her carefully to avoid the sleeping baby she held in her arms. "So this is the infant. I hoped he would have your looks. Or that he had inherited my looks and not those of my brother." He spoke in his careless way, but his eyes glowed with tenderness as he looked upon his nephew.

"Nigel is every bit as handsome as you are," she teased.

"Sadly, I have to admit that he is."

"You came all the way from Capri?" Nigel asked.

"I did. I had to meet my new nephew. It appears I have had excellent timing. Mother tells me the baby is only two days old."

Zoe laid her hand on her brother-in-law's arm. "You are happy in Capri?"

Sebastian gave her a gentle smile. "I am. I'm painting. I've sold a few of my pictures—to people who don't care that I'm a duke's son. They actually like the pictures. But don't tell Grandmama. I think she might expire from the shock. Fortunately, you are here, producing heirs and shouldering all of Brideswell's responsibilities. Makes up for having a bohemian artist in the family."

"Nigel is actually very bohemian—under that ducal surface." Zoe laughed at Sebastian's look of doubt. "I am glad you are happy, Sebastian."

"As am I, brother," Nigel said.

"I wouldn't have been if it had not been for you, Zoe. And I give my thanks to you, Nigel, for listening to this brilliant woman. The most intelligent thing you ever did was to marry her."

"I agree."

"What about Julia?" Sebastian asked. "I hope she isn't married yet. It would be just like Grandmama to forbid her to send me an invitation."

"No, she isn't married yet," Zoe said.

"Is she still in love with the surgeon?"

"He left at the end of February," Nigel said. "He was offered a post in a London hospital, and he took it. Apparently he didn't believe a marriage between a surgeon and a duke's daughter would work. Thought he couldn't give her the life she deserved."

"Is Julia brokenhearted?"

Zoe knew Julia was, but her sister-in-law had insisted she was not going to waste her life pining for love. "Julia wants to see the world before she settles down," Zoe told her brother-in-law. Julia glowed with confidence now. Zoe had been angry with Campbell, but Julia's decision to travel had made her very happy.

"And you're going to let her?" Sebastian gaped at his brother.

"Of course," Nigel said. "Why would I stop her?"

"I never believed you could change. Have to admit I was wrong."

"It took a Herculean effort on Zoe's part," Nigel admitted.

"It was the power of love all along." Sebastian grinned.

"It was," Nigel agreed.

There was a quick rap on the door, and then it flew open immediately, and dark-haired Isobel ran in. She threw herself into Sebastian's arms. "You didn't find me and tell me you'd arrived," she said accusingly.

"I wanted to see the baby, pest," Sebastian returned good-naturedly.

At that point, Maria walked in. She beamed at the sight of the baby. Nigel's mother had spent much time holding the little boy. Even in just a day, she had lost much of her sad, faded appearance. There was color in her cheeks. "Your grandmother is coming for dinner," she told Sebastian.

"Your grandmother has been seeing a gentleman," Zoe said, wearing an innocent smile. As soon as she had returned to Brideswell, she had convinced the dowager to stop avoiding the attentions of Sir Raynard, the gentleman who so obviously admired her.

The dowager had not had love in her marriage. Zoe had pointed out that if Nigel was willing to take a chance on love, the rest of his family should, too. Her other bright spot was Lily Bell—the girl was now attending school to become a secretary. Zoe wanted to use income from her wealth to better the futures of girls in America and in England through education. She had never had the chance to get much schooling. This was a change she could make. It was, in its own way, as exciting as flying. And in the end, she realized, it would touch many more lives.

"You look thoughtful," Nigel said to her.

She gazed around at the Hazeltons, now part of her family. Mother was going to come and see the baby, too. Mother was so aglow with happiness over a grandson, Zoe believed she could see the light of it gleaming in the sky all the way from New York. "I am happy," she said. "So very happy."

"We are going to have a wonderful future," he said softly.

Zoe caught her breath at the glow of happiness in her husband's blue eyes—the beautiful clear blue of the spring skies over Brideswell.

"To our future," she cried. "I love you, Nigel. And our baby. And I love this place. I think I love it as you do. It's in our son's blood now. It's in mine. It's steeped in the past and waiting for the future. Our future." She kissed her baby's head. "Welcome, Nicholas, to this remarkable new world."

* * * * *

Turn the page for a sneak peek at
THE WORTHINGTON WIFE,
the poignant and irresistibly entertaining
follow-up to AN AMERICAN DUCHESS,
featuring Lady Julia Hazelton and the
unconventional American artist who threatens
everything she seeks to protect while
stirring her deepest desires.

ACKNOWLEDGMENTS

MANY THANKS GO to Kate Dresser, my editor for *An American Duchess*. I so appreciated your excitement for this story, as well as your work in smoothing my path. I was truly blessed to benefit from your very keen editorial eye. I also wish to thank Susan Swinwood for her enthusiasm and guidance. I also want to thank my new editor, Allison Carroll, for making the transition so easy and seamless as *An American Duchess* comes out in a new format. Her enthusiasm for the series has been wonderful.

Huge thanks, of course, to the entire Harlequin team, especially for the gorgeous cover.

As always, thank you to my agent Jessica Faust, who looked at this story in its very early stages and helped me bring it to life.

Of course, thank you to the readers. I hope you fall in love with this story as much as I did.

As the butler led him to his bedroom, Calvin Patrick Robert Carstairs—now the 7th Earl of Worthington—remembered the shock on Lady Worthington's face when he'd walked into the drawing room and grinned.

A month ago, he'd been woken from a hangover, hauled out of his bed in his apartment in Paris and told by a pale, nervous young lawyer named Smithson that he had inherited a title, three estates and the contents of four modestly invested bank accounts from the family who thought he wasn't good enough to lick their boots.

The lawyer who tracked him down had stammered and blushed throughout the meeting. Cal's latest model, Simone, had been walking around the room half-naked. She liked to feel sunlight pouring through the window on her bare breasts, and she liked to keep Cal looking at her. The lawyer had looked as if his eyes were going to leap out of his head.

Cal had poured himself a glass of red wine to clear the hangover, then he'd let the lawyer explain his supposed good fortune—

"The master's apartments have been prepared, my lord."

The snooty tone of the butler brought Cal back to the present. The man had his hand on the door knob of the room, but wasn't opening it. Maybe he hoped to learn

THE WORTHINGTON WIFE

424

it was all a joke before he let Cal across the threshold of the earl's bedroom.

It was a double door, so Cal shoved the other door open and walked in.

His trunk and his case were already in the room. The butler pointed out the bed, probably assuming he had no idea what a bed looked like if it wasn't a dirty mattress on the floor. The man opened the doors to the bathing room and the dressing room, as well as a small room with large windows where the earl would traditionally retire to prepare his correspondence.

"It'll do," Cal said indifferently.

Haughtily, the butler tried to look down his nose at Cal—though his eyes came up to Cal's shoulders. "Is your manservant traveling with you?"

"Don't have one," Cal replied, and he laughed at the look of smug satisfaction on the butler's face. "I'm bohemian. Wild and uncouth. If you think you've been proven right about me because I don't have a valet, wait until I start holding orgies in the ballroom."

The butler turned several fascinating colours. His cheeks went vermilion, his forehead was puce, and he developed a fascinating blend of violet and scarlet on his neck.

It gave Cal the itch to create a modernist portrait of an English butler, done in severe blocks of color. Red, purple, yellow-green and stark white—the colors of a shocked servant.

"When should I tell the countess you will return downstairs?" the man asked, sounding as if his windpipe wasn't drawing air. "I will send a footman to unpack."

"I won't stay up here long. The footman can finish that job while I'm at dinner."

"Very good."

The butler turned away and stalked toward the door, but before he reached it, Cal called, "Wait."

The man turned, lifting his brow self-importantly.

"The dark-haired woman with the pretty blue eyes— Julia Hazelton. Was she really my cousin's fiancée? Anthony died at the Somme, isn't that so?"

"Yes. We lost Lord Anthony to that battle. Indeed, Lady Julia Hazelton was his intended. It was a tragedy, devastating to us all."

Yeah, Cal imagined it would be, since he was standing here now. "Why is she here?"

"Her family was invited to dine, and she is a close friend of the family."

"Did she find someone else—after my cousin died?"

"Lady Julia Hazelton is still unmarried, my lord. If I may ask, what is the purpose to these questions, my lord?"

"I'm curious," he answered easily. "And if you're going to ask a question anyway, don't waste time asking permission to do it."

The butler, whatever the hell his name was, glared snootily. "Very good, my lord." Bowing, he retreated.

The door closed behind the butler's stiff arse.

For the hell of it, Cal jumped on the bed, landing on his arse in his dusty trousers. He crossed his ankles, his boots on the bed.

He could just hear how his mother would berate him for that, so he slid off.

He went into the bathroom to wash and shave. Showing up scruffy had been his plan and it had served its purpose. The Countess of Worthington, his aunt, had looked as if she was going to faint. She would expect him to show up at dinner looking equally bohemian and she would expect that he would have the table manners of an orangutan.

His family had stared at him with suspicion. He's seen condescension on the countess's face, resentment on the faces of his female cousins. His family had all glared at him, sullen, angry...and scared.

Lady Julia had been the only one to welcome him. She had been the perfect English lady to him, polite and unflustered.

Traits he should have hated, given how he knew the aristocracy really behaved. She was likely no different than the rest of them. Masking her disdain behind a polite, reserved smile.

But she had been nice to him. And his mother would say that she didn't deserve to have him judge her—and dislike her—just because of who she was.

Cal opened the bag that contained his straight razor, and he filled the small sink with some water—

Hell, that was freezing cold. He ran the other tap, but it didn't get any warmer. Cold water shaving it would have to be.

He drew the sharp blade along his cheek, slicing off dark blond stubble. He had been looking forward to this ever since that morning when he'd been drinking while the lawyer was outlining the meaning of his new position.

At first he was going to tell the young lawyer with the slicked-back hair to go back to the damned countess and tell her where she and her snobby family could stick their title.

They had disowned his father; they had rejected and vilified his mother for the sin of being an honest, decent woman from a poor family. His mother, Molly Brody, had gone into service to a rich family on Fifth Avenue, his father had been a guest. The usual story. Except his father, Lawrence Carstairs, had been idealistic. He'd fallen in love with the maid he seduced and married her.

Then his father had died. And his mother had gotten sick…

Cal had been thirteen years of age, with a younger brother who was ten. That was the only reason he'd swallowed his pride and begged the damn Carstairs family for help. He'd been a desperate boy trying to save his mother's life. And they'd refused. To them, he and his mother and his brother, David, didn't exist.

Clearing his throat, the young lawyer had asked him when he would like to book passage back to England.

Cal had been ready to laugh in the face of Smithson Jr. of Landers, Williams, Kendrick and Smithson. Go to England? He liked painting. He liked Paris. He'd finally found a place where he felt he belonged. He was happy in Paris whether he was sober or drunk, which he felt was a hell of an accomplishment.

"When you take up residence at Worthington Park, there is a Dower house available for the countess," Smithson had explained, after pulling at his tie. Simone had come into the kitchen and stood in front of the window so the sunlight limned her naked breasts. Blushing, the lawyer had said, "Should I relay your instruction to have it made ready?"

"For what?" he'd asked.

"For the countess to move into, when you take up residence in your new home."

At that moment, Cal got it. He understood what he'd just been given.

Power.

Now, Cal sloshed the blade in the water and shaved the other side of his face. He patted his face with a wet cloth, then slapped on some witch hazel. He got dressed in his tuxedo, tied the white bow tie and put on his best, shined shoes.

From his trunk, he took out a faded snapshot. It was six years old. He didn't know why he'd brought it with him. He should have burned it a long time ago. It was a picture of a pretty girl with yellow-blond hair and a sweet face. Her name was Alice and she had nursed him when his plane had been shot down in France. His brother, David, had ended up in the same hospital, three days after Cal got there.

Alice took care of David when both of his legs had to be amputated below the knee. Cal had fallen in love with her. The problem was David fell in love with her, too, but without his legs, David wouldn't propose to Alice. And with his brother being in love with her, Cal wouldn't propose either.

Cal tucked Alice's photograph into the corner of the dressing table mirror.

David had wanted to come here, too. He supposed David had a right to see their father's home. He would bring David over from America.

The problem was, David was a forgiving kind of man. He was a stronger man than Cal. David wasn't going to like what he planned to do.

But Worthington Park was Cal's chance at revenge.

Shine your shoes, slip on your flapper dress
and prepare for the ride of your life in

Lauri Robinson's

rip-roaring new miniseries:

Daughters of the Roaring Twenties

Available August 2015   Available September 2015   Available October 2015

Turn your love of reading into rewards you'll love with
Harlequin My Rewards